In a volatile world ripped from tomorrow's headlines, David Morton, intelligence agent, returns.

In Russia, following the collapse of the Soviet Union, a ruthless military troika is in power. In Rome, Pope Nicholas the Sixth, preoccupied with uniting all the faiths and bringing world peace, selects South Africa's first black cardinal for a crucial mission. In California, a pastor is spreading global hatred with the aid of the powerful, sinister Wong Lee . . .

As international tension mounts, David Morton, the James Bond of the 90s, undertakes his new mission – to combat the cynical forces threatening the stability of the world.

# GODLESS ICON

## Gordon Thomas

ORION

An Orion paperback
First published in Great Britain by Chapmans Publishers Ltd, in 1992
This paperback edition published in 1993 by Orion Books Ltd,
Orion House, 5 Upper St Martin's Lane, London WC2H 9EA

A CIP catalogue record for this book is available from the
British Library.

ISBN: 1 85797 234 1

Printed in England by Clays Ltd, St Ives plc

In memory of my father-in-law
who served his country in more
ways than anyone knows

# Special thanks

To Ian and Marjory Chapman: who saw the potential of this story before anyone else and who have never wavered in their determination to make it work. I could not ask for more; they could not have given more.

To Russ Galen: who once more showed the care and understanding that makes him who he is.

To Victor O'Rourke: always there in every sense of the word, ready to perform all the roles asked of him.

To Andrew Berry: a good man in good times; an outstanding one in other times, and, as always, there were those times.

To Morgan O'Sullivan: who understands the dynamics of storytelling.

To David North: whose enthusiasm knows no bounds.

To Greg Hill: an exploiter in the very best sense of the word.

To Miranda Moriarty: once more she made the transition from my almost illegible scrawl to impeccable manuscript appear effortless. I owe a great debt to a very special person.

To Mary and Paul McGrath: my proverbial first readers, as gimlet-eyed as always.

To Edith: she brought her late father's eye to bear, making sure I walked that difficult line between what could happen and what will happen. In that sense this book is also dedicated to her.

And to my friends in the Vatican and elsewhere in the Church and those persons who serve in various intelligence services. Their help is reflected in these pages.

# 1

His words all but lost in the first burst of gunfire, the man shrieked, 'Long live the CIA!'

A young, incredibly good-looking, dark-skinned commando raced towards the building, miraculously unscathed by the murderous gunfire. The man appeared at several windows in quick succession, wielding a bazooka. The commando reached a door and slapped old-fashioned *plastique* and a timer on the frame before racing away.

The explosions sounded like firecrackers as the building erupted in a fireball of shattering glass, crumbling walls and ignited drapes and furniture. No *plastique* could have done that.

Bodies hurtled through the air, blood streaming from eyes and chests. The man with the bazooka, one hand a bleeding stump, staggered from the building, laughing crazily and still shouting, 'Long live the CIA!'

When the final credits rolled, David Morton reached forward and switched off the TV.

Nothing to show the film was made by a Turkish subsidiary of Wong Holdings. Or that Wong Lee's fingers were everywhere nowadays.

The founder, president and sole stockholder of the conglomerate which bore his name, ran an organisation more ruthless and profitable than any multinational. Wong Holdings made a greater profit in a day than all the Persian Gulf oil sheikdoms did in a month. Neither the Mafia, the Triads nor the Japanese underworld dealt as secretly as Wong Holdings.

Among much else, Wong Lee's money had allowed the Turks to corner the market in movies where Islam's young fighters cleansed the world of old bogeymen. Villains and heroes always looked the same, as if Balkan Central Casting had gone on the blip.

Morton had positioned the TV set in the hotel bedroom so that he still had a perfect view of the ships passing through the Golden Horn. He catnapped at low tide, when even the most foolhardy of the Bosporus pilots would not risk guiding a ship through the narrow seaway which led to and from the Black Sea.

Long ago he had taught himself to sleep when he could and to watch patently ridiculous movies without getting angry. It went with the job.

He was waiting for the *Eastern Rose*. A pretty name for a ship engaged in such a dirty business.

The sun was setting over the inky-black oily waters of the Sea of Marmara, creating the illusion that the rusty spans of the Galata Bridge were spun from pink icing. Morton shifted in his armchair to follow the progress of another of the water taxis. The ride was still the cheapest transcontinental journey he knew, a few cents to be ferried from East to West. In the distance blared the horn of a tanker moving out of the Black Sea.

The *Eastern Rose* would emerge from his right, from the Aegean, from behind the Dolmabahçe Palace.

He had heard, apocryphally perhaps, that at high noon on a summer's day the reflection from the palace's white marble walls was so bright it could sear eyeballs. This was September and the heat had gone. The sun dipped behind the twin fortresses guarding the opposite banks of the Bosporus at its narrowest point. Soon it would be time to strap on the spectra goggles Technical Services had developed to spot a target in the dark.

The Armenian had been certain about the *Eastern Rose* and its cargo. Morton trusted the Armenian because she was not a fieldmouse who felt it essential to regularly come up with something new. He had not heard from her for almost a year. Three days ago the woman spotted the fresh splash of grey paint on the gatepost of a graveyard in the suburbs of Yerevan, the Armenian capital. The daub looked like something a child had done, the numerals '5' and '0' barely decipherable.

The fieldmouse had bought a bunch of flowers and returned to the cemetery. Counting from the gate, at the fiftieth grave on the left side of the pathway, she knelt and arranged the flowers in the urn on top of the tomb. The message was beneath the urn.

She had gone home, encrypted the words, and transmitted them to Mossad's main communications centre on Oliphant Street in Jerusalem.

When the message was decoded it was immediately faxed to Tel Aviv, to the high-rise known as Morton's Kingdom. All who worked there were Morton's Men, even the women.

Once he'd read the message, Morton flew to Istanbul.

He now knew that the *Eastern Rose* had made two previous runs. The first with the explosives which collapsed an underground car park in Haifa, where four buses were unloading children on their way to a sports meeting. It took three days to dig out the last of the one hundred and sixty-four bodies. The second cargo had demolished the desalination plant producing drinking water from the Red Sea. The plant was Israel's first co-venture with Jordan. Both times the explosives were of a type only manufactured by a subsidiary of Wong Holdings.

Now Wong Lee was about to try again. The voyage of the *Eastern Rose* proved that.

The first hint came when a yak herdsman in the Tibetan capital, Lhasa, passed the few details to a trader with a permit from the country's Chinese occupiers to travel to Nepal. From there the news was telephoned to a voice-activated dead-letter drop Mossad maintained in Delhi. When the box was next electronically cleared – a simple process involving no more than pressing buttons in Tel Aviv – Morton was informed of its contents. He had ordered extra surveillance in the Lhasa area before coming to Istanbul. He had not told Bitburg where he had gone.

Walter Bitburg was Mossad's Director-General, with a banker's relish for paperwork, and no real understanding of counter-intelligence. Morton's work. Bitburg liked to quote Macaulay's dictum about the perfect historian never filling the gaps.

Morton always said, in counter-intelligence action could not wait for certainty. Informed conjecture was his rudder through the dark seas of motive and deception. If that made him a lousy historian, it fitted him for the vicissitudes of espionage.

He could hear the tanker's horn continuing to blare to clear a path through the sea lanes and, through the beaded window curtain, see ferries and water taxis bobbing like corks in its wake.

Over Istanbul the smog was thickening as people lit coal fires. Soon only the spires of the mosques would rise above the sulphurous blanket.

There was a knock on the door. Through the peep-hole the waiter looked like a gargoyle.

'Yes?'

Like any Arab determined to show his superiority, whenever possible Morton had addressed him without opening the door.

'Gentleman like dinner now?'

In less than an hour it would be dark.

'Bring it straight away.'

'Fish or meat?' intoned the waiter.

The lamb at lunch had tasted rancid despite the curry sauce.

'Fish. Grilled, no sauce. And pommes frites.'

'Gentleman maybe like whisky or beer?'

'A cola.' He never drank liquor on duty.

Morton saw the waiter sigh, then walk towards the elevator. When the cage began its noisy descent, Morton returned to the window.

The last sighting of the *Eastern Rose* was two days ago, when it passed through the Straits of Gibraltar. The fieldmouse in Cadiz radioed Jerusalem to report the freighter had a starboard list. The cargo must have shifted during another of the storms which had forced other ships rounding the Cape of Good Hope to seek shelter. The captain of the *Eastern Rose* would not have risked that. The South African security service might have become curious.

His cargo consisted of rockets and multiple warheads, both of which Wong Holdings manufactured. One fully armed missile could do more damage than all the Scuds Saddam Hussein had launched in the Persian Gulf war.

Saddam had survived so long because the West had been uncertain how to deal with the end of the Soviet Union. Morton had heard the agonising in Washington. Was it better to leave Saddam in place, a despot controlled by the threat of further military action? Or to remove him – only to confront an even more sinister power in the region?

With Gorbachev and Yeltsin gone, and the failure of the Russian Commonwealth, a powerful Islamic empire had emerged. It consisted of the old Soviet Union's Moslem republics, Afghanistan and Iran. It called itself the Islamic Confederation, and its

12

hatred for the West was only surpassed by that which it felt for Israel, and the contempt it had for Saddam.

The West continued to play a dangerous game of keeping Iraq and the Confederation at each other's throats in the hope they would be too preoccupied to attack Israel. As a result tension had surfaced within the Confederation.

Iran wanted to attack Iraq before it had a chance to rebuild its war machine destroyed in the Gulf War. The old Soviet Moslem republics who had once been forced to rubber-stamp Moscow's aspirations, had begun to resent Iran's dominance. Newly independent nations with names few outsiders could still pronounce, let alone find on the redrawn map of Asia – Turkmenia, Uzbekistan, Tadjikistan, Kirghizia and Kazakhstan – were talking of forming their own alliance. An alliance which would one day achieve more than that of their forefathers, not only sweeping westwards to capture Moscow, but this time bringing all of Russia, the Ukraine, Byelorussia and the other republics of the former Soviet Union under their control.

But who actually would be in control? The question bedevilled the discussions among the Moslem republics. They had started to posture among themselves. Daily the region had become more volatile and unpredictable – and the perfect melting pot for the ultra-secret machinations of Wong Lee. He intended the cargo of the *Eastern Rose* to be used by extremists. If they managed to launch only half of the consignment, they could succeed where all the Middle East wars had failed. They could destroy Israel, and in doing so fire the opening salvo in a world war more terrifying than any other.

The conflict would effectively wreck Pope Nicholas the Sixth's carefully thought-out vision of finally reconciling Christianity with Judaism and Islam by going first to the Holy Land and then to Moscow. He called his mission Operation Holy Cross.

It was more, far more than the Pope acting like a spiritual Hercules, trying to bring together the three great faiths, more even than a respected spiritual leader exercising his great moral authority. Pontiffs had done that before – and failed.

What Pope Nicholas planned was rooted early on in his pontificate. Then he had proclaimed there could be no real and lasting peace on earth until Church and State shared a common ground in confronting the great problems of the world in the closing years of the millennium. The scourge of AIDS, the deprivations of hunger, the pestilence which still pock-marked the earth: these blights, and more, could be finally eradicated only when the hostilities between differing ideologies ended. There would be an end to the retributive hatred of Northern Ireland, and all similar places, only when tackled from one standpoint: a total respect for the dignity of man. And that would only happen when the secular and religious worlds worked in tandem.

That was the genesis of Operation Holy Cross, making it a concept infinitely more powerful than any political manifesto or clarion call from the hustings. It went right to the very heart of man's own survival on earth, offering a blueprint for a peace the world had never known – and one which would end the machinations of Wong Lee.

The Pope intended to keep the details of Holy Cross secret until the last possible moment so as to lessen the chance of anything going wrong. Morton knew whenever they became public, it would draw fierce opposition – not least from inside the Vatican itself. Pope Nicholas had said so when they last met.

To ensure Operation Holy Cross succeeded was another reason to come to this execrable room.

Another ship had joined the line waiting to enter the Black Sea.

Only those who absolutely needed to, knew what he planned to do. Chantal, of course, and Danny, Mossad's surveillance supremo. He could not fight fire with fire without his help.

Danny Nagier had sent Saki from Ankara to operate the transmitter in the safe house on the hill behind Istanbul University campus. Saki was one of those Greeks who could look and sound like a Tartar, or an Azari, or just about anyone from the Balkans cockpit.

The elevator was returning, slowly clunking its way up from the kitchen. Morton strode to his door. There was somebody with the waiter.

The waiter was a low-level informer, his tip-money paid from a Dresdner Bank account in Pullach, where the BND, the German security service, had its headquarters. It helped reinforce in him the carefully nurtured belief he was working for old friends. After Morton had checked in, the waiter had faxed his report to what he believed was a BND office in Munich. From the Mossad safe house it was transmitted to Tel Aviv.

Chantal Bouquet had called Morton on the satellite phone.

She ran Foreign Intelligence, and her brief included controlling all informers. In her delectable French accent, she had read him the waiter's report.

'Gentleman is Aboud-Aziz Hamidi. Syrian passport. Described as director of a Damascus manufactory. Gentleman arrived with one suitcase.'

Chantal's forgers had created the passport. Technical Services had purpose-built the suitcase.

'The physical is especially good,' Chantal had said, continuing to read.

'Gentleman is tall, maybe one metre eighty-five. No visible physical scars and his face is without beard. Wears only khaki shirt and trousers. Age anywhere between forty and fifty. Does not speak much.'

'Not bad, *oui*?' Chantal had said.

'For sure. Make sure he gets a bonus,' Morton had replied. He had always gone for the minimum of disguise.

He slipped the security chain and pressed an ear to the door panelling. A woman's voice. As the elevator shuddered to a stop, she fell silent.

When the waiter opened the cage door Morton saw she was plump with hennaed hair. A Circassian in her late twenties with a face that no longer remembered innocence. He glimpsed gold-capped teeth as she whispered to the waiter. The man smiled, then, balancing his tray, minced towards the door. The woman remained leaning against the open cage, skirt taut across her thighs.

Morton unfastened a shirt button to give him immediate access to the Luger in the armpit holster strapped against his skin. He yanked open the door, catching the waiter by surprise. Recovering, the waiter walked into the room. He smelled of anise.

Morton watched him place the tray on the bed and, with a flourish, remove the tin cover over the plate. The chipped potatoes were the thickness of burnt fingers, the fish swam in a little pool of oil. The glass of cola was diluted by ice.

The waiter turned to Morton, smiling a sly smile.

'Gentleman like relax after dinner? I have very fine lady waiting to make all pleasures possible. I fetch nice bottle of wine, champagne maybe, and you relax. Lady very experienced but still nice. You like meet?'

'No.'

The waiter rubbed his chin with a hairy-backed hand and continued to disclose his stained teeth.

'Maybe gentleman like boy? I have very good boy, clean, no disease –'

'*Y'allah! Imshi!*' Morton said, moving to the door, careful to show no more anger than an Arab would display at such presumption.

'Maybe animal? I have good dog, well trained to –'

Morton grabbed the waiter by the scruff of his jacket, and shoved him out into the corridor. The woman was no longer smiling.

After closing the door, he could hear the waiter trying to placate the whore. They were still arguing as the lift began to descend.

Morton carried the plate to the bathroom and tipped the contents into the toilet and flushed the bowl. Afterwards he drank the cola.

He pulled the suitcase from under the bed and turned the keys in the locks anti-clockwise to deactivate the fuses in the two sodium–phosphorus charges built into the lid. They were designed to explode in the face of anyone who opened the case after turning the keys clockwise.

Morton removed the tray holding his clothes – clean chino shirts, underwear, socks. Beneath were the satellite telephone and the spectra goggles.

They were like a welder's, except for a cable connected to a metal strip above the lenses. The strip had several push buttons.

Morton plugged the cable into a socket of the suitcase's built-in computer. Its rhombic antennae, half-a-mile of fibre-optic wire, were tightly coiled to form a disc six inches in diameter. Splitters connected the disc to four dipoles bolted to the corners of the Samsonite.

Goggles over his eyes, Morton turned to the window. To check focus he looked at the great mosques of Istanbul – at the Aya Sofya and, for him, the most imposing of all, the Blue Mosque of Süleyman the Magnificent.

Smog was swirling around their massive domes. He pressed a button on the strip and instantly could clearly see the filigree around the spire of the Blue Mosque.

He settled in the armchair and began to once more scan ships in the Sea of Marmara, and wonder again what made Wong Lee the way he was?

He was rich enough to buy the debts of most Third World countries, and quite a few in Europe. Powerful enough to spurn the friendship of world leaders.

The Professor and his behaviourists in Psychological Assessment said it all came down to old-fashioned megalomania, that Wong Lee was the latest in a long line from Attila to Hitler and Stalin. But they had all wanted to publicly build in their image. Wong Lee only wished to destroy, and from a distance, always using others to do his evil work. His great skill was to leave his complicity hidden. The voyage of the *Eastern Rose* could never be traced to Wong Lee.

But Morton knew. Not in the way Bitburg understood in his neat and precise world. But in that other world, where an imaginative leap could bring him to a shabby bedroom which still offered a great view.

The tanker, its horn at last silent, had dropped its pilot and was speeding towards the Mediterranean. The pilot tender was heading through the sea lanes, the pilot standing in the stern, a full-bearded man in a white uniform.

Morton pressed another button. The computer made its calculations to bring the pilot's face into close focus. Morton fished in a shirt pocket. He held the snapshot close to the spectra goggles to compare the two faces. It was Tafik, for sure. The pilot had escorted the *Eastern Rose* through the Straits on her previous runs.

The Bosporus was settling down for the night, with only a handful of water taxis ferrying tourists on sightseeing tours. An Egyptian freighter had joined the queue waiting to enter the Black Sea. A French cargo ship was passing between the twin fortresses. A Spanish tanker was weighing anchor, ready to follow.

Then he saw a bulky outline further to the right of the Dolmabahçe Palace than he expected.

The *Eastern Rose* was in darkness except for her navigation lights. She was low in the water. From her stern pole flapped a Taiwanese flag of convenience. Adjusting the magnification on the spectra goggles to maximum, Morton swept her decks. They were empty.

The pilot boat had altered course to intercept the *Eastern Rose*. How much was Tafik getting for this run?

There were still six ships waiting to pass through the Straits ahead of the *Eastern Rose*. That gave Morton an hour.

He removed the spectra goggles and placed them in the suitcase. He used the satellite phone to dial a number on Istiklâl Avenue, Istanbul's answer to Times Square, or just about anywhere.

Morton let the number ring five times, hung up, redialled and let it ring three more times. Hamid Osman would be waiting for the call. He had provided the boat and whatever else he'd been asked for. Hamid was the local Mossad fixer.

Morton dialled the safe house. Two rings, repeated at once. The signal for Saki to programme the transponder. The satellite would do the rest.

Morton reset the locks, and shoved the Samsonite back under the bed. He switched on the TV. The man who had died shouting 'Long live the CIA!' was chanting 'Death to America!'

Morton opened the bedroom door enough to make sure the corridor was empty. The elevator was wheezing between the floors below. He did not bother to lock the door; the waiter would have a pass key. Morton strode to a window at the far end of the corridor. Beyond was a fire escape. He used it to reach the street. His eyes were beginning to smart from the smog.

The night-time population of pimps, prostitutes, transvestites, shoeshine boys and political agitators barely gave him a second glance.

It took ten minutes to reach the dock. Hamid was waiting in the doorway of the launch's wheelhouse. He was a small man with the dark, intense features of a Kurd, and a holdall at his feet. Hamid kissed Morton formally on both cheeks, then reached into the wheelhouse and produced a couple of styrofoam cups.

'It's going to be cold out there,' he said, handing one to Morton. They drank the spicy hot drink made from goats milk and salep root sweetened with cinnamon.

Then Hamid started the engine and eased the launch past the anchored water taxis. Morton stood beside him, staring into the night, watching the riding lights of the ships.

When they cleared the waterfront, Morton used the ship-to-shore radiophone to once more dial Saki. This time only two rings. The communications satellite would start to monitor the radio frequencies the *Eastern Rose* used.

'The moon will be up in an hour. That's why I've chosen a cave below Anadolu Hisar,' Hamid said.

The old fortress was on the European side of the Straits.

'This cave, how big is it?' Morton asked as they passed the stern of a Polish tanker. The sound of balalaika music carried across the water.

'It's an old smugglers' hole. Big enough to hide a couple of fast boats running drugs out of Asia before they started flying the stuff.'

Away to the left rose the massive silhouette of Topkapi Palace. Stored there were all the forgotten secrets of the Grand Viziers, the prime ministers who had effectively ruled the Ottoman Empire.

'How long is this cave? There'll be quite a ground swell when she passes.'

The riding lights of another anchored tanker loomed up. This time Hamid decided to cut across her bow.

'She runs back forty, forty-five feet,' he replied.

Morton nodded, satisfied.

In the faint glow that preceded moonrise the anchored ships seemed even bigger.

There was a continuous rumble of cars crossing the Galata Bridge, and from its far side, the tinny sound of music played over cheap loudspeakers. Asia going into another night.

There was no sign of the *Eastern Rose*.

'She'll have to do a dog leg to pick up the pilot,' Hamid explained, continuing to steer a diagonal course across the Bosporus.

Morton squatted on the wheelhouse floor and reached for the holdall. He carefully removed the packages wrapped in newspapers. In the bottom was a small crossbow. He laid the packages and bow on the floor and called to Hamid.

'Ease up a little.'

After Hamid throttled back Morton unwrapped the first package and laid the suction rocket on the floor. He quickly unwrapped the others.

Even though he had attended the sea trials in a restricted area off the coast of Haifa, he still found it astonishing how powerful something so small as the suction rocket could be. It had taken the chemists in Ordnance a year to work out how to reduce the length of the rockets from a cumbersome four feet to a tube just eleven inches long which still produced the same explosive force.

Each rocket was no thicker than the average torch casing, with a suction cone at the nose and a fan-tail machined from aluminium. Built into the tail was a tiny gyroscopically-stabilised, gimballed timer, wired to an equally small computer behind the suction pad. Once the pad attached itself to a target the computer activated the timer. The triggering mechanism was based on the one used in the bomb dropped on Hiroshima.

The timer sent a charge of a couple of ounces of Comp-B – a mixture of hexane and TNT – hurtling down the tube to impact with a larger charge made from nitro-glycerine and an explosive known as RDX. The sea trials had confirmed one rocket could probably sink a large tanker.

The darker mass of the fortress loomed out of the night.

'Once clear of the straits how long before she's in deep water?' Morton asked.

'Ten, fifteen minutes. It depends which channel she takes.'

'She'll be going right, heading for Georgia.'

'Set for ten.'

Morton began to rig the timers. When he finished he strung the first rocket in the crossbow and adjusted the tension.

'She's coming up on our port. About half a mile away,' Hamid called out.

Through the wheelhouse windows Morton could just make out the bow wave of the *Eastern Rose*.

Moments later the launch glided into the cave. Hamid stopped the engines. The boat's fenders bumped against one of the rock walls.

The sound of powerful engines churning through water gradually became louder. The *Eastern Rose* had been fitted with new turbines for her work.

Morton picked up the crossbow and climbed out of the wheelhouse. Hamid followed, carrying the other rockets. Fog was swirling across the mouth of the cave. The engine noise increased.

Morton sat on top of the wheelhouse, spreading his legs for balance, the crossbow firmly gripped in both hands. He could hear the first surge of water being driven by the ship's turbines against the sides of the straits. He raised the crossbow, a thumb on the timer button in the fan tail.

The sudden blast from the *Eastern Rose*'s horn reverberated around the cave. The pounding of her engines was even louder. The water in the cave began to eddy.

Then the freighter's hull was blocking out what light there was from the mouth of the cave.

Morton pressed the timer button and fired.

Even before the pad suctioned on to the hull a few feet above the waterline, Morton fired a second rocket. It stuck fast some twenty feet further along the hull.

The freighter's bow wave surged into the cave, sending the launch bobbing crazily. Hamid swore softly and handed Morton a third rocket. As Morton fired, the launch rose with the swell and the rocket barely cleared the mouth of the cave.

Morton loaded and fired once more. A fourth rocket hit the hull, below the bridge. The launch suddenly dropped in the water as the bow swell receded. Moments later a fifth rocket suctioned on the steel plates protecting the engine room.

Once more. The midships hold. Some of the missiles were stored there. Again. The aft hold with the warheads.

Twice more. Both hits close to the fan-tail. Nine so far.

The ship's horn screamed again. Then the *Eastern Rose* was gone, her wake sending another small tidal wave surging into the cave.

Morton and Hamid clung to the wheelhouse roof until the water was calm once more.

There were a couple of rockets left.

'Let's go,' Morton said.

They scrambled into the wheelhouse. While Hamid guided the launch out of the cave, Morton dialled Saki. A single ring. The signal for Saki to instruct the satellite to transmit a pre-recorded message to the ship's radio room ordering its crew to take to the life boats – and why. The satellite would then jam any attempt by the *Eastern Rose*'s operator to transmit.

The crew would have a full ten minutes to abandon ship. Ten minutes more warning than the Haifa schoolchildren received.

Morton had always fought fire with fire. But he'd never kill for the sake of killing. He'd seen too much of that.

When the launch was back in the sea lane he dropped the crossbow and unused rockets over the side. Thirty minutes later the two men reached the dock.

'You did fine,' Morton said after Hamid had once more kissed him on both cheeks.

Then they went their separate ways.

Morton chose to walk back to the hotel through the old city; he enjoyed being able to pick out the dialects of Central Asia.

The smog was thicker, burning not only his eyes but his throat. Then he realised it was not just smog, but the reek of smoke drifting in the air.

A couple of streets from the hotel he saw the glow in the sky. People were running, and shouting in half a dozen languages. In the distance came the wail of the first fire trucks.

When he arrived at the hotel, scruffy-looking policemen were struggling to make room for the trucks to reach the building. Its upper floor was ablaze. He could see flames licking the bead curtain on his window.

Only sodium phosphorus produced those intense blue-white flames. Only the waiter would have been curious enough to open the suitcase. By now he and the contents of the Samsonite would be charred beyond recognition.

They'd wonder, of course, the men in Turkish Intelligence, when they came to sift the debris. But they'd probably put it down to another bomb-maker. There were plenty of them in Istanbul these days.

Morton turned away. In the next street he picked up a cab. Forty minutes later he was at Yesilkov Airport. He took the second available flight, to Rome. Never rush.

The squat little man at passport control spent his time studying the document, looking at Morton's face, staring at the pages again, finally consulting a check list of passport numbers.

Morton never took his eyes from the official. Chantal's forgers were the very best. Finally the man stamped the passport and waved him through.

On the television set in the departure lounge the first reports were coming in of a ship exploding just beyond the Straits. Apart from the captain and an Istanbul pilot, it appeared the entire crew had abandoned ship shortly beforehand.

Half an hour later, as the Alitalia jet climbed out of Yesilkov, Morton saw nothing to disturb the placid surface of the Black Sea. But Wong Lee still had a hundred, and more, ships to do his bidding. One way to stop him was for Operation Holy Cross to succeed.

It was such a brilliantly simple idea – that one genuinely holy man would walk in the footsteps of his Christ and then pray in Red Square, and by doing so unite the world in a lasting peace – that Morton believed it could yet succeed. He also understood why Wong Lee would continue to do everything in his power to stop that happening.

Morton also knew what he must now do.

# 2

Another gale which had been building up out in the South Atlantic had finally found landfall during the night along the entire coast of South Africa. Springbok Radio reported a trail of devastation from Natal to Cape Province. Now at dawn the thunderclouds swirled ominously above the valley on the edge of the veldt, over two hundred miles inland.

Julius Enkomo switched off the radio. No one could remember such a spate of storms. Even the howlers of '41 which had drowned his grandfather's cattle had not been so severe. These storms had uprooted entire townships. The harvest had been decimated and the first food riots had already occurred. He had no doubt the extremists would exploit the damage to foment further trouble.

Tension between the races had not been higher since those days when the African National Congress had stomped through the streets, proclaiming their new found freedom which had eventually swept away State President de Klerk and Nelson Mandela.

He had once more come to this purpose-built retreat to pray, to ask God to help him find new ways to lead his people through these turbulent times.

From the first time he said the rosary in mission school he had believed in the power of prayer. And he had seen it work, many times in many places. He hoped that when he left this thatched-roof building, prayer would again have shown him how he could best serve the millions of blacks, whites and those of mixed race who looked to him for spiritual leadership.

Julius Enkomo was their cardinal-archbishop, Primate of

South Africa, the first appointed by Rome to the Republic. His elevation to the Sacred College of Cardinals had created a stir throughout the Catholic world. Not least because at the age of fifty-seven, he was its youngest member.

Religious commentators invariably referred to him as a liberal. And, it was perfectly true, he had mastered the intricate, subtle workings of the great theocracy of the Roman Curia, the Church's rule-making body, to whom even the Pope bent, to argue for a more open attitude on the part of the Vatican to its flock of a billion souls.

But what created the greatest buzz of excitement in South Africa was his being black. A child of the bush who had risen to dizzy heights. A boy born in a kraal, who had gone on to sit alongside the Supreme Pontiff in Rome before returning to South Africa as his representative.

The tabloids, he remembered ruefully, had presented him as the answer to all South Africa's troubles. The Peacemaker, the Bridge Builder, the Great Architect who would bring about the Perfect Union.

Even in the creeping grey, where night ends and another day begins, out here on the veldt, 5.00 a.m. by the wall clock, Julius Enkomo was a striking figure. His was a strong and handsome face, the cheekbones broad, the lips full. His eyes shone like a cat's. Even in repose, standing at the window, listening to the rain hammering against the glass, there was a litheness about him which the high-buttoning cassock trimmed with red could not hide. In his youth, he had been a magnificent track athlete. His body remained as fit and trim as in those days when the newspapers had dubbed him the Panther.

The tag had most recently appeared in press reports of how he had faced the new neo-Nazis when they had marched on his palace in Cape Town, chanting, 'Burn the Pope's Kaffir!'

The photographers and TV cameramen showed him calmly standing on the palace steps, ordering the police not to intervene. The rabble dispersed in the face of such fearlessness. The media noted approvingly that His Eminence had lost none of his charisma.

Only he knew how frightened he had felt; nothing was more precious than life.

The truth of that troubled him. Thirty-two years had passed since, on the day of his ordination, he had said that life on earth was no more than a passing imperfection, at best only a pale reflection of its Creator. That the real life was the Hereafter.

Thirty-two years since his first parish in Durban: the two years spent as a curate in Zimbabwe before being selected for four years' study at the Greg, the Church's own university in Rome; the postings as monsignor-secretary to the Papal Nuncio in Korea and then as auxiliary bishop to the Apostolic Delegate in Washington; the period back in Rome serving as a bishop on the Pontifical Commission for Justice and Peace and then the Sacred Congregation for the Clergy; the three momentous years as the Pope's personal envoy in Jerusalem before getting his Red Hat and returning to Cape Town. In all that time he had continuously reminded himself he was no more than a cipher, driving himself ruthlessly until the day finally came for his release into the all-embracing arms of the Almighty.

He had become a confidant to Pope Nicholas the Sixth. People said they were the nearest to father and son it was possible to be within a hierarchy like the Church's. But he still called the Pope 'Your Holiness', even in private.

They had sat together in the shambolic comfort of the pontiff's private study in the Apostolic Palace and spoken of the sheer satisfaction of serving God – whether it was saying Mass, hearing confessions or studying together the files sent up from the sacred archives on long dead candidates for canonisation.

They had spoken of worldly matters: the collapse of the Soviet empire; the emergence of the Islamic Confederation; the threat Saddam Hussein had posed; a hundred such deeply troubling issues.

These included the growing influence of the graduates of the Zimba campus in Zimbabwe. They were preaching an extreme radicalism not only in South Africa but throughout the entire continent. The campus was supported by huge grants from Wong Holdings.

He had suggested His Holiness should write to Wong Lee himself about what was happening. Weeks later came a cold reply from Lhasa stating that Wong Holdings never interfered in how its money was used.

Pope Nicholas had sighed and said he would continue to preach against the radicals, not just in Africa, but everywhere.

Afterwards His Holiness had revealed the details of Operation

Holy Cross, which he hoped would arrest the new and frighteningly dangerous godlessness sweeping the world.

Listening, Julius Enkomo had realised again that here was the one authentic voice calling for an end to hostility between differing ideologies. In the Pope's mouth words like truth and justice and freedom had not become debased. When he spoke of salvation it was not a tired noun, but a reminder of the dignity of man.

Julius Enkomo had found Operation Holy Cross both a moving and mysterious concept for reducing global tensions.

It presumed a great deal: that all societies had the spiritual capacity to accept the Pope's ideas. How would they be seen in Tehran, from where the Islamic Confederation ruled? In Moscow, where a troika clung to power? In Washington, London, Tokyo and Berlin, where other leaders clung just as desperately to old beliefs?

That night, as they once more prayed together, he had asked God to grant to the old man kneeling beside him success for his passionate commitment to end the self-destructive impulses of a world whose inhabitants so often seemed determined to accelerate Armageddon.

Yet, no matter how hard Cardinal Enkomo had tried, then or since, he could not shake off the feeling he still had to fulfil God's purpose for him. That was why he feared death. Nothing indeed was so precious as a life not yet fully used for the greater glory of God. But after days spent in prayer and meditation in this long, low-ceilinged and simply furnished room, there was no sign of what God wanted him to do next for his people.

A little while ago he had awoken after a short sleep and cooked breakfast on the primus stove in a corner of the kitchen. There was no electricity, no telephone or television. The only link with the outside world was the battery operated radio.

He ate his meal as he had done as a child, squatting on the floor's rush-woven mats, and washing-up under the cold water hand-pump outside the front door, the same pump he used for his own ablutions. There had been no need to perform them this morning; the rain had soaked him to the skin. He had changed into one of the spare cassocks he kept and lit fresh candles on the altar made from the trunk of the acacia tree from his parents' kraal. Before the altar was a prie-dieu.

After switching off the radio, he had remained at the room's

27

picture window which, on a fine day, provided a stunning view of the valley where he had grown up. Even now, lashed by the storm, there was a primaeval beauty to the landscape which held him in thrall.

He began to concentrate. Perhaps what he should do was confront the government over the food hoarders. Coaxing had not worked. There were dangers, of course. The government could refuse to listen, complain to Rome that he was meddling. The government could do anything it liked. But that risk had always been there.

He was about to return to the kneeler when, through the heavy, pitiless rain being driven across the valley by the vicious wind, he spotted headlights.

They were passing the kloof where he had sat as a child, minding cattle, the lights rising and falling with the dips in the road. He felt sudden sweat cold on his body.

Had some of those extremists learned of this place and followed him here? If so, he had no doubt they would kill him in cold blood, the way they had butchered so many others.

He stared through the downpour at the approaching lights and willed himself to become calm.

If he was to die, if indeed God had decided he had no further role on this earth, there was no more fitting place to die than here.

The headlights were moving faster across the floor of the valley.

The road was built the year after the arrival of the African Missionary. The priest had left a bible for each kraal, and promised he would teach every child to read.

He had heard his own mother say to his father, as they curled up on the hut floor that night, that education would be a wonderful thing. Nevertheless, it had needed weeks of persuasion on her part before his father agreed he could attend the mission school.

The schoolhouse had been destroyed by the police when they drove everyone from the valley after it was designated a Whites Only zone during the days of apartheid.

The headlights were closer now.

He walked to the prie-dieu and stared at the small stained-glass picture above the altar. He had painted the depiction of Christ on the Cross. It hung beside an icon of the Holy Family.

28

He lowered himself on the kneeler, and began to recite the Lord's Prayer. He opened his eyes and looked once more at how he had imagined the scene on Calvary to be.

If he was to die, he would do so in the grace of God, as a man who had never broken one of his sacred vows; who had never physically known a woman; whose personal possessions would barely fill a small trunk.

Despite the wind, the candle in its red glass cup, the altar's sanctuary lamp, remained steady. The crucifixes gleamed in the soft light.

On top of the kneeler was the heavy, embossed Bible Pope Nicholas had given Julius Enkomo on the day he became a cardinal.

Even then His Holiness had the look of a man who accepted that his death sentence was written on the day he was born – and now a tumour had begun to grow in the Pope's brain, like a mango-tree root, slowly but inexorably.

When Julius Enkomo had last asked what the doctors said, His Holiness had looked at him carefully before replying that we are all on earth for a little while, and our one hope must be that Death, when he comes, will come quietly and softly like his sister, Sleep.

Would he, in a few moments, be able to face death so calmly? Or would he, for the briefest of moments fear the wrenching separation of flesh from the spirit?

He opened the Bible at the Book of Matthew, his favourite, and began to read aloud, his voice deep and resonant delivering the words with certainty.

There was a knocking on the door. He continued reading, totally calm and controlled. The knocking grew louder and more urgent. The candles cast long thin shadows, so that the faces of the Holy Family in the icon looked as though they were alive.

Steve had presented him with the icon. He had added impishly it would be a constant reminder of the many arguments they had both enjoyed over scriptural interpretation. Steve had held the chair of Comparative Religion at Hebren University in Jerusalem. They had remained in touch to the very end – that shocking, awful moment when a terrorist bomb had killed Steve and Dolly Vaughan in London.

Morton had telephoned Cape Town with the news; no grief had been evident in his voice. Julius Enkomo had wondered again about Morton's inner control, both what it took to achieve and what it must have cost. He knew Morton was not a cold or unfeeling man, even if he could not share his feelings over the death of the old couple who had adopted him as a child.

The knocking was more insistent. Why didn't they simply burst in?

Morton had once told him that emotional reserve was very much his style. Once a bond of trust had been established, Morton had told him a lot of things he probably shared with few other outsiders. But then, he joked, their professions were very similar.

The hammering on the door came again.

Cardinal Enkomo rose, crossed himself and backed away from the altar. Through the window the morning light had begun to drain from the sky, as if squeezed out of the clouds by the downpour. The howl of the wind seemed louder. When he lifted the catch, the force of the gale almost drove him back into the room. Behind him, there was the sound of something falling. He glanced over his shoulder. One of the crucifixes had toppled. The candles were sending shadows dancing crazily on the walls.

The man had stepped back into the gloom. Behind him was the Mercedes which the diocesan chancellor used for formal visits. Then Cardinal Enkomo recognised the young priest – he had joined the chancellery staff a couple of weeks ago – Father O'Sullivan. Not too often the Irish came this far south nowadays. They were more intent on gathering souls in Central Africa.

Father O'Sullivan was holding something under his black raincoat.

'For God's sake, don't just stand there, Father!'

After the rain-sodden priest stepped into the room and Cardinal Enkomo shut the door, he turned to Father O'Sullivan. For a moment the priest reminded him of that African Missionary who had stood with the same uncertainty in his parents' kraal.

'I'm sorry to disturb you,' Father O'Sullivan began, glancing towards the altar. The candles' flames were once more steady.

'Has something happened?' asked Cardinal Enkomo, walking to the altar and repositioning the crucifix. He needed the moment to hide the relief he felt that his visitor had not come to harm him. He turned back to the priest.

Father O'Sullivan was unbuttoning his raincoat to reveal a packet wrapped in the familiar yellow waxed paper the Vatican used for protecting hand-carried messages. Father O'Sullivan handed the packet to the cardinal.

'The courier brought it on last night's plane. The chancellor said I should bring it straight to you. I would have been here before, but the road's gone at Umtata. I had to detour through –'

'They teach you to make tea at Clonliffe?'

He remembered reading in the transfer file that O'Sullivan had graduated top of his year from the Dublin seminary.

'Our rector said it was the best he'd drunk,' grinned the priest.

'Good. Get out of those wet clothes. You'll find a spare cassock in the trunk under the bed. Then brew up a pot your old rector would be proud of!'

Cardinal Enkomo squatted on the floor. The waxed paper bore the seal of the Fisherman's Ring His Holiness wore.

'I'm to take your reply back to the courier,' called out Father O'Sullivan.

'You're assuming, father, I need to reply,' the cardinal said.

'Anything from the Holy Father needs a response, Your Eminence.'

'You'd make a good Jesuit.'

He used a thumb to work loose the seal and unwrapped the paper. Inside was an envelope addressed to him. It bore the Vatican coat-of-arms, a set of embossed gold keys in the upper left corner. He recognised the familiar handwriting. The envelope was sealed with the same waxed imprint of the Pope's ring.

He heard Father O'Sullivan opening the trunk and the rustle as he changed his clothes before moving to the kitchen.

'You take milk and sugar, Your Eminence?'

'No sugar. And lemon. There's a slice in the cupboard.'

Cardinal Enkomo broke the seal. He extracted the letter and smoothed out the folds on his knees.

The kettle had started to whistle.

'Like something to eat, Your Eminence?'

'No. There's some bacon and eggs in the cupboard next to the lemon. Help yourself.'

'I must say I'm peckish.'

A note of asperity came into Cardinal Enkomo's voice.

'And I must say I'd be obliged if you'd let me read this in peace, father!'

'Sorry, Eminence. Only I've never carried a letter from the Vatican before –'

'Father,' came the warning voice.

At last there was silence in the room.

Pope Nicholas had begun the letter the way he addressed all his cardinals: 'My dear brother-in-Christ'. His Holiness had come to the point at once:

A few days ago the new American Ambassador to the Holy See conveyed to me the news that Israel is still opposed to my making a pilgrimage to the Holy Land. The reason given is the familiar one; the security risks are too great. I told the Ambassador I was saddened, but understood the Israeli response. It means, of course, that Holy Cross is still no more than a dream of mine. Yet the spirit of reconciliation remains as strong as ever in me. That is why I now seek your help.'

From the kitchen came the smell of bacon starting to sizzle. He continued to read.

Better than most of those around me, you understand there are perfectly valid reasons for the Israeli attitude. They still resent the words of my dear predecessor-in-Christ, my brother Pius the Tenth, who said that 'as the Jews had not recognised Our Lord, we cannot recognise the Jewish people'. Pius was never a strong theologian and what he wrote was, indeed, very suspect theology.

Sadly, there persists a powerful anti-Israeli lobby in the Secretariat of State. Many of its members are young. They could still be in high office well into the next century.

His Holiness was being as blunt as always. There was an anti-Semitism which continued to seep from the Secretariat to the nunciatures and papal missions through the local hierarchies down to the humblest parish priest and nun. From the beginning he had stamped hard on it in his own diocese. But it was still there.

He continued to read.

A more immediate predecessor-in-Christ, my brother John Paul, did not help matters by referring to the West Bank and the Gaza Strip as 'occupied territories' and the Golan Heights as being 'annexed'. Nor did he calm Jewish suspicions when he spoke of the need for Jerusalem itself to have 'international status', guaranteed by United Nations forces, and Curia priests in charge of shrines. While I can think of many a prelate I would dearly wish to send as a nightwatchman over Lazarus's tomb, I can also understand how the Jews would respond!

Cardinal Enkomo smiled. Once when asked how many people worked in the Vatican, His Holiness had replied, 'About half. And that's on a good day.'

I mention all this, not because you will be unfamiliar with such matters, but partly because it helps me to crystallise my own thoughts.

Quite apart from the very great importance I attach to Operation Holy Cross, the need to make my pilgrimage to the Holy Land has become increasingly important to me, both as a man and as leader of our Church.

To do so would, I hope, put an end to those who argue, even within our faith, even at times within our own ranks, that so much of what we believe is really an elaborate sham. A demented intellectualism, last seen over a century ago in Europe, seems to be on the loose.

The number of letters I now receive offering solutions to the question of the identity of Our Lord is on the increase. Not a day goes by without somebody sending me a genealogical chart intent on proving Christ Our Saviour was a Tibetan, a Hindu, a Mongolian or a Mead. Not to forget all those zoologists and biologists who continue to write that the Immaculate Conception is a scientific impossibility.

More than anything these claims only reaffirm my passion for *my* Jesus, who I know is also yours. More than anything I wish to kneel and pray beside His empty tomb, whose very emptiness fills my heart with certainty about His true identity.

It was true that people increasingly believed the heresies, all of them, accepting them as gospel more than the Gospels themselves. He continued to read.

As you know – though few others suspect – my days are limited. 'Still slow-growing but well established' is how the doctors describe my tumour. I do not wish to know more and they

33

do not wish to tell me more. But we all know the clock is ticking towards midnight. My guess is that there are only a few minutes left. I want to use that time to go to Israel and then to Moscow.

Those are my two great ambitions. To walk in the footsteps of Christ and to celebrate mass in Red Square.

I believe that if God will grant me these wishes, I will have played a modest part in healing the terrible pain of the past and make this sad world more joyful.

Julius Enkomo felt his eyes begin to smart. When he had last been in Rome, new furrows had appeared on His Holiness's face. He looked like a man who was enduring his own hell on earth. He read on.

I would go to Israel as a supplicant, mindful that our faith is based on theirs. That without the Old Testament there could be no New, and that Christ Our Saviour was born, raised and died a Jew on a cross that has for too long been used to vilify all Jews.

I would travel to Moscow to pray that God will allow Mother Russia, and the other republics where the Christian faith once burned brightly, to do so again. And I would also pray that the other religions of that land, especially Islam, will, in God's name, co-exist in peace.

To achieve that will give meaning to my time in this great office.

The last time they had spoken in private, His Holiness had said he hoped Holy Cross would be a fitting climax to the Christian humanity for which he wanted his pontificate remembered.

Cardinal Enkomo turned over the final page.

What I require from you is a position paper, setting out clearly all the reasons why the Holy See should now extend full diplomatic recognition to Israel. Your experience in Jerusalem will serve you well, but do not minimise the difficulty you will face, and therefore I will face, in persuading others here to accept your arguments.

This time you will challenge not the position-makers of some secular government, but some of the sharpest minds in our own Secretariat of State.

I need not trouble you here with the web and weft of their arguments. Suffice to say they have not changed since my predecessor-in-Christ, John Paul, told Yasser Arafat that Israel is an artificially created state.

After the PLO leader leaked details of his private audience with the Polish pontiff, Julius Enkomo had spent difficult months in Jerusalem patiently diffusing Israeli anger. He had been greatly helped by Steve Vaughan, and David Morton whom he had just met. Both had opened doors which would otherwise have remained firmly closed to him.

He read on.

Recently it has come to my notice that the Secretariat of State intend to once more raise an issue bound to inflame Israeli feelings. Within weeks of the Jewish state being created in 1948, my predecessor-in-Christ asked for the new Israel to re-stage the trial of Christ Our Saviour and, of course, reverse the original verdict. You will recall what I said to you about this.

His Holiness had once more refilled his coffee cup and said that in no instances were the skeletal bones of Jesus' biography more stridently rattled than over His trial. But that any review of the event would be both pointless and capricious.

Cardinal Enkomo glanced towards the window. The storm continued lashing the building. He found that its fury calmed his own sudden anger over what the Vatican bureaucrats once more wanted to do. He continued to remember.

Over dinner in Jerusalem, Steve had described how, in 1948, he had been given the task of rebutting the argument for a retrial. Morton had sat between them listening, radiating only a quiet, tightly wound energy. It was not the energy Julius Enkomo had often seen in some nervous, busy priest in the corridors of the Apostolic Palace, but the energy of someone who knew how much he has to expend, and conserved it until he was ready to do so. He had asked Steve if he could see the documents. Two nights later Morton had brought him to a room near Temple Mount. On the table was a steel box. It contained the contentious correspondence.

After reading the file, Julius Enkomo was in no doubt that the

Vatican lawyer-priests had been arrogant and patronising. But when he had started to say so, Morton smiled and said it was all in the past.

Now Cardinal Enkomo knew it was not. He turned to the final paragraph of the letter.

I cannot stop my brothers-in-Christ from presenting me with their arguments as to why Israel should remain beyond our diplomatic blessing. To deny them the right to so argue, would be to negate the open pontificate I have tried to create. The only way I can overcome them is with a more powerful argument. I can think of no one better equipped than you to provide me with one. I would ask you to put aside whatever else engages you, and concentrate only on this request. The very future of Holy Cross depends on you.

Cardinal Enkomo read the letter a second time. Then he folded the pages and put them in a pocket of his cassock. He rose to his feet.

In the kitchen, Father O'Sullivan was standing and watching him. He had a cup in his hand.

'Your tea, Your Eminence.'

Cardinal Enkomo shook his head.

'Father, will you pray with me? For me?'

Without waiting for a response, he walked over and knelt at the prie-dieu. Moments later, Father O'Sullivan knelt beside him.

'What are we praying for, Your Eminence? To comfort a soul?'

Cardinal Enkomo glanced sideways at the pale face.

'We're praying for the future of the world,' he replied, closing his eyes.

# 3

Six floors below the Oval office, Morton watched a screen in a bunker extending under the White House gardens to the edge of Pennsylvania Avenue. His face revealed nothing, except the tiredness he felt after two days of missed sleep since leaving Istanbul.

He had briefed Israel's Prime Minister, Isaac Karshov, his key aides, and Bitburg on Operation Holy Cross and Wong Lee's determination to stop it. The debate which followed reminded him of the Knesset at its worst.

Bitburg had said that to allow the Pope to visit Jerusalem would pave the way for Israel to lose control over the city. The Chief of the Air Force had urged pre-emptive strikes against known Wong Lee military subsidiaries in Syria and Iran.

The lunatic Right, Morton realised, was as entrenched as always in the middle echelon of Israel's power structure. There had been endless meetings and lengthy phone calls to the President before Karshov had finally silenced them with his Old Testament prophet's voice, and brought Morton and Bitburg to Washington.

An Air Force major standing beside Morton in the bunker's observation deck pointed to a digital clock blinking on the lower right-hand corner of the monitor. On the screen the tribesmen out on a plain in what had once been the Soviet Republic of Uzbekistan had dismounted from their horses and begun to herd the Red Army soldiers into line.

'Elapsed time is a minute fifty,' the major confirmed proudly.

Under two minutes for the sensors parked almost halfway to the moon to transmit the scene to a facility buried deep in the

Virginia countryside, for computers the size of a house to sift and shift the images to a data bank, which fed them through fibre-optic cable to one of the twenty-four screens suspended from the ceiling of the bunker.

Through his earpiece Morton heard the throaty voices of the Uzbeks; they always sounded as if they were clearing phlegm.

Below the glass-walled deck the watch-keepers worked in a temperature-controlled environment and a green half-light which never varied.

The major continued to speak in the same emotionless voice.

'Just 'bout anywhere from Central Asia elapsed time used to be fifteen minutes with satellites. Those KH-12s were slow monsters. Most times our antennae farms can now get us images inside two minutes of real time.'

Morton glanced at the major. His jacket had a splash of ribbons: Grenada, Panama, the Gulf. Was it after Desert Storm his face had been remodelled? Perhaps one of the unlucky few caught by a Saddam Scud? The surgery had left the major's face oddly angular. Is that why he'd ended up here, out of sight, as a guide to Star Trek come true?

'With the next generation of photo receptors, elapsed time will be down to under thirty seconds. Some general belches in the Kremlin, we'll see 'n' hear him before he closes his mouth. Other hand, way things going, won't be many of them left. You agree, colonel?'

Morton smiled non-committally. People were always trying to probe. Those who knew who he was knew better.

'You familiar with antenna farms?'

'Only that our people can't afford one, major.'

Morton's eyes flicked over the other screens. A view of the compound in downtown Beijing where China's aged leaders lived. The picture clarity was sharp enough to pick out the carp rippling the surface of their private lake. A string of mineral-mining camps in the Antarctic. A couple of Royal Navy frigates moving between the ice-floes; there had been renewed tension between Britain and Argentina over territorial rights. Another screen was filled with Berlin's rebuilt Reichstag, the new Parliament of reunified Germany. Other monitors carried equally high-resolution views of Cairo, Tripoli, Baghdad, Tehran, Damascus, Karachi, Lima, Caracas and San Salvador. All the expected places. The remaining monitors relayed images of

Moscow and other major cities of what had once been the Soviet Union.

The major continued to explain. 'The President's still insisting on maximum surveillance even if the fighting's supposed to have stopped. Want my opinion? Those people just like to fight. It's their nature. Lookit, they had so much going for them. All that manpower, water power, forests and precious minerals. If they'd put it together properly they could've conquered the world.'

Morton doubted if they'd taught the major at re-training school that there had always been problems. The oil, gas and forests were in Siberia. The manpower in Central Asia. Most of the land wasn't suitable for farming. Too hot or too cold, too wet or too dry. And the water flowed in the wrong direction.

But Stalin hadn't listened. He had set out to crush nature. Entire forests had been decimated, lakes drained and an inland sea diverted.

Gorbachev and Yeltsin had listened. But it was too late by then. Now tens of millions of acres of man-made farmland were polluted. The Black and Caspian Seas were little better than sewers. The ring of industrial cities around Moscow were under a permanent pall.

In Moscow itself the air pollution had produced birth defects fifty per cent higher than the national average and the life expectancy in the capital had dropped by ten years. People had blamed Gorbachev. It had become worse after he resigned. They blamed Yeltsin. When he went, the figures continued to worsen. Western Europe had virtually closed its borders to the hordes of Russian refugees trying to flee this ecological disorder.

Those forced to remain suffered a succession of crop failures. Two more Chernobyl-like disasters made thousands of square miles of the Urals permanently unusable. An area of tundra the size of England was a moonscape. Great rivers like the Volga were sluggish with toxic waste. An almost biblical blight had cast its shadow everywhere. Out of the darkness had come anarchy. Soon, close to 300 million people were at each other's throats. Serbs against Croats, Armenians fighting Lithuanians, Kazakhs slaughtering Slavs. Old feuds spilling new blood as Moslems confronted Christians.

The West had watched, appalled and fascinated, as this once most powerful of enemies had begun to devour itself. There was no question of intervention. Just making sure it didn't spill over, by giving sufficiently little in the way of aid.

This strategy perfectly suited Wong Lee. It allowed him to manipulate the troika in Moscow, and the leaders of the Islamic Confederation in Tehran. Those he could not manipulate he set about crushing.

The major turned from the screen.

'This could really have been over by now if we hadn't propped up Gorbachev for so long. The guy was a loser. A smile with no substance,' he said.

Morton kept his eye on the screen. Bunker strategists weren't exclusive to Washington.

Mikhail Gorbachev had tried to balance expectations with reality. After surviving the 1991 *putsch* which saw the end of the Communist Party, he had resigned. Yeltsin had taken power. He had not savoured it for long.

The demise of these two leaders signalled further steps on the road to the present chaos. The collapse of the Berlin Wall and the reunification of Germany. The dismembering of the Warsaw Pact. The end of the Soviet Union.

These events, Morton now knew, had been brilliantly and ruthlessly exploited by Wong Lee. But knowing that and proving it were very different matters.

The major was visibly gripped by what was happening on the plain in Uzbekistan.

'Thirtieth mass execution this week at this spot. Same time every day.'

'The Uzbeks have always killed their prisoners at sunset.'

The major pressed buttons on his keyboard to bring the image on the screen into closer focus.

'What beats me is why they bother to bring them out there to be killed.'

'There's the reason.'

Morton nodded towards a green-blue dome visible in the middle distance on the screen.

'The tomb of the great Uzbek leader, Timur. He once defeated the best Europe could put against him. He was tougher than Ghenghis Khan and all the Tartars rolled into one. His people like to remember that. So they dispose of their enemies in front of his tomb.'

'Strange people.'

'For sure.'

Morton adjusted the earpiece and continued watching the screen.

The choice had been coming to the bunker, or taking the other option on the schedule, a trip to Langley, while Karshov briefed the President in the Oval Office. He had told Karshov to hold back nothing. The Prime Minister's frown had deepened and he had growled it was going to be difficult.

Morton had suggested Karshov should begin by asking the President to threaten to cut off aid to Israel unless the Pope was allowed to launch Holy Cross by travelling from Nazareth to Jerusalem. Karshov's frown had deepened. Then he had nodded and displayed his predator's teeth. The sheer crudeness of the threat would concentrate wonderfully the minds of those who bedevilled his administration.

American dollars had paid for their fancy holidays outside Israel and the expensive mistresses they discreetly maintained within – and still left them enough for their wives to buy the latest Paris fashions from unnumbered Swiss deposit accounts.

Karshov had insisted that when he made his pitch to the President, he wanted to be alone. Morton understood. There would be the usual amount of horse-trading over who would silence the more vociferous voice of the Jewish lobby in America.

Bitburg had gone to Langley, to discuss the latest CIA trend, to recruit bank tellers as case officers. Bitburg would no doubt come away impressed. He always was by such things.

On the flight from Tel Aviv he had sat next to Bitburg listening to him fretting about Yoshi Kramer's decision to travel to Moscow, even if he was the first Jew invited to address the Soviet Academy of Sciences. Yoshi had invented a new surgical technique, using a laser which enabled him to eradicate a tumour deep in a patient's brain. The Academy had said, come and show us. Implicit in the invitation was – and we'll arrange freedom for another plane load of Soviet Jews. Some things hadn't changed in Russia.

Yoshi was still in Moscow, no doubt showing off his jars of pickled brain tumours, and animatedly explaining his new technique for removing them, especially to any pretty woman doctor. Yoshi's sexual conquests were as legendary as his skills. Bitburg had said it must be his Georgian blood. Morton suspected that was Bitburg's needling way of reminding Morton of his own past.

He and Ruth were among the first to leave the Soviet Union, in those post-Stalin years, in order to go to Israel; leaving their parents buried in unmarked graves in some forsaken part of Siberia.

It had taken years to grasp why Steve had changed Ruth's and his surname; that there'd be less chance of racial persecution for someone with a name like Morton. The change had not saved Ruth, like Steve and Dolly, from becoming a victim of terrorism. Or made it any easier for Morton to get along with the Bitburgs of this world.

Morton hadn't told the Director why he had wanted to come to the bunker. The skill, of course, was never to let anyone know exactly what it was you were searching for.

'Lemme show you what we can really do with resolution.' The major's hands flew over the keyboard.

An insert screen appeared in an upper corner of the monitor. The close-up was of a soldier with a strong, young face. Along with fear there was something else in those coal-black eyes.

'We can focus down to six inches. One day a sensor will be smart enough to see up a man's nose.'

The major was a clone of all the guides Morton had listened to at NASA and the other shrines to mechanical intelligence. They always forgot it needed human ingenuity to create that intelligence.

'Guess I'm not breaking security when I say this whole set-up was the White House response to the failure of our combined intelligence community to predict events before, during and after the Persian Gulf war.'

Morton gave another non-committal smile. Three months before Iraq invaded Kuwait, he had warned the CIA about Saddam Hussein's intentions. But Mossad was in another period of being cold-shouldered by Langley and the alert disappeared into a void.

After the war, the memo surfaced at a closed hearing of the Senate Select Committee on Intelligence. A furious President had ordered the bunker built so that he would have direct access to unedited intelligence and not the CIA's version of events.

The fear on the youth's face had been replaced by determination.

'The close-up's of the guy at the far end. Look at the way he's

42

bobbing up and down. You'd think he was out on the sprint track.'

Morton had seen this kind of tension in young Arabs in Gaza and the West Bank just before they threw rocks. One of the tribesmen was shouting, the wailing cry of a muezzin coming strikingly clear after its long journey through space.

'One of them always yells before they kill,' said the major in disgust.

'He's asking for God's grace. They've always given killing a religious significance,' Morton explained.

For sure, the muezzin was no graduate of one of Uzbekistan's *madrasahs*, the religious schools where they teach a wailing as distinctive as Gregorian plainchant. Probably a peasant who did not even own a Koran, and could not read it if he had.

The major squinted at Morton. 'You know a lot about them?'

'A little.'

'Yeah?'

'Yes,' Morton said in a voice designed to discourage further such questions.

The major turned back to the screen.

The mullah had stopped chanting to look towards the horizon.

'Taking longer than usual,' the major said.

'The muezzin wants the sun at head height so that it catches the soldiers' eyes. The last thing they're supposed to see on earth is the glory of Allah dazzling them.'

'Some god.'

The face on the insert screen had drawn a deep breath.

'Hey! Lookit!' cried the major.

At their work stations some of the watch keepers had paused to stare at the monitor.

The young soldier had broken from the line and was running towards the horses. Spumes of dust were being kicked up by his boots and the lappets of his field cap flapped in the wind.

'Go man, go!' a voice cried in the half light of the bunker.

The unexpectedness and sheer speed of the soldier's move gave him a flying start. He was a good thirty yards into his escape before the first of the tribesmen began to bring their rifles to bear.

'Ten he makes twenty more yards from – now!' a voice called from a work station to Morton's left.

43

The conscript was zig-zagging, a tiny figure against the evening sky spreading its shadow over the plain.

'You're on, Ollie. Marker's running. He's still got twelve to go!'

Across the base of the screen a strip of mercury was moving along its scale.

'Our new digitised stereoscopic sensors allow us to measure movement within a foot,' murmured the major.

'Ten, nine, eight . . . !' The chanting had begun to grow in the bunker.

The soldier had turned into the full glare of the sun, hoping to dazzle the aim of the tribesmen.

'Seven, six, five . . .' called out Ollie. 'He's gonna make it!'

Several of the Uzbeks had rifles at their shoulders.

'Three, two!'

Morton saw the soldier suddenly pitch forward. A split-second later the echo of rifle shots filled his earpiece.

A sigh, a little louder than the hiss of the filtered air circulating through the bunker, came from the watch keepers. The mercury had stopped moving. An electronic pointer appeared, flashing above a number – 20. It was like a TV game show.

The major looked embarrassed. 'It gets boring down here after a while.'

'I can imagine.'

From the work floor came Ollie's protest.

'Focal plane could have been distorted. It's too close to call. Guy could still have passed the marker.'

Morton could see Ollie, standing at his work station. A man in the foothills of middle age, waving a pudgy hand. A bad loser.

'Focal plane never distorts, Ollie. You know that,' called a watch keeper from the opposite end of the bunker.

'That's right,' said the major proudly. 'The sensors record the same scene from different angles. The computers do the rest.'

On the screen the firing squad had reformed. A moment later the row of condemned soldiers collapsed. By the time the sound of the volley reached Morton's earpiece, the Uzbeks had slung their rifles and were walking back to their horses.

'They leave the bodies as a warning –' The major broke off. 'Lookit, upper right on the screen!'

A plane, no bigger than a fly, was swooping down. The tribesmen were already scattering. The whine of engines at full pitch filled Morton's earpiece. He saw the faint white glow from rockets launched at the speed of sound. Then the flashes from their impact, followed by the unmistakable sound of high explosives detonating among the Uzbeks.

The major's fingers were working frantically at the keyboard. The insert screen was momentarily filled with a close-up of the Mig, then the fighter climbed and disappeared off the monitor. Afterwards the sound of the wind whistling over dead men and horses came to Morton.

"Kay, everyone. Playtime's over,' called the Navy captain from his desk behind the work stations. The watch officer sounded like someone with a lifetime of disappointment.

'It really does get quite boring down here,' repeated the major.

Morton thought things were actually going very well. Long ago he had learned never to rush; haste was to heed the call of the Mocking God.

The major pressed a button. The scene from Uzbekistan vanished from the screen.

'How about a little tour? You name it, we go there,' he offered, sounding like a fairground barker, used to showing off to some Congressman that the money was being well spent. 'Our version of a Sunday spin in the country.'

'Wherever you like.'

The major fingered the keyboard. A vast urban sprawl looking rather like a flower in bloom came on screen.

'Sixty thousand miles out, Mexico City looks kinda pretty. Now watch.'

At a key touch, the city came close enough to show buildings, avenues and streets, and the scars from the last earthquake. All were bathed in a rosy hue.

'Nicest looking pollution on earth. So thick you can bottle it. Yet over 25 million people still live down there, maybe more.'

A growing number worked for Wong Holdings. The conglomerate had underwritten a significant portion of Mexico's debt to the World Bank in return for exclusive manufacturing rights. Wong Lee had done the same in over two hundred other countries. It made him the world's largest employer of near-slave labour.

The major pressed a key and a busy street scene appeared. Girls in short black skirts and black suede thigh boots sprawled on bonnets of gridlocked cars. Kids bobbed up and down at wing mirror height, laughing and picking pockets. Morton's earpiece was filled with noise – sales patter and engine grunt.

'A breeding ground for terrorists and other troublemakers. Right in our own backyard, and more we try 'n' help them, more they abuse us.'

The major reflected a growing attitude. America was tired of being the world's provider. Or its policeman. The air waves were filled with the isolation of the thirties. Then it had been the radio preachers who thundered that Europe's problems were – Europe's.

Now it was the TV evangelists who spread the message. None did so with more power than the Reverend Edward Kingdom, pastor of the Church of True Belief. He was another reason why Morton had come to the bunker.

On the screen, Bangkok came and went. Then Vienna, Stockholm, Nairobi, Madrid and half a dozen other cities Morton knew well. He listened politely as the major continued his set lecture.

'We cover 173 countries on a regular basis. Apart from all the usual stuff, the sensors have a task list. Check for somebody in a key office being promoted or demoted. A mistress moved in or out. New peccadilloes for a ruling family. That kinda stuff gives us an overview the CIA likes to keep to itself.'

Morton nodded politely. No matter how sophisticated, intelligence gathering would always be a continuing education in human frailty.

The major organised another scene shift. The images on the other screens also constantly changed at the command of the watch keepers. From time to time Morton had seen their reel-to-reel tape decks spin.

'We put together a daily video for the President. He views it after the evening news,' said the major.

After they had peered down on Paris the major glanced at his watch. 'That's about it. Round the world in eighty minutes.'

'How about Tibet?' Morton kept his voice casual.

The major hesitated. 'It's middle of their night. All you'd see is the snow and the glow of candles in their shrines. Nothing moves, even in Lhasa, after sunset. Those monks are early to bed, early to rise. The Chinese follow suit.'

'I'd still like to see, if it's not too much trouble.' It was important not to push too hard.

The message in the Delhi drop had led to all the other pieces. The recent transfer of millions of dollars from the Bank of Southern California to equip the Kazakhs. Rockets heading down a six-lane highway on China's border with Tadjikistan. Arsenals which had turned up in Turkmenistan, Moldavia and Armenia. Caches of explosives moved up the River Don and out of the swamps of the Aral Sea. Enough to equip a dozen armies to wage unholy war to satisfy the megalomaniac who lived in Lhasa.

The major picked up a phone and spoke to the watch officer. The Navy captain half turned in his chair and stared up at the observation deck. On one of the screens had appeared the mass of Michelangelo's dome on the basilica of St Peter's.

Morton had first seen it on a visit to Rome with Steve. He had been eighteen, finished at Clifton and on his way to Cambridge, Ruth at medical school, their world at peace. Steve had said it must be an awesome thought for the man he had come to see, the Pope, to know he would be buried in a vault deep beneath the ground which supported this edifice. Even then Morton realised Steve could be touchingly naive.

Pope Paul the Sixth had been unable, or unwilling, to accept Steve's argument that it was time for the Holy See to recognise Israel's statehood. Steve had fared no better with Paul's successor.

The major replaced the phone. 'It'll take a few minutes to activate the Tibet farm.'

From Rome came the view of Bernini's awesome colonnade and St Peter's Square. The towering obelisk of Caligula in the centre of the piazza was in evening shadow.

The Turk who tried to assassinate Pope John Paul had used the towering granite pillar as cover. The Polish pontiff had recovered from his wounds and eventually died peacefully.

On screen appeared a terracotta coloured building, the Apostolic Palace. Lights glowed in the upper floor. Through one of the windows a familiar white cassocked figure sat at a desk, reading.

The major began to recite sonorously. 'Servant of the Servants of God, Patriarch of the West, Vicar of Christ, Archbishop and Metropolitan of the Province of Rome, State Governor of Vatican City, Supreme Pontifex Maximus of the Universal Church. His Holiness, Pope Nicholas the Sixth.'

'You spy on the Pope?' Morton made sure to sound properly impressed.

The major gave a man-of-the-world smile.

'Mostly we check on how he responds to his CIA briefings. The station chief drives over from our Rome Embassy and they have supper together. Afterwards the pontiff says his evening prayers and settles down with his Langley up-date. That's what he's doing right now.'

The image had tightened to show the old pontiff. He read slowly, one arthritic finger tracing the words on the paper, the other fingering the pectoral cross suspended around his neck on a gold chain.

Bitburg had recently circulated a memo that the cross and chain were currently insured by the Vatican at 450,000 dollars. That sort of detail always appealed to Bitburg.

'You a Catholic, major?'

'Born 'n' raised. Never missed a feast day.'

'You tell your confessor you bug the Pope?'

'No need to. All Catholics working in sensitive areas have special dispensation from the White House chaplain not to disclose.'

On the screen Pope Nicholas was hunched over his desk. He was already in his seventieth year when he ascended the Throne of St Peter.

Three months later, in the utmost secrecy, Morton had brought Yoshi Kramer to see the pontiff. Yoshi had diagnosed Nicholas the Sixth had a meningioma, a slow-growing brain tumour. Yoshi had explained to him that surgery carried too high a risk at his age. He had not mentioned his experimental work with lasers. There was no point. Nicholas the Sixth would in all probability be dead before the new technique was perfected.

Now, a year after Yoshi had performed his first successful laser operation in Paris, the Pope was still alive.

Watching the screen, Morton remembered the feeling of real warmth he had felt when he had accompanied a delegation of Israel's most senior rabbis to discuss Holy Cross.

After Pope Nicholas explained his vision, the head of the delegation had spoken. 'It will not be easy. You are a good man. But there are many who fear and even hate what that would represent.'

Pope Nicholas had sighed. 'If God had meant it to be easy, he would have fulfilled my wish a long time ago. I believe he will do so now because time is truly running out.'

The major once more picked up the phone, listened for a moment, then replaced the receiver.

'Lhasa's coming up on screen,' he said.

The towering Tanglha Hills flanking the city looked no bigger than hummocks. The Potala, once the palace of the pontiff-ruler of Tibet, the Dalai Lama, rose above the silent city.

The only signs of life were the flickering pin-pricks from yak-butter candles burning inside the Jokka Kang, the oldest and most sacred of the Lhasa temples.

Morton's eyes were drawn to a structure as imposing as any of the temples.

The pagoda-roofed building clung to a rock face eight hundred feet above the valley. On one side of the structure was a heli-pad, on the other a glassed-in garden. The complex was a feat unequalled in modern-day construction, built to withstand maelstrom winds, blizzarding snow, sub-zero temperatures and the intense sunlight of the rarefied crystal-pure air at this height.

It was Wong Lee's principal home.

'Here, lemme show you something.'

The major pushed keys. On screen the building slowly came closer. Then shutters began to lower on its windows and a canopy started to cover the enclosed garden.

'Best private security system in the world,' said the major, reluctant admiration in his voice.

'When our sensors focus down at around the thousand mile marker, when we'd expect to see the colour of someone's hair, or more important what he's reading, Wong's box of tricks really comes into play. See for yourself.'

The screen was filled with the kind of white-out a badly-tuned TV set emits.

'His system pumps out electronic chaff – an updated version of the stuff our bombers used to dump over the Ruhr and send German radar nuts. This stuff sends our sensors crazy. Best cosmic dirty trick in the business. The sensors can't stay more'n a minute in range or they panic to the point where they'll just shut down.'

The major punched keys and the picture returned to its previous clarity. The shutters and cover over the garden rolled back.

It really was a prime example of superb technology embedded in architectural boldness.

Ultimately every deal Wong Holdings made was approved in this building – including the one a year ago, when one of its Caracas-based banks had funnelled money through another of its Cayman Island registered corporations to a Malta-based private trust.

The trust had been set up by lawyers acting for the Church of True Belief. They used the money to buy a communications satellite which allowed the Reverend Kingdom to reach the remotest settlement on earth.

It was not simply the size of the donation, two billion dollars, which first attracted Morton's attention. Or that Wong Lee had no known religious affiliations. It was a question of why he had financed God's self-appointed messenger on earth. Was the Reverend Kingdom an integral part of Wong Lee's plans to wreck Operation Holy Cross?

The major grabbed Morton's arm.

'Oh Christ! Lookit!'

A red light was blinking above the screen relaying the scene from the Pope's office.

Over the bunker's speaker system the watch officer was calmly announcing, 'We have a Code One at the Vatican.'

On the screen Pope Nicholas sprawled on the floor. A moment later a cassocked figure entered his office. He punched a button on the desk console, then knelt beside the Pope, listening for a heart beat. Morton recognised the Pope's English-language secretary, Monsignor Sean Hanlon.

More priests were rushing into the office. An older man in the blood-red cassock of a cardinal arrived and began to wave the others back.

'Hubert Messner,' identified the major. 'Secretary of State, and the nearest thing the Vatican has to our Vice-President. Used to be in charge of exorcisms. His staff call him the Hun, and not just because he's from Bavaria.'

Steve had said there was nothing quite like a theologian who came grunting out of the Black Forest. Except a major who read the religious tabloids.

Morton's earpiece was filled with the hushed, stricken voices of those gathered around the Pope.

'Looks like a heart attack,' said the major.

On the screen a Swiss Guard in a billowy Renaissance costume of blue, orange and yellow stripes arrived with a dark-suited figure with a gold fob chain across his waistcoat. Even without his black bag, the man could be nothing but a doctor; he exuded that special bedside manner which only very successful physicians possess. Yoshi had said he wouldn't let Fortuti, the papal physician, treat a baby with colic.

'What are they saying?' the major demanded.

'Why don't you keep watching the screen?' suggested Morton, pulling out his earpiece and striding from the observation deck.


Once Morton explained why he had interrupted, the President placed the White House Communications Centre at his disposal. Morton called Yoshi in Moscow. Yoshi said he would call Fortuti.

Afterwards the President explained what he and Karshov had discussed so far. The President was a courteous man in his late fifties, well groomed and well spoken.

'This threat Wong Lee poses is the most difficult one I have faced since coming into office. He is beyond all the usual sanctions. If we move to censure him through the UN, all those countries he has in an economic arm-lock would simply be made to vote against us. We can't use military force. What would we attack? His Lhasa HQ? China would see that as a declaration of war. Wong Holdings is scattered across the globe. We couldn't touch it militarily. The best option would be squeezing him economically. But that's going to take careful working out. Wong Holdings suddenly collapses and we have a crash that would make '29 look like a piggybank going under.'

Karshov stirred in his chair. His voice was like a rasp working on metal.

'What we propose, David, is that you continue to monitor Wong Lee's operations while we see what's feasible.'

'You can have anyone or anything in my power to authorise, colonel,' the President said.

Morton turned to the President.

'I want that antenna farm over Tibet watching twenty-four hours a day. I want the other farms repositioned so they focus on Wong Holdings' operations. I want all CIA stations to concentrate on what Wong's people are doing on the ground –'

The President raised a hand, palm facing Morton.

'Hold it a moment, colonel. This is turning out to be quite a shopping list. I'd better take a note.'

He produced from his pocket a small memo pad and pen and made a note of what had been requested already. Then he looked at Morton and nodded.

'I want all the CIA operations to be run by Bill Gates. He reports directly to me.'

Gates had remained the agency's Director of Operations, the most clandestine branch, under three previous presidents. Morton regarded him as a total professional.

The President gave a quick nod, then waited, pen poised.

Morton looked at both men.

'I want to bring some others fully into the picture. Jacques Lacouste in Paris, for a start –'

'Who is he?' the President asked quickly.

'Number two in French Intelligence. He could have had the top job, but hates being chained to a desk.'

'I know the feeling,' the President said ruefully.

'Marcus Baader,' Morton continued. 'He runs Operations for the BND.'

'That I know,' the President smiled. 'When the Chancellor came here the other day I had Baader's men tramping all over the Rose Garden.'

'I'll want to talk to Norm Stratton who runs Canadian counter-intelligence and Anwar Salim who does the same for the Egyptians.'

'A good man,' Karshov rumbled. He was a smallish giant of six-five, with the movements of a boxer who still worked out.

'How about the Brits?' the President asked.

Morton hesitated. There had been another upheaval in Britain's Secret Intelligence Service following revelations that a number of its officers had close links to South African Security – who in turn had been passing sensitive material from London to neighbouring front-line states to try and buy peace. But West was still there as head of MI5's E-Branch, responsible for anti-terrorism.

'I'll need to talk to Percival West.'

The President nodded.

'What about the Soviets?' he asked.

'Since the KGB folded, its replacement set-up has leaked like a sieve. The only man I'd trust would be Savenko.'

The President nodded. 'I met Yuri Savenko with Gorbachev. Savenko seemed to know his business. You want to brief him, that's fine by me.'

'But not yet, Mr President. I want to keep this as tight as possible.'

'What about our own people?' Karshov asked.

'Danny and Chantal know some of it. So does the Professor. Lester Final's people are going to be essential. So are Humpty Dumpty's.'

The President's eyebrows arched.

'The Professor runs Psychological Assessment,' Morton explained quickly. 'Lester Final our computers, Humpty Dumpty, Voice Analysis.'

'How come such a nickname, colonel?'

Morton smiled briefly. 'He looks like he fell off a wall and nobody quite put him together again except they gave him two brains.'

'Sounds like quite a team, colonel.' The President glanced down at his notes. 'I can arrange my end without going to Congress.'

Morton looked at Karshov.

'There's one other matter, Prime Minister. The aid question.'

The President shook his head.

'Threatening to cut off aid to your country? That I would have to take to the Hill. And I'd never carry them with me. The way the Arabs torpedoed the peace conference has made even the doves into hawks.'

He smiled his politician's smile.

Karshov cleared his throat. 'I never thought the day would come when I'd regret that!'

The Prime Minister turned to Morton. 'You have the usual free hand.'

'Walter?'

'I'll speak to Bitburg.'

The President tapped his pen on the pad.

'All this, of course, could be academic, given what's just happened to the Pope.'

'If Pope Nicholas dies his successor should take over Holy Cross, Mr President.'

The President glanced sharply at Morton.

'He may, or he may not. You can't be certain. Personally, I've never given the idea much of a chance.'

The silence was broken when Yoshi called back and the President put him on the speaker phone.

'What's the prognosis, Dr Kramer?' asked the President.

'Fortuti couldn't diagnose a nose bleed. Luckily he had the sense to call in Carlo Poggi at the Gemelli. If I had a brain injury, he'd be the man I'd want. He says the meningioma's haemorrhaged close to the hippocampus –'

'Forgive me interrupting, but what exactly is that?' asked the President.

'It's that seahorse shaped structure we all have in our brain that controls emotions, learning and memory.'

'Could Poggi operate on that area, Dr Kramer?'

'With a younger, physically fitter man – possibly. Even then it would be a tough call. But with the Pope, Carlo says it's a non-starter. He physically wouldn't be able to withstand the surgery.'

'Where is Pope Nicholas now?'

'They've moved him to the hospital in the basement of the Apostolic Palace.'

'Could they transfer him to the Gemelli? I recall they did a pretty good job in fixing Pope John Paul's gunshot wounds,' said the President.

'To move him would only increase the risk of further cranial bleeding.'

The President looked at Karshov, then continued.

'This new technique of yours, Dr Kramer. Is it suitable for this kind of surgical intervention?'

'Of course. It's far quicker and there's less stress risk. But I am in Moscow –'

'Could you operate in the Vatican, Yoshi?' Karshov interrupted.

'I can operate just about anywhere, Prime Minister.'

Morton smiled. Yoshi was quick to take offence.

'Then you don't have a problem. I'm sure Dr Poggi can give you any help you want with nurses and back-up equipment. So how quickly can you get to Rome?' Karshov demanded.

'There's still a problem. Aeroflot's once more cancelled most of its flights because it can't get fuel. The few foreign carriers still operating out of here are also running a restricted service.'

Morton turned to Karshov. 'Let me take the Dove.'

The El Al Concorde was parked at Andrews Air Force Base waiting to fly the Israeli delegation back to Tel Aviv.

'It's yours.'

At that moment the door of the Oval Office opened.

'Hello, Walter,' said Morton evenly.

Bitburg was already nodding obsequiously to the President and Karshov. Despite the warmth of the day he wore a dark grey winter flannel suit.

'I came as soon as I heard,' Bitburg said.

'So here you are,' Karshov rumbled. 'You're just in time to say goodbye to David.'

Bitburg's fussy banker's walk propelled him to an uncertain halt between the armchairs of the President and Karshov.

'How was Langley?' the President asked politely.

'As always, Mr President, impressive. They've recruited some fine young business men and women.' Bitburg glanced quickly at Karshov. 'Where's David going?'

'Moscow.'

Bitburg's eyes began to carom behind his glasses.

'Moscow? Why, Prime Minister?'

'I take it you're not bringing Walter,' came Yoshi's voice from the speaker phone.

'Why are you on this phone, Dr Kramer?' Bitburg demanded.

'Ask David.'

Bitburg finally addressed Morton. 'Why are you going to Moscow?'

'To pick up Yoshi and take him to Rome to operate on the Pope.'

'*What?*' Bitburg spun round to Karshov.

'Prime Minister, I don't think this is wise, and not just in the historical context.'

'The historical context?' murmured the President, surprised.

Bitburg's eyes settled briefly on the President. 'We Jews have spent two thousand years living down the calumny that our ancestors killed Christ. Not just a handful of rabbis and a madman called Herod. But the whole Jewish people!'

Bitburg turned back to Karshov. 'For Dr Kramer, or any Jew, to become directly involved in trying to save the life of the leader of the largest Christian faith is sheer madness! The Pope dies and we'll be accused of murdering him! I must absolutely urge that we have no direct part in any of this. Consultation is one thing. Dr Kramer will then be just another voice. But for him to be the one to actually use the knife –'

'It'll be a laser, Walter,' came Yoshi's suddenly irritated voice. 'And please don't tell me what I can do!'

'Quite simply the world needs Pope Nicholas to live, Director Bitburg,' the President said quietly.

Bitburg turned to Karshov. His eyes resembled balls being repeatedly struck by a cue in his head.

'You know my views on this Holy Cross operation? Until the Vatican sends us all the paperwork to evaluate, we should not get involved.'

Engraved on Bitburg's brain was the maxim that if something was not on paper, it should be avoided.

'There's nothing on paper, Walter,' Morton began.

'I thought not.'

'You remember that trip Danny and I made to Kathmandu?' The balls continued to carom.

'That you never really told me about afterwards.'

'I knew about it, Walter,' Karshov said.

Bitburg had lost the struggle for mastery over his eyes.

'We went to the border with Tibet and buried in the perma-snow those receivers Lester and Humpty Dumpty came up with,' Morton told Bitburg.

'So? I still don't see –'

'The receivers were programmed to trigger data from our weather satellite,' Morton continued.

The satellite was equipped with the latest light-sensitive silicon diodes and phased-array radars for photographic and electronic intelligence gathering.

Morton stared at Bitburg, at the manicured fingers, into the eyes. What else was going on in there, going round and round? Bitburg's way was to keep everything in separate compartments, each labelled with the amount of proof they contained.

'Remember that memo I sent you about reorbiting the satellite?' Morton asked.

Every ninety minutes the satellite made an orbital cycle of the earth, each time covering a 600-mile track.

'And I queried the cost. You remember that!' Bitburg snapped.

'For sure.'

The President smiled.

'Our own intelligence folk were a little concerned about the new orbit, colonel. We don't usually allow foreign satellites, even if they're only supposed to be for weather purposes, to pass over the United States.'

'Thanks for your understanding, Mr President,' Karshov said quickly.

'I suspect if I hadn't agreed, the colonel would have found some other way, Isaac.'

Morton had ordered the orbits to be reset so that, fourteen times a day, the satellite passed close to Lhasa and immediately above the world headquarters of the Church of True Belief in Malibu, California.

'So what have you learned from that extra half million dollars a day it's costing us?' Bitburg demanded.

Morton felt suddenly tired – tired and wasted. He wanted an end to this bickering.

'Wong Lee is planning the final destabilisation of what was the Soviet Union. Part of his plan is to stop Holy Cross happening. If he succeeds, not only Israel but a lot of other countries will be in danger.'

There was still complete silence in the Oval Office when Morton opened the door and left.

# 4

The Reverend Doctor Edward Patrick Kingdom waited for his cue.

To his right, his best profile for a close-up, the red transmission light had stopped glowing on one of the RCA cameras. He had long learned complete mastery over a lens, knowing exactly the angle to make him look ten years younger than his fifty-five years and leaner than one-eighty pounds. A permanent suntan and a thousand dollars a year spent on dental fees helped.

The Reverend Kingdom rapped one of the mikes with a manicured finger.

'What's the problem?' he demanded.

In the glass-walled production gallery high above the organ loft, one of the faces quickly leaned forward and spoke into a microphone.

'Sorry, Reverend Kingdom, we're getting feedback.' The voice came from a speaker built into the pulpit. 'We're doing a sound check.'

'Just hurry it along, Alan. God loves you.'

'Will do,' Alan Milton promised before obediently completing the obligatory mantra, 'And bless His name.'

The credits listed him as producer of the *Voice of Truth Hour*. In reality he was only the show's director. The real power lay with the executive producer, Edward Kingdom, Doctor of Divinity and First Pastor of the Church of True Belief.

That credit always came immediately before the final one: A Production Of The Tabernacle Broadcasting Network Bringing God To The People.

The Reverend Kingdom waited, silent and motionless in his

custom-made cassock and surplice, lantern-jaw firm and deep blue eyes unswerving. He looked exactly like his photograph on the cover of the Church of True Belief Salvation Handbook each convert received upon joining.

He glanced up at the gallery. Martha wanted Tom out as sound man. She had said put him in Records, the library, any place where perfect hearing didn't matter.

That was after she discovered their eldest brother's deafness. The doctors said it was only marginally worse than in anyone of Tom's age. Martha still insisted the margin was unacceptable in someone responsible for making sure there was no glitch in recording the Word.

'Eddie?' a reedy voice came from a speaker built into the pulpit.

'Yes, Tom.'

'Sorry about this.'

'It's okay. God loves you.'

'And bless His name.'

The Reverend Kingdom tapped the mike again. 'Alan, make sure you get wide-angles of the pulpit. People write and tell me it gives them a sense of God's power.'

The pulpit rose from the church floor, rising half-way towards where the stained glass windows began to form the base of a crown of glass thorns at the apex of the pyramid-shaped Tabernacle. A dozen hand-cut marble steps, each one dedicated to an Apostle, led to the carpeted platform on which the Reverend Kingdom stood. The Salvation Handbook explained they symbolised his own climb to spiritual rebirth as well as providing a reminder he was here to carry on the work of the original Twelve.

The Reverend Kingdom bowed his head as in prayer. It was his favourite shot.

Built into the pulpit was a small monitor on which he could see the transmission picture. Concealed microphones enabled him to move freely around the area without voice-fade. The cue bulbs were wired into the base of the lectern supporting the open, leather-tooled Bible. Resting on the Book of Job was the typed script which reminded him at what passages of his sermon he should smile and spread his hands, or frown and fold his arms, and when to knit those magnificent jet-black eyebrows, or use any of the other gestures from his repertoire appropriate to the moment. On the ledge was a telephone. He'd use it during live broadcasts, interrupting a service to receive and then repeat some earth-shattering news. During Sunday morning services one of the staff constantly monitored CNN.

There was always a rush of converts after he stood in the pulpit, phone in hand, warning of Armageddon drawing ever closer for the godless. For the faithful the sight was affirmation of his claim that God did indeed speak to the world through him.

At this moment, mid-morning on a Wednesday, the Reverend Kingdom's fleshy lips began to tighten. This business with the sound was taking too long. He raised his head and once more tapped a mike.

'Alan, I've got an eleven-thirty I can't break even for you.'

Martha had insisted he mustn't miss the appointment with the realtors. The chance would not come again to buy those seven hundred acres adjoining the church's present land holding. On them he would build a university campus to surpass all those erected by other evangelists.

'Nearly there, Reverend Kingdom. We've found the problem. Just need to switch the feeder input –'

'Spare me the technical details.'

'Absolutely, Reverend Kingdom. God loves you.'

'And bless His name. But let's get this show in the can!'

The Reverend Kingdom began to compose his face as one of the cameras started to slowly track in.

This was the twentieth year of his electronic ministry. He had begun with a single radio hour. Then a Sunday morning TV show he'd shared with another preacher. He'd bought him out, then bought the station.

The Tabernacle Broadcasting Network now owned 645 TV stations across the nation, plus another 1,055 radio stations, and broadcast to 97 countries. Coming here this morning he'd been told another two million Soviets could hear his voice now that the relay station in Finland was at full power. Worldwide that meant over 700 million were listening.

'All set here, Reverend Kingdom. You need a playback?'

'Thank you, Alan. I know exactly where I was interrupted.'

He had built to the point of attack. No one he knew did it better.

'Terrific. We'll start with a medium shot, than a slow creep out.'

'Fine.'

The lights returned to full power and he felt his skin begin to glisten. The air conditioning was turned off during recording because the machinery had a built-in low-frequency murmur which the mikes amplified.

When he suggested replacing the equipment, Martha had said the cost was prohibitive, given the time he spent in the pulpit. She had never been able to shake off her Belfast penny-pinching ways. Perhaps it was no bad thing. With the tens of millions of dollars tithed every year, it would be easy to splash out recklessly.

Martha had also persuaded him to accept Wong Lee's gift of the satellite. Never mind he was an atheist. His money was as good as any of those Midwest tycoons. All Wong Lee had asked was for the Word to be spread through the old Soviet empire. And look what had happened. Communism had been swept away, literally overnight. True, the factions were still killing each other. But that meant the cleansing sword of the Almighty would have less work to do. The Only Book, Martha had said, was full of such examples of God using someone like Wong Lee to finance His work.

His sister could rationalise everything. Without Martha he would be half the man, only able to do half the amount of God's work. But he would never tell her that. God forbid.

Alan's voice came through the pulpit's speaker. 'Cheryl, fix the Reverend Kingdom's make-up.'

The girl crouching at the back of the pulpit with a make-up kit scrambled to her feet and dabbed the Reverend Kingdom's face with a puff and applied fresh lip gloss.

'Thank you, Cheryl. God loves you,' he smiled.

He'd long given up calculating how many converts that smile had brought.

'And bless His name,' Cheryl murmured, resuming her position.

He composed himself and grasped the sides of the lectern firmly, a towering black-robed figure.

Alan's voice once more broke the silence.

'One minute. Settle down everyone. Let's make this a good one.'

The Reverend Kingdom glanced towards the gallery. He always found a taping more demanding. With a live broadcast, with all the Tabernacle's three thousand seats filled, the presence of the congregation always fired him. But Wednesday morning was when he recorded a sermon to sustain his vast electronic flock from whom there was no instant feedback.

The precise number of his global congregation was stored on computer tape in Records. The Communications Centre, from where the satellite was controlled, the editing suites, and the Finance Office were also buried within that part of the complex hewn out of one of the canyons above Malibu.

On top of the canyon was the manse where Martha and he occupied adjoining suites on the upper floor. The twelve Elders of the Church, its full-time associate pastors, lived beneath. The rest of the permanent staff occupied a compound behind the manse.

From Pacific Coast Highway only the soaring pyramid of the Tabernacle was visible and its gold-plated cross rising another forty feet. At night it was neon lit.

'Thirty seconds.'

A red light was blinking above the lens. Cameramen at other positions around the Tabernacle would be lining up their shots. He glanced quickly at the monitor.

'Twenty seconds.'

The Reverend Kingdom stared into the camera, concentrating totally. He deepened the frown a little, trying to remember the way he'd looked before the sound fault. It didn't really matter. Alan would be covering with a cutaway of his hands framing the Only Book.

'Ten seconds! Tape rolling.'

The Reverend Kingdom began to count down silently. The cue light steadied. He waited two more seconds. Then,

EACH AND ALL OF YOU! ASK YOURSELVES THIS. WHY HAS GOD, FOR WHOM ALL THINGS ARE POSSIBLE, TURNED HIS FACE AWAY FROM THIS EARTH? ASK THAT NOW OF YOURSELF! OF THOSE WITH YOU! ASK IT!

He had allowed the brogue to creep in, knowing it was a pleasant reminder to Americans that they too were of immigrant stock, while for all his other listeners it was proof that he had never forgotten his roots. Once more the richly resonant voice echoed around the Tabernacle.

When I was a child in Belfast, there was no talk of the ozone layer or acid rain, or all the other pollutants and toxins which plague us today. The words 'mugger' and 'drug pusher' were not part of our language any more than 'serial killer', 'gang rape', or 'gays'. And we had never heard rap music on our radio, or had to allow live sex shows in our towns and cities. For all this I can only say, thank you Lord for sparing us for so long.

But ask yourself again. Why has God allowed all this to infect our lives?

It was forty years since he had walked the streets of Belfast, a lad not yet fifteen on his way to listen to the young Reverend Ian Paisley. He had known then that he too wanted to be a preacher, to have the same total power and respect Paisley commanded from his flock.

He realised later that Paisley's vision had been too narrow in that he merely wanted to solve Ulster's problems. The Almighty had whispered in Reverend Kingdom's own ear that he had been chosen to resolve the world's.

God has turned His back because He is warning us that this godless decline must be stopped. Here and now! It must be halted.'

The Reverend Kingdom paused and touched the Bible, a quick, deferential gesture.

Those of you who know the Only Book will know that God has turned his back on the world before. Chronicles, twenty-six. 'And the Lord God of their fathers sent to them his messenger. To warn them to change. But they mocked the messenger of God and despised his words. Then the wrath of the Lord rose against his people.' It's all there! And we know what happened! Those who survived the sword were exiled to Babylon. But did they learn? Mend their ways? Become better people?

He clasped his hands.

NO!

He hurled the word from the pulpit, knowing the startle it would create.

No! No, they did not! The epistle of the Apostle Paul to the Ephesians, says they did not. They thought they could fool the Lord God Almighty! But what does Paul say? 'God is not deceived. For whatever a person soweth, that shall he also reap.'

Today, my brothers and sisters, we are indeed reaping a terrible God-given punishment. Because we have allowed others to sully His name.

Look around you, we have filth on a scale Paul could never have imagined. He spoke only about adultery and fornication. But a satellite, just like the one which brings you these words, in the hands of others brings filth into your homes. Plants it in the minds of your loved ones! In the minds of your children, corrupting them even before they can speak! Today any child who can reach the button on a television set is exposed to this all-pervasive filth. Filth which is so evil it will destroy that little child for ever.

He glanced at the cue sheet on the Book of Job and spread his hands.

Jesus said 'Suffer the little children to come unto me'. That's what He said, and what He meant.

The Reverend Kingdom placed his hands palms down on the Bible.

But how can our children even begin to see the way to Jesus in the face of the squalid mountain of garbage that blocks their view? Not just on television. But in newspapers and books. In the movies. On videos. In all they can see, hear or read there is this great sickness, this terrible cancer, this stifling corruption. Yet from who and where do we hear the voice of protest? Who speaks out today to make sure there will be a tomorrow? Who says enough? That this must stop?

He paused.

I DO! I HAVE SAID IT BEFORE. I SAY IT AGAIN. IN THE NAME OF
GOD, THIS MUST STOP!

He glanced down at the script. A tight close-up. He screwed his
eyes as if he was in pain. When he continued to speak his voice
was suddenly soft and defeated.

But who else? Who else joins his voice with mine? Serving
Him in the way He has always asked in return for His love –
without flinching.

He let the silence lengthen. At Bible college he had always come
top of pulpit class. After ordination he had left Ulster to spread the
Word in the United States. Two years in Georgia had softened his
accent. After another year of preaching on the stomp, he'd landed
the radio show which marked the beginning of his mastery of the
microphone. The TV programme that followed taught him how
to dominate the camera. After he'd bought the station he'd sent
for Martha to keep the books. The rest was history.

In the beginning when people asked how he had achieved so
much so quickly, he had said, 'God looks after his own'. In those
days he welcomed publicity.

After scandal emptied the churches of many of his fellow evangelists in the Bible Belt, he stopped all media interviews and
moved his ministry to the very edge of the Pacific.

Martha had selected the builders for the Tabernacle, Complex
Construction Inc., and arranged the finance through the Bank
of Southern California. Later, Complex built replica Tabernacles
in scores of countries, and the bank underwrote the costs. By then
he had learned both were wholly-owned by Wong Holdings.

On a visit to consecrate the Tabernacle in Jakarta, he had
finally met Wong Lee. The tycoon had impressed him greatly
in the short time they spent together. Since then they had only
spoken on the telephone. The last time was after the troika seized
power in Moscow.

He bowed his head to glance at the cue script. A close shot.
Time to tighten the jaw. Lifting his head, he managed to quickly
brush the dampness from his brow before looking steadfastly into
the camera.

I ask again who else speaks for a better world? Says enough? Says that this evil must stop?

It was his policy, proven by requests, to return time and again to familiar targets. He did so once more, attacking the World Council of Churches, the Church of England, the Lutherans and all the other churches of Europe. He raised and lowered his voice as he castigated them over their ordination of women and liberal attitudes towards homosexuality.

In between the telling silences, he worked in his standard attack on the failure of other churches to deal with pollution, and all the other man-made perils of life on earth today. He knew his audience would know where all this was leading.

He paused again. The camera lens would be creeping in, so only his face filled the screen, so that nothing would detract from the message.

There is, of course, a preacher who has more titles than any others, more than God himself. The man I still simply prefer to call the Roman pontiff. Do we hear his voice? Do we hear what he wrongly calls his Universal Church raising its voice in one unified and universal way? No! The Church of Rome today is more divided than ever. Over divorce and contraception. Some practise it, some don't. Over abortion and homosexuality. Again, some do it, some don't. But no matter how divided it is, the Church of Rome still insists it knows best!

He allowed the pain to once more cross his face. People always wrote in their hundreds to say how moved they were to see him again close to tears for the failings of others.

Rome certainly knows best when it comes to Rome's interests. Do you know that the Vatican's investment portfolio is still among the largest in the world? Do you know the Vatican is still among the largest property owners on earth? Do you know that every day its income is greater than the debts of many Third World countries? Do you know that the Roman pontiff is the keeper of more priceless art and jewels than even the Royal Family of England and all of Europe's surviving royalty?

He spread his hands, a man baffled by the ways of the world.

And the rest of that vast Roman treasure trove of wealth? Let me assure you, it is not lying idle! It is being used to once more spread the power of the Roman pontiff as it never was, not even in the heyday of Rome when it ruled through the terror of the Inquisition!

This time the pause was only a breath. Once more the thunderous denunciation rolled from the pulpit.

THE ROMAN PONTIFF, AND ALL THE OTHER SO-CALLED RELIGIOUS LEADERS, ARE TOO BUSY WITH THEIR OWN AGENDAS! TOO BUSY TO DO GOD'S REAL WORK! TOO BUSY TO CARE ABOUT WHAT IS REALLY HAPPENING IN THE WORLD! TOO BUSY TO CARE ABOUT YOU! THESE RICH AND POWERFUL PEOPLE WHO PROFESS TO WORK IN CHRIST'S NAME HAVE FORGOTTEN WHAT HE SAID. 'VERILY, VERILY, I SAY UNTO THEE, EXCEPT A MAN BE BORN AGAIN, HE CANNOT SEE THE KINGDOM OF GOD'!

When the Reverend Kingdom next spoke, the change of voice was truly striking, a relaxed, conversational tone.

My brothers and sisters. There is a verse in the Only Book which has been translated into over a thousand languages. Let me say it to you one more time. 'For God so loved the world that He gave His only begotten Son, that whosoever believeth in Him should not perish but have everlasting life.' So how can we, you and I, prepare for that life?

He felt the smile soften his face and the tension lift. The camera would have pulled back so as not to show the dampness around his collar and armpits.

There are today over seven hundred million of you who have pledged to me you will obey the Word. I am proud and humble to know that. We are a great army waiting to carry out God's work. The time is fast coming when we must do so in a more vigorous way to save the world from itself. I must warn you, a great deal will be asked of each one of you. For my part I will not flinch in telling you what God expects. That is my job. Your task is to obey – absolutely. No hesitation. No doubting. No 'is this right for me?' Only 'this *is* right for God!'

Today the world is that much darker than it was yesterday. It will be that much darker tomorrow – unless we act. Each one of us, here and now.

Almost two thousand years ago the Crusaders seized Jerusalem from the godless. They did not hesitate to use the sword. They cleansed in the name of the Lord. Now we must do the same. We must prepare for a new Crusade, a Moral Crusade. And where better to start than in the godless pit of what was once the Soviet empire?

Over a year ago it would not have been possible to say that. But now millions of God-fearing Soviets have accepted the Word I have been privileged to bring them. They are ready to rise. But they need help. Your help. So let me tell you exactly –

At that moment the telephone in the pulpit started its soft, insistent ringing.

The Reverend Kingdom frowned.

The switchboard had absolute instructions never to interrupt a taping. The show was totally scripted and there was no place for sudden news about some fresh disaster afflicting disbelievers.

He picked up the receiver.

'Yes?'

'Eddie, it's me.' Martha never identified herself.

'What is it?'

'There's a call for you.'

He gave an exasperated sigh.

'Martha, you know I don't allow –'

'It's him.'

The Reverend Kingdom felt a sudden surge of excitement.

'Did he say what he –'

'No. Only that he must speak to you. I wouldn't have interrupted if it was anyone else.'

'Of course.'

'God loves you, Eddie.'

'And bless His name.'

There was a click on the line.

'Mr Kingdom?'

'Reverend Kingdom speaking.'

'You have heard?'

There was no mistaking that voice.

'I'm not sure. Heard what?'

'The Roman pontiff has suffered a brain haemorrhage,' continued the voice in the same unearthly tone.

'It's God's will,' the Reverend Kingdom replied instinctively. 'A sign from the Almighty –'

'The Zionists are rushing to save him!' the robot-like voice bore on.

'Why would the Jews do that?'

There was an impatient tongue-clicking in the Reverend Kingdom's ear.

'You have prepared everything?'

The Reverend Kingdom bit back his anger. The hand that pays is a hand to heed; Martha had a homily for everything. When he spoke his voice was reassuring.

'Just about to finish taping. It's probably the most powerful sermon I've ever preached. It'll have a huge impact once transmitted. There's a great hunger out there to hear the Word –'

'Have you heard of Operation Holy Cross?' the impatient voice demanded.

'No, but it sounds like some new fund-raising scheme by Rome –'

The Reverend Kingdom heard the connection being broken by Wong Lee.

# 5

Ninety air miles out from the west coast of Ireland, the Concorde's Communications Centre Officer informed Morton that General Yuri Savenko was once more about to come on screen. The general was handling Yoshi's departure from Moscow.

Morton turned to the CCO. 'How's Alitalia doing?'

The officer glanced at a screen built into his desk on the other side of the aircraft cabin.

'Should be on the ground ten minutes after us.'

A summer storm over the Alps had slowed the chartered 737 from Rome bringing the two passengers Morton had asked to join the Concorde at Shannon. Monsignor Sean Hanlon was bringing X-rays of Nicholas the Sixth's head for Yoshi. Morton had asked Claudio Morelli, the Vatican's head of security to travel with him.

Static began to appear on one of the six-inch monitors built into a bulkhead.

'We're still getting trouble locking on. Pollution over Moscow today is bad enough to affect transmission,' apologised the CCO.

'Think what it's doing to their lungs.'

'Lungs can be replaced, David. Not so easy to find replacement perceptors now they've lost their Gorky facility.'

A month ago saboteurs had destroyed the plant producing microchips. The loss had put a further strain on Russia's telecommunications network.

'I thought your new pixels had built-in compensation.'

The CCO grinned, 'Don't believe all the Yanks say in their publicity. Still, let's see what can be done.'

He turned back to his keyboard.

Israel's flying battle headquarters had been refurbished by the United States as part of its thank you to Tel Aviv for not becoming openly involved in fighting Saddam. The Concorde's onboard gadgetry was the most sophisticated in the world.

'We've got the general visually,' the CCO reported.

Yuri Savenko's fleshy, florid face filled the monitor. A veteran from the days of Brezhnev, Gorbachev and Yeltsin, he survived because he delivered. When the troika took over, Savenko went on delivering. Morton respected a man who did that.

'Yuri, can you hear me?'

'I see you better.'

Static still spotted the screen. Behind him Morton heard the CCO humming as he made adjustments.

'I am sorry Comrade David, but it is not possible for you to land at Sheremetievo,' came Savenko's crackly boom.

Morton leaned towards the screen to hear better. Sheremetievo was Moscow's main international airport.

'We're locked on,' the CCO called.

Picture and sound from Moscow were suddenly pristine-clear.

'What's the problem, Yuri?' Morton asked.

'Kazakh terrorists trying a hijack. The pilot had the courage to refuse. But a lot of passengers are dead and there was a big fireball on the runway. Nothing lands or takes off for the next day at Sheremetievo.'

Despite his accent, Savenko spoke good English.

'Where were your *Spetsnaz*?'

The elite force had been placed on internal security duty since the crisis worsened.

Savenko sighed, 'The Kazakhs made a diversion. Our *Spetsnaz* rushed to a little explosion on the far side of the airport.'

'That's an old trick, Yuri.'

Savenko shrugged. 'For you, yes. For us, no. In old times no one would have dared try that. So we have no experience.'

It had been like that in the early days in Israel. You learned fast once you started counting bodies.

'It's not only Kazakhs who are very clever. In Kiev, another Uzbek bomb has killed more people. No one knows how the bomb passed the guards. In Baku, Armenian terrorists fired rockets at a Red Army base. In daylight!'

Morton stared at Savenko's troubled face. But nothing must get in the way of the immediate priority.

'I've got to get Dr Kramer out, Yuri. What about that military air base north of Moscow? The one Tsuigun used to smuggle his millions to Switzerland?'

Savenko looked pained. 'You are not supposed to know that!'

'That sort of scam gets around.'

Semyon Tsuigun had been First Deputy Chairman of the KGB. He'd been allowed to commit suicide after Savenko had confronted him with incontrovertible evidence of his involvement with the black market economy.

'*Da*, okay. We haven't used the base since Gorbachev flew back there to end his first coup.'

Savenko grinned. 'Maybe your landing will be a little smoother than his!'

As Savenko dictated new co-ordinates, Morton quickly typed them on a VDU screen and keyed them to the cockpit.

Savenko had a question. 'You want a fighter escort once you enter our air space?'

'The less attention we attract, the better.'

'*Da*, okay. We move Dr Kramer by car. Driver and two men. They arrive just as you land. Thirty minutes to refuel, then you go again. Just enough time for us to have a drink.'

'How's Dr Kramer?'

Savenko chuckled. 'His libido's like his ego – big. So far a dozen of our prettiest young doctors go to his room and personally inspect his pickled tumours. Then he inspects them. He's a bull.'

Even a couple of years ago Yoshi's behaviour could have left him open to blackmail. But like so much else unravelling in Russia, the security police had been forced to throw away the handbook.

'The Holy Father, can Dr Kramer save him?'

'I don't know, Yuri. But the sooner we get our doctor to Rome, the better.'

Savenko nodded. 'My wife's Russian Orthodox. She has been lighting candles for the Pope. Many people are doing the same.'

Morton's eyes softened. 'He's a good man, Yuri. He wants what we all want. A better world.'

'*Da*, okay. *Mir*. Peace.'

Abruptly the image from Moscow faded. Below the Aran Islands passed, then came the unbelievably green fields of Ireland.

He and Ruth had spent their only holiday together somewhere

down there, renting a thatched cottage and living off the catch-of-the-day and some of the best meat he'd eaten. In the evenings they'd sat in pubs and listened to the fiddlers and the ballads which sounded as if they were being sung in Yiddish. Ruth had shared her dreams of becoming a doctor good enough to work with Yoshi. Six months later the terrorist bomb had killed her.

'Buckle up everybody,' came the order from the flight deck. Moments later the Concorde was rolling down the runway at Shannon.

Standing in the aircraft's open cabin door Morton watched two men hurry down the steps from the Alitalia jet parked nearby. A ground crew was refuelling the Concorde.

Monsignor Sean Hanlon looked like a recruiting poster for the priesthood. He was tall, tanned, his hair a streaky burnished blond. There was power in the way he moved. In one hand he had a large, slim carrying case – the Pope's X-rays.

Claudio Morelli was a couple of inches shorter, his face dark as his hair. He walked with the quick, careful steps of a man who spent his time protecting the lives of others. In serving three Popes he'd prowled the back corridors of power. Morelli had instantly become a friend of Steve's, and the friendship had been extended to Morton.

'*Ciao*, David,' Morelli said, embracing Morton quickly.

'Good to see you Claudio.'

Morton turned to Monsignor Hanlon. 'And you, Father.'

'Call me Sean. The Boss always says formality gets in the way of a good working relationship.'

Morelli smiled. 'Sean calls most people in authority "Boss". Very Irish. In this case he means the Holy Father.'

'Any change in his condition?' Morton asked, leading them into the plane.

'He's regained consciousness, and instructed me to say he agrees to Dr Kramer operating,' said Monsignor Hanlon. 'He'll agree to anything as long as it means the delay to Holy Cross will be minimal.'

Morton glanced at Morelli. 'I take it there's nothing suspicious about what happened, Claudio?'

'Nothing. Poggi says he's surprised it didn't happen sooner.'

'I gather Pope Nicholas was reading something just before he collapsed. Could that have helped bring it on?'

73

Monsignor Hanlon looked at Morton thoughtfully. 'The Boss was studying a submission from the Secretariat of State opposing diplomatic recognition for your own country. Given his determination to go to Israel, that sort of thing could have burst a blood vessel.'

'The Americans tell you he was reading, David?'

'Yes.' He never lied to Morelli.

'Damn their spies in the sky,' Morelli said forcefully.

'Try closing your windows,' Morton suggested.

Monsignor Hanlon grinned. 'We've just learned to open them to the world. Anyway if we close the shutters, they'd find a way through the floorboards.'

The priest looked at Morelli mischievously. 'But what would you do if you didn't spend your time sweeping the place for bugs with those funny little machines of yours?'

The security chief shrugged good humouredly.

Morton led them into a small but comfortable cabin behind the flight deck. There was a bed, a couple of armchairs and a telephone console on a desk. The carpet, like the walls and ceiling, was pale blue. The cabin was normally only used by Prime Minister Karshov.

'Reminds me of my first room in the Vatican,' grinned Monsignor Hanlon. He propped the X-ray case against a wall.

'Now he has a palace. And two of the prettiest nuns you'll ever see to look after him, not to mention the best wine cellar in Rome,' Morelli said.

Monsignor Hanlon nodded happily. 'All true. But you don't do so bad yourself, Claudio. Offhand, I can't think of any other police chief who works in a building ranked as a work of art. Or with a couple of Michelangelos hanging on his walls!'

Morton detected mutual respect behind the teasing. He motioned them to be seated, then turned to Monsignor Hanlon.

'Yoshi Kramer will do his best. But we have to be realistic. Pope Nicholas could die. If he survives, he'll certainly need a long convalescence. In either case Holy Cross could be doomed – especially if its opponents in the Vatican have their way.'

Monsignor Hanlon nodded.

'Right now the opposition is still muted. Whispers in back corridors. Or over the post-dinner brandy. But you're absolutely correct, once they see the lie of the land, they'll come out of the woodwork. As it is, we'd hardly moved the Boss to the basement before the papabili and their handlers were preparing for the next conclave.'

Papabili were cardinals deemed to be serious candidates to become Pope, their handlers the equivalent of secular campaign managers. Conclave was the ancient forum where the secret balloting took place.

'It fits very well in a system where democracy is still about as popular as it is in Beijing, David.'

Morton had forgotten how waspish Morelli could be. Twenty years of dividing his time between the deal makers and the holy men must affect any man.

'Any new front runners, Sean?' Morton asked.

'Muller of Berlin still leads the pack. Coming from the old East Germany he's been promoted as the symbol of unification the Church needs. The man to reconcile Eskimos scratching the *Ave Maria* on whalebones and Chinese using gongs to sound the Angelus. And, while I've no doubt His Eminence from Berlin has faith, humility he does not possess. I fear if Jesus ever returned to the Vatican and Muller was Pope, he wouldn't allow Christ to enter. At times His Eminence sounds as if he'd be happier running God Incorporated rather than God's first church on earth.'

'Messner?'

'He worries some of us even more. He's the old Hun running the younger Hun. They're a perfect example that celibates can give birth to clones. What Messner thinks, Muller says.'

'Neither of them want to change the status quo over Israel,' Morelli added.

Monsignor Hanlon nodded vigorously.

'The Huns are also totally opposed to the Boss's passion to see Mother Russia and all her siblings returned to the sanctity of Rome. They say it would have the same effect as the Trojan Horse had on Troy. We'll be inviting the enemy to destroy us from within. Incredibly, they've managed to convince half the members of the Sacred Congregations and several of those on the Commissions. The only real support the Boss has is from the Cause of Saints. He used to be Prefect there, so there's an element of personal loyalty involved. But with the Boss off the scene, that could change. When it comes to switching positions the people in Saints have an illustrious record.'

'Are there any papabili who could stop Cardinal Muller?' Morton asked.

Monsignor Hanlon gave an elegant little shrug.

'There's Leutens of Marseilles. The right age and background. Mid-sixties, worked in the Curia, widely travelled, five languages. But probably a little too timid when the knives come out of the cassocks.'

'Anyone from North America?'

'Canada – no. Their bishops blew their chance by taking the wrong decision over Quebec Libre. They should have known Rome didn't want that pimple on its rump. And as far as the United States goes, the hierarchy there's almost lost control of its charismatics. Nobody's going to want the next Pope waving a tambourine on the Chair of St Peter.'

Morton smiled. Sean was a refreshingly different priest to most of those he'd met in the Vatican.

'How about Cardinal Lopez?'

Monsignor Hanlon shook his head ruefully.

'A month ago he was in with a real chance. Not just because he's got a power base that runs from Buenos Aires to Mexico, but because he knows how the system works at head office. Who pulls which strings in which Sacred Congregation. He's served on all the right Pontifical Commissions, and has friends in the Apostolic Signatura. But none of them are going to vote for him when the time comes.'

Monsignor Hanlon glanced at Morelli.

'The old story, David. The flesh is weak. Cardinal Lopez was discovered having an affair with one of his nun housekeepers. It probably wouldn't have mattered, but she's pregnant.'

'So what's going to happen to him?' Morton asked.

Monsignor Hanlon sighed. 'What's happened before. The baby will be taken into one of our homes. The nun will go into a cloistered order. His Eminence will be given an all-male domestic staff. It may not be exactly equitable in terms of punishment. But then we've never been strong on equality, sexual or otherwise.'

Morton looked quizzically at the Pope's secretary. Could a cardinal's sexual peccadillo be one more reason why the Church, once unified and monolithic, was now split from top to bottom and sideways not only on high-minded theological concepts but over personal morals?

'How about Africa?' Morton asked.

Monsignor Hanlon shook his head. 'Enkomo's doing a good

job in South Africa. But he's out in left field. When it comes to votes, he probably couldn't count on more than two or three. I think it could be another decade before we can see a serious candidate come out of Africa.'

'Cardinal Enkomo's a good man,' Morton said softly.

'Indeed so,' Monsignor Hanlon said brusquely. 'But sadly, just being a good man has never been enough to make it to the Chair of St Peter.'

Morelli exhaled. 'Given the way things are, David, I'd prefer another Italian. John Paul the Second showed what happened when you elect a foreigner. You thought you were getting someone who'd open the door on change. Instead we ended up with the door firmly locked.

'All Pope Nicholas has been really able to do is get the key in the lock. His successor will find it even harder to actually get it to turn. He moves it one way and he'll lose the traditionalists. Turn it the other way, and all the radicals will be off. If we get an Italian, at least he'll understand that the key's been in the lock a long time and needs a careful oiling.'

Morton decided the time had come to probe in a different direction.

'How seriously does the Vatican take these attacks by the Reverend Kingdom?'

Monsignor Hanlon laughed. 'On that we're all agreed, except Claudio. The Reverend Kingdom is just another pinprick in the crown of thorns Rome has always worn.'

'Seven hundred million followers are a lot of thorns, Sean,' Morelli said quietly.

Monsignor Hanlon shook his head. 'The numbers game doesn't mean anything. Our people at Christian Unity say a lot of the Reverend Kingdom's followers are what we call "lip servicers". They bang the drums and rattle the castanets. But they have no real faith base. We learned our lesson in China about those kind of people. Before Mao took power the Church used to give everyone who came to Mass a bowl of rice. When the Communists came in, they offered two bowls to everyone who gave up their faith. Our churches were empty from one Sunday to the next. Promoting belief through hunger was never a good idea. Using blind hatred as the Reverend Kingdom does has even less of a chance of success.'

Morton leaned against a bulkhead and looked at them both.

'Has the Church had any dealings with Wong Lee?'

Monsignor Hanlon gave another of his little shrugs.

'Is the Pope a Catholic? Of course we have! Wong Holdings has rebuilt some of our finest churches in South America and Asia which were destroyed by those who fear our faith.'

'Did you know, Sean, that the profits Wong Lee makes help finance the very people bent on destroying the Church? And that he's also the Reverend Kingdom's financial backer, almost certainly his biggest?' Morton asked.

There was a sudden silence.

'We had no idea. The Boss, none of us. Simply none at all. This is disturbing news,' Monsignor Hanlon finally said.

'There's more, Sean.'

Morton told them quietly and without emotion, the way he always gave especially bad news, all he knew about Wong Lee's plan to wreck Operation Holy Cross.

'Surely the United Nations could do something?' Monsignor Hanlon asked.

Morton shook his head. 'Wong Holdings is certainly more powerful than a lot of UN member countries, Sean.'

'But surely if it can be proven that Wong Lee is behind it all –'

'In his case knowing and proving are about as far apart as the Reverend Kingdom is from Pope Nicholas,' Morton said.

'Where does Kingdom fit in?' Morelli asked.

'It's not clear if he's just a pawn. But his kind of rabid preaching could touch off a backlash which could finally tear things apart. We could have a rerun of the crusades and all the jihads rolled into one.'

The stricken silence was broken by a knock on the door. The CCO said Danny was on screen from Tel Aviv.

'I'll send coffee,' Morton said as he left.

'Tea please, David. I know your coffee,' Morelli sighed.

Pausing at the galley to give the order to the steward, Morton strode into the Communications Centre. The black patch covering Danny's left eye was the result of the Yom Kippur war, when he'd lost half his sight.

Morton bent towards the screen. 'What's new, Danny?'

'Our receivers in Nepal aren't operating. Not a peep as the weather satellite went by. I've triggered the spoilers. It has to be Wong Lee's people.'

'Any idea how they found out?'

'Not yet. But it's punched a hole in our net.'

'Can we reprogramme to work off Samson?' Morton asked.

Samson was the Israeli satellite positioned in geosynchronous orbit to pick-up Arab missile telemetry.

'That would mean giving up something else.'

'That's always going to be a problem, Danny.'

'We could ask the Americans to cover for us.'

'I'd rather not. They've got their own agenda. It may not be ours.'

'Things go badly in Washington?'

'With the President, no. But some of the old guard at Langley want to actually help the whole house of cards to fall. They're convinced that the best thing would be if everywhere between the Buryat Republic and the Black Sea were chopped into pieces. That way there won't be a chance for Communism to ever take root again. They think that with the whole country becoming little more than a collection of tribal states, it wouldn't need more than a Third World army to keep them in check if they get any big ideas. The problem with that scenario is that someone always wants to be top dog.'

'With Wong Lee wagging the tail?'

'For sure.'

Morton glanced at an adjoining VDU screen. It displayed a radar image of the Middle East in delicate green tracery: the scanning range of Samson.

'How about dropping Beirut?' Danny suggested.

Morton shook his head. 'If things finally break loose those Shias are going to be rushing to join in. The only warning we'll get is what Samson gives us.'

'Damascus? Walter says the Syrians are being almost civilised nowadays,' Danny said.

'That's when they can be at their most dangerous.'

Morton came to a decision. 'Here's what you do. Use the Kabul sensors to work with the weather satellite'.

'Right.'

Morton nodded at Danny and walked to his seat as the flight deck announced take-off. Minutes later the Concorde rolled out to the edge of the runway. The throttle was released and the big bird began to hurtle down the tarmac.

Morton felt the nose tyre lift off the ground, saw the wings cant skywards and for a brief moment he remembered Dolly's question. *Why should anyone fly?*

They'd been sitting, Steve, Dolly, Ruth and himself, in the Jerusalem apartment on that Sunday afternoon when the programme of classical music was interrupted. It had been the Israeli Philharmonic, playing Steve's favourite, Mozart.

Morton could still remember how the radio announcer had cleared his throat before saying a planeload of Jews had been hijacked to Entebbe. After he'd finished, no one in the apartment had spoken until Dolly's question. Then Steve had reached out and grasped her hand tightly. *That's what they want*, he had said. *To isolate us.*

Below him Morton felt the main wheels rise and the aircraft bank slightly. Moments later they were above the clouds, heading east towards France. Morton continued to work his way through the names he had given to the President.

He had asked Bill Gates to order the antenna farms to be repositioned and scores of CIA operatives deployed. Jacques Lacouste had agreed to assign a dozen of his men to begin electronic surveillance on Wong Holdings' companies in France. Marcus Baader was doing the same in Germany. Anwar Salim would send a team from Cairo to try and probe the conglomerate's installations in Iran. Norm Stratton's operatives would check subsidiaries in Canada, while agents stationed at the Canadian embassy in Beijing would begin to probe Wong Lee's influence with the Chinese regime. In Tel Aviv Lester Final's programmers had already begun checking the employees of the conglomerate. World-wide they totalled over 600,000. The programmers were looking for those with any previous terrorist connections. Chantal had sent some of her operatives to Hong Kong, Seoul, Karachi, Rangoon and Kathmandu to listen out for anything coming out of Lhasa. Humpty Dumpty's specialists were working on new receivers to be positioned on Nepal's border with Tibet. The Professor and his behaviourists were up-dating Wong Lee's psycho-profile.

As Concorde crossed the French coast Morton began to brief Percival West on one of the telephones on his desk in the Communications Centre.

'I want a breakdown of all Wong Lee's investments in UK arms, electronics and shipping firms. Also a picture of his investment portfolios in Commodities, Futures and the Institutions.

Once we see where the money is, your people can put on the squeeze. No fund manager's going to want you breathing down his neck.'

'I'll get the Fraud Squad people moving,' promised West.

East of Frankfurt, General Savenko was back on screen. He looked bleak.

'We have a bad situation, Comrade David. A big, bad situation. Dr Kramer's been taken.'

The technicians around Morton paused to stare at the screen.

'What happened, Yuri?'

'A roadblock. Our car stopped and the driver got out –'

'What they do with Dr Kramer?'

'Took him away in the car.'

'They have any idea who he is?'

Savenko shrugged.

'Do you know where they took him?'

'To a dacha that's very close to the base where you'll land.'

'Where was Dr Kramer's laser equipment?'

'In the car trunk.'

'Any idea who they are, Yuri?'

It was a long shot. There were now more terrorist groups in Russia than there had ever been in Lebanon.

'*Niet*. Only that they are your people. But that still makes them terrorists.'

Morton heard the surprised murmurs from the technicians.

'What are you saying, Yuri?'

'Your people, Comrade David. From Omsk ghetto. Jews. They came to Moscow for exit visas. Foreign Ministry say no more until next month –'

'They don't sound like professionals. More like a bunch of amateurs who've done a stupid thing.'

Savenko shook his head. 'They're still terrorists.'

'How many are there?'

'Five. Two women. Three men.'

'How'd they know about the car?' Morton asked.

'One woman, she's a doctor who visited your Dr Kramer.'

'And he told her about the change of flight plan?'

Indiscretion was as natural to Yoshi as sex.

'*Da*. Maybe. It's not important now.'

Nor was it important to know where they obtained the

81

uniforms and the equipment for a roadblock. Only why they had taken Yoshi.

'Do you know what they want?'

Savenko grunted. 'To leave the country with him, Comrade David. He's their exit visa!'

The murmurs from the technicians this time were sympathetic.

'Will they be allowed to go, Yuri?'

'*Niet*. Even if I said okay, others would say that was not possible. These people must be made an example for other terrorists!'

'So what's been done?'

'Our *Spetsnaz* have surrounded the dacha. They gave the terrorists the order to surrender. They say they'd rather die.'

Morton kept his voice low and steady.

'Pull your troops back, Yuri. Do nothing until I get there. Like you said, these are my people. Let me deal with them. I just want Dr Kramer on this plane – whatever it takes.'

Savenko's shoulders heaved. 'I'll see if it's possible. But no promises.'

# 6

The shamaness held the taper between thumb and forefinger and blew noisily through the gap in her teeth until the tip of the wax glowed. Then the old sorceress lowered the stick and there was the sound of hair sizzling. The flesh reddened. She glanced at Wong Lee.

'Hold yourself still,' she scolded, before again blowing on the taper and applying it to remove more of the frizzle of grey pubic hair, the only evidence of his advancing years.

'Pleasure only comes from control,' she reminded him. 'Or have you forgotten?'

She continued to singe.

No one but the old crone dared speak to him so insolently. It amused him to allow her to do so. Though he was careful never to show it, the shamaness also intimidated him. She was the most skilled of the few surviving exponents of Dark Taoism, the black magic of ancient China.

When he had found her in the fastness where the Yangtze rises, she was already famous throughout the land. After she accepted his offer of a small fortune to perform her magic only for him, he explained she would also have other duties. These included removing all traces of his body hair.

'Your hand is cold. It is not easy to lie still,' he protested.

She made a dismissive noise. 'Your blood is still too warm from anger. You are like a young man.'

They spoke the broad Mandarin of the mountains, the language of their ancestors.

'Attend to your work, woman,' he grunted, pleased.

No one would take him for a man in his early sixties. The hair

83

on his head was still naturally sleek and black, his teeth white and free from cavities. His skin was supple and without an ounce of surplus fat. His body was a testament to the rigorous regime the shamaness made him follow. This included swallowing crushed tiger bone to ward off hypertension and drinking extract of yak penis to keep his blood purified.

'Your hair grows fast, singsung,' she said singeing. 'It is another sign of your vitality.'

He enjoyed the carefully-controlled pain she applied. The sensation was like an aphrodisiac, travelling through his body and making his eyes smart. He felt himself begin to harden.

'Control!' the shamaness said, more sharply. 'Concentrate on something else, but not to make you angry, singsung.'

He forced himself not to think of the last of those phone calls during the night. The earlier ones had brought good news. The powder which the shamaness had prepared had entered the digestive system of that meddlesome *gweillo* in Rome, dissolving in his coffee, and travelling through his vascular system to his brain. There it burst one of the blood vessels already partly constricted by his tumour. It had needed months of careful planning and the expenditure of a large sum of money to arrange for the coffee to reach the *gweillo's* kitchen in his drab-looking palace.

Next came the news that one of the tracking teams had located the Zionist receivers buried in the permasnow of Nepal. The search followed the successful torturing of a Tibetan trader and an elderly Nepalese. Both had been left to hang in the wind for the vultures to pick clean.

With the discovery of the equipment, he hoped to learn the Zionists' intentions. Whether they would really fight to the bitter end – or negotiate? For him it would not really matter. Jew, Arab, Mongol, Christian – they were all the same to him. Puppets.

Then came the news the receivers had self-destructed. Only Fung would have dared phone with such news. But, like the shamaness, Fung had served him a very long time as his principal secretary.

Later Fung called to say the Zionists were offering the services of their famous brain surgeon to try and save the life of the *gweillo* in Rome. Even Fung had not risked calling after that.

Lying on the bed, he had waited until he felt calm enough to telephone the *gweillo* in Malibu who, for the moment, was still important.

After that call he had sent for the shamaness and told her what he wanted. The pleasure from receiving and giving pain was the only way Wong Lee knew how to regain total control over himself.

'You are getting excited again,' chided the crone.

Wong Lee looked towards the window. The dense pink glow of dawn was beginning to bathe the glass. He tried to concentrate on the sound of the bells on the yak herds being driven to fresh pastures. The rarefied air enhanced sound, vision and smell at this hour, when the sun was only a faint glow touching the gold on the roofs of Lhasa's temples and sanctuaries in the valley below.

During the night antenna farms of the American *gweillo* had again triggered the security system. Hadn't they learned by now? Wong Lee felt himself continue to harden.

'How old is she?' he asked.

'Young enough. She is still intact. But do not think about that yet, singsung.'

He glanced at the clocks mounted on a relief map completely covering one wall. The map showed Lhasa as the centre of the world.

In the United States it was still yesterday. But in a thousand places he controlled from coast-to-coast, from banks to meat processing plants, more profits would be accruing.

In Europe, the day was already well advanced. By evening his fortune would have grown by another 20 million dollars. From luxury hotels around the Mediterranean and factories in the German Ruhr. In France, it would come from wine; Portugal, shoes; in Spain, olive oil. In Italy he had a controlling interest in car manufacturing. In Scotland, forty per cent of the whisky-distilling industry was his. Ireland's meat barons did his bidding, just as others obeyed in Australia, New Zealand and on the tundra of Argentina.

Bad weather had provided an unexpected bonus in South Africa. The food manufacturing and distribution companies he controlled continued to increase their profits. Elsewhere in Africa, entire governments depended on Wong Holdings. In return for its continued support he had insisted the brightest of the Zimba graduates must have key positions in those regimes. It was another way to control from a distance. The *gweillo* in Rome had written to protest about the graduates from Zimba.

85

Someone who really understood power would never write.

Even Japan had fallen under his power. One in every ten of all electronic items it manufactured produced a further income for Wong Holdings.

World-wide that amounted to a million US dollars every fifteen minutes of every hour. Day and night.

To produce it, galleries had been hewn deep in the rock to house the computers running the financial operations and telecommunications equipment for him to instantly reach his furthest outpost. One gallery housed the satellite jammer. Others contained storage areas, canteens and staff living quarters. A thousand hand-picked people ran the high-tec complex. He paid them double what they could possibly earn elsewhere. He had always believed financial loyalty was the best of all. The only hint of their presence was the faint hum of the air-circulating pumps.

That was another reason why the discovery of the Israeli receivers had enraged him. Their very presence was an affront to his privacy. None of his experts were able to say how long the equipment had been buried in the snow. Or whether the Zionists were engaged upon another of their probe-and-hope operations. Or if there was some more disturbing reason – a precursor of what had happened to the *Eastern Rose*?

They were only certain the ship had been sunk by the new kind of explosive developed by the Israelis. The ship's company had been flown back to their home port of Shanghai for questioning by Chung-Shi, the head of security. Several seamen recalled the sound of something hitting the side of the ship. They'd thought it was driftwood.

Chung-Shi was a painstaking interrogator and had the radio officer flown to Lhasa for further questioning. After two days the man finally confessed he was asleep when the warning came the ship was about to be destroyed. Chung-Shi knew in the end it would have made no difference. The Israeli satellite would have blocked all out-going radio traffic. But the officer had to be taught a lesson. He too had been hung from a gibbet for the vultures to devour.

Chung-Shi had sent his best men to Istanbul. They'd bribed the Turks to let them inspect the remains of the suitcase salvaged from the hotel room. Whatever it contained had been totally destroyed. The Turks said it was a bomb-maker crossing the wrong wires. That had alerted Chung-Shi. A bomber always left something.

His men questioned the whore who worked the hotel. She described the glimpse she had of the man who had occupied the room. Chung-Shi had fed the description through his computer. It did not exactly match anyone on file. Only the khaki chinos came close. It had been enough to send Chung-Shi himself to Istanbul.

The sizzle of singed hair made Wong Lee tremble anew. The more he tried not to think of the pleasure ahead, the harder it became not to do so. By now the girl would have bathed in warm yak milk. He liked the faintly sweet taste it left on the skin.

'Singsung! You really will be finished before she comes.'

'The camera –' he began.

'It is ready,' the shamaness assured him.

Wong Lee glanced towards the lacquer framed screen in a corner of the bedroom. In one of the stamens of the flowers painted on the silk panes he could just make out the lens. Everything was indeed ready.

He gave a long, low sigh of satisfaction which always came when he lay on this huge bed. Raised from the floor by four exquisitely carved dragons, the bed was carved from the hardwood of the humid jungles of Vietnam.

The pair of dragons at the foot were the guardians of one of the two mighty primal energy forces which governed his life. *Yang*, the male, represented the sun and all things forceful and fiery. *Yin*, the female, depicted by the pair supporting the head of the bed, was cold, covert and mysterious. Managing to balance the delicate interplay of these elemental forces had made him undisputed master of all he touched. How else to explain how he, the illegitimate son of a treacherous merchant and a licentious concubine, had achieved such power? How else had he been able to deal with those who sought his help and promised undying fealty in return – and then had broken their word? Men like Mafia bosses in the United States and the drug barons from the Golden Triangle and Colombia. The bankers in Wall Street and the City of London. They had come to him in the greatest secrecy as supplicants, offering deals in return for his help. When he had honoured his part, they had reneged. They had all been severely punished.

Gorbachev and Yeltsin had forgotten that. When the West

failed to help them, he had stepped in to save the Russian economy. For a while it had actually prospered. When the leaders went back on their promise to let him take his substantial profits, he had simply removed his support, collapsing Russia and the republics into even greater chaos. First Gorbachev and then Yeltsin had paid the price.

Soon the mullahs of the Islamic Confederation would suffer the same fate. He had financed them on the promise they would launch a new holy war. But they had vacillated, unable to agree when to attack Iraq. Soon it would be too late. He planned to arm Saddam in return for sixty per cent of the revenue from Iraq's oil which the West had agreed could once more flow. The money did not really interest him, only the prospect of finally having a properly malleable surrogate in the region.

In Moscow the troika was struggling to hold together the remnants of central government, while in the Moslem republics factions continued to bicker as they prepared to sweep westwards.

He had supported a number of the more militant republics. He would offer a deal to those who emerged triumphant. The glory would be theirs, the real power his. It was the way he had always worked.

All this had been threatened by the *gweillo* in Rome, with his grandiose dream of a great act of reconciliation. That would bring about a peace which would destroy Wong Lee's one unfulfilled dream. To be the temporal emperor of a kingdom stretching from the Pacific to the Baltic. Not even Genghis Khan had achieved that. No one had.

'Your powder,' Wong Lee asked. 'There is no antidote?'

'There is nothing in our medicine. So there can be nothing in theirs,' assured the shamaness.

In the strengthening light he saw the look of complete certainty on her wrinkled face.

Wong Lee lay back as she began to oil his body, working with long, quick movements until he gleamed from head to toe.

Ever since he had learned about Operation Holy Cross, he had planned how to destroy it.

First the *gweillo* had to be removed. Hopefully, his plan would now die with him. If not, his successor as Pope must be made to understand he could not succeed. But after studying the procedure of a conclave, Wong Lee realised there was no real way of knowing who the next Pope would be. He had drawn up a short list of cardinals he would like to see elected. He had learnt all he could about them. One by one he had crossed out the names. Finally only one remained. Cardinal Hans-Dietrich Muller.

'You are ready.' She gave him a broad, insolent grin. The shamaness straightened and gathered up her lacquered box filled with tapers and bottles. She padded across the polished wood floor and went behind the screen. He could hear her soft clucking as she reached the camera. It had taken him months to teach her how to correctly frame and zoom.

Now that the time had almost come, he was in no hurry. He rose from the bed and walked to the window. The sun was above the peaks, bathing the room in its warm glow. Outside it was still below zero. In the valley the first horsemen were leaving the city, tiny figures wrapped in pale leather, their heads covered with the felt hats which was the headgear of all Tibetan males. They would spend the day fishing in their yak-skin conches or in the fields. On a ledge in the rock face he could see the vultures breakfasting off the remains of the radio officer and the other two bodies hanging from the multiple gibbet.

Behind Wong Lee came a faint, hesitant tap on the door. He walked quickly to the bed and lay on the black silk sheet. The knocking was repeated.

'Enter,' he called.

The heavy lacquered door slowly opened. A figure stood silhouetted in the sunlight. She was smaller than he had expected. He felt his tumescence grow.

'Singsung?' A peasant's voice.

'Come. Close the door.'

She did as told and stood, her back pressed against the door, breathing nervously. She wore only a light silk robe to conceal her nakedness.

'Come!' he said, more loudly.

When the girl reached the bed she stopped, saying nothing, watching him with her peripheral vision.

He continued to observe, noting her tremble. He snapped his fingers.

'Take off your robe.'

When she had done so, he stared at her through half-closed eyes.

'Where are you from?'

'Chamdo District, singsung.'

From one of the villages along the banks of the Yalutsango.

'When did you come to Lhasa?'

'A moon ago. To find work.'

He had always said to choose girls who had been in the city only a short while; no one would miss them.

'Turn and face that screen.'

'Singsung?'

'The screen with the flowers. Face it and smile.'

She turned and smiled at the hidden camera. It was always important to have a record, to remember one from another, to capture this moment of unsuspecting innocence.

With the speed of a man half his years Wong Lee rose from the bed and stood behind her, encircling her with his sinewy arms, forcing her back to arch forward so that he could enter her more easily.

She gasped. He drove deeper into her, his fingers brutally squeezing her breasts. The girl began to whimper.

'Stop crying,' he commanded, half dragging her backwards to the bed, still remaining inside her.

'Singsung, please,' she cried, 'it's painful.'

He grunted and hurt her again. When he reached the bed, he hauled her on to the sheet, twisting himself so that she straddled him. He saw her quickly glance down between his legs.

'He is all yours,' Wong Lee said coarsely.

'What would you wish me to do?' she whimpered.

The shamaness would have instructed her.

'Amuse me! But do not satisfy me too quickly.'

She looked down at him, a new, hopeful look in her eyes.

'If I please you, singsung, you will keep me here and treat me well?'

He looked up at her. 'First show me what you can do.'

The aroma of the yak milk mingled with the girl's perspiration. She began to handle him, hesitantly at first, then with growing confidence. He was astonished at her skill, as she ran her hands and lips over his body, teasing him in all sorts of ways. The camera would be capturing every one of her movements as she encouraged him to follow her rhythm.

But he was a man of experience, with perfect control. Time and again, when she thought they were approaching the climax, he'd pause and force her to remain perfectly still. Then he would nudge her and she would resume, attempting to vary her thrusts and motion, coaxing him along, moving faster and faster, thinking surely he must finish now.

He watched her face, bathed with sweat, knowing she would soon no longer be able to control herself. She began to give loud, half-animal shrieks and started to sob uncontrollably. Tensing his body, catching her in the midst of a run of twitchy little movements he allowed himself to finish. She thrust down on him to take in every drop deeply, suddenly smiling slyly at him.

'Singsung, did I satisfy you?' she murmured, moving to curl her body beside his.

'Not yet,' he said. 'But now!'

Wong Lee hurled the girl from him, so that she sprawled on her back. He jerked her by the hair so that she faced the camera.

'Singsung,' she gasped. 'Please, singsung. It hurts! Please –'

He choked off her protests with the fingers of one hand pressed against her throat. A look of total panic, then terror came into the girl's eyes. She began to struggle. He slowly increased the pressure. Her thrashing became more desperate. Her hands clawed at him and her legs kept up a discordant drumming on the sheet. As his pressure increased her movements weakened. He continued to stare fixedly into her haemorrhaging eyes as he slowly strangled her. Her movements grew still more feeble and then she was still. He pushed the lifeless body to the floor and lay back. He was finally fulfilled.

To kill for pleasure, to kill without mercy because of the total personal satisfaction it brought him, was a deeply ingrained part of his personality. Sex was only an enjoyable by-product. In his lifetime he had methodically killed hundreds of women whose names he never knew; their sheer anonymity added to his pleasure.

He could hear the shamaness unloading the camera. The video would join his collection. The films were a satisfying reminder of how far he was removed from the ordinary world of men, that the slightest sentimentality and softness were emotions unknown to him. That was another reason for his success.

A light began to wink on the console beside the tank of carp on the far side of the room. He clapped his hands twice; the console was designed to respond to the sound.

'What is it, Fung?'

'There has been further news from Moscow, singsung. They

have delayed the attack on the dacha. We could still have the plane destroyed. There are many portable missiles on the flight path.'

She had assured him there was no antidote. To have the plane destroyed would be taking a pointless risk. Like a swarm of disturbed bees, the Zionists would be stung to fury.

'Fung, you are a good secretary, but no historian. You forget what the Emperor Qin said, "To kill only one enemy is to allow many more to live." Always remember that.'

'Yes, singsung,' said Fung obediently.

A soft, appreciative cackling came from behind the screen. Wong Lee clapped his hands and the console light went out. He put on a robe and walked over to the fish tank. The carp drifted in the aerated water, only their fin tips undulating slightly, so as not to stir the muck in the bottom.

Wong Lee fished in his robe pocket and produced one of the pieces of dried meat he kept there. He tossed the morsel into the tank. The water churned as the carp fought for possession. In moments the meat was gone. But the fish continued to surge greedily back and forth. Unable to find more food, they nibbled viciously at each other.

'They are like rats,' cackled the shamaness coming from behind the screen. 'If there is not enough, they devour each other.'

'They are like people,' he corrected, dropping another piece of meat into the tank. The feeding frenzy increased.

Behind them they heard the bedroom door open, and the shuffle of footsteps crossing the floor. Then came the sound of the body being dragged, followed by that of the door softly closing.

Wong Lee dropped another pellet into the tank.

'Just like people,' he murmured. 'They can so easily be manipulated.'

The console light blinked again. Fung announced that Chung-Shi was on the line from Istanbul.

'The attack on the ship was no lucky chance,' began the hoarse voice of the security chief. 'The description of a passport officer on duty at the airport fits perfectly. It was Morton.'

Now he knew, Wong Lee felt strangely calm.

# 7

The Concorde swept towards Moscow. Even on such a fine day, one that Monsignor Hanlon had said was a day to forgive all sins, the ground was half hidden by a haze of pollution. In the Communications Centre, the technicians continued to monitor frequencies.

The CCO shook his head and looked at Morton. 'Still can't raise the general.'

'How about MMC? It's still supposed to link all senior officers in the capital.'

Mikhail Gorbachev had used the Moscow Military Command radio network to summon loyal army officers to help him counter the 1991 military coup. It still had not saved him.

'MMC says Savenko's using a civilian mobile phone not on their frequency.'

Sometimes Yuri could carry security too far.

'What about his field set,' Morton prompted.

'For some reason he's got it switched off.'

'Maybe the ELF can get lucky?' The onboard Extremely Low Frequency search computer could scan for all the mobile phones in Moscow.

'I wouldn't hold your breath. The fug down there's so bad even the ELF's going to find it difficult.'

'Keep trying,' Morton said.

As they had entered Soviet air space, Savenko had come on screen to say he was leaving for the airfield. He'd sounded bleaker than before. New orders had come from the Moscow Chief Public Prosecutor. The dacha would be stormed at nightfall, and not by the *Spetsnaz*, but a platoon of the even more feared Black

Berets. As Savenko started to explain why Prosecutor Comrade Kramskay had the authority to use them, the transmission broke down.

While the CCO tried to find a way to resume contact, Morton continued studying the profile he had ordered on to his screen from the data bank in Tel Aviv of the Chief Public Prosecutor.

Valentin Nikolayevitch Kramskay had been the Special Investigator in Gorbachev's Kremlin who conducted the now notorious investigation into Boris Yeltsin's personal life. When that yielded nothing except embarrassing headlines for Gorbachev, following Yeltsin's well publicised claim that he was the victim of a witch-hunt, Kramskay was offered up as the pacifying scapegoat. He had been posted as head of security to the Soviet embassy in Ulan Bator, the capital of Mongolia. His career seemed over. Then he had been invited to China to meet Wong Lee.

What precisely happened between them would never be known. The meeting occurred a full eighteen months before the first orbit of the weather satellite.

However Chantal was satisfied that when the troika recalled Kramskay to become Chief Public Prosecutor, he was already Wong Lee's man. Her staff had checked Kramskay's personal life. A dull childless marriage. Yet no mistress, not even a casual affair. No hobbies to relieve his workaholic pattern. Nothing. Only a Credit Suisse deposit account in Geneva which grew by 5,000 dollars each month. The money was deposited by telex transfer from the Bank of Southern California. Kramskay had made no withdrawals. The Prosecutor was already a rouble millionaire, yet there was no clue what he planned to do with the money.

One of the technicians had begun to speak softly into a lip mike. Morton cupped his hands under his jaw and continued to read. Humpty Dumpty had done his usual job of interpreting what the weather satellite had picked up.

Using a voice print of Kramskay which Covert Action had obtained in Moscow, Humpty Dumpty had matched it with one taken off the satellite. Measuring speech patterns and spectroscoping for pitch variations, he had established the calls were from the Chief Public Prosecutor's office to Wong Lee's secretary, Fung. In the last one Kramskay gave the frequencies the Church of True Belief was using for its Finnish transmissions into the Soviet Union. Another piece in the jigsaw?

Morton swivelled to face the CCO. 'Get me the Prime Minister.'

Moments later Karshov's face appeared on screen aboard Air Force One. The President had loaned his official aircraft for the Israeli delegation to fly home from Washington.

'Shalom, David. A problem?'

'Shalom, Prime Minister. A problem.'

Morton told Karshov about Kramskay's order for the Black Berets to assault the dacha at nightfall.

'I'll get the President to call the troika,' Karshov promised.

Morton could see the Prime Minister searching for the next words. The scar tissue over his eyes furrowed.

'David, it's going to be a strange feeling when you step on that ground, even after all those years. I felt the same when I went back to my Polish village. It gets to your guts.'

Morton smiled.

'Thanks, Prime Minister.'

In all honesty he did not know how he would feel. His work had made him rootless; the loss of Ruth, Steve and Dolly more so. People said he was colder since their deaths. He did not know if that was true, only that his private deadness had become an integral part of him. The smile, he knew, had not gone beyond his lips.

Karshov's face stared for a moment longer at Morton, then disappeared off the screen. The CCO and technicians busied themselves at their work. They understood what it meant for a man to come home to his birthplace.

Morton stared out of the window. The Concorde was following the river, heading towards the domes of the Kremlin. They reminded him of Jerusalem without the bells.

How many more potholes were there since he'd last been driven through those broad streets, being taken with Ruth to the airport to begin their journey to Israel? They'd shared a suitcase filled with second-hand clothing. It hadn't mattered. They were leaving. Clutching a brand new Israeli passport each with its Russian exit stamp, they had received five roubles apiece after signing a paper; the money was also a gift from the State. At the airport an official took two of the roubles from each of them. He had not said why. When Ruth started to cry, the man threatened to stop her boarding the plane. On the flight to Tel Aviv, Morton had promised Ruth they would never return. As proof he left their remaining roubles in the seat pocket.

The CCO behind Morton sounded apologetic. 'We're going to have to give up on the general.'

'We'll be down soon.'

On Red Square, he could see the Ladas darting between the black government Chaikas and Zils.

He went to the cabin. Monsignor Hanlon nodded, but didn't break off his description to Morelli of an ecological holocaust.

'If anything, the break-up of the Soviet Union has made things worse. There was a semblance of control then. Now, none. In Minsk, industrial waste belching into the air has led to a huge increase in mental disorders. In Odessa, it's lung disease. In Kiev, heart problems. In Moscow the pollution's so bad, it's making people lose their hair. Two-thirds of their water is seriously contaminated. Last year there were a million new cases of hepatitis.'

Morton looked out of the window. They were passing over Moscow's Ratelvo district. Fifty thousand people forced to live beside an oil refinery and scores of industrial chimneys.

Morton turned to Monsignor Hanlon. 'So what's the Third Floor doing to change all this, Sean?'

The Third Floor was how everyone in the Vatican referred to the Pope's office.

'It's still very hush-hush, but the Boss has been trying to persuade the West that they've got to tackle the problem as if they're fighting a forest fire. All hands to the pumps now, and settle who pays what part of the bill later. His idea is to first create a pollution free zone around all the old republics. Then he wants the United States, Britain, France, Japan and Germany to provide the technology, training and expertise to clean up the Russians' own backyard.'

Morelli sighed. 'You're probably talking of more money than was ever going to be invested in Star Wars. The bill for cleaning up Kuwait will be small change compared to this.'

Monsignor Hanlon gave another elegant shrug of his shoulders.

'What's the alternative, Claudio? If everybody just goes on sitting back the problem will eventually engulf us all. It's already a real horror story: in Siberia, where they used to do their nuclear testing, the lichen's so seriously contaminated it's creating a whole breed of mutating reindeer. The animals are part of the basic diet for the people up there. Now they're beginning to see the first terrible congenital effects in humans. It's going to get worse, a lot worse. The Boss says that ultimately the Russians must learn to keep their own backyard clean.'

'Is Pope Nicholas planning to tell them that when he goes to Moscow?' Morton asked.

Monsignor Hanlon nodded vigorously.

'The Boss intends to read the riot act. To Christian and non-Christian alike. They've all got to stop playing Russian roulette with the environment. It's *ours* as well!'

The cabin telephone purred. The CCO told Morton the Prime Minister was on line. There was a click, then Karshov's voice.

'I spoke to the President. He called the Kremlin. The troika's still in closed session. It'll be another half hour before they can take the President's call.'

'Thank you, Prime Minister.'

Morton replaced the receiver. In less than an hour it would be dark. Then the attack on the dacha would begin.

The lengthening silence was broken by the pilot announcing they were landing.


Morton walked quickly down the aircraft steps followed by Morelli and Monsignor Hanlon. For one fleeting moment he felt how this earth had been home. The place where his mother had secretly baked the *challah* loaves for Friday evenings and insisted the family observed the Shabbat and kept the festivals, even if behind drawn curtains and closed doors. It still made no difference. The KGB had taken his parents away. That night, too, the air had contained the same noxious smell.

Monsignor Hanlon murmured the last days of Pompeii must have smelled like this.

Only the area around Concorde was floodlit. Hangars and maintenance buildings loomed in the murk.

Morton stood for a few moments longer, each one distinct and yet interlinked with the one before and after. Then he breathed out deeply as if to exhale the past, though no one would have known.

From the edge of the light, Savenko came forward to greet them, bear-hugging Morton and kissing the others formally on both cheeks. The general was dressed in combat fatigues with a blue beret on his head and a star on his shoulder. He held a cellular phone in one hand and a snub-nosed light machine-gun in the other.

Savenko glanced at Morton's waist. 'Not even a pistol?'

'I don't expect to be doing any shooting, Yuri.'

Morton nodded at the phone. 'I was trying to call you. What's the latest?'

'Dr Kramer is still okay in the villa.' Savenko looked at the phone in disgust. 'Japanese batteries aren't so good now.'

'We couldn't raise your field set either.'

Savenko gave a quick bark of a laugh. 'I keep it switched off. Then the Black Berets can't hear.'

He lobbed the phone to one of several combat-uniformed men hovering in the background, then beckoned to a figure standing a little apart. The man stepped swiftly forward.

Savenko boomed the introduction. 'Major Yalkov, *Spetsnaz* commander.'

Yalkov's biceps rippled when he saluted.

'You speak English, major?' Morton asked.

'I was for one year Assistant Military Attaché in London,' Yalkov replied in clear though accented English.

He'd probably spent his spare time pumping iron in the embassy's basement gym.

'What's their status at the dacha?' Morton asked.

'A platoon. More than enough to storm the place. They're in position and ready to go.'

Yalkov had the look of a man who understood the first rule of close combat warfare – that there isn't a second.

'Where are your men?'

'Here.'

Yalkov nodded towards a hangar.

'How many?'

'Two platoons. Our speciality is getting into places,' the major said. 'It's what we're trained to do.'

Morton briefly studied Yalkov's name stencilled over his heart on the mud-and-slime pattern of the camouflage.

'No one goes in before I get Dr Kramer out.'

Yalkov stared at Morton then turned to Savenko. If the major was about to say something he'd changed his mind.

'I want that clearly understood,' Morton added.

Savenko gripped him by the arm. 'Come, Comrade David.'

The general headed across the tarmac at a brisk trot, passing a tanker and its crew on the way to refuel Concorde. Morton saw a couple of army trucks and several black KGB Volgas with radio aerials parked in the lee of a hangar. *Spetsnaz* commandoes in full battle kit stood around the vehicles.

The air was filled with the soft snicking and clicking of magazines being locked. The sounds special-op units always make. Nearby was a field ambulance.

'What are you going to do with these *Spetsnaz*, Yuri?' Morton asked.

'They will see Dr Kramer comes out safely.'

At Yalkov's command, the commandoes were scrambling aboard the trucks. He had seen that look before in the eyes of men steeled to do battle.

'We're not going to war, Yuri.'

Savenko took a tense breath. 'Comrade David, this is still Russia,' he began, then started again. 'When the President speaks to the troika, there'll be no problem. Everything will be fine. You'll see.'

Still offering reassurance, Savenko strode towards the ambulance. After a moment's hesitation, Morton followed.

A tall figure in a long white doctor's coat climbed down from behind the wheel. Morton hadn't been close to such a beautiful woman in a long time. She had one of those Russian faces which come from centuries of careful breeding. Her cheek bones were high, her lips full and her eyes dark and widely spaced. No single photograph could have quite caught all her fine angles. Not even her shapeless uniform completely hid the fullness of her body. Her forage cap was perched on top of a mass of black hair. There was a bright, watchful intelligence in her eyes which somehow seemed to animate everything around her.

'Captain Doctor Ogodnikova,' Savenko boomed.

She saluted and then continued to look at Morton.

'She's one of your people. Jews are now allowed to serve in the army.'

Morton remembered Gorbachev introducing the scheme as part of his perestroika.

'Why is she here?'

'Dr Kramer will possibly need help after what he's been through,' Savenko replied.

Morton looked at him. Then he looked at her. Her eyes never left his. It had been even longer since he'd met such directness in a woman.

'You bear a distinguished name, doctor. Nikòlai Ivanovich Ogodnikova helped draft the constitution of my country, Israel.'

'He was my father's uncle.' She spoke English with almost no accent, almost too perfect, from learning it in the language laboratory, from reading aloud the permitted classics of the past.

'You should be proud of him.'

'I am. But I am also proud to be Russian.'

He glanced at the name tag stitched above her left breast. 'What do the initials stand for?'

After a moment's hesitation she replied, 'Carina Leonidovana'.

'After the ballerina?'

Carina was looking at Morton steadily.

'My mother,' she acknowledged.

Nan had taken him to see Carina Leonidovana dance with the Bolshoi in Paris. She had been close to the end of her career, but even then she had danced magnificently.

He had known Nan for three months and he had thought then that he had waited with purpose, and kept faith with good reason. He'd believed Nan was the start of a new dawn; he'd truly believed that. It had made no difference.

'Have you seen action before, doctor?'

Carina gave him what could only be described as a withering glance.

'Don't patronise me, Colonel Israeli,' she began.

'Morton. David Morton –'

'Very well, Colonel David Morton,' she continued. 'Yes. I've seen battles. That is my job – to deal with battlefield casualties. For the record, I have four years' military service. I served in the Baltic States before their independence. Also in Armenia. Is there more you wish to know?'

He felt his colour rise. He glanced at her hands. There was a paler circle of skin on her wedding ring finger.

'Are you married, doctor?'

'No,' her voice was harder. 'Widowed. My husband was killed on duty at Alma-Ata. He was a physicist.'

A smaller version of Chernobyl had occurred there.

'I'm sorry. You . . . you don't look old enough to be a widow.'
Her voice was even harder when she spoke again.

'I am thirty-two years old. But what has that to do with anything? You have women in your army who are even younger who
go to battle!'

Morton wondered if she was this touchy with everyone.

'For sure,' he said. That was all he said.

When she finally broke the silence, her voice was softer.

'I'm sorry for sounding angry. You have a right to ask questions. But can I ask you one?'

He nodded.

'Are you a practising Jew, Colonel Morton?'

The question surprised him. He hadn't worn a *yarmulka* or
prayer shawl since the day he'd buried Steve and Dolly. He was
still a Jew, but not in any religious sense.

'No. Why do you ask?'

She looked at him steadily. 'Just curious. Until recently we did
not have the right to practise our faith openly.'

Carina paused to look again at Savenko. He was still listening.
She turned back to Morton.

'You're the first outside Jew I've met. And you tell me you
don't practise!' she said in a quiet voice.

He remained silent. During the festivals he'd watched Steve
and the other men singing and dancing, and some of them would
have tears in their eyes. But he hadn't felt anything.

How could he tell her that when it came to his faith, there was
now so much which left him untouched. It wasn't just the way
Zionism had a near stranglehold. It was something deeper.
People were using their faith, the faith which had sustained them
in the Diaspora and through the Holocaust, as an excuse to justify
so much he found indefensible. He loved his country still, but
he was not blind to its failings.

The trucks had started their engines.

'Time to go,' Savenko said.

Reaching one of the Volgas he turned to Monsignor Hanlon.

'You better stay here. Say a prayer for the Holy Father.'

'You too, Claudio,' Morton added. The dacha would be no
place for men travelling on Vatican diplomatic passports.

'Luck, David,' murmured Monsignor Hanlon. 'And God be
with you.'

The priest walked with Morelli towards the Concorde.

Morton glanced at the ambulance. Carina was watching him intently. She smiled, and after a moment, he smiled back, then climbed into the back of the Volga beside Savenko.

He hadn't really smiled at a woman since that dinner in London with Nan. When she'd sat down he hadn't suspected, not for a moment, she had come to tell him there was someone else. There was no one who could surprise like a woman you're in love with.

The convoy drove from the airfield.

Morton nodded at the field radio on the seat beside the driver.

'I'd like to open a channel to my people, so we'll know the moment the President's contacted the troika.'

Savenko nodded. Now they were under way he seemed relieved and almost cheerful. Morton switched on the set and tuned to Concorde's frequency band. One of the technicians instantly responded and was instructed to remain on station.

Morton turned to Savenko. 'Okay, Yuri. Just tell me, what's really going to happen?'

Savenko fished in the door pocket beside him and produced a bottle.

'Like a drink? Our vodka's still the best.' He pronounced it wod-ka.

'Thank you, no. Just tell me what's going on.'

Savenko sighed, replaced the bottle and glanced out of the window. This was still open country, the outskirts of Moscow a sodium glow in the distance. Savenko abruptly turned to Morton.

'If the troika doesn't order the Black Berets to stop, my *Spetsnaz* will attack them. But you try to talk your people into letting Dr Kramer go. The *Spetsnaz* will protect you.'

'It's not Yalkov's people I'm concerned about, Yuri. Those Black Berets will kill Dr Kramer.'

'The *Spetsnaz* will kill them first!'

'So you are going to war?' Morton said.

'Maybe it's the only way to free Dr Kramer. If we move quickly, we'll win.'

Morton was listening for a hint of anything else. He found none.

'What about the consequences for you, Yuri?'

Savenko shrugged.

'Maybe bad, maybe not. That's not important now. It's only important to free Dr Kramer.'

'Where's Kramskay?'

'At the dacha.'

'Let me talk to him.'

Savenko shrugged.

They rode in silence. Industrial pollution filled the car with a rancid smell. Away to their left loomed the first of the dachas. A squat, low-fronted building, partly hidden by trees, standing well back from the road in its own park.

'Comrade Gorbachev used to live there,' Savenko said briefly.

'Is our dacha like that?'

'*Da*. But with more trees and bushes. Yalkov says there's plenty of good cover.'

A little further on Savenko ordered the driver to stop. In the wing mirror Morton glimpsed a couple of *Spetsnaz* jumping from the lead truck. They sprinted past the car, the swift slapping sound of their boots loud on the road surface. Each commando carried a laser-sighted carbine fitted with a silencer. They disappeared into a copse just before a bend in the road.

The car drove on, leaving the two trucks, Volgas and ambulance stationary. A quarter of a mile beyond the bend, the Black Berets had set up a control point, a couple of soldiers crouching by the verge. They rose to face the oncoming car. One raised his carbine to signal it forward. The other stood to one side, gun at the ready. Morton suddenly saw spots of red light appear on the chests of both men. Then they pitched forward. Savenko grunted. They were going to war. Now he was sure, Morton knew what he must do.

By the time the car reached the bodies, the *Spetsnaz* marksmen were running back up the road. Moments later the convoy came around the bend and parked behind Savenko's vehicle.

Yalkov and his men jumped down onto the road. Two of the *Spetsnaz* rolled the bodies into the undergrowth, then joined the others gathered around Yalkov. They listened intently to him, then moved off with swiftness and silence into the gathering darkness.

Savenko's car drove on down the road. A mile later, Morton spotted the black Zil limousine parked across a pillared gateway.

'Prosecutor Comrade Kramskay,' Savenko said.

Morton saw the iron gates to the dacha hung crookedly, as if they'd been burst open. Yoshi's captors had probably used the car as a battering ram.

The Volga came to a stop near the Zil. Morton climbed out, opened the front passenger door and hoisted the field radio on his back. Savenko emerged, holding his machine gun. He spoke to the driver who reached under the dashboard and unclipped a Uzi. He handed the weapon to the general. Savenko walked around the car.

'You'll feel better with a gun.'

He thrust the weapon into Morton's hand.

'I'd feel better if I knew I wouldn't need to use it, Yuri.'

They walked to the limousine. Still a few feet away, a rear window was lowered. Morton stared at the face. It was a clever, arrogant face, and handsome in a dark, saturnine way.

Valentin Nikolayevich Kramskay ignored Morton.

'Why have you returned, general?' the Chief Public Prosecutor asked in Russian. Kramskay had a soft, almost a feminine voice.

Savenko waved his gun towards the gateway.

'The Black Berets are not to attack, comrade prosecutor. We are awaiting further orders from the Kremlin. Until then, nothing will be done.'

In his own language, the general's Crimean accent was more pronounced.

'I know nothing of this. My orders to arrest the terrorists remain.' Kramskay continued to speak Russian.

'Mr Kramskay,' Morton said quietly in English. 'Why don't you call the Kremlin on your radio?'

'Who is this man?' Kramskay demanded, still speaking Russian, still staring at Savenko.

'He has come to collect Dr Kramer.'

'You know perfectly well who I am, Mr Kramskay,' Morton continued. 'And I've come to collect Dr Kramer on the orders of my Prime Minister and the President of the United States.'

Kramskay looked at Morton for the first time.

'I know you, Jew,' Kramskay acknowledged in American-accented English.

'I know you, too, Mr Kramskay. And I want you to understand one thing. I am leaving here with Dr Kramer.'

The prosecutor turned back to Savenko and spoke in Russian.

'This Jew has no jurisdiction here. Nor do those who sent him. And tell him that here in Russia, he should speak our language!'

'I speak English. You speak the same!' Savenko rumbled. There's no time to play games, comrade prosecutor.'

The gathering darkness made it harder to see Kramskay's face. Speaking English increased the fury in his voice.

'These Jews have committed serious crimes. They must be arrested, tried and punished. That means this other Jew, Kramer, must remain here so that a statement can be taken. That will then be examined by both me and any defence attorney the court will appoint –'

'How long do you need for this, Mr Kramskay?' Morton asked.

'Days. Probably a week.'

'Dr Kramer must go to Rome as soon as possible,' Morton said.

'That is not a concern for me! I am concerned only with dealing with dangerous terrorists –'

The voice had an odd, high-pitched squeak. Morton had heard it before in men dangerously close to losing control.

'They're hardly that, Mr Kramskay. More like a bunch of stupid people who wouldn't wait for their visas. What they did, for sure, breaks the law. But it doesn't justify the steps you've taken. Or the need to keep Dr Kramer here.'

'Don't tell me what is right or wrong!' Kramskay's voice continued to rise.

Morton stared at him. 'I wouldn't even try to teach you that. But I will arrange for Dr Kramer to make a full statement in Rome to your legal attaché at the Russian embassy. I will also guarantee that Dr Kramer will return here to give evidence after he has performed his operation –'

'Don't tell me what you can do! I am not interested! I am only interested in dealing with these terrorists!'

Morton made a slight hand movement and continued in the same low firm voice.

'I am going in there to persuade these people to let Dr Kramer go.'

'You cannot go in there! The Black Berets have orders to attack –'

'My *Spetsnaz* will shoot them first!' roared Savenko. '*My* orders! *Don't* forget my authority is greater than yours! You remember that!'

Morton felt the darkness was like a living, tangible thing.

'Russians fighting Russians – for Jews?' Kramskay asked viciously.

'*Da*! If it's good for our country!' Savenko roared again.

From inside the limousine came a sudden burst of radio traffic. The Black Berets radioman was reporting the arrival of *Spetsnaz*.

Morton pulled the hand mike from the backpack and stepped closer to the car.

'Mr Kramskay. I'm going to give you ten seconds to agree to give me time to talk to these people. Otherwise I'm going to ask General Savenko to radio his *Spetsnaz* to attack your Black Berets. It's two to one in there, and your people wouldn't have a chance –'

'You threaten me, Jew?'

'No. Just stating a fact. I'm starting to count from now.'

Morton's voice was cold, impersonal, without the warmth of Kramskay's hatred.

'One.'

Savenko raised his gun.

'And after I give the order, I will then kill you personally, comrade prosecutor!'

Morton stared at Kramskay out of flat, emotionless eyes.

'Four . . . five.'

Savenko's gun barrel was trained on Kramskay's face.

'Six . . . seven.' Savenko would pull the trigger. There never was any point in bluffing.

'Eight.'

'All right, Jew. You have ten minutes,' screeched the prosecutor.

Kramskay turned and relayed an order to his driver.

By then Morton was already sprinting through the gateway, the field radio bumping on his back, the Uzi clutched in one hand.

# 8

Inside the gateway, Morton moved into the foliage. He switched off the field radio and put on night vision goggles. He pulled the strap tight. Research and Development had explained how to adjust eye-screws on either side of the frame. When he had done so, he could see with aquamarine clarity. The road shimmered away to his right.

He took a tube from another pocket and daubed his face, neck and hands with the camouflage paste. He moved through the undergrowth with a hunter's speed and stealth. Only the soft sucking of mulch under his feet marked his progress.

Several yards deeper into the overgrowth he stopped by a thick tree trunk. A moment ago had come the sound of something moving over a piece of fallen wood ahead and to his left. Moving and stopping. Then moving again.

Morton darted from trunk to trunk in a half crouch, constantly turning to present a more elusive target. The noise had stopped, started and stopped again. He saw dark spots on a bush. He rubbed the leaves between his fingers and put them to his lips. Blood.

A few yards further on he found the body. The face was shattered, blood coagulated over every feature, the skull a mass of broken bone and cartilage. A six-pointed star on the neck chain glinted brightly through the goggles. One of Yoshi's kidnappers. Russian Jews had started to wear their stars again with pride.

Morton stood up and stepped back into the overgrowth. Another cracking. Too heavy for an animal.

He edged to the right, away from the sound, one hand carefully pushing the branches from his face and body, the other clutching the Uzi. He had helped write the rules of evasion.

Morton was moving so fast he almost passed the track. The few corn seeds the birds had missed glittered like tiny jewels. He sniffed the air. No smell of alcohol. The still had either been abandoned, or destroyed by one of the special police squads formed to hunt bootleggers. It wasn't the illegal brewing the authorities objected to, but the loss of revenue.

A few yards along the track he came to a brick archway and a ramp leading down to where there had once been a door. He could see rusty hinges set in the stonework. The sound of a footstep bearing down on the mulch was perhaps no more than fifty feet away.

Morton ran down the ramp and through the opening. He adjusted the eye-screws to compensate for the blackness. The air was as cold as a tomb.

He was confronted by a low-ceilinged, brick-lined passage with recesses on either side: an abandoned underground winter storage area. Some forty feet ahead it disappeared around a bend. Behind him the passage extended back another twenty feet. The bootleggers had set up their equipment here. The floor was littered with broken glass and overturned vats. An old-fashioned stove lay in bits. Through the chimney hole came the sound of another footfall.

Morton began to move swiftly along the passage, looking into the recesses. The shelves were empty. He reached the bend and looked behind him. Something was blocking what little natural light had indicated the opening.

He made another adjustment to the eye-screws. Black boots and the lower half of black combat fatigues were visible. The soldier was standing with his machine pistol thrust forward in one hand. With the other he removed one of the grenades clipped to his field jacket.

The Black Beret pulled the pin and rolled the grenade along the passage, then ran back up the ramp. At the same time Morton dived into a recess. A moment later the explosion came, echoing and re-echoing against the walls, bringing down bricks. Dust was billowing everywhere. Even before it settled, long bursts of automatic fire raked the passage.

After the gunfire stopped, Morton lay perfectly still on the floor, allowing the hammering in his chest to subside. Then infinitely slowly he rose to his feet and moved to the front of the recess.

The bullets had gouged furrows in the brickwork. Hugging the wall, he edged back to the bend in the passage. The Black Beret was standing in the arched opening.

Morton could smell the man from here – deep-brain nerve cells releasing body odour. Fear and tension. Always the hardest to control. Morton silently moved deeper into the passage.

He heard the soldier stepping over the rubble. The footsteps stopped. Then resumed. Three steps forward. Pause. Another three steps. Pause. The way the manual said.

Morton passed a recess on his left and saw another opening ahead on the opposite side. Reaching it, he slipped off the packset and placed it at the back of the storage area. He switched on the radio. The faint hiss of squelch sounded as if someone was breathing nervously through his teeth.

Morton doubled back to the first opening. He stood motionless and silent in the dark, willing his body into the walls. The soldier had stopped again. Morton could hear the man's shallow breathing. Then he was moving more quickly, lured by the sound.

Morton raised the Uzi, one hand on the steel stock, the other gripping the top of the snubby barrel. He held the weapon slightly extended.

The Black Beret had stopped just before reaching the opening. The only sound was the hissing. The soldier was moving across the face of the recess, weapon close to his hip, no more than a different shade of aquamarine.

Morton moved with astonishing force and speed. He rammed the Uzi against the trooper's jaw and neck, breaking the bone and crushing his wind pipe. The man was dead before he reached the ground.

After dragging the body into the recess, Morton ran to retrieve the radio set. He switched it off and humped the pack onto his back.

Ahead was a faint blur. Moments later he emerged from the passage through another arched entrance. He switched on the radio.

Yalkov appeared from behind a bush. Around his neck was a headset and a surveillance stethoscope.

'What happened?' he asked urgently. 'I thought we weren't going to war!'

'There was a problem,' Morton said briefly. 'I had no choice.'

The dacha was in complete darkness, its windows shuttered and a steel-mesh grille lowered over the entrance porch.

'Dr Kramer and his captors are in the kitchen,' the major whispered.

'How well are they armed?'

'A couple of shotguns they took from Dr Kramer's escort. They've also found a hunting rifle.'

'Where's the car?'

'On the other side. The keys are still in the ignition. I've posted a man there.'

'I want to take a look.'

Yalkov turned and led Morton back into the undergrowth. The major knew how to use the dark, how to put out his hand to feel the air, to brush aside a branch, to sidestep a piece of fallen branch.

They reached the far side of the dacha. Behind the main building were a couple of smaller ones, also in darkness. Staff quarters probably. A place like this would have needed a retinue to function properly. To the left of the buildings was a high wall with an opening. The gateway to the fruit and vegetable gardens. The dacha would have been completely self-sufficient.

The stolen Volga stood in the middle of a parking area big enough to hold a dozen vehicles. The car's grille and fender were badly crushed from forcing open the entrance gates.

'Black Berets are on the other side of the wall,' Yalkov whispered. 'They've planted charges at the dacha windows. The cables run back to a firing point.'

'Cut them.'

Yalkov grinned. 'I already have.'

A *Spetsnaz* was crouching by the Volga's rear wheel. As they ran towards him, Morton heard the snick of the trooper checking the safety catch on his carbine. The noise sounded like a door slamming.

Reaching the car, Morton opened the trunk. A large case filled most of the space. Stencilled on the top were bold words in red:

DEPARTMENT OF SURGERY
UNIVERSITY OF TEL AVIV

Yoshi's laser. It would take a couple of men to move it. As Morton closed the trunk the sound of urgent whispering came from behind the walls. Someone was radioing for instructions.

At that moment the set on Morton's back came to life.

'El Al One to El Al Two,' came the CCO's voice.

Morton grabbed the hand mike. 'Go ahead, El Al One.'

'We have the Prime Minister on line.'

'Has the President reached the troika?'

'He was still arguing with them when the line broke down. The President's back on to Moscow now.'

'Tell the Prime Minister I'm going in.'

Morton thrust the mike back into its holder. He and Yalkov ran towards the rear of the dacha.

The major nodded to a shuttered window. 'Kitchen.'

Yalkov placed the headphones over his ears and the stethoscope disc against the wooden shutters. He listened intently and began to shake his head, perplexed. The major removed the headphones and handed them to Morton. He positioned the disc against the wood. Through the headphones he heard a woman's intense voice.

'Is that why you want to get out of here – just to save the Pope's life?'

'I'm a doctor. I'll save any life I can,' Morton heard Yoshi say wearily.

'No Pope's ever been a friend of the Jews!'

'I doubt if those Jews the Pope saved in World War Two would agree with that!'

'What about all the Nazis the Vatican helped to escape?' the woman flared.

Morton sensed the effort Yoshi was making to stay calm.

'Lady, you've chosen an odd time and place for such a discussion.'

Morton rapped quickly with the disc on the shutters. There was sudden silence in the kitchen. Morton pressed his mouth against the shutters.

'Yoshi?'

The silence lasted a moment longer.

'David?'

'Yes.'

'How in God's name did you –'

'Are you okay, Yoshi?'

Yoshi gave a mirthless laugh.

'Not exactly a term I would choose under the circumstances.'

'Who are you, out there?' the woman demanded.

'This place is completely surrounded. You all have a couple of minutes to let Dr Kramer go, and come out with your hands on your heads. I'll guarantee your safety,' Morton replied.

He pressed the disc against the shutters. Angry, protesting voices. Finally the woman's voice.

'You out there! We want to go with Dr Kramer to Israel, to anywhere not to remain in this country. It's our only chance to build a new life.'

Morton heard the sobs through her words. His voice was gentler as he pressed his mouth one more time against the shutters.

'Just come out with your hands on your heads. No one will hurt you.'

Yalkov lifted one of the headphones from Morton's ear and whispered. 'We're almost out of time.'

Morton looked towards the garden wall. Vague forms were moving through the arched opening. He turned to Yalkov.

'Get the car up here.'

The major spoke to a commando. The man ran towards the Volga.

Morton turned back to the shuttered window. 'Yoshi, start walking towards the door.'

The woman's voice was more fearful. 'We will only let Dr Kramer go if you promise we can go to Israel.'

Morton ignored her. The time for negotiation was over.

'Yoshi, are you free to move?'

'Yes.'

'We will surrender our weapons to you,' the woman cried out. 'Just promise we can leave.' Her voice wobbled from fright.

'Yoshi, start moving – *now!*' Morton ordered.

He pressed the disc against the shutters. Through the headphones he heard footsteps crossing the floor. Then the creak of a door opening.

'Please, sir! Promise us!' the woman implored from behind the shutters.

Yoshi was making calming noises, repeatedly promising everything would be all right.

Morton removed the head set and let the stethoscope dangle from his neck.

The car was lurching towards him without lights. The impact with the gates had destroyed them. The driver stopped at the far end of the dacha, leaving the engine running. He came running back to join the other commandoes.

Yalkov pointed to a door beyond the window. Morton tried the handle. Locked. He could hear footsteps approaching and Yoshi's calming voice.

At that moment the CCO's voice came over the field radio.

'El Al One to El Al Two.'

Morton grabbed the mike. 'Read you.'

'The troika's agreed to cancel the attack until dawn. But those people have to stand trial.'

The CCO's voice sounded as if it was coming over a loud-speaker.

Morton slammed the mike back into its holder and switched off the radio.

Behind the door the woman was shouting.

'No trial! They kill us! No trial! You promised!'

From beyond the garden wall came the sound of radio traffic.

Morton addressed the door. 'Yoshi, keep walking. And everyone do exactly what I tell you to do. First, open that door.'

The woman wailed. 'You promised us –'

'Just open that door,' Morton said as if she had no other choice.

'Please, sir –'

'Yoshi, get that door open,' Morton ordered.

The radio transmission had ceased.

Yalkov motioned his men to form an outward facing ring extending in a semi-circle from the door to the Volga. Professionals making a professional deployment.

Still the door remained closed.

'Yoshi! Open it – *now!*'

There was the sound of bolts being drawn, then a key turning in a lock. The door swung slowly open. Yoshi was bunched between a bearded man and a woman. They each had one hand on their head and a shotgun in the other. Behind them were the others.

In the light from the corridor they all looked so young and vulnerable. One of the men held a hunting rifle.

'Please, sir,' whispered the woman. 'You promised.'

She was quite a pretty woman, Morton thought, but the fear in her eyes gave her a haggard look.

'Throw out your weapons,' Morton instructed. 'Yoshi, step forward.'

'Please, sir. We only –'

'Throw out those guns! Yoshi – move!'

As Yoshi obeyed, there was a clatter as the shotguns and rifle fell to the ground.

'Now, one at a time, both hands on your heads –'

'Look out!' shrieked the woman. 'They are going to kill us!'

Morton whirled. As he did so the first blast knocked the woman to her knees. Blood was streaming from her eyes and ears. The second struck the bearded man full in the face and throat, almost severing his head from his body. The couple continued to make strange twitching movements where they fell.

Morton charged Yoshi to the ground. Then, he spun on his back and fired a long burst with the Uzi at the aquamarine figures emerging through the wall opening. He saw one drop, then another.

The *Spetsnaz* were pouring automatic fire into the wall opening. From beyond came the dull crump of a mortar.

The radio on Morton's back exploded and burst into flames under the impact of a splinter from the phosphorus shell. He wriggled out of the harness and continued firing, at the same time yelling at Yoshi to crawl to the car. The man and woman had stopped moving.

Yalkov was moving like a swift night lizard among his men, directing their fire, sending them to new positions.

The two other men and the woman came running from the doorway, screaming. One of the men's heads became a small fireball when a phosphorus shell burst in his face. Morton saw the crazed look in the woman's eyes, saw Yoshi grab her and pull her down, saw him crawling with her towards the Volga.

The stonework and wooden frame around the door splintered under a hail of bullets. A phosphorus shell landed in the passage-way and the flames quickly took hold.

All around him Morton could hear men dying. The Black

Berets kept coming on low and hard, but they were no match for the *Spetsnaz*.

Flames came from behind the kitchen shutters. A sudden explosion followed as its entire window hurtled out of its frame.

In the glare, he saw Yoshi and the woman reach the car. The second man was dragging himself along by one arm. The other hung uselessly.

As Morton began to fire another burst, there was a click. The magazine was empty. He dropped the Uzi and sprinted to the man, lifted him across his shoulders, and ran to the car.

The Black Berets' attack was faltering. Yalkov was shouting through a loudspeaker that they should surrender and receive medical attention. The major was still repeating his offer when a burst of gunfire cut him down.

When he reached the car, Morton found Yoshi and the woman sprawled in the back. He lowered the man on to the front seat, then got behind the wheel. The entire rear of the dacha was now blazing.

Savenko's voice came over the radio under the dash.

'Yalkov, report your situation.'

Morton gunned the engine. The car bumped over the ground and around the side of the dacha. Flames were attacking the front of the building. A Black Beret stepped out of the undergrowth. Morton drove full tilt at him. At the same moment, dots of light appeared on the man's black fatigues, on the centre of his chest, and the material burst apart. The trooper flew back under the force of the bullets.

A couple of *Spetsnaz* were running behind the car, searching for new targets with their laser-sighted guns.

'Yalkov! Report your present situation!' Savenko roared in Russian.

Morton grabbed the mike. 'Yalkov's dead, Yuri. We're coming out. We've got casualties.'

'Dr Kramer?'

The car roared down the driveway.

'He's okay. Call the airfield for Concorde to start engines.'

Through the goggles Morton saw the dacha gateway ahead, saw Savenko standing in the opening, saw the Black Beret down on one knee on the driveway aiming at the general. He slammed down on the accelerator and the Volga hurtled forward. Even as the commando rose and tried to leap for safety, the car struck him, snapping the man's spine. The body hurtled over the Volga and landed behind on the driveway.

Morton stopped outside the gateway beside Savenko.

'You drive good. You saved my life,' Savenko said.

'Where's Kramskay?' Morton asked, pulling off his goggles.

'The first sound of shooting, he was gone,' Savenko roared.

He stuck his head into the car.

'Dr Kramer?'

'That's me,' acknowledged Yoshi.

The injured woman groaned.

'She's hurt and needs medical attention,' Yoshi added.

Savenko grunted and glanced at the man beside Morton.

'He also needs help, Yuri.'

Savenko turned and yelled. The ambulance appeared moments later and parked beside the Volga.

Carina sprang from the cabin. Two orderlies carrying a stretcher emerged from the back.

Morton climbed out of the car. Carina looked at him quickly.

'You are not hurt?'

'No.'

'I'm glad,' she said softly, continuing to supervise the removal of the injured kidnappers.

Morton turned to Savenko. 'Yuri, I need your men to move Dr Kramer's equipment to your car.'

Savenko gave the order. The sky over the dacha was a fiery glow. The shooting had stopped and *Spetsnaz* were running down the drive to the gate. A couple of commandoes lugged Yoshi's laser to Savenko's car. *Spetsnaz* appeared carrying the body of Yalkov.

While the orderlies stretcher-carried the man, Yoshi and Carina supported the woman to the ambulance. Morton took Savenko by the arm and pulled him aside.

'What's going to happen to these two, Yuri?'

'The troika says they must face trial, Comrade David,' Savenko grunted.

'The troika isn't here, Yuri. It's your decision.'

Morton watched Yoshi and Carina lead the woman into the ambulance.

'Once Kramskay gets his hands on them, they won't have a chance.'

Savenko gave a grunt which rose from his belly.

'*Da*. But the law –'

'A lot of your laws were broken tonight when I killed that Black Beret who would have killed you, for sure.'

Savenko rocked his head from side to side. Not a headshake. More a decision weighing movement.

'How you say, I owe one to you?'

'Maybe.'

The head movement stopped. Savenko gave a barking laugh and turned and faced Morton.

'*Da*, okay. They can go with you.'

'Thank you, Yuri.'

'No problem. A general still has some power.'

He took Morton by the elbow and they began to walk towards Savenko's car.

'They'll need a doctor to go with them, Yuri. We've only a paramedic on board.'

Savenko glanced sideways at Morton. 'Dr Kramer's a doctor.'

'He'll need to rest. He's going to need all his strength when he gets to Rome.'

Morton thought again how Savenko's pauses were like no one else's.

'*Da*, okay. You take her. She's our best doctor.'

Savenko gave another sideways glance. 'Also the prettiest.'

Morton smiled, but there was no way of telling why.

# 9

Martha Kingdom realised that when Eddie came into the conference room on the ground floor of the Communications Building, he was tightly wound, the way he always was after a telephone call from Wong Lee. She had stayed on the line, as she did with all his important calls. One of Eddie's little faults was that he often imagined what he had been told, rather than what was actually said.

Wong Lee's reference to some operation called Holy Cross concerned her. Why had he not explained it to Eddie? And why had he hung up like that? He had never done that before. Whatever it was, this Holy Cross plan had upset Wong Lee mightily. They had both searched everywhere. Nothing in the Only Book. A computer check on the words 'Holy Cross' yielded nothing resembling an operation.

She had told Eddie to call Wong Lee back. He had been unable to get through. That would account for why Eddie was so wound up. One thing he hated more than not knowing, was being thwarted. Some of his tension would have been dissipated under the ice-cold shower he took three times a day before putting on another of his sky-blue linen suits, white silk shirts and blood-red ties, which he always wore when not in the pulpit.

Eddie moved quickly among the realtors, shaking their hands and saying how glad he was to see them. But he sounded inattentive and ineffective.

Roland Tinker, the senior of the realtors, a patrician in a formal suit, frowned and said loudly that he had just settled a multi-million dollar land deal with the state governor.

Martha smiled brightly at Roland Tinker. 'The governor's an old friend of the Reverend Kingdom.'

'That so?' smiled Tinker. The smile spread his sunken cheeks, a humourless smile, the smile of a basking shark.

Martha led them out of the conference room into the Hallway of Support. The walls of the long corridor were completely covered with plaques and citations and photographs of the rich and famous. They all appeared to be listening attentively to the Reverend Kingdom. The state governor with his arm around the pastor's shoulders. Scrawled across the photo in the governor's child-like writing was the inscription: 'Your prayers helped elect me. Anything I can do to spread the Word, just holler.'

Martha gave Roland Tinker an even brighter smile. Then she continued to point out the Reverend Doctor Kingdom – in public she always referred to Eddie formally – posing with stars on a movie set and singers in a recording studio. Beside the German Chancellor outside the Berlin Reichstag. Towering over the Secretary-General in front of the United Nations Building. On board the private yacht of a European King. Praying before the altar of the chapel in the Pentagon, with the Joint Chiefs of Staff; at an open-air rally, with Mr Universe; on a Mississippi river boat, crowded with the stars of daytime television; on a plane, hand raised in benediction over the Vice-President of the United States.

By the time she had led them half-way down the Hallway of Support, Martha knew even the snooty Roland Tinker was totally overwhelmed. More importantly, Eddie was returning to his old self, smiling modestly, and murmuring that God's work opened all sorts of doors.

Roland Tinker turned to Martha. 'I don't see any photos of you, Miss Kingdom.'

She shook her head and smiled. 'I'm just one of many doing the Lord's work through the Reverend Kingdom. The Almighty has chosen to shine His light on him and we are all happy to be part of the reflected glow.'

'That's very ennobling', Roland Tinker said. 'Very ennobling and impressive.'

Martha had long accepted men were impressed by her. Partly, it was the way she always dressed, in a full-length white gown, trimmed with red lace at collar and cuffs. She had a dozen to choose from, each tailored to carefully flatter her height and figure. Partly, it was the way she wore her red hair in a braid pinned into a regal tiara above her piercing blue eyes which, like the rest of her face, never received a touch of make-up. The natural glow of her skin made her look considerably younger than her forty-five years. But what impressed men most of all was her obvious devotion to Eddie. She had heard more than one muse why such an attractive and vital woman had sacrificed marriage and motherhood for her brother. Not even Eddie suspected anything about her relationship with Clara Stevens who ran the Mail Department. They had been lovers for a year.

At first Clara had been content for them to meet once a week, when she would walk over to Martha's top floor suite in the manse, with a bundle of computer print-outs under her arm to allay suspicion. After drinking a bottle of the good wine Eddie kept for specially important guests he entertained, they made love.

Then Clara started to come to the manse twice, and even three times a week. The last time she had arrived tipsy, drooling on about being truly in love with Martha.

Martha had known then the relationship was doomed to end like all the others. Why did her lovers always need to complicate a situation? The sheer act of physical sex was enough for her. Why not for anyone else?

They had quarrelled, and Clara ran sobbing from the apartment.

'Is that the President of France?' asked Roland Tinker, pointing to a photograph of Eddie receiving a plaque from a stout man in full morning dress.

'You're perceptive, Mr Tinker,' Martha smiled graciously. 'The President's always inviting the Reverend Kingdom over to Paris for a prayer rally. But if he accepted every invitation, there just would be no time for him to do God's work here.'

'That's right,' the Reverend Kingdom nodded humbly. 'God brought me here for a purpose.'

He turned and glanced at Roland Tinker. 'We're all here for a purpose. To do His work.'

'And bless His name,' Martha added.

They had reached the centrepiece of the Hallway of Support; a large coloured photograph of the Reverend Kingdom standing in the Oval Office with the former President.

Roland Tinker and the others peered at the small, spidery inscription.

'He sure couldn't have gotten many marks at school for hand-writing,' Roland Tinker murmured.

'Let me read it to you,' Martha said. 'I was there when the President wrote it, so the words are enshrined in my heart.'

She read in the same strong voice as when reading a scripture passage in the Tabernacle.

'May the handmaidens help the Reverend Kingdom spread the Word to all corners of the world. With sincere admiration and great affection.'

'Wow,' said one of the realtors. 'Isn't that just something?'

'I'm intrigued by the reference to handmaidens,' Roland Tinker began. 'Sounds like there's a story behind that.'

'There surely is,' the Reverend Kingdom said, smiling broadly, effortlessly moving back to centre stage. 'There surely is.'

His voice was now relaxed, folksy almost, in complete contrast to Martha's controlled formality.

'Martha and I had gone to Washington to present the President with a new edition of the Only Book. I'd had the cover specially hand-tooled with a piece of goat hide from Galilee, and it looked really fantastic. The kind of finish Jesus Himself would have been proud of.

'Anyways, after I'd prayed over the President to always be guided by the Only Book, he called in the official photographer.'

The Reverend Kingdom paused and looked affectionately at Martha. She lowered her eyes.

'Martha here said she didn't want her photo taken. That she was just a handmaiden of the Word. At that moment, the First Lady came in, and having overhead what Martha said, she added she knew just what Martha meant. Then the First Lady turned to the President and told him exactly what he must write on the photo.'

'Wow,' said the realtor again. 'That's really something.'

'Indeed so,' Roland Tinker added.

Martha and the Reverend Kingdom smiled at them all.

She had instructed the photographer after they had left the Oval Office what the inscription should be. But then, the parables and miracles in the Only Book were also largely apocryphal.

Allowing the group to pause to admire the three separate *Time* Man of the Year covers devoted to the Reverend Kingdom and the plaque from the Religious Broadcasters Association voting him God's Voice Of The Year, Martha led them to the current jewel in the display.

It was a photograph of one of Britain's Royal princes listening attentively to Eddie at a fund-raising dinner.

'He didn't sign it,' Roland Tinker said, disappointed.

Martha smiled knowledgeably. 'Only the head of the Royal Family is allowed to sign photographs publicly, and then only for bank notes and official portraits. But the prince told the Reverend Kingdom something very wonderful.'

She turned to Eddie. 'Would you care to share it with our friends?'

'Well, after dinner His Highness took me aside. Just the two of us, real informal like. He said next time I came to England he'd like to arrange for me to preach in Westminster Abbey.'

'Wow!' said the realtor.

'Not even Billy Graham's done that,' Roland Tinker said in an even more impressed voice.

The Reverend Kingdom nodded his head modestly. Martha had signed the 100,000 dollar cheque for the prince's latest interest, preserving the Amazon, once His Highness agreed to attend the dinner.

Out of a corner of his eye he saw Martha nod quickly. He smiled at Roland Tinker and his associates.

'I bet some of you are thinking that if this fella knows so many famous folk, he should have no problem rustling up the money needed to buy those seven hundred acres for our new campus.'

Roland Tinker gave his basking shark smile.

'Well, I must say the thought –'

The Reverend Kingdom focussed totally on Roland Tinker.

'Let me share something with you, Mr Tinker. People just think the money rolls in and stays here. No one ever figures what it costs to keep all this going. Twenty-four hours a day, seven days a week, our television and radio network brings the Word. Then there's all those millions of videos we sell at cost only, and the millions of copies of the Only Book itself we also sell at cost only. Our regular mailing to all our members makes us the highest private Post Office user in the country, second only to government. They just send out garbage. We mail the Word. Believe you me, Mr Tinker, when we pay for all that, we are most certainly not rich in earthly terms. Only in God's grace!'

'And bless His name,' Martha murmured.

She had spent a full two years doing nothing else but setting up the complex financial structure which no amount of IRS probing had been able to penetrate. At the base of the financial pyramid were the hundred offshore corporations. They controlled all the commercial operations. The management of the tithes, now running at over a billion dollars a year, required investment portfolios on every major stockmarket in the world. The buying and selling of property on a global scale had earned last year over 60 million dollars in pure profit. Like all the other profits, the money was deposited with Credit Suisse in Geneva, to earn still more profits.

The Reverend Kingdom flapped a hand towards more photographs.

'These people, all rich folk, often expect *us* to support them! To give money to their favourite charities! To donate to something they have an interest in. Last year we gave away over two million dollars. We were glad to do so because it's what God wants!'

'And bless His name,' Martha intoned.

The Reverend Kingdom clasped his hands together.

'All this giving leaves us mighty short to do all His other work: spreading the Word, showing the way. We broadcast now in twenty-nine languages, in all the important tongues of the world. But that still leaves another thousand, and translators come expensive. We've still a long way to go to see the Only Book translated so that everyone can read it. To publish and ship the Word to all those godless countries that still need to hear it. And to train our Ministers in the Word so that they can go forth and correctly spread the teachings of the Only Book.'

He paused to allow the enormity of the task ahead to be fully appreciated.

'But no one here at the Church of True Belief ever stops and asks "Can we afford this?" All we say is, "God will provide". And you know why? Because He's the best deal-maker there is! Surprised to hear me speak of the Almighty like that? Then think about it. Who else can you deal with who says "Do My work and you will never want"? I'll be there when you're lonely, in danger, suffering, weary or just not knowing what to do. That's the kind of deal-maker He is. He offers us all a cradle-to-the-grave-and-beyond deal just so long as we follow Him. And I'm proud and privileged and, if I may add, humbled too, that all of us here have been chosen by Him to deal here on earth on His behalf.'

He stopped and let the silence grow. Several of the others had taken their cue from Roland Tinker and were also nodding fervently.

The Reverend Kingdom unclasped his hands and spread them in a gesture of beseechment. When he spoke next his voice was as rich and resonant as it was in the Tabernacle.

'Before we go any further, let me clear up one thing. If you have some fancy price in mind for those acres God wants, then I am sorry, but you will be wasting your time. God knows I am ready to pay a fair price. He also knows what I can afford to pay. And He will not allow me to go a dime over that figure. Because if I do, I will be breaking His solemn commandment.'

The Reverend Kingdom paused for a moment to close his eyes. When he opened them they shone with certainty.

'The Only Book says, in Romans 12:8, that "he that giveth, let him do it with simplicity". In other words, don't rip anyone off.'

He smiled at them then turned and walked to a door bearing the words MODEL ROOM.

The Reverend Kingdom opened the door and walked in. After a moment, Martha led the others after him. Inside the door, the visitors stood transfixed. Almost the entire room was covered with a scale model raised on trestles of the Church of True Belief complex.

Each building was faithfully reproduced to the last detail and set in landscaping which followed the curve and slope of the actual ground. As in real scale, the Tabernacle towered above the other structures. A replica of the canyon had been cut away to show how far the work area extended back into the rock. To the left of the complex's boundary chain-link fence was another set of buildings, fashioned from moulded perspex.

Standing at the far end of the model display, the Reverend Kingdom allowed the visitors a moment longer to familiarise themselves. Then he pressed buttons on a console before him. The perspex structures were instantly bathed in a diffused ethereal light emanating from spotlights in the ceiling.

'Wow!' breathed the realtor. 'Eat your heart out Hollywood.'

At that same instant the air was filled with the singing on disc of the Kingdom Angels. The choir of two hundred voices led the Sunday morning service. They began to render a medley of old and well-loved hymns which had made the compact disc a perennial favourite.

The Reverend Kingdom pressed another button and the harmony swelled out of the loudspeakers built into the ceiling and floor. He stood perfectly still, eyes closed, arms extended as wide as the Christ overlooking Rio.

Across the room he heard Martha's voice join in the singing of 'Jerusalem'. She had a resonant voice, none more so when she sang his favourite hymn.

The Reverend Kingdom felt his eyes begin to sting. The emotion of the moment always reached him. He opened his eyes, lowered his arms, and pressed more buttons. Instantly the disc stopped and the spotlights went out. Martha had already stopped singing. The Reverend Kingdom looked across the table.

'Some folk have toy trains to remind them of their childhood. But when I was a boy in Belfast our family couldn't even afford to buy a cardboard cutout. Compared to us, church mice were positively rich!'

The Reverend Kingdom paused only long enough for Roland Tinker to lead the sympathetic smiles.

'But all that poverty couldn't deny me one thing. A right to dream. Not to dream about train sets for Christmas or a birthday, or later finding the money to get drunk, but dreaming what I like to call God's Dream. In that dream, He came to me and said that one day I would have the chance to do something really worthwhile for His greater glory.'

He swept a hand over the model display.

'I have tried. God knows I have tried to do what He wanted. But in that dream, the Almighty also told me that I would build even more than this. That I would create a place where His Word would be studied for all time. Until the very Day of Judgement! A place where future generations could be trained to spread the Word to all corners of this all too godless world of ours. A place where they would be able to learn Hindi, Sinhalese, Tamil, Malay, Korean, Icelandic! And all the other tongues God gave man to speak His Word!'

The Reverend Kingdom extended his hand towards the lifeless perspex buildings.

'Today, it is still no more than a dream. Waiting to be raised up to the glory of His work! On those seven hundred acres of ground which are in your gift to sell – not to me – but to God! At God's price!'

'And bless His name,' Martha said loudly.

'God, folks! That is who you will be selling to. I'm only His channel. No more. It is God with whom you will be dealing.'

The Reverend Kingdom's hand began to move slowly over the perspex structures, as if he was blessing them in turn.

'It is God who needs you to build these classrooms where our theologians can learn how to argue against the godless, these laboratories where our physicists and scientists will learn how to cure only within the parameters of the Only Book, these student halls where they can sleep secure in the knowledge that He will be watching over them, these gymnasiums and sports arenas where they can learn to keep their bodies and souls healthy, these kitchens where they will have prepared for them only God's given food. All these places God wants built!

'When you come to decide the price I would only ask you to remember the words of the psalm of David. "Lord who shall abide in Thy tabernacle? Who shall dwell in Thy holy hill? He that putteth not out his money to usury!"'

The Reverend Kingdom paused to look first at Roland Tinker and then at the others, each in turn. He resumed speaking in a voice more certain than ever.

'Be guided by the psalmist. By the Word of the Only Book. Be sure God is listening. Don't disappoint Him!'

'And bless His name,' Martha said even louder than before.

The Reverend Kingdom bowed his head in prayer. Martha followed. The realtors murmured among themselves.

'Reverend Kingdom?' came the nasal voice of Roland Tinker, 'is there some place where my colleagues and I could confer for a few minutes?'

Martha lifted her head. 'The conference room,' she said promptly.

'That'll do fine.'

Roland Tinker looked across the room. The Reverend Kingdom had not raised his head.

In silence Martha led them out. When she returned Eddie was staring anxiously at the door. She closed it behind her and leaned against the frame.

'Tinker's the proverbial pain,' Martha said briskly. 'I think you did fine after a slow start. You shouldn't have let that call from Wong Lee get to you –'

'It wasn't just that. It was Tom. There was another sound foul-up.'

'Okay, that's it. Tom goes.'

'Agreed. I'll send him to Correspondence.'

'No,' she said sharply. Correspondence was part of Clara's department.

'Put Tom in charge of Tours. The public will like the idea one of the family's their guide. And that way Tom can tell us what people are saying.'

He shrugged. He didn't really care where Tom ended up.

'Okay. Tours.'

He nodded towards the door. 'Think they'll go for it?'

'I don't know. It's prime building land.'

'If they don't come through, I'll call Wong Lee. I'll promise him a finer campus than the one he built in Africa. I'll even name a building after him. Something like the Wong Holdings Faculty of Comparative Scripture.'

She winced. Eddie could be gross at times.

'I've been thinking about this business of Holy Cross, Eddie. It sounds like it could be part of the Moral Crusade the Roman pontiff is so keen on. You know, everybody marching behind the Cross of Jesus. That sort of thing.'

'Maybe I should start working in some references to the Holy Cross in my sermons.'

'I'll have Research look out some suitable texts,' she promised.

There was a knock on the door. When Martha opened it Roland Tinker stood there. His associates were grouped behind him.

'We've come to a decision,' Roland Tinker said, walking into the room. The Reverend Kingdom seemed not to have stirred, still standing with his head bowed.

'I should be glad to hear it.' The Reverend Kingdom slowly raised his head.

'The way we see it,' Tinker continued, 'is that you're doing good work here.'

'God's work,' Martha interrupted quickly.

'Exactly, Miss Kingdom. Exactly so,' Tinker smiled at her. He thought her an attractive woman. He turned back to the Reverend Kingdom.

'We'd like to play our part in helping you spread the work, Reverend.'

'The Word,' the Reverend Kingdom gently corrected.

'Exactly so. The Word. Accordingly, we propose to offer you the seven hundred acres at a price we feel will satisfy both our business instincts and, if I may say so, God Himself.'

'And bless His name,' Martha said.

'Exactly so.'

'What sort of figure do you have in mind?' asked the Reverend Kingdom carefully.

'A dollar an acre. With the provision the land will only be used for the purpose expressed to us here today.'

Martha made a little whimpering sound, suppressed almost as soon as it emerged.

'God bless you, Mr Tinker. All of you,' the Reverend Kingdom said in a half whisper which carried clearly across the model display.

'And bless His name,' Martha added in her normal voice. She turned and bestowed a radiant smile on Roland Tinker and his associates.

'You'll be remembered in our prayers, now and for always,' Martha assured them.

'Amen,' intoned the Reverend Kingdom.

'Coffee, gentlemen?' Martha said graciously, leading the realtors out of the room, closing the door after her.

The Reverend Kingdom allowed tears to roll down his cheeks. He'd always cried when things were going really well. He picked up one of the perspex models. This would be the language laboratory where the god-forsaken languages of the godless Soviets would be taught. He tried to remember how many there were. Russian itself, of course. Then Uygur and Turkic, Uzbek and Caucasian, Moldavian and Ukranian . . .

# 10

The broad accent of the Ukranian air traffic controller at Kiev's Borispol airport ordered the Concorde to switch to the radio beacon at Ivano-Frankovsk, the next sector.

'Roger, Kiev,' acknowledged the pilot into his lip microphone.

At Mach two, twice the speed of sound, El Al One continued to hurtle through the night sky at a height of 60,000 feet. The industrial pollution of Kiev gave way to the lighter strip of the River Dnieper on one side and Byelorussia on the other. The pilot pressed a switch to reset one of the computers and shook his head.

'I once spent a couple of nights at Borispol. We were fog-bound, trying to bring out a couple of hundred Ukranian Jews. When it comes to complainers there's only one kind worse than a Ukranian Jew. That's a Russian Jew. Those Ukranians complained so hard the airport authorities made us keep them on board the second night. Have you ever sat on the tarmac with everybody yelling to tell you to take off before the weather gets worse?'

The co-pilot nodded sympathetically. 'We've become the natural home for complainers. I remember when an immigrant was just glad to arrive. Now before he's even set foot on the ground, he's looking for all kinds of promises.'

The flight engineer grinned. 'That's why they call it the Promised Land. And you two sound like a pair of anti-Semites!'

'Just anti-immigrant,' growled the pilot.

'We're all immigrants,' sighed the engineer.

'He's right,' said Morton softly. He was standing in the open door to the flight deck.

The pilot turned quickly in his seat. 'Didn't know you were there, David.'

There was a sudden awkward silence among the crew. He didn't want to embarrass them.

'It's okay,' Morton said.

Behind him he heard the door to the Prime Minister's cabin opening, then Carina's voice.

'You like coffee, Colonel Morton?'

'Thank you.'

He wished he hadn't sounded so formal.

She came forward from the galley, holding a cup, still wearing her doctor's long white coat, a stethoscope around her neck.

'Everything okay?' he asked, taking the cup.

She nodded. 'You drink too much coffee.'

'I know.'

He watched her light another cigarette. Her directness continued to disconcert him. It had been a long time since a woman had behaved like that towards him. Yet it was also pleasing.

She smiled at him. He had Russian eyes, like Andrei's. Andrei had been the kind of man women were not supposed to go for: puny and diffident. But in bed Andrei had been masterful and tireless. He had shown her how to develop on all levels. Then suddenly he was no longer there – literally incinerated in the meltdown. They buried him with the rest of the reactor under a concrete mountain, leaving her a widow after barely a year of married bliss.

Since then there had been one or two other men, experienced and capable of physically arousing her, but as blunt in bed as they were at work. Andrei had made a conspiracy of love with his eyes. No one had looked at her the way he did, in turn creating in her the skill to communicate with glances, to convey a world of secrets without so much as a word. They had been lovers in the true sense of the word: physically, emotionally, intellectually. She had thought it could never happen again. But there was something about this stranger which surpassed her understanding.

Knowing Morton was still watching her, Carina stared into the flight deck. Ahead, through the cockpit plexiglass windshield, rose the peaks of the Carpathian Mountains. Beyond lay Hungary. In forty minutes they would be over the Adriatic and in Italian air space.

'Counter's started up again,' called out the flight engineer.

The pilot grunted. 'Those UN inspectors are supposed to have got into this area by now.'

'Last I heard they were still poking around Odessa,' the co-pilot said. He pressed another switch to computer check the course bearing.

Twice already, as the Concorde passed over the industrial cities of Smolensk and Gomel, the on-board geiger-counter had recorded radioactive emissions. The only way of telling whether they were from waste or part of the old Soviet Union's nuclear arsenal would be when the print-out was analysed in Tel Aviv. If the emissions were from a weapons facility, the evidence would be passed to the United Nations inspection teams.

'They're facing an uphill task,' Morton said.

The teams were created after the Minsk Agreement when the former Soviet Republics, anxious to convince the world they were politically mature, had agreed to allow control over all nuclear weapons within their borders to remain with Moscow.

When the troika seized power, the Islamic republics withdrew from the pact, bluntly saying they must take control over their nuclear arsenals for fear Moscow would once again try to dominate them.

The suspicion had helped create the Islamic Confederation. But, so far, the Moslem Republics had refused Tehran's demand to have control over the weapons. Within their own turbulent borders no one knew whose finger was on the trigger – or how many triggers there were.

'By the time those inspectors get here, some of those weapons could have been sold to our immediate neighbours,' the pilot said sourly.

Once more he turned in his seat. 'What do you think, David?'

'It's something I try not to think about.'

The nightmare had been there since the break-up of the Soviet Union. How long before it became reality?

The engineer turned from his control panel.

'The counter's stopped. Has to be a waste dump. The reading's too low for even a single warhead.'

From a transponder came the rapidly fading voice of the Kiev controller.

'God guide you through the sky, El Al One.'

'Thanks, Kiev,' acknowledged the pilot.

Carina turned to Morton. 'He probably grew up not even knowing there was a God. The State was God.'

She tapped ash from her cigarette into the palm of her hand.

'It takes more than that to remove God from the human psyche,' Morton replied. 'Here, use this.'

Draining his coffee, he handed her the cup. She carefully tipped in the ash.

'Do women in the West smoke much?' she asked.

'Less and less. The annual lung cancer statistics are great for concentrating minds.'

'We never publish that sort of thing. Moscow decided it would be bad for morale.'

She squinted at him. 'You don't approve of women who smoke?'

'Especially not when they've their whole life before them.'

He felt the warmth of her breath when she exhaled.

'Very well. I will try and behave like a Western woman.'

Carina dropped the cigarette in the coffee cup.

'I saw Madonna do that in a movie.'

Morton smiled.

'She's not actually your average Western woman.'

'Do you think she's attractive?'

'She's not really my type.'

'What is your "type"?'

He laughed. 'I thought you were a doctor, not a psychiatrist!'

'All good doctors are psychiatrists, Colonel Morton.'

He hadn't skirmished like this with a woman since those first weeks with Nan. That had been different. Nan had said she was on a crash course of discovery. She had wanted to know everything, at once. Nan had never understood he needed time to allow himself to be probed. Instinctively, he felt Carina realised that. His feeling of pleasure grew.

'How's the patient?' Morton asked.

'She'll survive. She's been telling me about this Reverend Kingdom. You know him?'

'Only of him. There's not much to choose between him and a godless state. The Reverend Kingdom uses religion as a means to spread his own poison. What he preaches has precious little to do with God.'

Carina lifted her chin and stared at him.

'The woman says many millions now listen to him in all the republics, like they used to listen to Stalin.'

'Probably most of them need something to cope with the withdrawal symptoms after Communism. Kingdom knows how to do that. How to make what he offers seem attractive.'

Carina looked doubtful. 'But surely only to Christians? I can't imagine he'll have much appeal in our Moslem republics.'

He looked squarely into her eyes.

'That's the real danger. They'll see Kingdom as fomenting hatred against Islam. That could trigger a violence we haven't seen since the Mongols went on the rampage. Only this time, instead of swords they'll have missiles.'

'But why would Kingdom want that to happen?' She touched him briefly on the arm.

For a moment he was tempted to tell her.

'Probably only God knows what drives Kingdom,' he said.

Carina was silent for a moment. 'I'm not sure I actually believe God exists.'

'If there's no God, there's probably no point.'

For long moments Carina continued to look at him, then turned back to watch the quiet activity on the flight deck.

After Andrei, after the shock and anger had been followed by numbness and then the gradual acceptance she would never feel his powerful embrace again, she had recognised her own sexuality would not die. Each time she would close her eyes and ask to be used, knowing it was she who was using him. And afterwards she would whisper to herself that she would never love another man. It had been almost a year now since she had done that, done anything.

Carina gave no response when Morton took the cup from her hand and walked to the galley.

The purser was preparing meal trays for the technicians in the Communications Centre. He nodded to where Monsignor Hanlon and Claudio Morelli sat in the small conference area immediately behind the Prime Minister's cabin.

'Think our guests will mind eating kosher?'

Morton grinned. 'I doubt if they'll be able to tell the difference. Those microwaves of yours make everything taste the same.'

'For a man who can't boil an egg, may you be forgiven,' sighed the purser.

Pouring himself more coffee, Morton raised the pot, but both men shook their heads.

Yoshi was still in the Centre, on the phone to the Vatican: questioning, ordering, preparing in his mind for what lay ahead. A man like that could be forgiven his sexual peccadilloes, could be forgiven most things for his brilliance. With it came a sense of reality bordering on the ruthless. Yoshi had shown that shortly after take-off.

As the Concorde levelled out of its steep graceful climb the injured man had suffered a massive heart attack as Carina struggled to control his internal bleeding. Yoshi had worked like a demon alongside her to stimulate the man's heart. After a quarter of an hour he had stopped. When Carina continued, Yoshi pulled her away. She had looked angrily at him.

'It's over,' Yoshi said. 'Anyway, if he was still alive, he'd be better off dead. Who wants to be a vegetable?'

Morton had helped carry the body to the small storage area at the rear. The trunk with Yoshi's laser had been stowed there. Afterwards, when Morton had shown Yoshi the X-rays of Pope Nicholas, the surgeon said sombrely he had seen better. Since then he had been continually on the phone.

Collecting fresh coffees, Morton walked back to Carina. The foothills of the Carpathians were below. He handed her a cup and continued to listen to the exchanges between the ground and the flight deck.

'Hello, El Al One. This is ground control at Ivano-Frankovsk,' came the voice from the transponder.

'Read you ten-ten,' the co-pilot reported.

'Maintain present height, speed and course. No other traffic except a Turkish Airlines outgoing from Bucharest.'

The pilot pointed to one of the radar screens. The 200 kilometre band showed a blip. The Turk would pass well to starboard and 20,000 feet below.

'Thank you, Ivano-Frankovsk,' the co-pilot replied.

Carina turned to Morton. He saw the sudden sadness in her eyes.

'My grandparents came from Ivano-Frankovsk,' she said quietly. 'My grandfather was a doctor, a specialist in children's illnesses. He came from a family of doctors, all the way back to Peter the First. No one asked if they were Jews or Catholics. They were Ukranians and proud of it. They couldn't understand why my uncle, the lawyer, insisted on going to live in what was then Palestine. He must have seen what was going to happen.

'When the Nazis came, they took every other Jew in the town to one of the smaller concentration camps. Nothing special, like Auschwitz or Treblinka, just another concentration camp with enough gas chambers.'

She paused and looked at him steadily. When she spoke again, her voice sank even lower.

'My grandmother was gassed early on. She was already too crippled to work, so they must have carried her into the chamber. My grandfather's reputation kept him alive. The guards needed him to treat their own children. He somehow did a deal for my father to be his assistant. My father was fifteen at the time, but big and strong for his age.'

Carina gave Morton another searching look. 'You want to hear all this?'

'Yes.'

He knew the flight deck crew was also listening. Everyone had a memory of the Holocaust. Yet, like flakes of snow, no two were quite alike. Each memory had its own distinctive horror.

'In the last months of the war, they gave my father an extra job. He was put in one of the squads dragging out the bodies from the chambers. One day he dragged out his own father.'

When she paused again he asked no questions, made no gesture. He knew better than that. She continued her monologue in the same flat voice, and he wondered at the effort it must be costing her to remain so emotionless.

'By then my father had met my mother. She was already famous, in a way, as the girl who had danced Swan Lake for Himmler. She was thirteen and tall and the camp commandant had spotted her practising. God knows where she found the time or energy. Anyway he was impressed enough to take her off all duties to rehearse for Himmler's visit. He liked to visit all the camps at least once a year. So my mother danced for him. The commandant allowed her parents to watch from the wings. The day afterwards he made her watch them going into the chamber.

'To try and comfort my mother, my father gave her some of his food. That's how it began for them. And when she said she wouldn't dance any more, he became really angry with her. He said she had to dance to stay alive. Not just for herself, but to live so that she could tell the world what had happened. So she went on dancing for the Nazis.

'Then my father discovered they were all going to be killed in a few days and the whole camp burned to the ground. The Red Army was advancing and the Nazis didn't want to leave any evidence. But the army arrived unexpectedly early. They killed every German man, woman and child.'

Once more she looked at Morton. 'You really want to hear all this?'

He nodded, still not wanting to speak.

She resumed in the same low voice.

'What happened then was quite usual. The political commissars with the army ordered all the prisoners to be taken to one of the special camps where they could be assessed. Anyone the commissars decided had become the slightest bit infected with Nazi ideology was simply shot on the spot.'

Carina paused again.

'That should have happened to my parents. No matter that they'd been forced to, they had worked for the Nazis. But the day before they were to go before the commissar, the mayor of Ivano-Frankovsk visited the camp. He was looking for labourers to help rebuild the town. Among those he selected was my father. He somehow persuaded the mayor to let him bring my mother along as a cook.

'One day she was seen rehearsing her ballet by a visitor from Moscow. The man was sufficiently impressed to send a recommendation to the Bolshoi. At that time they were always on the lookout to replace all those dancers they'd lost in the war.

'My mother was taken to Moscow and my father spent the next three years building highways all over the Ukraine. In her fourth year in Moscow my mother made the touring company. The Bolshoi in those days performed all over the Soviet Union. The tour came to Lvov. You know, the place where Stalin ordered the statue of Neptune pulled down in case anyone used its trident as a weapon.'

'My own parents came from there,' Morton finally said.

Carina smiled quickly. 'My mother, too. So you'll know how headstrong those people can be. My father was working in Lvov at the time. He went to the ballet, saw my mother and somehow managed to get backstage. A week later they were married in one of those collective ceremonies the Party used to encourage. I was born a year later. Now I'm here.'

Carina stared into the flight deck. The engineer was checking fuel consumption and present gross weight. He smiled and she smiled back, grateful for his understanding.

Behind her Morton spoke. 'It still leaves quite a gap in how the baby became a doctor.'

Carina turned and looked at him. A shadowy thing moved in the depths of her eyes.

'It was the way it is with all babies. I grew up, Colonel Morton.'

'I'd prefer you call me David. Unless you want me to go on calling you Doctor Ogodnikova.'

After a moment's hesitation, she nodded. 'Okay, David. Most people call me Cari.'

'I think I prefer Carina.'

She gave a little shrug. 'Okay. Now I think it is time to check on my patient.'

When she entered the Prime Minister's cabin and closed the door behind her he made his own way back towards the Communications Centre. On the flight deck the co-pilot was once more retuning radio frequencies, this time to Belgrade.

The rain had eased. Cardinal Enkomo thought that somehow the grey drizzle was worse, like moisture being squeezed from a cold sponge against the windscreen.

'There's a hotel a couple of miles down the road. We could grab a bite there,' Father O'Sullivan suggested.

'You can't be hungry again, not after all that bacon and eggs.'

'That was eight hours ago, Your Eminence,' protested the priest.

The cardinal leaned forward to see better through the mud, with which the windscreen wipers were fighting a losing battle. The hotel was off the track, a place for safari stopovers en route to the game reserve further north. In these conditions it would be crazy to even attempt to reach it. They'd get bogged down in the first few yards.

'We'll keep going. If you don't think about food, you won't feel hungry. Didn't they teach you that at Clonliffe?'

Father O'Sullivan grinned. 'They also taught us you do God's work better on a full stomach.'

'Abstinence is good for the soul,' Cardinal Enkomo firmly reminded the young priest.

He liked O'Sullivan. He had vitality and verve. The Church needed more like him. He was also a good driver.

After they had knelt before the altar in the retreat and prayed together, Cardinal Enkomo had spent a couple of hours making notes for the report Pope Nicholas wanted. Once he had started, he had been pleased at how powerfully he could argue the cause for the Holy See to finally grant Israel full diplomatic recognition, and why it would be completely nonsensical to demand a staging of the retrial of Jesus. Satisfied he had the back of the argument broken, they had set out for Cape Town. He would hone and polish the report there, reducing it to no more than the few pages Pope Nicholas always preferred.

They had kept the radio tuned to an all-news station until lightning had zipped between the kloofs and the station went off the air. Only when Father O'Sullivan tried to retune the set had they realised the radio itself had been put out of action.

Several hours later, as they approached the edge of the veldt, the rain had turned into drizzle. The Mercedes continued to slide and slither through the mud. Shortly beyond the turn-off to the hotel the car joined the main Johannesburg to Cape Town freeway.

'Home in a couple of hours,' promised Father O'Sullivan.

The cardinal knew it would still be a close call as to whether he would have the report ready for the courier to catch the evening flight to Rome.

Ahead the traffic had started to build.

'Could be an accident,' suggested Father O'Sullivan. 'They drive even worse here than they do back home.'

'It's still a new thing for most black people to have a car, father. Now they want to go faster than white people.'

'You think it's as simple as that?'

Julius Enkomo smiled. 'No. But if we get into a serious debate here, we could end up in another accident.'

'Point taken, Your Eminence,' Father O'Sullivan said cheerfully. He edged the Mercedes past a truck. The way ahead was blocked by more vehicles.

In the oncoming lane, a car, its horn blaring, rushed past and was swallowed up in the drizzle.

'There's a road block ahead,' Cardinal Enkomo said.

'How do you know?'

'When you've been here long enough you'll recognise that horn blast, father.'

The signal, like so much else, had emerged from the

townships. Now everybody used it to give warning. The police were universally hated. It was, thought Cardinal Enkomo, a symptom of the great malaise afflicting his country.

A mile further on the red warning lights loomed out of the mist. Then the two armoured personnel carriers, deployed to leave only a gap for single lane traffic. Policemen in slickers were checking every vehicle.

Behind the APCs was a black Ford with government licence plates. A man stood beside the car, trenchcoat collar up and fedora brim down.

'Special Branch,' murmured Cardinal Enkomo. 'They all seem to go to the same hatter.'

He turned to Father O'Sullivan. 'You have your passport, father?'

The priest tapped his jacket pockets, then gave an embarrassed smile. 'It must be in my other suit.'

The cardinal sighed. 'You should carry it with you at all times, father. It's supposed to help the police fight crime.'

The law had recently been introduced that foreigners must carry their passports in public. Only accredited diplomats were exempt.

'I guess we don't actually look like a couple of burglars,' Father O'Sullivan said.

'Let's hope not.' Cardinal Enkomo produced from his cassock his purple covered Vatican passport, which granted him full diplomatic immunity.

A policeman tapped on the glass and ordered Father O'Sullivan to lower the window.

'Your passport, reverend.'

'I'm sorry, I don't have it with me.'

'Step out onto the road. Both of you.'

Cardinal Enkomo reached across, extending his passport to the policeman.

'I don't think that will be necessary, constable. I am Cardinal Enkomo and this is my driver.'

The policeman flipped open the passport. He stepped back and waved to the Special Branch officer. The man started to run towards the car.

'Trouble?' Father O'Sullivan began.

'Leave it to me,' Cardinal Enkomo murmured quietly.

The officer took the passport, glanced inside, looked at the car's registration number and ran around to the passenger side.

Cardinal Enkomo lowered the window.

'Good afternoon, Your Excellency. I've been waiting for you.' His English had only a faint trace of an Afrikaan accent.

Cardinal Enkomo raised an eyebrow. 'Why would you be waiting for me, especially out here, Superintendent Van Kruger?'

Van Kruger looked at him in surprise. 'You don't know?'

Cardinal Enkomo sighed. 'I was never very good at guessing games. Now if you'll just tell me what all this is about –'

'Your Pope. He's dying. We're here to escort you as quickly as possible back to your palace. I'm sorry, I thought you knew.' Van Kruger nodded at the car radio. 'It's been on all the news bulletins.'

'Our radio got knocked out,' interrupted Father O'Sullivan.

The superintendent nodded. That he could understand. What was beyond him was the response of a grown man to the news someone was dying. It was not even as if the Pope was related to this black. Yet here he was, close to tears. You wouldn't catch a minister of the Dutch Reform Church, dewy-eyed in public if the Moderator was dying. But then, the blacks had always been very emotional.

Cardinal Enkomo blinked. 'Do you know what happened to Pope Nicholas?'

'The radio says he just collapsed. Your chancellor said it was probably a stroke.'

It had to be the tumour. He had read somewhere the slower growing ones were the deadliest.

'Oh my God,' Father O'Sullivan murmured. 'We should pray for His Holiness at his hour of need.'

'You can do that later,' Van Kruger said brusquely. 'Right now you just concentrate on following my car.'

'I think I know the way without you having to show me,' Cardinal Enkomo said.

Van Kruger gave a brittle laugh. 'I'm sure you do. After all you led a protest march along this very road. All the way to Jo'burg and back. Ten thousand of you.'

The cardinal remembered. 'By the time we completed the round trip, we'd twice as many. But you've still got a good memory, superintendent. That was thirty years ago and I was still a curate.'

'I ought to remember. I was supposed to arrest you. Then at

the last minute the Minister cancelled the order. Now I'm here to protect you.'

Cardinal Enkomo did not bother to conceal his surprise. 'Protect? Against what?'

'Your people. They're out on the streets again. Using the weather as an excuse to run riot. They've been looting food shops all over the city. Blaming everybody for the shortages. The government, the farmers. Everybody. Probably even your Pope! No point exposing you to that violence, Your Excellency.'

Cardinal Enkomo looked calmly at Van Kruger. 'I'm not afraid of my people.'

'I'm afraid of what would happen if one of them forgot that. So let's get you home as quickly and safely as possible.'

The superintendent touched his hat-brim and walked back to his car. One of the armoured carriers took up position in front of the Ford, the other behind the Mercedes. At full speed the convoy set off.

'His Holiness,' Father O'Sullivan began. 'Were you expecting this?'

'Yes. And don't ask any more questions!'

Cardinal Enkomo closed his eyes and began to consider what he should do.


In the Concorde's Communications Centre Morton listened on an extension earpiece to the conversation Yoshi was having with Carlo Poggi. The Italian neurosurgeon was speaking from an ante-room in the Apostolic Palace.

'Think he'll remain stable?' Yoshi asked.

'Hard to say. I've brought in my best team. If anything happens between now and the time you get here, we'll have to move straight in.'

'Understood.' Yoshi glanced at a pad filled with copious notes.

'I'll need a couple of technicians who've done some basic laser work.'

'I'll hunt around.' Poggi spoke Oxford English, a legacy of the days he had been head of the Department of Neurosurgery at the Radcliffe.

'What's that basement like, Carlo?'

'Not bad.'

Morton's earpiece was filled with a throat-clearing protest from Rome.

'It's the best, Dr Kramer. I have personally made sure of that.'

'That's good to know, Dr Fortuti,' Yoshi said briskly.

'I will remind you, gentlemen, that the Holy Father is still my patient,' the Pope's personal physician added in his prissy voice.

'Understood, Dr Fortuti. But as I'm going to operate, he's temporarily also my patient.'

'I still wish to be consulted,' Dr Fortuti continued. 'At every stage.'

Yoshi snorted disbelievingly. 'You mean you want me to stop during a procedure and consult you? What do you think we're dealing with here, Fortuti, some sort of experiment? This technique's been tried and tested. And it works! And one of the reasons it works is because it's fast, which makes it safer. And one of the reasons it's fast and safe is because I don't stop and consult at every twist and turn!'

'Easy, Yoshi,' Morton called softly.

Yoshi rolled his eyes. When he spoke next he was calmer.

'Okay, Dr Fortuti. You want to be consulted? Understood. But I'll consult you when I think it's appropriate. Understood?'

'*Si*,' Dr Fortuti's hiss sounded like steam being released from a valve.

'Anything else, Carlo?' Yoshi asked, once more completely in control.

Poggi chuckled. 'Secretary of State Messner wants to know if you'll describe the procedure to the Sacred College of Cardinals. A couple of dozen of their Eminences have already arrived in Rome and he thinks they ought to know what's involved.'

'Any of them medically qualified?'

'Not that I know of.'

'Any with a degree in medical engineering?'

'I doubt it, Yoshi.'

'Then it's going to be a pretty short presentation.'

Poggi's chuckle and Dr Fortuti's hiss came together in Morton's ears at the same moment as the pilot announced they would be landing in Rome in ten minutes.

Cardinal Enkomo saw the signs of a mob on the rampage as soon as the convoy reached the suburbs of Cape Town. Burnt-out vehicles. Smashed shop windows. Rubble everywhere. The crew of the APCs began to swivel their machine guns.

'My God,' Father O'Sullivan said in a stricken voice. 'This place was okay when I drove through here last night.'

'It doesn't take long to get a riot going, father. You should know that from Belfast.'

The convoy was travelling down the street when the protesters came sweeping out of a side road. There were about thirty, arms linked, completely filling the road. They were chanting as they marched, the old chants of the kraal. Some of the men were dressed in suits, the women in dresses, others wore only pieces of cast-off clothing or blankets. Some looked well fed, others starved. Some were white haired and stiff in their movements, others were young and moved with the litheness of animals. And they were all united by a chanting born in an earlier time of hatred.

'*Jee-ka!*' They roared in unison, a battle cry which had once driven their forefathers' spears against the white man's guns. '*Jee-ka!*'

There was a crash of breaking glass. Across the street another shop window shattered.

'You have one minute to disperse,' came a voice from a loud-speaker on top of the APC. 'Otherwise we will open fire!'

The marchers came to an uncertain stop. So did the chanting. Then a single voice rose defiantly.

'We are on our way to Parliament to protest at the unfair way food is distributed.'

Cardinal Enkomo could make out the speaker – a short man in a jacket and shorts with no shoes on his feet. There was a certain dignity about his deeply lined face.

The loudspeaker voice continued to give orders.

'That man! Step forward! You're under arrest! The rest of you disperse at once!'

The chanting resumed. Not just '*Jee-ka*', but '*Amandala*!' – Arrest me too!

Slowly the mob began to advance towards the convoy.

'Prepare to fire on command,' came the strident voice over the loudspeaker.

Policemen jumped from the vehicles, rifles at the ready. The machine-guns began to swivel over the crowd.

Superintendent Van Kruger emerged from the Ford, a pump action shotgun in his hand.

The crowd roared.

*'Jee-ka! Amandala! Jee-ka! Amandala!'*

Guns began to line up on targets.

More deep-throated came the cry which had launched a thousand and more attacks.

*'Bulala!'* – Kill!

Cardinal Enkomo jumped from the Mercedes and ran towards the mob.

'Stop! In the name of God, I command you to stop!'

'Fire! Warning burst!'

The metallic voice was followed by the sudden chatter of a machine-gun firing above the crowd.

Instinctively the marchers fell back. Cardinal Enkomo stepped into the vacated space and turned to face the armoured carriers.

'Stop firing! Father O'Sullivan! Come and stand with me! They might as well kill us if they're going to kill anyone!'

Cardinal Enkomo pointed a hand at Van Kruger.

'Superintendent, if there is any more shooting I will personally see to it that you will spend the rest of your career in some godforsaken border post.'

Van Kruger stared impassively at Cardinal Enkomo. Then he motioned to the policemen. They lowered their weapons.

Cardinal Enkomo turned to the crowd.

'Are you mad? You think this is the way to get food? By recklessly breaking the law? Is that all you've learned? To go on breaking the law?'

He grabbed the barefooted man by the arm and hauled him forward.

'You have a wife?'

The man nodded.

'And children?'

Another nod.

'You think they will eat better because you are going to deliver a protest to Parliament? You think that will put food in their stomachs?'

The man stared sullenly.

'I don't know, baas cardinal. But we must eat.'

A low chorus came from those behind him. Cardinal Enkomo looked at the shining black faces. When he spoke it was in that deep, thrilling voice they knew so well.

'I have never lied to you. I am not going to lie to you now. There is sufficient food for all of you. The people who tell you there is not are troublemakers. They want you to make trouble so that they can profit.'

Some of the marchers had begun to nod.

'Those people know the only way they can succeed is if they continue to divide the races. They have been doing that for over fifty years. Turning Tembu against Zulu. Xuma against Oumba. And always black against white!

'But I tell you this. The only hope for this country, your country, my country, is for us all to be one people! We will not achieve that by your kind of behaviour. I tell you again. There is plenty of food!'

He paused, aware of the impression he was making, able to see the respect and growing agreement on their faces.

Then from the back of the crowd came the renewed chant. '*Jee-ka! Jee-ka!*'

'No!' Cardinal Enkomo shouted. 'I'll give you something better to chant!'

He turned and motioned for Father O'Sullivan to kneel beside him. With his head held high and eyes closed, Cardinal Enkomo began to recite the Our Father. Father O'Sullivan picked up the cadence.

The crowd took up the words as if with a single voice.

When they finished, there was complete silence. Cardinal Enkomo rose to his feet.

'Go home,' he urged the crowd. 'Go home to your families.'

The barefoot man turned to the crowd. 'You heard the baas cardinal. Let's go home.'

He began to walk away. The crowd followed him.

Cardinal Enkomo turned and looked at the policemen and Van Kruger standing beside the Ford.

'You, too, superintendent. Go home. All of you.'

Van Kruger lowered his shotgun.

'Very impressive, Your Excellency. I'm sure you won't need our protection to get you home.'

The superintendent nodded to the policemen who began to climb back into the armoured carriers. Then he got into the Ford and drove off.

Cardinal Enkomo walked slowly back to the Mercedes. He was shivering.

'Are you all right, Your Eminence?' asked Father O'Sullivan anxiously.

'Perfectly fine.'

How could he begin to explain he had once more feared death would claim him before he completed whatever else God wanted from him? How could he begin to rationalise that though he loved his people, he must also leave them for a little while to be with the man he loved equally?

'Father,' he said as he climbed into the car. 'When we get back, book me on tonight's flight to Rome.'

Wong Lee's office, immediately below his bedroom, was unlike any other tycoon's. There was no massive desk, or art gallery of rare paintings adorning the walls; no deep pile carpets or doors which opened and closed at the touch of a button, or floor to ceiling shelves of books, or even a personal computer. Above all, there were no windows offering distracting views. Floor, walls and ceiling were made from the same hardwood. There were only two pieces of furniture in the room. A log and an onyx slab.

The log's natural shape was that of a seat. The wood had been carbon dated as being over half-a-million years old. There was no other piece of timber like it on earth. The sphere was a communications receiver. Like the log, it was unique. The sphere had cost almost as much as the satellite he had given the *gweillo*.

The fool had called again, leaving a message on the sphere's memory to say he now had the money to build his university. Wong Lee had instructed the memory to place the call in limbo.

In communication terms, the sphere could do anything he commanded. Merely by speaking a number, it would instantly connect him to any telephone on earth. It could sort and divert calls. Its voice recognition capability allowed the sphere to decide which caller was currently important and which was not.

This morning a caller from Rome had been assigned the top spot – above the Prime Minister of Japan who was seeking a loan, and a cattle breeder in Argentina who was due to call with news of his experiment to produce a new strain of beef; above a dozen other equally important calls.

Waiting for the call from Rome, Wong Lee sat cross-legged and perfectly still on the log, silently repeating the mantra the shamaness had given him. He was in the middle of a new recitation when a tiny spot on the sphere's surface suddenly glowed.

'Speak,' Wong Lee commanded.

'They have landed. There is no change in his condition,' reported the voice.

Wong Lee clapped his hands and the light instantly faded. What made him smile was that the *gweillo* in Rome really believed he was helping his Church.

# 11

As the Concorde landed at Leonardo da Vinci, Rome's principal airport, Yoshi turned to Monsignor Hanlon.

'Is that the Pope's chopper?'

The papal secretary squinted through the window. Parked on the tarmac outside the arrivals terminal was the familiar white helicopter. He sighed.

'Yes. And I know who sent it, our Cardinal-Secretary of State. It's not just to impress you, it's Messner's way of showing he's in charge. The Hun wants to remind everyone he's camerlengo-in-waiting.'

Yoshi looked puzzled.

'Camerlengo? Makes him sound a bit like an Italian cheese.'

'And in his case, just as unpalatable,' Monsignor Hanlon said wearily. 'In practice the camerlengo's our version of the old secular court chamberlain. It means the Hun runs the shop when the Boss is away on a pilgrimage or at a time like this.'

'That must give Messner a lot of power.'

Monsignor Hanlon gave another of his elegant shrugs.

'In theory, the Hun can order all sorts of things done. Like having the bells of St Peter's remain silent, as the camerlengo did when Paul the Sixth was dying. Or equipping the Swiss Guards with machine guns, as happened after the attempt on John Paul the Second's life. And he can send something he doesn't like back for further study by the Congregations and Tribunals. That's usually the kiss of death for a good idea. All this muscle flexing is good practice for the Hun in case a *sede vacante* is declared.'

Once more Yoshi looked puzzled.

'It's what we call the period between one Pope dying and another being elected. Then Messner will really come into his own – and God help us.'

Yoshi grinned. 'I take it you don't like His Eminence?'

Monsignor Hanlon wrinkled his nose. 'How can you like someone who still thinks the Inquisition was too soft?'

The seat-belt sign went out, and around them people started to stand up. The CCO stepped out of the Communications Centre and told Yoshi Dr Carlo Poggi was once more on the phone.

'Keeping you busy?' Monsignor Hanlon said.

'So what's new?' Yoshi replied as he hurried after the CCO.

When the Concorde reached its parking stand, two ambulances drove slowly forward, one to remove the man's body, the other to convey the woman to hospital.

Outside the door of the Prime Minister's cabin, Carina turned to Morton.

'I have given her a sedative and she is drowsy. But shouldn't I go with her?' she asked.

He shook his head. 'No point. You've done all you can. And she'll be in good hands.'

Carina nodded quickly. 'Of course. But what shall I do now? There's probably not an immediate flight back to Moscow.'

The fuselage door was opening.

Morton smiled. 'Come with us. Probably be the only chance you'll get to see the Vatican.'

'I don't want to just tag along, David.'

He immediately regretted saying it.

'I'm sorry. I didn't mean to sound so gauche.'

She looked at him. 'I think it's a long time since you have been around a woman.'

After a moment, he nodded. 'I'll tell you about it one day.'

'I'd like to hear.' This was not a man who would let her use him, nor one she would want to use.

Yoshi emerged from the Communications Centre, a look of concern on his face, the case with the Pope's X-rays in his hands.

'You ever done any laser work, doctor?' he called out, coming towards them.

'I spent a year attached to Academician Morav,' Carina said proudly.

Yoshi looked relieved. 'Then you'll do! Morav was getting close to a breakthrough in laser surgery before he died.'

A month after she had left his team, the chief surgeon of the Moscow Neurosurgical Institute had been killed in a motor accident.

Yoshi turned to Morton. 'Carlo's only been able to come up with one technician. The doctor here's solved my problem. And she's probably prettier than any technician!'

Carina coloured. 'Dr Kramer, you're a sexist!'

Yoshi grinned broadly. 'Just sex-motivated, lady. Just one hundred per cent sex-motivated!'

The purser turned from the fuselage door. 'Quite a reception committee, colonel.'

Morton strode to the door.

The area around the papal helicopter and Concorde was cordoned off by men in combat fatigues and flak jackets. There was something flashy and self-assured in the way they toted their Uzi machine guns and regularly muttered into handsets. More armed figures could be glimpsed on the roof of the terminal building.

Behind him Morelli grunted. '*Digos*.'

The anti-terrorist squad's brief extended to airport protection.

'By now they'll have everybody running scared in the terminals, and road blocks on all the approach roads. They haven't quite got over the mess they made last time,' Morelli growled.

Morton remembered that, despite Morelli's warning that there would be an attempted assassination of Pope John Paul the Second in 1981, the *Digos* failed to stop a Turk unleashing a fusillade of gunshots into the pontiff in St Peter's Square in May of that year. Some people said it was a miracle the Polish Pope had survived.

Claudio was right. Why shouldn't they fail again? They were just too cocky, not like the cassocked figure standing beside the helicopter. He was positively imperious.

'Well, well. The Hun's hitman,' murmured Monsignor Hanlon over Morton's shoulder.

Across the tarmac the dark obsidian eyes of Cardinal Messner's secretary continued to stare at the Concorde.

'Heinrich Linde's been with the cardinal so long he behaves just like him,' Morelli said.

'And with all the charm of a pit bull terrier,' added Monsignor Hanlon.

'I know people just like that,' Morton said, thinking of Bitburg. As the Concorde entered Italian air space, the Director had called to say he expected a full report on what had happened at the dacha.

Morton led the group down the landing steps and across the tarmac towards the helicopter. Two cabin stewards carried the box with Yoshi's laser.

As Monsignor Hanlon made the introductions, Monsignor Linde's hooded eyes remained cold and hostile. For a moment they flicked over Carina.

'There are more of you than we expected.' He spoke English with the thick accent of Bavaria.

'Dr Ogodnikova is Dr Kramer's assistant,' Morton explained.

'I see.' The priest-secretary's eyes looked as if a membrane had been drawn over them. He turned and climbed the three red-carpeted steps into the helicopter. Shrugging, Monsignor Hanlon led the others on board.

The cabin was surprisingly spacious and lavishly appointed. The walls and ceiling were lined with a thick white quilting to provide insulation and sound-proofing. The floor was covered with the same red carpet. A throne-like heavily-padded leather armchair faced smaller armchairs.

Monsignor Linde sat in the Pope's seat, the others facing him. Yoshi held the case of X-rays on his knee. The stewards stored the box on the floor and left. Moments later the door was electronically closed from the flight deck and the helicopter lifted off.

Carina turned to Morton. 'The last helicopter I flew in wasn't like this one.'

Monsignor Hanlon smiled. 'Actually we lease it from Alitalia.'

'At an exorbitant price,' snapped Monsignor Linde. He looked like a predator about to strike.

Yoshi grinned at him. 'Wait until you get my fee.'

'I'm sure it will be no more than we would expect,' Monsignor Linde said icily.

'I'll try and surprise you,' Yoshi said cheerfully. 'Of course, I'm perfectly happy to take payment in kind. I'd settle for one of those Giottos or Raphaels I hear are gathering dust in the basement now you've run out of wall space in your museum.'

'Yoshi,' Morton said quietly, 'I don't think the monsignor appreciates your sense of humour.'

He looked at Monsignor Linde. 'Israel is pleased to waive all our costs.'

No one spoke again until, in the distance, appeared the dome of St Peter's. Monsignor Hanlon turned to Carina.

'Michelangelo planned it so that the dome would be seen from every quarter of Rome. Fifty years of gerrymandering building practices put an end to that.'

Below rose the first of the highrises. Homes for the city's growing migrant community from North Africa and the Balkans; Moslems and Coptic Christians living cheek-by-jowl.

'The whole place is a tinder box,' Monsignor Hanlon continued. 'One day they'll tear each other apart.'

'It's the same in my country,' Carina said softly.

Monsignor Linde's eyes flicked towards her, then flicked away again. Carina wondered if it was just her he disliked, or was it all women.

The helicopter began to pass above the red-tiled Renaissance roofs of the inner city, frequently changing course. Morelli turned to Morton, frowning.

'The *Digos* say this makes it harder to take a pot shot at us. I've given up telling them it would be a waste of time against a heat-seeking Stinger. All someone would have to do is carry his shoulder launcher up on one of those flat roofs. But in security terms this is *Digos* air space, so they go on playing their little games.'

Once more the helicopter banked, this time following the course of the Tiber. Monsignor Hanlon began to point out to Carina the more important basilicas of Rome.

'In the old days the Boss liked to say Mass in as many as he could over a year. Then someone decided half the places weren't safe.'

'*Digos* again,' Morelli grunted.

'You'll have to patch up things, Claudio,' Morton said quietly, 'otherwise you'll end up with the Pope being little more than a prisoner in his own city.'

'Some people would like that,' Morelli replied, glancing at Monsignor Linde.

The hooded eyes remained expressionless.

Below was the Via della Conciliazione. As the helicopter banked, Morton saw at the end of the long, broad avenue the colonnades and pilasters of Bernini's three-quarter circle embracing

St Peter's Square. Above its cobblestones rose the pillared facade of the basilica, capped by that awe-inspiring dome.

Although it was still early morning, the pilgrim buses were already beginning to fill the side streets. Tourists looked up and pointed towards the helicopter as it passed over the ancient walls of the Vatican. Below was a jumble of close-packed roofs and glimpses of tiny courtyards.

Carina turned to Monsignor Hanlon.

'Which is your palace?' she asked seriously.

He smiled deprecatingly. 'It's not really a palace.'

'Just the next best thing,' Morelli said dryly.

Something came and went in Monsignor Linde's eyes. In another man Morton thought, they would be killer eyes.

'Welcome, everybody,' Monsignor Hanlon said formally. 'In size we've a little over a hundred acres, and in number close to four thousand souls. Not quite as crowded as down-town Tokyo, but getting there.'

'How many women?' Carina asked.

'About a couple of hundred nuns.'

'And none, I bet, as attractive as you,' Yoshi teased.

Monsignor Hanlon inclined his head in agreement. Monsignor Linde appeared not to have heard.

The helicopter passed over the Secret Archives and the stuccoed villa of the Pontifical Academy of Science before landing on the helipad near the representation of the grotto of Lourdes.

Waiting on the edge of the tarmac square were several blue-suited *Vigili*, part of Morelli's security force to protect the tiny city state. A couple of black limousines were parked on the roadway beside the landing strip. With them, shielding his face with an arm from the down draught of the rotors, was a plumpish figure in a black suit with a gold fob chain across his vest.

'Dr Fortuti,' Monsignor Hanlon murmured.

'A perfect example that God moves in mysterious ways when he hands out medical qualifications,' Yoshi said.

The anger was back in the hooded eyes.

'Dr Fortuti has never forgotten his prime duty under the Hippocratic Oath is never to do harm to his patient,' Monsignor Linde snapped.

'Our oath also sanctions doing everything to help a patient,' Yoshi replied, his irritation plain. 'I would imagine that gives us the same sort of freedom you have in deciding what kind of penance to exact after a confession. But I can't assume results any more than you can guarantee confession secures a place in Heaven.'

There was a sudden livid flash of anger in the hooded eyes. Then, as swiftly as it appeared, it was gone. Monsignor Linde's eyes remained expressionless as he led them out of the helicopter.

Waiting for his caller to end another of the silences which had punctuated his telephone call, Cardinal Enkomo turned in his chair to look out of the window with its splendid view of Table Mountain. The rain had stopped, leaving the sky a pale washed blue.

Immediately he returned to his office, he had telephoned the Vatican and was connected to Monsignor Linde's office. The secretary sounded as if he was reading from a prepared script. Pope Nicholas had suffered a brain haemorrhage. Surgery was planned. Upon its outcome there would be a statement. His Eminence should remain close to a radio.

Julius Enkomo promptly called Colonel Harald Asmusson, commandant of the Swiss Guard, an old friend. Harald explained His Holiness's only hope was the famous Israeli surgeon being rushed from Moscow. Cardinal Enkomo had asked if a Colonel Morton was on the flight. Harald said he was.

He would talk to Morton about Operation Holy Cross, about the growing influence of Wong Holdings throughout Africa, about the broadcasts of the Reverend Kingdom increasingly being quoted with approval by racists of both colours. These were dangerously unpredictable times, he could tell Morton, like the weather itself.

A mattress of cloud had begun to settle over the flat-topped mountain, a precursor of another storm building out in the Atlantic.

As Minister of Interior Piet Van der Vaal resumed speaking in that slow, heavy tone, as if he disliked using English, Cardinal Enkomo turned back from the window.

'I hear what you're saying, Your Eminence. And it may well be that some suppliers are not prepared to sell until the prices climb a little more. I grant you that may not be very Christian. But these people are not breaking the law. Your people are. You have just seen that yourself. That could have been a very

154

unpleasant situation for those policemen who were only trying to get you home safely, Your Eminence.

'But to go back to your question. My government cannot order food suppliers to sell when they feel market forces are against them. After all, we are not speaking here of starvation. You yourself have said there is ample food.'

'But a lot of it's being hoarded, minister, by people who just want to make bigger profits.'

The minister gave a mirthless little laugh over the phone, gone as swiftly as it had come.

'Responding to market forces would perhaps be a better way to describe it, Your Eminence. Neither your family nor your good self have ever been in business, I imagine.'

Cardinal Enkomo felt his anger stir. He pushed it down.

'When I grew up, we weren't exactly encouraged to set up in business – especially in competition with the white man.'

Another small laugh came and went.

'Times have changed, and a good thing, too. Nothing like competition to keep people on their toes. But I am certain that if we checked, we'd find that some of those people you say are hoarding are actually your own people. In my experience no one is more exploitative than black of black.'

The anger in the cardinal stirred again. He tried to focus on something to settle it, his eyes going from the crucifix on one wall to the formal portrait of Pope Nicholas on another.

The night before he had left Rome to come to South Africa, his mentor had warned they would try and goad him. Be firm, but not angry, His Holiness had counselled.

'I'm sure you're right that some of the hoarders are blacks. And I want you to deal with them just as firmly, minister.'

A note of acerbity entered the minister's voice.

'I keep trying to tell you, Your Eminence, these people – black, coloured or whatever colour you think they are – are not breaking the law. Your people are when they take to the streets.'

'They're not just my people. They are *our* people,' Cardinal Enkomo said firmly. 'Unless we accept that simple fact, there is no way to bring a proper and lasting peace to this country. And one way to start is to recognise that some of *our* people – these food producers and middle men – are hoarding so that they can make bigger profits out of the rest of *our* people. That's what's at the root of this trouble – the greed and exploitation by a few of the majority.'

He paused for a moment.

'The good and the bad, minister. They're all *our* people. It doesn't matter what colour they are. They are all *our* people.'

As the silence returned, Cardinal Enkomo glanced at the small neat stack of typescript on his desk. The report now only had to be proof-read.

'So what do you expect me to do?' the minister finally asked. 'You can hardly expect me to let people break into warehouses and just take what they want!'

'Of course not.'

'Then what do you want?'

Cardinal Enkomo knew that his patience was all but gone.

'Minister Van der Vaal, unless you act now, people will continue to take the law into their own hands. I've told them I am against that. But I know there is sufficient food for them all, all *our* people. My staff have spent the last two hours checking on all the food depots between here and Durban, and Durban and Pretoria. The places are filled to overflowing.

'All you have to do is introduce an emergency regulation that it is an offence for any producer to hoard. I'm not asking for this to be a permanent measure. Only until the next harvest is in. These storms are far more severe than usual.'

There was another mirthless laugh.

'We can't be blamed for the weather, Your Eminence. But perhaps a few more prayers from you would help.'

Cardinal Enkomo forced himself to remain calm.

'I've been doing that, minister. All I am asking from you is to use the law to support those prayers.'

'That could take weeks!' protested the minister. 'You know how slow Parliament can be!'

'It only took hours to pass the old emergency regulations in the sixties –'

'A different time, Your Eminence!'

'Stop prevaricating, minister! Unless you do something now, these food riots will spread. We could see bloodshed on a scale we haven't had since Soweto. To avoid that happening, you must introduce an emergency regulation now that it is an offence for any producer to hoard. Suitable penalties will have a wonderful effect on concentrating minds. The food is there. It must be distributed at a fair price. That's all I'm asking for – for all our people!'

The biggest hoarder was South African Food Consolidated. He had discovered it was owned by Wong Holdings. Last year, he had also learned, Food Consolidated had donated ten million rand to the Zimba campus.

'I'll see what is possible,' the minister said at last.

'Thank you.'

The minister put a question. 'How is your Pope, Your Eminence?'

'I'm sorry to say there's no change.'

'I see. That means Cardinal-Secretary Messner will be in charge?'

'Yes. Until His Holiness recovers.'

'If I may say so, the cardinal-secretary has a clearer under-standing of our problems than does the Pope. His Eminence recognises there was too much of a rush by de Klerk and Mandela to break down the barriers.'

'I'm familiar with the cardinal's views.'

'You don't share them?' the minister asked quickly.

'Right now what I am sure I do share with the cardinal-secretary is a wish for His Holiness's full recovery.'

Cardinal Enkomo pressed a knee against the top of his desk. Could Van der Vaal have possibly learned that His Holiness had been planning to visit Zimbabwe to confront the radicals of Zimba campus, and then come on to South Africa? The visit would be a pastoral one, not as head of state, to cut down the government's opportunity to object. But it would have a galvanis-ing effect on those millions of all races who wanted only peace. Their voices welcoming His Holiness could finally drown the evil cries of the racists.

The minister interrupted his reverie.

'Are you going to Rome, Your Eminence?'

'Tonight. But I'll be staying in touch. And I hope to hear good news soon about what is going to happen to all those hoarders.'

Once more the mirthless laugh filled his ears.

'Have a safe trip, Your Eminence.'

The minister hung up.

Cardinal Enkomo sighed. These clashes with government went directly to the heart of the old argument of the need to keep Church and State separate. But so often nowadays there was no way to do so. The report he had prepared for His Holiness showed that.

He picked up the typed pages and began to read.

At the core of the question of whether Israel should now receive our formal recognition, lies one indisputable fact. Hundreds of generations of Jews throughout the Christian world, have been indiscriminately mulcted for a crime which neither they nor their ancestors committed.

If there can be found a grain of consolation for this perversion of justice, it is in the work of Jesus Himself as recorded by Matthew 5:10-12.

'Blessed are they which are persecuted for righteousness' sake; for theirs is the Kingdom of Heaven. Blessed are ye, when men shall revile you, and persecute you, and shall say all manner of evil against you falsely, for My sake. Rejoice, and be exceeding glad; for great is your reward in heaven.'

This will be the text from which I will argue the case for Israel to be now recognised by the Holy See.

He had begun by showing how, since the third and fourth Councils of the Lateran, the Church had enforced a system of apartheid against Jews every bit as odious as that once practised in South Africa. He had cited the scores of anti-Semitic documents published by the Church over fourteen centuries. Identified each conciliar decree, papal encyclical, papal bull and pastoral directive which had heaped further odium on the Jews.

After showing an unchallengeable link between past papal legislation and the pogroms of Hitler and Stalin and the other persecutors, he had concluded by quoting the words of Pope John the Thirteenth after he had studied the evidence of the Holocaust. 'The mark of Cain is stamped upon our foreheads!'

Julius Enkomo was satisfied he had presented an argument strong enough to withstand anything the present mandarins of the State's Middle East Desk would produce. After correcting a few punctuation points, he took the report to his outer office for one of the nun-secretaries to produce the final clean copy he would take with him to Rome.

Returning to his office, he once more stood at the window. The cloud was thickening over Table Mountain. He hoped the storm would not come before take-off. At the best of times he disliked flying.

The telephone rang. Cardinal Enkomo frowned. Probably Van der Vaal with some new reason why his government would do nothing about food hoarders. He picked up the receiver.

'Cardinal Enkomo?'

'Speaking.'

He slowly lowered himself into his chair.

'I understand you received a letter from the Holy Father?'

He would recognise that cold and distant voice anywhere. Messner was never one to waste time on the niceties.

'That is correct, cardinal-secretary.'

'In which you were asked to offer an opinion on the policy of the Holy See?'

'I would prefer to call it a considered judgement based on the reality we live in.'

The laugh from Rome verged on the supercilious.

'Given all the other problems you have down there, I would have thought you would not have found the time to write anything for the Holy Father.'

Had Van der Vaal called Messner?

'I'm advised, Cardinal Enkomo, one of the pre-symptoms with the kind of haemorrhage the Holy Father has experienced is a clouding of the faculties. In someone of his years the effect often manifests itself in *folie de grandeur*.'

Julius Enkomo sighed. Years as a professor at the Pontifical Academy had given Messner ample scope to practise turning the knife. Climbing the Secretariat ladder to its very top had allowed him to perfect how far to twist.

'His Holiness's letter was perfectly lucid,' Cardinal Enkomo said firmly. 'How is he?'

From Rome came a sniffing sound. Messner suffered from hay fever. It was the only human frailty anyone had detected in him.

'Certainly not what I would call lucid. He's saying some rather strange things about still being determined to walk the shores of Galilee, then kneel and pray in Red Square. Frankly, I wouldn't rate his chances of making a full recovery, even though he seems to think this wunderkind Jew can work a miracle.'

'Perhaps we should all pray for one?'

There was another sniff. 'Until we know the outcome of his surgery, this whole matter of the Holy Father's request to you is academic. It can all be looked at later. I am sure you enjoyed the exercise. But I fear that's all it was for the moment. Certainly, I see no point in giving your report to the courier.'

Cardinal Enkomo leaned forward in his chair and placed his elbows on the desk.

'I don't intend to. I will be bringing it myself.'

'You are coming to Rome?'

Julius Enkomo felt a moment of satisfaction at the total surprise in the cardinal-secretary's voice.

'Yes. On tonight's plane.'

'Now more than ever, you should be devoting your time to calming down those food rioters. And supporting what their government's trying to do.'

Cardinal Enkomo spoke in a firm measured tone.

'I've made my suggestions to the minister on what his government must do. If there is no response, I'll go directly to the State President. But most important of all to me, cardinal-secretary, His Holiness is more than just my former confessor. He's my spiritual guiding force, who brought me through the pitfalls and who always showed me there was a way forward.'

'I know all that, Enkomo. I know all that!'

'Then you will also understand why I regard His Holiness's letter as more than a request for a position paper. It's a small chance to repay in a very modest way, a little of all he has done for me – as well as an opportunity to further serve the Church we both love. If he recovers, and I pray for nothing else, then I am certain he will still wish to go to Israel and Moscow.'

'And if he dies? What happens to your report then?'

'Then I will do everything possible to ensure it will reach the hands of his successor.'

Cardinal-Secretary Messner replaced the telephone in his salon in the Third Loggia overlooking the St Damaso Courtyard in the Apostolic Palace. For a moment he sat perfectly still, a stocky, bull-necked figure who wore his iron-grey hair cropped close, so that his zucchetto, his small purple skull cap, fitted tightly on his scalp. Muller and the others who had said the African was harmless, were wrong. Utterly wrong. He was that most dangerous of all men – a man with a commitment.

Abruptly, the cardinal-secretary stood up. The broad peasant face that masked a formidable intellect, was as suffused as the scarlet of the sash into which was tucked a heavy brass pectoral cross. As he walked from behind his desk there was a quick knock on the door, then a cleric appeared.

'Your Eminence, the helicopter is back.'

'I know. Now get out! And stay out!'

The discomfited priest withdrew. It was going to be another of those days. It must be something serious to have upset His Eminence so early.

Glaring for a moment longer at the closed door, the cardinal-secretary walked to a fourteenth century Bavarian wooden cabinet in a corner of the salon. He opened the ornately painted door to reveal a safe. He turned the dial, listening to the clicking of the combination only he knew. Finally he pulled open the solid steel door. From a shelf he removed an envelope, thinking again how his extraordinary sixth sense had not failed him.

The envelope had come into the Vatican mail room a month ago. Neatly typed and correctly addressed, listing after his name his religious order, Dominican, and the Papal honours he held: Knight of the Grand Cross of St Sylvester and the Cross Pro Ecclesia et Pontifice. The envelope had been brought unopened to Linde's office.

When his secretary read the contents, he had immediately brought him the letter. He had trained Linde well; he had the nose of a rat-catcher.

'No address or signature, only that it was posted in Rome,' Linde had apologised. 'But still interesting.'

The anonymous letter listed the times and places Julius Enkomo had met Morton during his time in Israel. Though the letter explained, the cardinal-secretary already knew who Morton was.

He had immediately ordered Linde to check on all the reports Enkomo had sent from Israel. Not one contained a reference to Morton. His highly attuned sixth sense had still told him the letter could be valuable one day, and it had gone into the safe.

Walking around the salon which he had personally furnished with some of the finest pieces from the past six centuries, he read it one more time. At first he had wondered if someone was trying to make mischief for Enkomo. God knows who he might have crossed in his career. Then Muller, after one of his meetings with Wong Lee to settle another building contract, said he believed the letter had come from Wong Lee. He had hinted as much.

All that really mattered was that Enkomo's secret meetings must have been part of the dangerous madness of Nicholas to reconcile the faiths. But this business of righting some imagined wrong Rome had done to the Jews was as great a threat as Luther.

Cardinal Messner paused at a window. The cars from the helipad were arriving in the courtyard. Linde was leading several figures across the cobbles to an entrance on the far side of the Apostolic Palace. A couple of Vigili were carrying a large box.

The cardinal-secretary continued to stare down at the group. He would recognise Fortuti anywhere with that quick little stride. Hanlon was talking animatedly to a woman in a white coat. The man staring about him like any tourist had to be the wunderkind. Then the other figure was Morton.

# 12

As he walked through the high arched doorway, the contrast with the exterior appearance of the Apostolic Palace struck Morton. The terracotta paint was peeling from the outside walls and the drain pipes were pitted with rust. Inside the door was another world, one few outsiders saw.

Morelli was instructing the *Vigili* carrying Yoshi's laser to use another door. Probably the palace version of a tradesman's entrance.

Like Yoshi and Carina, Morton stood for a moment taking in his surrounds. They were in a broad corridor whose barrel-vaulted ceiling was covered with a mural of biblical figures with robes picked out in gold-leaf. The ochre-coloured walls were hung with gilt-framed portraits.

'Our gallery of saints and rogues,' Monsignor Hanlon said cheerfully.

Monsignor Linde's eyes flicked towards him.

Yoshi turned to a framed portrait of a robed figure with a low forehead, puffed cheeks and jaws, and a misshapen nose. The lips had a sensual twist.

'Pinturicchio's depiction of Alexander the Sixth! I know collectors who would kill to have this hanging on their walls!' Yoshi said.

Monsignor Hanlon looked pleased.

'You are clearly an art lover, Dr Kramer, and you're absolutely right. This is one of Pinturicchio's finest works. Not least because it captures so perfectly the personality of the greatest of our Borgia Popes.'

He turned to Carina.

'Alexander's eye for a pretty woman was infallible. So much so that when he was Pope no fewer than ten bore him children. Two are remembered still as Cesare and Lucretia Borgia. Right to his dying breath Alexander lived by St Augustin's prayer: "Lord make me chaste, but not yet!"'

Carina laughed and looked at Morton.

Monsignor Hanlon led them towards two Swiss Guards standing at attention further down the corridor, pointing out various pontiffs. Morton paused to study a crucifix scene on the ceiling mural. As usual, Christ's loins were covered with a cloth.

That evening in Jerusalem, Julius Enkomo had agreed with Steve that the cloth hid the reality that Christ was born, raised and died a Jew with the cut of His circumcision in His flesh. Making Him an honorary Gentile, Steve had argued, was the beginning of a cover-up which finally enabled Hitler to claim in *Mein Kampf* that Christ Himself supported Nazism. It was not only the monstrosity of such a statement which appalled – but that millions who read it, believed it. Tears in his eyes, Julius Enkomo had taken Steve's hand and asked his forgiveness for what had been done to the Jews.

As they reached the Swiss Guards, a man in a black morning suit emerged from a side room and bowed deeply to the Monsignori. Then, still without saying a word, he led them on down the corridor.

Yoshi pointed to a portrait of a floridly handsome pontiff.

'He looks like a man who had a full life.'

Monsignor Hanlon chuckled. 'Doctor, you clearly have an instinct for such matters. And you're right again. That's Pope John the Twelfth. The day he assumed the burden of office, entire monasteries did nothing else but pray for his death!'

'Monsignor, please! We have no time for these discussions!' Dr Fortuti protested.

Carina looked at Monsignor Hanlon. 'Why did they pray for him to die?'

He smiled at her. 'Well, apart from his harem and his stables of a thousand racing stallions, John had an unquenchable passion for attractive married women!'

'How do you know all this?' she asked.

'It's all in our Secret Archives.'

'Is that where you keep the Third Secret of Fatima?'

He looked at her, surprised. As Lenin was seizing power in Russia in 1917, the Mother of God appeared to children at Fatima in Portugal to disclose three secrets. The first predicted World War Two. The second foretold first the spread, then the collapse, of Communism. The Third Secret remained the most closely guarded of all the secrets in the papal archives.

Monsignor Hanlon shrugged. 'Some things have to remain secret, I fear. So let's just stick with John the Naughty. He went to his death the way he lived – caught in flagrante delicto by a jealous husband.'

'And I thought our tsars were wild,' breathed Carina.

A few yards further on, the corridor forked. Monsignor Linde's eyes flicked over them one more time. Then he turned on his heels and walked away.

The official led the others down the opposite corridor, the ceiling of which was covered with a map of the old Holy Roman Empire, its borders outlined in gold. Morton remembered Steve had said that every year the Vatican melted down twenty gold bars to make paint.

Immediately ahead was an elevator door, guarded by a blue-suited *Vigili*. He gave a quick nod towards Morelli, at the same time sweeping his eyes over the others. Still not having said a word, the official turned and walked solemnly back along the corridor.

'It's how we remain the only state on earth with zero unemployment,' Monsignor Hanlon murmured.

The *Vigili* pushed a button and the elevator door slid open. Monsignor Hanlon motioned the others to enter, then followed. The door closed and the elevator began to descend.

Moments later it opened on to a white-walled corridor. The recessed ceiling lights cast no shadows. The floor was made from a dark-green composition material. In the air was the faint but unmistakable whiff of anaesthetic all hospitals have. Waiting in the corridor was a tall man with a leonine head, bifocals and a goatee. He wore a blue scrub-suit and hat and white operating room clogs.

'Carlo!' Yoshi said warmly, stepping forward to greet Dr Poggi.

'Good to see you, Yoshi. Very good to see you.'

While Dr Fortuti hovered, Yoshi introduced Morton and Carina. Dr Poggi gave Morton a quick handshake and an appraising look, then brushed his lips against the back of Carina's extended hand.

Monsignor Hanlon turned to Morton. 'I'll be on the Third Floor most of the day. I'll sort out sleeping accommodation. If you need anything else, just yell.'

He smiled at Carina. 'I can't promise you a palace, but I think we can rustle up a change of clothing.'

She smiled her thanks. The secretary stepped back into the elevator.

Dr Fortuti addressed Dr Poggi. 'How is my patient?' the papal physician asked importantly.

'The same.'

Dr Poggi turned to Yoshi. 'A lifetime of high-fibre intake has helped him keep in good physical shape. Given what happened, he is surprisingly alert.'

They walked down the corridor towards swing-doors which led to the hospital proper. Beyond the doors the *Vigili* waited with Yoshi's box. He asked Dr Poggi to have it taken to the operating theatre.

Yoshi looked at Dr Fortuti. 'I'd like to see His Holiness alone, please,' he said.

'I don't think I can allow –' Dr Fortuti began.

Yoshi took him by the arm and led him aside.

'I had this conversation with you when I first examined the Pope. I agreed to you being present then because there was no question of surgery. Now that I am going to operate, he's going to be frightened –'

'He's the Holy Father –'

'He's first a man! And I haven't met one who doesn't have some fear when it comes to major surgery. An important part of my pre-operative work is to try and remove that. And I do that best on a one-to-one. Understood?'

After a moment Dr Fortuti nodded. Yoshi released his arm and nodded to Dr Poggi. He led him to a door further along the corridor.

Yoshi opened the door and walked into the room. A nurse seated in a corner jumped to her feet. After she'd left, he closed the door and walked to the foot of the oversize bed.

'Good morning, Your Holiness.'

Pope Nicholas inclined his head.

'Thank you for coming again so quickly, Dr Kramer.'

The voice was low but clear. A good sign.

Yoshi glanced at the monitors around the bed, each recording a different life function. The most important was the continuous graph of the electrical output of the Pope's brain from the electrodes pasted to his scalp. The trace showed no abnormal activity.

'How have you been since I last saw you?'

'Until this, very well. No headache or nausea. Just a little difficulty with my reading. But you warned me about that, didn't you?'

'That's right, Your Holiness.'

There was nothing wrong with his memory. Another good sign.

As he continued to gently question, Yoshi pressed the readout buttons on the monitors and received an immediate update.

Clinically, the Vicar of Christ was in better shape than he had dared to expect. But there was still more probing to be done.

'How's your appetite?'

'It was never very good.'

'What about your digestion?'

'A little difficult.'

The tumour itself had begun to affect the brain's parasympathetic nervous system, which controlled bodily functions.

Pope Nicholas looked at him, a ghost of a smile at the corner of his mouth.

'Well?'

Yoshi walked to the head of the bed and continued to study Pope Nicholas. His skin was pallid and the veins stood out on the back of his long, thin hands, the fingers tapering to nails which needed paring. Yet, in the winter of his years, there was still something left which age had not dimmed.

The Pope's eyes retained their brilliant blue colour, their luminosity and, above all, their look of piercing inquiry.

'Well?' he asked again. 'What do you see?'

'A sick man, but a determined one as well. That's very important. Your determination to come through this is going to be crucial. As critical as the surgical procedure itself. I can't stress that too strongly.'

Pope Nicholas glanced at a cheap alarm clock with a lacquered brass frame and roman numerals on its plain white dial. Then he looked up at Yoshi.

'I bought it the day I was posted as *addetto*, second secretary, to the nunciature in Warsaw. I wanted to make sure I didn't oversleep.'

Yoshi smiled. 'And did you?'

'Of course. We are all fallible.'

'I think you are asking me if this is going to work?'

The smile had gone.

'That, Dr Kramer, is a matter for God. But what I want you to clearly understand is that if your intervention is not successful, you will not place me on a life support system so as to uselessly prolong my life. The sooner my successor is elected the better.'

Yoshi could not quite conceal his surprise. 'Your Holiness, does that not go against the teachings of the Church about all life being sacred?'

There was a sudden sharpness to Pope Nicholas's voice.

'Leave the theology to me, Dr Kramer. Just give me your undertaking to obey my wish.'

Yoshi looked into those piercing eyes for a long moment.

'Very well, Your Holiness. You have my word.'

'Thank you.'

They continued to look at one another in silence.

'Would you like me to explain the procedure?' Yoshi finally asked.

Pope Nicholas shook his head. 'The mechanics do not interest me. All I wish to know is if there will be any side effects and how long it will take me to overcome them.'

'There will be pain, Your Holiness. But that is controllable,' Yoshi began. 'We have drugs that guarantee that.'

Once more there was an edge in the Pope's voice.

'I am not concerned about the pain. I want to know how soon afterwards can I start to make decisions.'

Yoshi stared down into that determined face. He'd been wrong. There was no hint of fear there.

'I can't put an exact time on it. A month or so and you should be able to take up the reins again. Some light reading would be acceptable but you will need to convalesce. I would hope that you will be fully able to resume your duties after, say, six months.'

Pope Nicholas did not take his eyes off Yoshi. When he finally spoke there was a new tension in his voice.

'I understand you have been told about my plan to go to your country and Moscow?'

Yoshi nodded.

'Then you will know I cannot wait six months. I must travel in a month from now. Sooner, if at all possible.'

Yoshi reached down and placed his finger on the Pope's wrist. It was only a gesture for the screen across the bed told him the pulse rate with absolute accuracy. He must do something to avoid the look in the pontiff's eyes, to give him time to deliver words which had suddenly caught in his throat.

'Your Holiness,' he began, taking his finger away. 'I am here because I have the most experience and have achieved the best results with this technique. I developed and perfected it. But I also know its limitations. I cannot say to you that in a month you can travel, especially by plane. Even in a pressurised cabin you could suffer another haemorrhage.'

'That's a risk I must take.'

'It's not one I can be party to, Your Holiness,' Yoshi said firmly.

'I shall absolve you of that responsibility.'

Yoshi shook his head. 'You can't absolve me in a clinical sense. That's a responsibility that rests only between me and my Maker, Your Holiness.'

'You know how to get your own way, Dr Kramer.'

Yoshi shrugged and smiled.

'It's the only way I know.'

The smile was once more tugging at the corner of the Pope's mouth.

'Very well. I suggest a compromise, Dr Kramer. We shall say no more now until after the operation. Then I will make the decision. Agreed?'

'Agreed.'

'Very good. Now when do you propose to operate?'

Yoshi glanced at one of the monitors. The Pope's blood pressure had increased, but not seriously. Such iron control would help during recuperation.

'This afternoon. I will arrange for you to have premedication shortly.'

'Before that I must be clear minded. I need to see my confessor.'

Yoshi laughed quickly. 'Hedging your bets, Your Holiness?'

'Don't be so impertinent, Dr Kramer!' The smile had spread. 'You are an honest man. I appreciate that. When you first diagnosed my tumour, you told me the truth. Give it to me again. What are my chances?'

For the first time he could sense the anxiety in the Pope.

'They're good, Your Holiness.'

'I have to believe you.'

Pope Nicholas seemed to suddenly withdraw into himself.

'Please, leave me now so that I can compose myself for confession,' he murmured.

'I am already here to hear it,' Cardinal Messner said loudly from the doorway.


Half-way down the long conference table, the Reverend Kingdom leaned back in his high-backed leather chair, steepled his fingers and closed his eyes. A point always came during the weekly Investment Committee meeting when he felt no longer able to look, as well as listen, to Hal Lockman. How could someone, who could so easily afford the best, settle for teeth so patently false and hair so visibly a wig? Hal was financial controller of the Church of True Belief. Next to Martha, who sat beside him, no one knew more about its fiscal affairs.

Across the table, the Reverend Kingdom heard Hal once more shuffle his papers before continuing.

'Domestically, our investments in Dow Chemicals and Du Pont look good again this week, a clear three point improvement in both cases. In Europe, we should see a couple of extra points each from Krupp and Aerospace, which means a million-five to reinvest. I recommend we place that in Singapore preference bonds. That'll round off our portfolio down there to ten million.'

Hal paused to clear his throat noisily. Martha had said that, in Hal's case, personal appearances and mannerisms did not matter. That was after she'd spent six months coaxing him to leave Wall Street. What finally clinched the deal was agreeing to double Hal's salary and pay it directly to the Bank of Southern California branch in Freeport in the Bahamas.

'I've pulled us out of the London Futures market so we'll be well clear of the investigation into its misconduct that's about to begin. I've put most of that money into Eurotunnel Units and Whyte and Mackay, the drinks group. Right now the profits to be earned from its whisky are under valued.'

Hal gave another throat-clearing exhibition. He relished being able to show his total mastery over the Church's investments.

He could feel the warmth from Martha's body as she shifted in her chair. There was a musky fragrance about her he found distracting. It was the same way he felt in the presence of the prettier of the Kingdom Angels. They had the same, almost intrusive sexuality. But he must not be tempted now that things were going so well.

Not even Martha had spotted that in a year he had diverted 350,000 dollars of Church money to the account he'd secretly established in his name with Credit Suisse in Geneva. Every day it increased by another thousand dollars, money that was diverted from one of the four thousand portfolios he controlled. It really wasn't stealing, he'd told himself. Just another variation on the computer games he played. Anyway, a thousand dollars was less than the price of that jacket Eddie wore.

'The buys and sells for Tokyo and Hong Kong remain as before – a steady withdrawal from software and into grain and timber. It'll take another month to complete, that way we won't raise any eyebrows. We've still got seventy million currently spread over thirty companies on the Hang Seng, a little less on the Nikkei Average. I'm proposing to move some of that into the Weighted Price.'

'That's the Taiwan Stock Exchange, Eddie,' Martha said quickly.

'Thank you,' he murmured politely.

'Taiwan's a comer,' said Hal. 'Its spot rate is steady and its Futures and Commodities look good. I say we should pump as much as we can into the Weighted Price. Agreed, Eddie?'

Closing his eyes also enabled the Reverend Kingdom to avoid the look of complete certainty Hal often wore. How could anyone be that certain?

'Sounds okay to me, Hal.'

Hal made a note on a pad and gave Martha a smile. He wondered if she would even understand that certain needs in certain people are beyond logical restraint? Here he was, in his fiftieth year and the great desire for physical satisfaction refused to slacken. There was a caged beast in the back of his mind, as untamable now as it had always been since he had had his first woman. He had been fourteen and he had saved for a whole six months to visit her in that house on the far side of town.

'The Trusts,' Martha prompted. Though Hal was superb at what he did, that smell was getting to be unbearable. It seemed to seep out of his sallow skin, from those bags under his pale grey eyes all the way down to the coarse curly hair which grew in tufts on the back of his finger knuckles.

'The Trusts,' Hal repeated. 'Since last week we've bought into nine more. A further investment of one-o-nine million. That gives us a spread over sixty-three Trusts, divided a third each in stocks, bonds and money market funds. We're positioned for long and short, depending on the market.'

'What's Vatican Bank doing?' the Reverend Kingdom asked abruptly.

Hal glanced up from his computer print-out.

'I'm not sure I quite follow you, Eddie.'

'The Roman pontiff's dying. That could affect their market strategy.' When Paul the Sixth was dying, Vatican Bank had lost a billion dollars in speculations.

Hal ran his finger down the activity indicator column. If there was any change, he would expect to see it on the Milan Banca Commerce indicator which listed the movement of Italian stocks. Since the banking scandal of the seventies, Vatican Bank had kept its portfolios close to home.

'Nothing here, Eddie.'

The Reverend Kingdom rocked gently back and forth in his chair. One day he'd catch Hal out. It really wasn't good for anyone to be as certain as that.

'As I predicted, our investments in the securities market remain healthy. We're up in pharmaceuticals and engineering. Allowing for the usual seasonally adjusted figures, I predict we'll continue right on target.'

Hal continued his global tour of the market place. They were in profit in Australia, breaking even in South Africa and Canada, up in Spain and South America.

Martha looked across the table. 'We still don't think it's time to move into the Russian market, Eddie.'

'Well that's your decision.'

'And if you opened your eyes, we could at least see if you agree it's the right one,' Martha said, her voice a little sharper.

The Reverend Kingdom kept his eyes shut.

'This way I concentrate better. Figures were never my strong point.'

Hal smiled across the table. 'All you need to know, Eddie, is the bottom line figure is better than last week.'

He began to gather together his sheets of paper.

'There's just one thing,' the Reverend Kingdom said, continuing to rock in his seat. 'We need money to make sure the building foundations of our new campus will be more earthquake proof than is laid down in the California building code.'

Hal paused putting paper back into his briefcase. He glanced at Martha. She looked as surprised as he felt.

'The code's pretty strict, Eddie,' she said.

'I know it, I know it. But I still want to be on the safe side.'

Hal frowned. 'I can't see no place where the money could come from.'

'I can,' the Reverend Kingdom continued. 'Why don't you pull us out of South African Food Consolidated? That'll free up four, five million. More than enough.'

Hal spread the paper back on the table and his fingers raced down and then across the columns of figures. He'd been nurturing investments in South Africa, not least because it was easy to transfer 1,000 dollars a time from that volatile market to Geneva. He'd taken 50,000 dollars in the past two months. That was something Martha would spot if she looked over the South African portfolio.

'Actually Eddie, it's only three point seven million,' Hal said.

'Fine, Hal. That's still more than enough.'

'Taking out that money from Food Consolidated is certainly a possibility, Eddie, but it could present a problem further down the road. We suddenly produce three point seven million extra for the building project and the IRS will, sure as the devil hisself, come sniffing around.

'On the other hand, Eddie, here's what we could do. We could leave that money where it is and let it go on producing its guaranteed yield over one year which the IRS will never be able to touch. Right now food industry shares in South Africa are about to go through the roof. Every time there's another storm, which knocks over more of their harvest, they go up a few more points. There's never been a better time to stay in. In twelve months' time I can structure the profit as a tax-deductible gift. Then, if you still want, you can use that to pay for your extra building foundation.'

In a year's time he planned to be gone from here. By then he'd be 1,000,000 dollars better off. More than enough to finally unleash the caged beast.

The Reverend Kingdom had stopped rocking.

'A year's too long, Hal. By then I want the campus up and the first students in class. I really need that money now.'

He heard Martha exhaling slowly. 'I still don't see why you want to spend more money just to exceed what the building code says is perfectly adequate. And Hal's right. Why risk having the IRS come poking their nose in?'

He knew they were both looking at him, waiting for a response. But how could he possibly tell them the dream had once more returned, in exactly the same terrifying sequence as before.

He was standing on top of the canyon, dressed in a cassock and surplice, knowing that thousands of people were staring up at him, waiting for him to dedicate the University of True Belief. Below he could make out the President of the United States and other world leaders. To one side stood Wong Lee. Anybody who was anybody had come. Then, as he extended his arms, the sea beyond the Pacific Coast Highway suddenly heaved. A split second later, first the Tabernacle, then all the other buildings, swayed and toppled. The canyon itself divided asunder as the long overdue Great Earthquake of Southern California swept inland, leaving him crushed beneath the rock.

It had been a year since he had last experienced the awful dream. In those months it had gradually faded from his consciousness until this afternoon. He had been cat-napping after the meeting with the realtors when, once again, he awoke in sweat-soaked terror as the rocks buried him alive. Not even an extra-long cold shower had expunged the horror of that moment.

The Reverend Kingdom opened his eyes and smiled at Martha and Hal.

'The building code specifies only minimum standards. I want the campus to be able to withstand a nine on the Richter scale.'

'But we didn't do that for the Tabernacle or the Manse, Eddie,' Martha said.

'I know it, I know it! But I hadn't studied the building code then. And we all know the Only Book says those who go on making mistakes are not looked on kindly by God.'

'And bless His name,' Hal and Martha murmured in unison.

'You really think there is a risk, Eddie?' Hal asked.

The Reverend Kingdom once more made a fingertip tent. As he prepared to answer he leaned forward and spoke gently.

'The Only Book says no man knows the day or the hour. This

campus will be an offering to the Lord, so we have to make it extra safe. We can make a virtue of how safety conscious we are about our students. That will be another way to reassure all those who tithe, that their money's being used wisely.'

He paused and looked at them and shook his head sadly.

'Once upon a time that was never an issue. It still shouldn't be, but it's threatening to become one.'

'It's only a small number, Eddie,' Martha said reasonably.

'I know it, I know it. But small things grow. It's like cancer. One cell divides and multiplies. Before you know where you are, the whole body's infected.'

'But they seem satisfied once they get the standard letter over your signature,' Martha said

She had composed the words herself. That a tithe is a gift to the Lord, an acceptance that to be born again into His Kingdom on earth, it was necessary to give up a portion of your income. The Only Book itself asserted that money was a tangible way to measure the effort made to be born again.

'In tithing part of their income, they're tithing themselves for God,' Martha cried.

'And bless His name,' her listeners responded.

The Reverend Kingdom continued to look at them with penetrating directness

'Martha, Hal. I accept what you say. But this campus must not only be the most glorious to His name, but the safest.'

He spread his hands.

'Okay. So we don't take the money out of South Africa. Where else can we do a little robbing Peter to pay Paul?'

Hal grinned. He was back on safe ground.

'Well we could get out of Pulpmac Industries. I could switch our holdings there to that trust in Malta we used for the satellite purchase. That way it could come back in here as a donation.'

The Reverend Kingdom frowned.

'Pulpmac? Don't they own the Eternal Life Casket Company?'

'Yes. They bought it six months ago.'

'Then we stay in Pulpmac! Half our membership get a discount on their coffins from Eternal Life.'

Hal peered at his papers. There was nothing there.

'I didn't know, Eddie –' he began uncertainly.

The Reverend Kingdom smiled. He had caught Hal out! If that wasn't close to upset in Hal's voice, it was close enough.

'It's okay, Hal. I made the deal before your time.'

'Before my time, too,' Martha said pointedly.

Hal looked up from his papers.

'I still say we should not touch anything, Eddie. What we've tried to do is create an intricate financial structure which depends on each buy and sell order, each investment, each infusion of new money being carefully managed. To start changing that makes me nervous.'

'You get paid to be nervous, Hal,' smiled the Reverend Kingdom.

Hal turned to Martha for support. She stared steadily back at him. He was on his own. So be it. He set his face and looked at the Reverend Kingdom.

'The IRS are not going to give up; we both know that. What we could do is outflank them, even catch them totally unprepared.'

'How do we do that, Hal?' the Reverend Kingdom asked.

Hal took a breath and plunged.

'Relocate! The entire operation! Move to Utah, Kansas, Ohio. It doesn't really matter where. The whole thing would be a tax write-off that we could carry forward for ten years, maybe even longer! The time the IRS could work out what is deductible and what isn't, we'd be home and dry! And you could build your university without all this extra earthquake proofing you need here!'

The Reverend Kingdom continued to stare at Hal. He'd always had a question mark about him as to whether he was a cut-and-run man. He was. Too damn right he was.

'No way, Hal!' Martha cried. 'If I didn't know you better, I'd say the very devil has been whispering to you in your sleep!'

The sheer fury of her words made Hal go white.

'Martha, it was only a suggestion. I'm sorry if it offended you –'

She turned in her seat to glare at him.

'You offended God, Hal Lockman! That's what you have just done – offended and insulted Him. Do you think God would have made those realtors give us their land for nothing if He wanted us to move? Is that what you think? Then let me tell you something! Just sit there and listen, d'you hear me?'

Hal nodded miserably.

The Reverend Kingdom composed himself. He had always let

Martha deal with these matters. There was no one better at crushing a bad idea before it could get going.

She raged on.

'God – and bless His name – brought us here because this is the furthest point we can be in this country from what is happening in Europe! The furthest point, Hal, from all that godlessness and evil! From all that pollution and filth! From just about everything we abhor in His name!'

'And bless His name!'

The Reverend Kingdom's injunction overrode Hal's whisper. Martha continued to pour a torrent of words over him.

'When you took this job, I gave you a copy of the Only Book. Right?'

Hal nodded.

'And I said read it! All of it. A chapter a night. Right?'

Hal gave another nod.

'So you would have read what the Prophet Joel said? About the Good Lord gathering together His forces in a great canyon? And those people who dwelled there would go forth and destroy all the forces of darkness? You remember reading that, Hal?'

'Yes,' he whispered.

'This is that canyon! We are those people! From here we will go forth! Do you understand that, Hal?'

'Yes, Martha.'

'Very well. Never, ever, again, say we should move!' She sat back, arms folded.

In the silence the Reverend Kingdom stared across at her. He could not fault what she had said, or how she sat, like a statue raised to His greater glory. Yet, so often nowadays, she would erupt over something quite trivial.

Last Sunday it had been the choir missing a beat. She had made them practise all afternoon. Before that it had been some problem in Mail. Martha had had that pretty young Clara Stevens bring work over to the manse. The last time, after he had gone to bed, he had been awoken by Martha yelling at Clara. He had heard the supervisor running tearfully from the manse.

'I'm sorry, Martha,' Hal said.

The Reverend Kingdom nodded. What Hal had proposed was foolish. Moving from here *was* out of the question. But no point in punishing him further.

'It's okay, Hal. But Martha's right to remind us all of how important is our work here.'

Hal smiled gratefully. 'Thanks, Eddie.'

The worst part was having to sound contrite to those two monsters.

The Reverend Kingdom stood up.

'I rejoice the Lord has given me such wonderful helpers. Now why don't you both just go through the portfolios one more time to see if there just isn't some way you can come up with the money to pay for that extra earthquake proofing?'

Hal gave another throat clearing performance.

'We'll do our best, Eddie,' he said fervently.

'I know it, I know it,' the Reverend Kingdom replied.

He walked from the conference room. In the Hallway of Support a blonde-haired young woman was dusting the photographs. She wore the white blouse, blue skirt and sensible shoes required of all female staff.

She smiled and he smiled back.

'It's Jenny, isn't it?' He prided himself on knowing the names of all the staff.

'Penny-Jane, Reverend Kingdom.' She hesitated as if not knowing what else to say.

'Of course,' he smiled again. 'Penny-Jane.'

The girl from the detention centre. The Church employed several after Martha decided it would help to emphasise its community commitment.

'I thought you were assigned to Mail?'

She nodded.

'So?' He raised an eyebrow.

'I didn't get on with Clara Stevens.'

'How so?'

Penny-Jane looked discomfited.

'She work you too hard?'

'Oh no, nothing like that, Reverend Kingdom. I like to work.'

'Then what was it, child?'

'Well ... she was always touching me, giving me little squeezes, paying me compliments. It made me feel ... uncomfortable and embarrassed.'

The Reverend Kingdom smiled. 'Clara's a very affectionate person, Penny-Jane. She probably just wanted to make you feel welcome. Probably her way of saying you're safe here.'

'You really think so?'

'Of course. It's Clara's way of showing she loves you. We all love each other here. It's part of living together in His name.'

She looked at him in relief.

He waved a hand towards the photographs. 'But if you're happy dusting then that's fine. It's all part of the Lord's work.'

'And bless His name,' Penny-Jane said obediently.

He bestowed another smile on her and walked on. Kids could get strange ideas, especially teenage girls. But it was a sad old world when they felt unable to accept some old-fashioned affection.

He turned into the executive offices. Martha and he had adjoining offices and shared a secretary. Lena was not at her desk. The Reverend Kingdom sighed. She was probably off on another errand for Martha. He would really have to speak to her about getting a second secretary and counter her argument that it was an unnecessary expense.

He picked up his messages off Lena's desk. Wong Lee still had not phoned back. Now he had another reason to call him. Between them Martha and Hal would find some plausible reason why they could not provide the money for the extra earthquake proofing. He'd ask Wong Lee to provide it. That sort of money was probably petty cash to him.

He walked into his own office, shut the door and began to dial the long series of digits to connect him to the special telephone number he had been given. As he did so he began to rehearse what he would say. First, he would quote the words of John the Apostle that the Lord's mansions must be suitably furnished. Then he would explain what a good deal he had made with the realtors. Afterwards, he would make his pitch.

He could hear the phone ringing. But no one answered.

In Lhasa, Wong Lee watched the light on the communications sphere disappear as the call from Malibu disconnected. He continued to sit cross-legged and perfectly still on the log in his office.

Behind him the shamaness stirred and spoke.

'It is good that they now operate on him,' she murmured.

'You are certain?'

'I am very certain, singsung. It will allow the powder to complete its work.'

# 13

When Yoshi returned from briefing the Cardinals of the Sacred College, the tension markedly increased in the basement hospital. Outside the elevator door he turned to Cardinal Messner.

'I'm sorry, Your Eminence. This is as far as you go. I have a strict rule. No outsiders while I operate. That way if something goes wrong, no one else gets blamed. If it goes right, I take all the credit!'

The cardinal-secretary looked past him to where Morton stood in full theatre garb.

'He is not a doctor,' Cardinal Messner said.

'No. But he stays,' Yoshi replied.

For a moment Morton thought Cardinal Messner was about to argue. Instead he turned on his heels and the door of the elevator closed behind him. Morelli posted himself at the door to stop anyone else from passing.

'How'd the briefing go?' Morton asked.

'As you'd expect. A lot of questions of the how-long-is-a-piece-of-string variety. For holy men they certainly need a lot of earthly assurance. After I'd done my best, one of the Germans stood up and said in his view God should decide the outcome!'

Morton glanced at Yoshi. 'A tall, thin man with thick glasses?'

'That's him. And skin like he's one of the walking dead. You know him?'

'Hans-Dietrich Muller, Cardinal-Archbishop of Berlin.' The prelate Sean said was Messner's clone.

Dr Poggi and Carina emerged from Pope Nicholas's room.

He carried a kidney bowl and a used syringe and vial. She had a tray which held a small pile of human hair, a cut throat razor, and an old-fashioned shaving mug and brush.

Like Dr Poggi, Carina was fully gowned though not yet scrubbed.

'He's nicely relaxed. We've started the IV with the steroids. He's also on Dilantin,' Dr Poggi told Yoshi.

'Good.' The steroids would help reduce intracranial pressure, the second drug would guard against a seizure.

Yoshi turned to Carina. 'Not every day you get to shave a Pope's head. Probably helps we're all descended from barbers.'

Carina smiled. 'Not to forget wizards, bone-setters and sow-gelders.'

'*Eco*,' murmured Dr Poggi.

They all entered the surgeons' dressing room. Dr Fortuti sat on a bench, a small plastic bag in his hand. He walked over to Carina and took the tray from her. He carefully swept the Pope's hair into the bag.

Yoshi watched curiously.

'What are you going to do with that?'

'If the Holy Father dies this will go into his coffin,' Dr Fortuti said, tying the bag.

'You've got some funny customs, doctor,' Yoshi said.

He started to whistle tonelessly.

Morton looked at him. There was a tension about Yoshi not there before. Was he finally reacting to the strain his nervous system had endured – his kidnap and his brush with death before being spirited out of Moscow? Since then he had worked non-stop.

'You got a moment, Yoshi?' he asked quietly.

'Sure.'

They walked out of the room. In the corridor, Morton reached out and gripped Yoshi by both arms, running his hands up and down, feeling the muscles beneath the skin. They were taut, like a man going into combat.

'What are you doing, David?'

Slowly, without embarrassment, Morton looked into Yoshi's face, searching for any sign of weakness, the merest flicker or twitch which could, during the operation, deepen and expand and finally crack open.

He stepped back and looked at Yoshi seriously.

'There's a lot riding on you, Yoshi.'

Yoshi grinned. 'Not least my reputation.'

Morton knew then that if anything did go wrong, it would not be Yoshi's fault. All he had felt and seen in the neurosurgeon was strength and total self-confidence.


In his office Cardinal-Secretary Messner sat perfectly still in one of a pair of armchairs. Carved on the armrests was the Borgia family crest of unicorns rampant. Seated opposite was the cadaverous figure of Hans-Dietrich Muller.

His pallor would have aged him further except for his bouffant hair style. His skull cap was perched on the peak of a steel-grey wave.

The Cardinal-Archbishop of Berlin drew on a cigarette through a long ebony holder.

'But you say there's still no independent proof Enkomo and Morton did meet?'

He spoke the *hoch-Deutsch* they used when alone together.

The cardinal-secretary turned to a side table beside the armchair and picked up his coffee cup. Sipping, he peered over the rim.

'Proof could actually be a disadvantage. If Enkomo had sent detailed explanations of why he had met with Morton, we might well have nothing. But properly presented, we can suggest their meetings were the tip of the proverbial iceberg. At the right time, that will be all that's needed.'

On the credenza against one damask-papered wall a sixteenth century Venetian clock chimed the hour.

'You have no doubt, Hubert, that Enkomo met this Jewish spy?'

'None at all.'

The cardinal-secretary drained his cup. 'Our African liberal would be the perfect bridge between Jerusalem and the Third Floor. And sometimes Enkomo sounds as if God really intended him to be a Jew!'

Cardinal Muller inhaled, savoured the smoke, then slowly exhaled through his nose.

'Yes. Yes,' he said again. 'Do we know any more about this Morton?'

The cardinal-secretary leaned back in his chair and sniffed The smoke irritated his hay fever.

'He's the best Mossad has. That means he's probably the best in the world at what he does.'

'Do you think his presence here is deliberate, Hubert? That he's come to meet Enkomo again?'

Cardinal Messner paused. With Morton, anything was possible. He'd shown that when he had turned up with those rabbis who had come to express support for Holy Cross. In no time Morton had managed to get the pontiff's ear. But Morton had already been airborne before Enkomo had decided to come to Rome.

The cardinal-secretary shook his head. 'I think that's giving Morton more credit for deviousness than even he deserves. But I think their presence here is a coincidence we can use.'

Smoke continued to drift out of Cardinal Muller's nose.

'Yes. Yes of course,' he said.

The cardinal-secretary rose to his feet and walked to a window. He began to move his head from side to side. Dr Fortuti had recommended the neck exercises for his arthritis. So far they had not helped any more than his pills for the hay fever.

Below in the courtyard a bishop was being saluted by a Swiss Guard as he passed under one of the arched openings. Cardinal Messner turned back to the room, continuing to move his head and sniffing from time to time.

Hans-Dietrich Muller stared at him dispassionately. 'Perhaps if this wunderkind fails, we may never have to do anything?'

'You are not worried, are you, about any action we might have to take, Hans-Dietrich?'

The cardinal-secretary resumed his seat and continued to study Cardinal Muller's face.

'No. No, of course not, Hubert.'

'Good.' The merest flicker of relief crossed the cardinal-secretary's lips.

He had backed Muller from the beginning, spending time to make sure each of the other cardinals in the Sacred College knew why he felt Muller was papable. Being a realist, he had not expected them all to agree – certainly not the liberal Nicholas had placed as head of the church in Romania with its Byzantine rites, or the Jesuit who was cardinal of the Slovakian part of Czechoslovakia. But enough had listened: thirty-five Europeans, most of whom were Curia-trained cardinals; some of the Americans; a surprising number from Latin America.

They were not only shocked by the sexual misbehaviour of

that fool, Lopez, but also wanted their next pontiff to be strong enough to face up to the Protestant evangelists sweeping through what was once the most secure of Catholic continents. Nicholas, with his policy of religious co-existence, had let the tub-thumpers run riot.

The cardinal-secretary had promised all those who listened that Hans-Dietrich would put an end to such nonsense. Just as he would stop Operation Holy Cross.

'The time to move will be before the next conclave. By then we will know who is for you, who is against you.'

Cardinal Muller's skeletal fingers stroked the carved unicorns.

'That could still be some time away. If Nicholas recovers, he will want to continue as before.'

He sucked in another lungful of smoke.

'Fortuti says if he recovers, he will need a lengthy convalescence. A great deal can be achieved in that time. If he returns to the throne, Nicholas will find there is much he cannot undo. So whether he lives or dies, Hans-Dietrich, is not really a concern. Either way we make sure to end his nonsense of recognising Israel and going to Moscow.

'When the time comes we'll tell the waverers Nicholas's illness made him a tool of the Jews. Merely to suggest that will be enough. But as proof, we let them see Enkomo's report. I can't imagine even our most liberal-minded brothers-in-Christ will be pleased to discover what was going on behind their backs.'

Cardinal Muller lit a fresh cigarette.

'With a little luck we could see the papacy back on course, Hubert.'

Cardinal Messner smiled.

'And with a little more luck, I will live long enough to see the day you are elected.'

He had found the carrot always worked better than the stick with Hans-Dietrich.

Before Cardinal Muller could respond, one of the telephones on the cardinal-secretary's desk rang. He walked over and picked up the receiver.

'*Danke*,' he said, replacing the handset. He turned to Cardinal Muller.

'The operation is about to start. Perhaps the outcome will save us all a lot of trouble.'

*

Morton held open the door to Pope Nicholas's room to allow Carina and members of Dr Poggi's surgical team to wheel in a trolley. They quickly transferred the pontiff from his bed to the gurney. The Pope wore a white gown and a tubagauze cap to protect his partly shaved head.

Carina checked the intravenous drip containing the steroid solution. She made an adjustment to reduce the flow, then hooked the bottle to the trolley's built-in stand.

As the gurney passed, Morton saw the Pope's eyes were still clear, moving from side to side, staring up at the faces.

'Colonel Morton, what are you doing here?' he called out in surprise.

The pontiff's voice had thickened slightly with the drugs.

'I came with Dr Kramer, Your Holiness.'

'I am glad to see you again, colonel.'

'I'm glad to see you so determined.'

Pope Nicholas gave a wry smile.

'At a time like this what else could I be?'

The doors to the Induction Room swung open and Morton helped push in the trolley.

Dr Poggi was waiting with the anaesthetist, going over her report. Pope Nicholas had no loose or cracked teeth. There was no history of previous serious illness. His blood-pressure was average for a man of his years.

Dr Poggi came forward and smiled a surgeon's reassurance.

'It's time for you to go to sleep, Your Holiness.'

'Before I do, could you please let me have a private word with Colonel Morton.'

Dr Poggi hesitated. Then he beckoned Morton forward and nodded for the others to follow him out into the corridor.

Morton stood beside the trolley. Pope Nicholas reached out and held Morton's hand. The grip was surprisingly strong.

'Colonel, if this is not successful, I want you to contact Cardinal Enkomo and help him all you can to make sure the world knows about his report.'

'What report is this, Your Holiness?' Morton asked gently.

He felt the grip tighten, as if the Pope wanted to reinforce what he was going to say.

'The one I hope successfully argues why the Holy See must now recognise Israel. It was intended as the precursor to my visit there.'

'Shouldn't that news be released by your own people, Your Holiness?'

The Pope's grip increased. 'I fear that's the last thing some of them'll want to do!'

Pope Nicholas stared at Morton intently. There was a new urgency in his voice when he spoke again.

'If my surgery fails, I must make sure my successor continues my policy of reconciliation. The best possible way to do that is to have Enkomo's report made public. That will make it more difficult for those who oppose this act of coming together. We both know there is little time left for that. So will you help?'

Morton smiled down at Pope Nicholas. 'Yes. But you're still going to make those journeys yourself, Your Holiness.'

Pope Nicholas released his grip.

'It's a pleasant thought to go to sleep on. Now fetch the others so that they can get started.'

Morton walked to the door. Dr Poggi, Carina and the anaesthetist returned.

Carina followed Dr Poggi into the side room where Yoshi was already vigorously scrubbing his hands. A nurse wheeled a trolley of bottles, cylinders and tubes to the side of the gurney. The anaesthetist selected a needle, pierced the back of the Pope's hand, then deftly aspirated blood into a syringe. She placed the syringe on the trolley and connected a fresh one to the lumen of the needle. The syringe was filled with a colourless liquid.

'Count backwards from ten,' she instructed, steadily depressing the plunger for a measured amount of Pentothal to enter the vein.

Almost at once the supreme pontiff began to snore. The nurse extended his neck. The anaesthetist continued to watch until Pope Nicholas's eyeballs stopped moving.

'Okay, let's tube him,' she said brusquely.

From the trolley the anaesthetist took a tongue depresser fitted with a small but powerful light at one end and swiftly inserted it over the Pope's tongue to inspect his throat. A puff of hot chemicalised air came from the pontiff's vocal cords. The anaesthetic was on its way through his system.

The anaesthetist injected a muscle relaxant into the larynx to prevent convulsive reactions. Next she slipped a tube down the throat to provide an airway into the Pope's lungs. She connected the tube to one of the cylinders on the trolley and piped oxygen directly into the lungs. Satisfied, she packed each side of the tube with gauze strips. She squeezed a rubber bag a few times. If the Pope was properly anaesthetised, he would stop breathing when she stopped squeezing. She gave the bag one more squeeze, then waited. The pontiff did not breathe. The anaesthetist turned to the nurse.

'Keep it going, will you.'

The nurse continued to squeeze the bag.

The anaesthetist glanced towards Morton then continued her work. She had heard he was some sort of bodyguard, but she was not curious.

She connected an intravenous line, so that during the operation she could provide drugs which would immobilise every muscle except the heart. There would be no chance of the supreme pontiff moving during surgery.

'Ready when you are, OR,' the anaesthetist called out.

The doors to the operating room swung back and two assistants emerged to wheel in Pope Nicholas, while the anaesthetist pushed the trolley and the nurse kept squeezing the bag.

Morton walked behind them. The last time he'd been in an OR was to watch Ruth perform her first operation. Then, as now, he was struck by the range of diagnostic and monitoring equipment. There were almost as many screens as in Concorde's Communications Centre.

The operating room was thirty feet square, with a green, anti-static floor and green tiled walls. Suspended from the ceiling was a kettledrum surgical light. It could be moved on tracks. For the moment the light was tilted down over the black surface of the operating table.

Attached to the frame of the kettledrum was the fibre optic microscope Yoshi had brought from Moscow. It resembled a submarine periscope and its base was connected by cables to a steel-framed chair with armrests and foot-pedals. More power lines ran to the square sealed box housing the laser unit. The microscope and chair were draped with sterilised towels so that only the two separate eye pieces remained uncovered. The lenses were set at right angles to each other.

In one movement Pope Nicholas was lifted from the gurney onto the table. He lay face up. His gown was removed, leaving him totally naked.

The surgical assistants attached electrical leads on his chest and a blood pressure unit to an arm. A heart monitor on a trolley beside the table at once began to display information. The spiky trail reminded Morton of a continuously moving city skyline.

While one assistant slid a greased catheter into the Pope's ureter, another taped thick pieces of wadding over his eyes and then inserted a needle into the femoral artery in the right thigh. This would provide an immediate pathway to transfer blood in case of an emergency.

The assistants positioned a copper plate under the Pope's buttocks as an earth against any shock from the high voltages and currents to be used during the operation. A rectal thermometer was inserted.

The Pope was now fully anaesthetised and prepared for surgery. All his vital signs read normal on the various monitors around the table.

In the door of the scrub room, Yoshi stood with his arms held up so that the last drops of water flowed safely away to the crook of his elbows. A nurse stepped forward and worked white, skintight rubber gloves over his hands. Yoshi flexed them and then stepped into the OR. The nurse tied on his mask.

'*Buongiorno*,' he said.

Murmured responses came from the surgical team. Dr Fortuti remained impassive to one side of the operating area.

'That's all the Italian I know,' Yoshi said cheerfully.

His eyes swept over the activity. The anaesthetist was partly hidden behind sterile curtains which isolated her from the top end of the table. Nurses were wheeling tall instrument-trolleys into position directly over the operating area to form a large square-topped table covered with green sterile cloths.

Pope Nicholas disappeared from view, apart from his feet and the shaved area of his scalp. It gleamed in the overhead light.

Carina emerged from the scrub room and, when the nurse had gloved her and tied on her mask, she walked over to where Yoshi stood before a backlit display panel on one wall. Clipped to it were X-rays of the Pope's brain.

He turned to Carina.

'Your classic basal meningioma. Deep seated and hard to get to.'

He began to move a finger over one of the negatives.

'We'll go in this way. Slip past the ganglia so as not to leave him paralysed. And stay well clear of the limbic system so we don't leave him without his full complement of emotions. To here.'

He had indicated a surgical pathway of a few centimetres.

Yoshi's finger stopped at a darker area on the print.

'That's our target. We'll need at least two hours, possibly longer.'

Carina glanced at the table. She turned back to the X-rays.

'Can he stand that? He's an old man.'

'It's either that or being a dead old man.'

He turned to watch the activity. Nurses were laying out sterilised dressings, towels, needles and instruments on the square top.

Dr Poggi walked into the OR, extended his hand to receive his gloves and allowed the nurse to tie his mask. He glanced up at one of the four video cameras mounted at various points on the ceiling.

'Messner wants a visual record,' he said to Yoshi. 'And they want us to provide a commentary.'

'What's he going to do, Carlo? Run it as movie of the week on Vatican Television?'

Dr Poggi smiled behind his mask and looked at Morton.

'Colonel, would you like to operate the video end of things?'

'No problem.' Morton walked over to a TV monitor and VCR unit in a corner of the OR. He inserted a tape and pressed buttons. Lights on the cameras blinked red.

On the quarto-split screen he had a choice of images from the scene around the table. He chose one showing a close-up of the Pope's skull, pressed a button and the image was recorded on tape.

A moment later, Yoshi, Dr Poggi and Carina were at the table. Dr Poggi looked up at a camera.

'Your Eminences. The procedure today will be lengthy. I will now open the head and begin to prepare the way for Dr Kramer.'

Dr Poggi sat in the chair. Yoshi was to his immediate right, Carina on his left. The chief instrument nurse stood at the high table. The rest of the team were positioned around the table to fetch and carry.

Dr Poggi glanced towards the anaesthetist hidden behind her green screen.

'Everything okay?'

'No problem,' she acknowledged.

The only sound in the OR was the rustling of a nurse's gown as she moved to the steriliser against the wall.

'Let's do it,' Dr Poggi said.

The instrument nurse slapped a scalpel into his extended hand. Dr Poggi began to make a scratch mark on the skin. A tiny crimson trickle appeared. By the time he had completed a roughly spherical outline, the scalp tissue was covered with blood.

'Adrenalin.'

From a trolley beside her, Carina handed Dr Poggi a syringe already filled with the anaesthetic.

He quickly injected around the cut area. The skin began to bubble from the effect of the drug as it reduced the bleeding.

'Gauze.'

Carina handed Dr Poggi a forceps with a piece coated in antiseptic solution. He placed it over the cut area.

'Towel.'

Yoshi began to pass him small sterile squares. Dr Poggi placed these on top of the gauze.

He glanced up at a camera. Then he continued to work.

Monsignor Hanlon cradled the phone to his shoulder.

'Thank you, Excellency,' he murmured to the Indian Ambassador to the Holy See.

The Pope's secretary scribbled on the pad before him: Indian government offering convalescence in the foothills of Himalayas.

In the past few hours he had received offers for Pope Nicholas to recuperate in places as varied as an island in the South China Sea to a ranch in California. The Japanese had offered a cruise liner, the Canadians a cabin in the mountains.

'No . . .' Monsignor Hanlon continued, 'we don't really expect news for several hours. But I'll make sure you will be among the first to know, Excellency. Yes . . . thank you again. It's a very generous offer and I'll be sure to convey it to His Holiness.'

He put down the telephone.

As well as heads of missions, over two dozen presidents, rulers and prime ministers had also telephoned personally. The Archbishop of Canterbury had called. So had Rupert Murdoch, Billy Graham and the Dalai Lama. The Queen had sent a message.

Beyond his open office door, the dozen monsignori of the papal secretariat were dealing with other calls. The nuns at the Vatican switchboard were handling over three thousand incoming calls an hour. Media enquiries were switched to the Press Office; reporters heard a pre-recorded message. There would be a further announcement after the operation.

Calls from cardinals were routed to the Secretariat of State. They were read a statement drafted by the cardinal-secretary. It was identical to the one Monsignor Linde had read to Julius Enkomo. Prelates who tried to ask questions were firmly told to be patient. All other callers were thanked by the switchboard operators and asked to pray for the Holy Father.

Monsignor Hanlon walked to his office window on the third floor of the Apostolic Palace and looked down at the scene in St Peter's Square. He estimated there were now at least 20,000 people keeping vigil. The silent, watchful crowd stretched all the way across the piazza to the Arch of the Bells.

Swiss Guards standing before the heavy wrought-iron gates continued to receive flowers. The same was happening at the other two principal entrances to the city-state, the Bronze Door and the Santa Anna Gateway.

Monsignor Hanlon had arranged for the flowers to be distributed among Rome's hospitals. The way things were going, there would be enough to give a bunch to each patient. He felt a sudden lump in his throat at this great outpouring of concern and affection for a man few of the tribute givers had personally met.

Behind him the phone on his desk had started to ring again. He turned and walked quickly to answer it.

'*Pronto*,' he murmured into the receiver.

'Secretary Hanlon?' demanded a high-pitched voice.

'Speaking.'

'This is Fung, secretary to Mr Wong Lee, president of Wong Holdings. He desires to obtain any information you can provide on the Pope's condition . . .'

# 14

Dr Poggi once more turned to a steel basin mounted on a stand and washed his gloved hands in an antiseptic solution. He shook the water from them and turned back to the table. He found it easier to work with his gloves damp. They gave more sensitivity to his fingers.

Forty minutes had passed since he made the first scratch mark. In that time he had pared back a skin-flap which was now carefully covered with a sterile pad.

Yoshi and Carina kept the operating area free of blood and fluid. He used a diathermic electrode to cauterise blood-vessels. She wielded a suction-tube which carried blood into a bottle, graduated to show how much fluid the Pope was losing. He had already had his first transfusion.

There were now three holes neatly bored in his skull. An assistant once more handed Dr Poggi a high-speed surgeon's drill. Moments later he made a fourth hole. As the bit was retracted, Yoshi collected the bone shavings and placed them in a small pot. They would be used to refill the holes later.

Carina rinsed out the cavity.

'Martel's,' Dr Poggi said.

The nurse handed him the thin flexible instrument.

The surgeon glanced up.

'I'm going to separate the skull cap from the brain,' he said into a camera.

Morton began to record a close-up of Dr Poggi passing the protector down one hole and up through the adjoining one.

When Dr Poggi finished, he handed the protector to the clear-away nurse.

'Gigli.'

The instrument nurse handed him a strip of wire not unlike a cheese cutter. He fed the surgical saw blade between two of the holes.

Morton briefly wondered who Martel and Gigli had been to have instruments named after them.

Yoshi fixed a t-shaped steel handle to one end of the saw, the surgeon an identical one to the other end. They started to pull in tandem and, in a few moments, the bone between the two holes was severed.

They repeated the process with the other pair of holes.

When they finished Yoshi looked up at the camera.

'What we have to do now, Your Eminences, is to make sure His Holiness's brain doesn't just pop out of his skull.'

He glanced at Carina and smiled. She wondered again why he always had to be on stage?

'Elevators,' Dr Poggi called.

He took one of the inch-long blades the nurse proffered Angling it in through a hole, he levered upwards. He repeated the process hole by hole. The loosened bone began to rise from the dura mater, the membrane covering the brain.

'Pad!'

Carina handed Dr Poggi a gauze square which he placed on the exposed dura mater. Then another, and a third.

'Blood-pressure?' he demanded.

'Ninety-eight over seventy-two,' the anaesthetist replied.

Dr Poggi did not look up from his work. 'Try and drop him at least a couple of points.'

Yoshi grinned up at a camera. 'That's blood-pressure points, not stock market points.'

Morton could see a few smiles behind the surgical masks.

Dr Poggi asked for a tenotome. The nurse handed him the small scalpel with a finely honed blade. The surgeon nicked a corner of the dura mater. He passed the knife to the clear-away nurse.

'Dural.'

Dr Poggi was handed the long fine-edged scissors. With infinite care he started to snip away, fraction by fraction, the membranous skin. When he finished snipping he carefully peeled back the dura mater.

Yoshi irrigated and dried the exposed brain. It was milky

pinkish in colour except in one part which was a greyish purple.

'The site of the tumour,' Yoshi said to a camera.

He turned and called across to Morton.

'You got this on camera?'

'For sure.'

Yoshi turned back to stare at the gently throbbing brain of Pope Nicholas the Sixth.

Once Fung had typed into his computer the report of his telephone call to Monsignor Hanlon, he immediately transmitted it through the electrical network of Wong Holdings in Lhasa. After the report was deposited in Wong Lee's personal modem, it simultaneously appeared on screens in Telecommunications, Security and Surveillance, Data Bank and on those in Central Operations.

Set three hundred feet back from the rock face, Central Operations was housed in a chamber the shape and size of an ice-skating rink. Its floor rose forty feet to a steel-girder grid, containing the air conditioning plant which cooled the computers. Some were the size of a domestic living room, others as big as a house. The largest ran the length of one side of the chamber.

Day and night the computers sifted and scanned millions of pieces of information, slotting them into place with billions of items already stored on tape. Armed guards were posted on the computers.

It needed a moment for one of the computers to assess Fung's report and direct it to the terminal of one of two hundred operatives on the floor.

This operator's name was Zong. Because of his analytical skills, he had been assigned to Tracking – the unit which kept watch for significant shifts of stocks anywhere in the world. Zong worked at station 127 – a desk, terminal and display screen, all enclosed by a head-high plastic wall to ensure a modicum of privacy. His brief was to watch for movements on the Hang Seng, the Weighted Price of the Taiwan Stock Exchange and the Banca Commerce indicator in Milan.

A few minutes ago he had recorded on his computer another 14 million dollar sale of computer stocks in Hong Kong by Eternal Investments. That now made 60 million dollars of software holdings divested by Eternal Investments in the past month. Eternal Investments had used the money to buy shares in a number of timber-producing corporations on the Taiwan Exchange.

As instructed, Zong keyed the details on to his supervisor's screen. From there the operative knew it would be routed to Wong Lee's own computer. The supervisor was the only man in Central Operations who had its access code.

In many ways Zong was no different from all the other operatives in Central Operations – except he was more curious than them to know how all this information was used. His questions at first had been politely side-stepped by his supervisor. Finally the man had warned Zong such inquiries would lead to his dismissal. That had only made Zong more curious.

He now knew that, despite its imposing name, Eternal Investments was in reality only Hal Lockman seated before his modem in Malibu. The financial controller was on Zong's watch-and-trace list; all the analysts in Tracking had instructions to follow the dealings of traders who were leaders in their field. A precise record of Hal's transfers to Credit Suisse had also been keyed by Zong to his supervisor. The young operative had briefly wondered why someone like Hal Lockman who was most certainly very well paid, should be stealing such trifling amounts.

Monitoring the Banca Commerce indicator gave Zong a clear overview of the market strategy of Vatican Bank. The heady days were gone, when the bank invested in high-risk stocks for even higher yields. Instead the bank had returned to its cautious gilt-edged ways.

Though Vatican Bank formed only a small part of his brief, Zong automatically received all related data. Since Pope Nicholas's collapse, there had been a continuous flow, far too much for even Zong's retentive memory to remember.

When Fung's report reached his modem, the operative called up the most recent input for comparison. On screen came the latest statement from the Vatican press office announcing that the Pope was undergoing surgery. There followed a short selection of newspaper reports, a description of the Vatican hospital and profiles of the surgeons. None of this interested Zong.

Next came a fulsome statement from the President of the Banca Commerce expressing his members' hopes that the pontiff would make a swift recovery, then adding that the Italian stock market would be unaffected by the Pope's illness.

Zong smiled. It always amused him how God and Mammon co-existed in places like Rome and Malibu.

He was about to return the information to Data Bank when a series of numbers and letters appeared on screen. Zong stared transfixed. Though he had only glimpsed the sequence once before, on his supervisor's screen, he recognised Wong Lee's access code.

The operative realised at once what must have happened. When Fung used the code to key his report to Wong Lee's modem, its computer had failed to remove the numbers before retransmitting. Zong had always said no one should expect computers to be infallible.

For a moment longer he stared at the screen. He knew what he should do: press a key and consign the ultra-secret code to limbo. Instead he glanced quickly around. The other operatives in Tracking were bent to their work. The guards standing in front of the computers seemed as bored as usual.

Zong glanced quickly up to the catwalks high above the floor. The two men who constantly monitored the activity below were over on the far side, peering down on the South African and Latin American analysts.

He pressed a key on his board. The code moved to the top of the screen. He tapped another key. In the screen's centre appeared the words: READY TO PROCEED.

Zong quickly typed on screen. RECALL.

A moment later came the acknowledgement: COMMAND ACCEPTED. PROCEED.

Zong glanced about and above him. Still no one realised he had accessed the most secure of all the computers in Wong Holdings.

He typed in the command: PROCEED NOW.

At once the screen began to fill with details of the plot to kill the Pope, and how his death would be used to unleash further serious unrest.

Despite the pleasant air temperature, Zong began to shiver. He was looking at a blueprint for Armageddon which had begun with the doping of the pontiff's coffee and would end with a civil war across a quarter of the globe. He was staring into the mind of Wong Lee.

Suddenly the screen went blank.

Even as Zong began to move his fingers over the keyboard to

try and retrieve the words, a harsh and totally terrifying voice roared down from the catwalk.

'Guards! Arrest the operative of station 127!'

On the catwalk, Chung-Shi, the security chief of Wong Holdings, checked the squelcher in his hand. A moment previously, the gadget – in shape and size like a TV channel-changer – had located the screen which had somehow obtained Wong Lee's access code. How, he would discover later. Right now, the important thing was to retrieve it.

As soon as Wong Lee had raised the alarm, the security chief had led a team of sweepers to electronically comb the galleries. Instinct had told Chung-Shi that if anyone would try and use the code, then it would be one of the operatives in Central Operations. He watched the first of the guards reach Station 127. Then he spoke into a mobile telephone.

'Everything is secured. The prisoner had only started to read.'

Through the receiver came the cold, implacable voice.

'I want a check made on everything he has done since coming here. I shall be gone for a few days. I want the report by my return.'

There was a click as Wong Lee disconnected.

Ninety minutes into the operation there was complete silence in the OR as Yoshi made yet another fractional adjustment to the microscope lens by the merest touch on a foot-pedal at the base of the chair.

Hunched forward, eyes glued to the periscope-like device jutting from the main central stem, the neurosurgeon resembled a submarine captain searching for a target. Another fraction of a millimetre of the brain of Pope Nicholas came into focus.

Dr Poggi stood at the other eye-piece, Carina was on Yoshi's left, holding the power-operated diathermic probe.

'Irrigation,' Dr Poggi called out.

After checking with a thermometer, the instrument nurse handed him a glass syringe to douse the operating area with a mild antiseptic which exactly matched the Pope's body temperature. Dr Poggi sprayed and then sucked the liquid away from the area.

Fresh blood welled from a corner of the brain. Carina immediately electro-cauterised the vessel with the probe. Until all the blood vessels had been carefully sealed, Yoshi could not proceed.

From the TV monitor screen, Morton selected another image to record. This one showed the Pope's brain as resembling a large scale road map criss-crossed with red and blue streets and avenues; veins, running through rolling countryside; contours of muscle.

Yoshi resumed his lecture for the benefit of Hubert Messner and the other cardinals.

'Haemorrhage is the best way a surgeon can show his incompetency. So we never miss one little bleeder. It's what I was saying earlier, about not being surprised. When you drive a car in winter you expect icy patches, when you get this far, you expect bleeding. But you never hurry.'

After Carina completed cauterising, Yoshi's foot once more worked the pedal to move the microscope another fraction.

'There's no easy way in,' he muttered. 'But there was never going to be . . .'

From behind the curtain, the anaesthetist suddenly called.

'Pressure's dropping. Ninety over seventy!'

'Let it drop further,' Yoshi ordered calmly.

'Dr Kramer –,' the anaesthetist protested

'Don't argue!'

Dr Poggi raised his eyes to the monitor recording the Pope's blood-pressure.

He knew exactly what Yoshi was trying to do. He could better control the cranial bleeding if the pressure was reduced. Against that there was the risk of the Pope going into shock. The skill was to balance one against the other.

The pressure dipped down through the eighties, hovered on eighty for a moment, then continued on down into the upper seventies.

'No lower, Yoshi,' Dr Poggi called out.

'I see it, Carlo. The road in!'

At that moment blood welled up from around the tumour. Another blood vessel had burst.

Yoshi swore softly.

Dr Fortuti edged closer to the table.

'Keep away!' Dr Poggi snapped. 'We need this area clear!'

The physician stepped back.

'He's starting to drop again,' Dr Poggi called out. 'Connect the pump.'

The anaesthetist grabbed a pump handle and began to spin it, expressing blood intravenously from the bottle on the stand beside her trolley into the Pope's femoral artery.

'The big sucker,' Dr Poggi called out.

The instrument nurse handed him the wide-nozzled tube connected to the suction pump at his feet. He began to vacuum away the blood.

'Irrigation!'

The nurse slapped a syringe into Dr Poggi's hand. He sluiced the area.

'How's the pressure now?' Yoshi called, his eyes glued to the lens.

'Steadying at eighty.'

'Diathermy!' he ordered.

'On!' Carina replied.

She touched a blood vessel. There was a quick hissing.

'Good,' Yoshi growled. 'Pressure?'

'Eighty-two,' replied the anaesthetist.

'Keep that handle turning!'

Already half a litre of blood had been pumped into the Pope's arteries. Most of it had welled out through the ruptured vessel.

'Pressure?' Yoshi demanded again a moment later.

'Eighty-six, eighty-seven ... eighty-nine ... ninety.'

'Right! Try to hold him there!'

'Disconnecting the pump,' reported the anaesthetist.

Now the crisis was over, if blood was forced into the Pope's body too rapidly, it would send up his blood-pressure, which could cause another haemorrhage.

'You want to wait to see how he settles?' Dr Poggi asked.

Yoshi gave a quick head shake.

'I can't afford the time, Carlo. Once this thing starts to bleed, there's no knowing where we'll end up. The sac's starting to perforate. I wait any longer and I could rupture the whole thing. Then the whole exercise will have been pointless.'

Morton stared at the group around the table. He felt for Yoshi. He knew too well the kind of loneliness that now isolated the neurosurgeon from those around him. It always came with decision-taking.

For a moment longer the tableau remained frozen around the top of the table. Then Yoshi was giving rapid orders.

'Beam setting at one-o-six.'

'One-o-six microns setting,' confirmed the technician beside the laser unit.

'Cutting at one thousand.'

'One thousand watts it is.'

'Glasses on.'

A nurse stepped forward and quickly fitted modified safety glasses over the eyes of those around the table. The other members of the team moved away to avoid exposure to the beam.

Through the lens Yoshi continued to guide the laser image to the precise location of the tumour.

'Set for separate short pulses,' he called out.

'All set for separate short pulses,' the technician reported.

Yoshi continued to calculate the track for the beam.

He gave another touch on the foot pedal to bring the cutting edge directly over the tumour.

'Stand by!'

The beam that shot out from the laser was the purest white Carina had ever seen. The searing rod of light was no thicker than a pinhead. As swiftly as it appeared, it vanished. Yoshi had turned off the power by raising his foot off the pedal.

There was the pungent smell of burnt tissue in the air.

'Get the hell back, Fortuti!' Yoshi barked.

The Pope's physician drew back.

'There's nothing to see, Dr Fortuti,' Dr Poggi said patiently.

'Let's go again,' Yoshi ordered.

Another beam of white-hot light entered the Pope's brain. A second tiny cut, the shape of a half-moon, was made in the base of the meningioma.

'I'm going to try and cleave it free,' Yoshi said.

A third finger of light shot out of the laser. The smell of burnt tissue increased as another piece of tumour was incinerated.

'Cannula.'

The nurse passed the long thin micro-instrument to Yoshi. It was designed to pass through brain tissues without damaging them. It would not pass through the malignant growth.

Moving the cannula around the edges of the tumour, Yoshi obtained an exact outline of the meningioma.

He worked with infinite patience: a fraction of a centimetre, a pause and then on again.

He handed the instrument to the clear-away nurse.

'Blood-pressure?'

'Ninety over seventy,' the anaesthetist called.

'Going again!'

The beam came and went in a fraction of a second.

The acrid smell grew stronger as another sliver of malignant tissue was burned in the Pope's brain.


The chauffeur of the dark blue Fiat limousine grunted as he entered Via della Conciliazione. St Peter's Square was filled to overflowing.

'Where do they all come from, Your Eminence?' asked the chauffeur.

'Probably from all over the world,' Cardinal Enkomo replied wearily.

The flight from Johannesburg had been delayed; a twelve hour journey had become almost twenty. For the last mile, all the roads around the Vatican had been jammed with people hurrying to the square. From time to time the piazza was lit by bursts of light from the TV news crews.

As the car passed the forbidding palace of the old Holy Office, from where the Inquisition had been conducted, Julius Enkomo saw a reporter standing on the steps, talking into a camera. The cameraman panned to film the passing car. There were more newsmen at the gate of the Arch of the Bells.

Spotting the Fiat's Vatican registration, they surged forward, seeking comment from the cardinal. He smiled politely but said nothing.

The car was swiftly inside the gate. Moments later it had skirted the south side of the basilica and passed under the arch-way into St Damaso Courtyard. It stopped before the entrance to an arcade which had been glazed-in and its windows covered with white muslin curtains.

As Cardinal Enkomo stepped from the Fiat, a Swiss Guard brought his halberd to the vertical in salute. A sallow-faced figure in formal morning dress emerged from the entrance way and gave a reverential nod.

'What news?' Cardinal Enkomo asked.

The flunkey looked startled. He could not remember when a cardinal had last spoken to him.

'No news yet, Your Eminence,' he said, turning and leading the way into the Apostolic Palace.

Behind them the chauffeur carried Cardinal Enkomo's small

suitcase. In silence they walked up the wide, gently-sloping marble-floored corridor which led to a long straight staircase. Waiting at the top was Monsignor Linde.

When they reached him, the secretary gave Cardinal Enkomo a wintery smile. 'Welcome, Your Eminence.'

'How is the Holy Father?'

'He is still undergoing surgery.'

Monsignor Linde turned and led the way along a corridor. 'You are in your usual suite,' he explained. 'When you have settled in, the cardinal-secretary wants you to join him for dinner.'

Cardinal Enkomo sighed and looked at his watch. 'It's been a long day, Monsignor.'

Cardinal Linde gave another cold smile. 'We are used to long days here.'

He stopped outside a door. The flunkey opened the door, bowed formally and walked back down the corridor. The chauffeur deposited the bag inside the door and followed him.

'His Eminence will receive you at eight thirty in his apartment,' Monsignor Linde said.

With the merest inclination of his head, Monsignor Linde followed the others.

Cardinal Enkomo sighed and walked into his suite. Nowhere else except in the Vatican would he expect such a petty display of authority as the secretary had shown.

Once more the searing white laser beam shot into the Pope's brain.

'Almost there,' Yoshi murmured.

The brain beat a weak rhythm.

'Pressure?'

'Still at ninety over seventy,' the anaesthetist reported.

Yoshi touched the foot-pedal to release another beam.

Morton glanced at the wall clock. Almost three hours had passed.

While the anaesthetist controlled the Pope's bleeding and the surgical assistants monitored equipment and the flow of blood from the plastic bag on the drip stand, those not involved in essential tasks continued to watch the incredible skill and care Yoshi displayed.

The neurosurgeon lifted his eye from the microscope lens and turned in his chair. A nurse stepped forward and quickly wiped perspiration from around his eyes.

'Another drink,' Yoshi said.

A second nurse brought a bottle of orange juice. Carina pulled down Yoshi's mask and guided the straw between his lips. She had done so twice already in the past hour. Yoshi drank noisily and quickly.

Dr Poggi's eyes remained glued to his lens, studying the remains of the tumour.

The nurse removed the empty bottle and Carina adjusted Yoshi's mask. His eyes swept over the monitoring equipment. The Pope's vital signs remained stable.

Yoshi placed his eye to the lens. His foot worked the pedals. Another beam was followed by the stench of burnt tissue.

'Sucker!'

Carina handed him the suction funnel. Yoshi delicately worked it around the base of the tumour. His eyes still glued to the lens, he handed her back the instrument.

The magnifying power of the microscope showed a small discoloured area of brain. It was all that remained of the tumour.

'What do you think, Carlo?'

'It's freed.'

'Then I'm going for a removal!'

He looked up at the instrument nurse

'Bifurcater!'

She handed him a slim micro-instrument with scissor grip and tiny serrated clamps at the end.

Holding the instrument firmly, Yoshi gazed through the lens and began to manoeuvre the instrument down into the brain. On the screen Morton watched the grips being positioned either side of the meningioma. Then, in one steady pull, Yoshi lifted out the sac. He turned and dropped it into a stainless steel basin.

Dr Poggi's words signalled the onset of a second crisis.

'Another bleeder! Cautery on!'

'Pressure's dropping,' the anaesthetist said.

By then Yoshi had his eyes already back at the lens.

Morton followed the tight clipped dialogue around the table, a wealth of meaning in each phrase, all delivered with an economy he admired.

'Irrigation!'

'Blood up!'

'Pump running!'

'Irrigation!'

'Eighty-four!'

'Cautery!'

There was a quick hiss.

'Pressure no longer dropping!'

'Irrigation!'

'Cautery! I have it!'

Another hiss of coagulating blood.

'Climbing. Eighty-six . . . seven . . . ninety . . . steadying off,' reported the anaesthetist.

'Irrigation,' ordered Yoshi again.

Once more he sucked out blood and antiseptic fluid.

The tumour had left a cavity in the brain. In time this would fill with healthy tissue.

'Seems good to me. Carlo?'

Dr Poggi lifted his eyes from the lens.

'For me too. Very well done, Yoshi.'

'Is that it?' Carina asked. She could not quite believe it was finally over.

'That's it!' Yoshi said. 'Shelled and picked just like the textbook says!'

There was a spontaneous cheer from the others around the table. Only Dr Fortuti remained professionally solemn.

Yoshi eased himself off the chair and stood up and stretched.

'I'll close up,' Dr Poggi said. 'You've done all you said you would.'

Dr Fortuti walked over.

'I congratulate you, Dr Kramer. A truly remarkable achievement,' he said with a sudden and unexpected warmth.

'Thank you, doctor,' Yoshi murmured, surprised and pleased. 'But we're still not out of the woods yet. It'll be another twenty-four hours before we can say that.'

Yoshi turned to Carina. 'You did good.' He looked around the team. 'You all did good.'

Then he stared up one more time at a camera.

'Your Eminences, a little praying from now on won't go amiss.'

As Yoshi walked from the OR, Dr Poggi and Carina began the slow process of closing the pontiff's skull.

'You get good pictures?' Yoshi asked as he passed Morton.

Morton smiled and nodded.

The flood of calls had disrupted the routine of the Vatican switchboard. After logging 10,000 calls in a few hours, the nuns had given up. They had also abandoned their spot checks on outgoing calls.

The system had been introduced by Cardinal Messner as a cost-cutting exercise. Several of the Irish priests at Vatican Radio had been caught making lengthy international calls to relations back home and had been transferred to other duties.

At a little after six o'clock in the evening, the operators were too exhausted to be listening in to the outgoing call from the Apostolic Palace reporting that the operation was over and appeared to have been a success.

'Thank you for calling,' said Wong Lee in Lhasa.

He then left his office and walked the short distance to the helipad to begin the first stage of his long journey.

# 15

Another hour had passed since Chief Public Prosecutor Kramskay was chauffeur driven into the Kremlin.

The troika had listened impassively to his version of events at the dacha. Even when he placed all the blame on General Savenko, they asked no questions. Their silence planted in him the first seeds of concern. Finally the senior member of the troika, Ivanovitch Leonid Borakin – once Gorbachev's deputy and who bore an almost identical birthmark on his forehead to the former President – ordered Kramskay to wait in a side room.

The prosecutor tried to control his anxiety by dividing his time studying the frescoes on the ceiling of what once was Catherine the Great's bedroom and looking out of the window at the monstrous Emperor Cannon. The largest field artillery piece ever cast was designed to fire the pile of one-ton cannonballs stacked beside the barrel. The nearest it came to being fired was when the Tsar wondered if the cannon could be used to execute Rasputin, ensuring the monk's influence was removed from the face of the earth.

The lengthening wait made Kramskay wonder if he would himself soon face a firing squad over what happened at the dacha. Nowadays people were being executed for less. He was mildly surprised to realise that if he was to die, his one regret was never making use of the considerable fortune deposited in his name with Credit Suisse in Geneva. He wondered if there would be time to give his wife the account number. The money could realise her dream to travel. He owed her that much; he had given her so little.

In truth, he also knew he had not done a great deal to earn the money. Most of the information he had given Fung, the secretary could have obtained elsewhere.

Fung had called again shortly before the prosecutor was summoned to the Kremlin. He wanted a description of all those who had come with General Savenko to the dacha. When Kramskay had mentioned the Jew there was a low intake of breath on the line from Lhasa.

'Ah, Morton,' Fung said.

There was a deadness in the secretary's voice Kramskay had not heard before.

If the Jew returned to Moscow, he had assured Fung, he would be dealt with.

'Prosecutor Kramskay!' a new voice had interjected. 'You will do nothing to Morton or to anyone associated with him. That is a matter for others.'

Even now in this stuffy and over-heated room, Kramskay felt a chill as he remembered Wong Lee's voice.

He returned to the window. The weak afternoon sun had lengthened the shadow of the cannon barrel, so that it reached towards the Secret Garden where Stalin had walked in solitude. They said the fate of millions of people was decided in that small plot.

Kramskay heard the heavy arched door open behind him.

'Comrade prosecutor,' intoned the aide, 'they are ready for you.'

The staff officer led Kramskay back into the salon Napoleon used as his headquarters when he briefly occupied the Kremlin during the war of 1812.

Seated at the long oak table on which Bonaparte planned his ignominious retreat from Moscow were Borakin and the two other members of the troika. One was a former chairman of the KGB; the other the last but one Party secretary. All wore the uniforms of five star generals; a reminder they ruled as a military junta.

They stared at Kramskay as he came to attention before the table. It was stacked with neat piles of papers and files. He recognised one file: execution orders. Each death sentence was in its own black-bordered folder.

'Comrade Kramskay,' Borakin began, 'what happened at the dacha was most regrettable.'

Kramskay's eye flicked towards the death sentence files. Was his own already there?

'Comrade general. Can I at least –'

'Wait!' Borakin raised a hand. 'Your zealousness, while commendable, could have killed more than just a few *Spetsnaz* or Black Berets.'

Kramskay became silent and perfectly still, fearful now to destroy the sudden flicker of hope in those words. Zealousness and commendable.

Yet Borakin's cat-and-mouse cruelty was renowned. Many a man and woman had stood here, believing they were going to be spared, only to see their death warrant signed by Borakin.

'Comrade Kramskay,' Borakin continued. 'I want you to listen very carefully to what I am now going to ask you. Answer only when you are ready. And I need hardly remind you that if you lie it will be most regrettable.'

He paused then repeated, 'most regrettable'.

The others continued to stare fixedly at Kramskay.

'I understand, comrade general,' Kramskay whispered.

Borakin reached for a folder from a pile at his elbow. He opened it and began to read, nodding as he did so. He closed the file and looked at the prosecutor.

'What do you know of Operation Holy Cross?' Borakin abruptly asked.

His red epaulettes and lapel flashes gleamed in the chandelier's lights.

'Comrade general, I have never heard of such a thing,' Kramskay said clearly, his voice tinged with relief. Whatever this operation was, it had nothing to do with him. If it had gone wrong, he could not be held responsible.

'What do you think it is?' The question was politely enough put by Borakin.

Kramskay's feeling of relief grew. Surely he would not be executed for expressing an opinion?

'Has it anything to do with the religious revival organised by this American demagogue, Kingdom?'

'What do you know about him?'

'Really, nothing,' Kramskay said quickly.

'Really? Nothing?' Borakin asked in the same polite voice.

Kramskay flushed. He had answered too quickly. He forced himself to become calm.

'Well, only what many people know. Kingdom is preying on those who miss the security of the Party.'

He glanced towards the former Party secretary. The man's hard eyes stared back.

Kramskay continued. 'Kingdom uses a satellite which allows him to reach all the republics. In the old days, he would have been jammed. But now –'

He shrugged at the ex-chairman of the KGB. There was no reaction.

'Who paid for that satellite?' Borakin asked.

Kramskay counted up to five under his breath.

'I really don't know, comrade general.' He really had no idea.

'You hesitated, comrade prosecutor.'

'I was thinking, comrade general.'

Borakin smiled. It was not a reassuring smile.

He abruptly stood up and walked over to a wall map. It still bore the legend boldly stamped across its face: USSR. Borakin picked up a pointer leaning against the wall and began to jab at the map.

'You will know, of course, comrade prosecutor, what is happening here ... here ... and here ...'

The cue touched the half dozen Moslem republics.

'Religious fanaticism,' continued Borakin. 'Ready to sweep all before it.'

Borakin began to indicate spots on the rest of the map.

'The last time they came, monasteries were founded to act as regional strongholds to stop the hordes from reaching Moscow. To show that one faith could resist another. At one time there were 100,000 churches between the Black Sea and the Baltic. No wonder Marx called religion the opium of the people.'

The pointer came to rest on Moscow.

'Now there are only 10,000 churches. But still enough to make Operation Holy Cross a success.'

Borakin walked slowly back to the table and sat down.

'I will tell you now what this operation is. Depending on how you answer afterwards, I will decide whether you live or die, comrade prosecutor.'

There was a long moment of silence before Borakin continued.

'Operation Holy Cross is the code name for the Roman Pope to come and proclaim his faith on *Krusnaya Ploschad*.'

'Here, on Red Square?' Kramskay gasped.

'Do you have trouble in hearing?' the former Party secretary demanded sharply.

Kramskay shook his head.

Borakin placed his palms on the table and leaned forward.

'Comrade Kramskay! Just listen!'

Kramskay nodded, too stunned to speak. Why were they telling him this?

'We have known of this plan for some time. But until now it has not pleased us to discuss it with anyone. Until what happened at the dacha. If you had succeeded in delaying Dr Kramer, the Pope would almost certainly have had no chance to come here.'

'You want him to come?' Kramskay asked faintly.

'Yes.'

'Why, comrade general?'

Borakin reached for another file, opened it and flicked through the pages. Without looking up he asked his next question.

'Why do you work for Wong Lee?'

Borakin looked up. 'Take your time, comrade prosecutor. After all, your life depends on your answer.'

Kramskay's mouth worked but no words came.


In the Recovery Room adjoining the OR, Dr Poggi crouched beside the pontiff's bed. An hour had passed since the operation had ended. Pope Nicholas was lying on his side so as not to place pressure on his operation wound. Dr Poggi was holding and squeezing the Pope's hand and calling out.

'Your Holiness, can you hear me? If you can, try and open your eyes.'

Another squeeze. 'Can you feel that, Your Holiness? Just move your head if you can feel my hand.'

A further squeeze. 'Try and open your eyes.'

As soon as Pope Nicholas responded to commands, the neurosurgeon would have some reassurance there was no brain damage.

Dr Poggi squeezed the Pope's hand harder.

'Come on, Your Holiness. You can hear me!'

Pope Nicholas stirred.

Dr Poggi rose from his crouching position and turned to Carina and Dr Fortuti.

'Keep talking and squeezing.'

Dr Fortuti knelt beside the bed and clasped the Pope's hand.

'*Sanctissimo Padre*,' he said. 'This is Dr Fortuti. Can you hear me?'

Carina bent her head close to the pontiff's face.

'He's trying to say something,' she cried.

Dr Poggi bent to listen. A low groan came from the Pope.

'*Sanctissimo Padre*, can you hear me?' continued Dr Fortuti.

Carina lifted one of the Pope's eyelids. The pupil was still dilated.

'He's coming round.'

Dr Poggi looked at the anaesthetist standing on the other side of the bed beside her trolley.

'Another fifteen minutes and you should be able to disconnect.'

'*Sanctissimo Padre* –' Dr Fortuti repeated.

As Dr Poggi walked from the room a weak mumble came from Pope Nicholas's lips.

Carina once more bent to listen. She lifted her head and looked at Dr Fortuti.

'He is trying to say something. About his operation and a Holy Cross –'

Standing inside the door Morton marvelled at the Pope's willpower and commitment.


'What you have committed is treason!' rumbled the former head of the KGB. He put down the pen he had used for writing down Kramskay's answers.

For the past hour Borakin had carefully extracted every detail of the prosecutor's contacts with Wong Lee and Fung. From time to time the general had checked a time or date with the file before him.

'Our records show you have at least answered truthfully,' he had finally said.

The silence was broken by the former Party secretary.

'Treason for money. The worst kind of treason,' he said pitilessly.

'I will repay the money,' Kramskay whispered.

They continued to stare at him. It took him a while to realise there was something else in their eyes except contempt. It was calculation.

When Borakin spoke his voice was as polite as always.

'Comrade Kramskay, we want you to go on working for Wong Lee.'

The prosecutor's mouth worked once more and, once more, no words came.

'But from now on you will report everything he says and does to us. You will be given a permit that allows you access to any one of us day or night,' continued Borakin.

He reached for a sheet of paper and began to write.

Kramskay looked at the former Party secretary. 'I will take no more money from Wong Lee.'

Borakin looked up. 'You will continue exactly as before. Otherwise he will become suspicious.'

He thrust the sheet of paper across the table. 'Your permit.'

The troika continued to study the prosecutor.

'Because it is important you clearly understand what is involved, I will explain to you why your treason is being overlooked,' Borakin said.

Kramskay picked up the permit and quickly folded and pocketed it as Borakin flicked open the folder he had consulted previously, as if to check his facts. He looked up.

'Wong Lee has been arming our Moslems. Like us, he knows the Islamic Confederation is doomed. Soon the republics will be powerful enough to try and overcome the rest of us. As you know, this once great nation is still divided: Ukraine against Moldavia, Byelorussia against Georgia, the Baltic Republics against everyone, especially Mother Russia herself.'

Kramskay nodded. 'Gorbachev should never have –'

'Forget that!' the former KGB chairman rasped. 'Just listen!'

Borakin glanced at the file before continuing.

'With his Holy Cross operation, the Pope hopes to unify them – and at the same time extend the proverbial olive branch to the Moslems. He wants their mullahs and imams to join the Patriarch of the Russian Orthodox Church and his priests in a great act of reconciliation in Red Square.

'From what you have told us, it is clear that Wong Lee fears this. So he will do everything to stop Holy Cross succeeding. It is in our interests to allow him to succeed.'

Kramskay waited, transfixed. An hour ago he had felt close to death, now he was being made privy to the inner secrets of the troika.

Borakin glanced at his colleagues before continuing.

'We do not know yet precisely how Wong Lee will try to

destroy the operation. But we are certain he will stage some incident – General Savenko has told us.'

Kramskay's mouth began to work once more.

Borakin looked to his left, at the former chairman of the KGB.

'We all remember the world outcry after the KGB was accused of staging the attempted assassination of the Polish pontiff because he was meddling where he had no business. Think of the reaction there will be if Pope Nicholas is assassinated before the world's television cameras – and we can say categorically it was the work of Islamic fundamentalists?

'That would create an outcry throughout the entire Christian world against our Moslem republics. With no more than the minimum of manoeuvring we will be able to persuade the Americans, the British and French, even the Germans, to help us deal with them. In many ways, it would be no different to the successful appeal Kuwait made after Iraq invaded. And the threat we now face from the Moslem republics would be over.

'And, of course, the other republics would understand why the power must remain where it always was, here in Moscow. There would be an end to this talk of secession. Instead, there would be a return to the days when the world looked with proper respect at us.'

'And Wong Lee?' Kramskay managed to whisper.

Borakin did not hesitate.

'We would enter into our own arrangement with him to make us sufficiently strong again to challenge the West. And next time we will not fail!'

Yoshi had returned to the Recovery Room. He had changed into a clean scrub suit. Like the others he wore a mask.

Plastic prongs inserted in the Pope's nostrils were connected to a rubber pipe running to a wall socket from which flowed oxygen to assist his breathing. Electrodes pasted to his chest were connected to a heart monitor. A clear liquid trickled from an IV bottle into an arm.

The anaesthetist had left, replaced by the team of specialist post-operative nurses. Carina and Dr Fortuti remained at the bedside.

Pope Nicholas's eyes were open.

'How do you feel, Your Holiness?' Yoshi asked.

There was a slight pause before Pope Nicholas answered. 'Very tired.'

'Would you like a drink?' Yoshi asked. The meningioma had been near the vagus which controlled swallowing. He needed to check the function.

Dr Fortuti held a glass from which the Pope sipped.

Carina noted on the chart. 'Patient swallowed easily, did not seem very thirsty.'

Pope Nicholas allowed his hand to stray towards the head-dressing. Yoshi was pleased. The pontiff was continuing to regain full movement.

The neurosurgeon continued to engage him in conversation.

'Is your head beginning to hurt?'

'Yes.'

'Do you feel nausea?'

'No.'

'Can you grip my hand?'

The grip was stronger than an hour ago. Yoshi told Carina to give Pope Nicholas something to combat the headache. He looked down at his patient.

'You're doing fine, Your Holiness.'

'Has Cardinal Enkomo arrived?' The voice was low but clear.

'Yes. You'll see him later. Right now, I just want you to sleep.'

Carina injected the sedative and, after a moment, the Pope closed his eyes and began to breathe deeply.

After Cardinal Messner appeared on the balcony above the main door of the basilica and read out a brief statement that the Supreme Pontiff had regained consciousness and his doctors were satisfied with his condition, the atmosphere in St Peter's Square became almost carnival.

Around Caligula's Obelisk thousands of people began a sing-along. Inside Bernini's colonnade a charismatic persuaded hundreds to kneel around him in prayer. Long lines of people waited to leave flowers at the Arch of the Bells and the Bronze Door. Food and drink sellers kept everyone supplied. The first vendors of T-shirts displaying the Pope's head appeared and did a brisk trade. There was also a steady sale for postcards of the pontiff's portrait. Other peddlers offered fake papal coins and plastic cruci-fixes and rosaries. The junk was being fingered by many of the devout as they wended their way into the basilica.

Extra police had been drafted in. They helped carry those in the throng who had fainted to first aid posts and cleared the way for ambulances. From time to time the police pulled a pickpocket from the crowd and hustled him to one of the waiting paddy wagons.

While the cardinal-secretary was on the balcony, the American bishop in charge of the Vatican Press Office walked on to the stage of the Audience Hall adjoining the Holy Office. As a back-drop he had the largest bronze sculpture on earth – 'The Risen Christ'.

After he had read an identical statement to Cardinal Messner's, the bishop refused to answer any questions from the twelve thousand print and electronic media journalists in the hall. He walked off stage to a great howl of protest.

'Journalists on the rampage are not a pretty sight,' Morelli growled. He picked up one of the phones on his desk and gave orders for the *Vigili* to clear the chamber.

'You should have seen the peace conference in Madrid,' Morton said. 'The press behaved worse than the delegates.'

Since coming from the hospital they had been in Morelli's office in the small palace behind the basilica.

On the office walls medieval paintings in heavy gilt frames were interspersed with state-of-the-art surveillance screens pro-viding pictures from all over the Vatican's public areas. One of the screens was now linked to the Concorde's Communications Centre. The aircraft was still parked at Rome Airport and the Communications Centre enabled Morton to see and speak to anyone, and be spoken to, on a secure circuit.

He had already used it to inform Prime Minister Karshov in Tel Aviv about the outcome of the operation, adding that Yoshi was staying on to monitor the Pope's progress and he would remain with him.

Morton watched the picture from cameras high in the nave of St Peter's of the praying multitude. Beside him, Morelli spoke into a phone.

'There's a couple of pickpockets over by the Pietà. Go grab them, Antonio.'

On the screen they watched a *Vigili* moving towards Michel-angelo's best-loved work, the only one in the Basilica to bear his name.

'I've only got ten men to cover six acres of floor,' growled

Morelli. 'Without the cameras they wouldn't have a chance.'

Other cameras, sited between the statues on top of Bernini's colonnade relayed the scene from the square.

'They'll stay all night,' Morelli predicted. 'Nothing like an old-fashioned drama to pack them in.'

He turned to Morton. 'Think he'll really pull through?'

'Yoshi's hopeful.'

'If he's wrong, we could have a real problem, David. Not just with Holy Cross, but the whole direction the Church will go.'

Morelli walked over to his desk and picked up a sheet of paper.

'One of the switchboard sisters does a bit of eavesdropping for me. She overheard this while you were still in the OR.'

He handed the paper to Morton. In a neat hand was the message.

15.00 hours. Secretary of Wong Lee telephoned to invite Cardinal Muller to meet Mr Wong in Hawaii. His Eminence said he would be happy to do so, but it depends on what happens here.

Morton handed back the paper.

'How do they know each other?' he asked.

'His Eminence has the Council for Public Affairs in his brief. Part of the job includes supervising all our rebuilding. Wong Holdings has had the world-wide contract for the past couple of years. Muller went all the way to Manila to negotiate it. It's due to be looked at again in a few weeks. That's probably what all this is about – Wong Lee wanting to get in first.'

'Maybe.'

Morton went to the keyboard that linked the screen to Concorde. He punched buttons and at once the face of the CCO appeared. Morton asked to be connected to Chantal Bouquet in Tel Aviv.

Moments later she was on his screen, sitting at her desk in that corner of the fourth floor of Morton's Kingdom which Chantal had made her own.

'I hear Yoshi did a good job,' she said.

'For sure.'

Chantal adjusted her turquoise-framed glasses and waited. He told her about the intercept and what Morelli had just said.

'Tell Lester I want his operatives to check for all past contacts

Muller has had with Wong Lee. Not just the building side of things. But other times they could have met. Religious conferences Muller would have attended. That sort of thing. See if Wong Lee was there, or that secretary of his, Fung. Then run the same checks on the Reverend Kingdom. Then for contacts between the troika and Muller. I want His Eminence checked against pretty well everyone Lester has on tape. I want him to repeat the whole process for Cardinal-Secretary Messner.

'I want Danny to send a surveillance team here to keep track of Muller and Messner and anyone else who turns up.'

Morton glanced at Morelli.

'Okay with you, Claudio?'

After a moment's hesitation Morelli nodded. 'But they'll have to operate outside the Vatican.'

Morton turned back to the screen.

'Tell Danny it's a long-pole job. I want another team locked into Kingdom in Malibu. Make sure Bill Gates knows. He doesn't take kindly to the unannounced.'

'I'll double-flash Swift Renovations in Los Angeles.'

Morton had created the company to handle all Mossad's work in the United States, and its staff were experts at anything from refurbishing a safe house to providing back-up for a take-out – an assassination by Covert Action of a known terrorist. But their speciality was surveillance.

'I want the weather satellite re-orbited so that we get double the passes over Lhasa. Have Humpty Dumpty put extra men on to sifting everything the sat picks up.'

'Bitburg's not going to like this, David. You're blowing away his budget.'

'Right now there are more important things to worry about than whether Walter gets to balance the books,' Morton said.


A little before eight o'clock, Cardinal Enkomo strode through the maze of the Apostolic Palace. The steel tips on his shoes rang on the marble as he passed antechambers, meeting halls and storage places.

Harald Asmusson had once said there were a thousand rooms in the palace. He had tried to call Harald but the duty sergeant explained the commandant was down in St Peter's Square. When he tried to phone Morton, the switchboard operator said she had no record of him. He had smiled; that would be Morton. If he made it to heaven St Peter himself would probably never know Morton had passed through the gates. When he tried to phone the hospital, the nun said she had orders to connect no calls.

He had managed to get through to Cape Town. Father O'Sullivan had said the crisis with the food distributors was over, after the government had suddenly announced it was considering introducing legislation ordering all the distributors to release supplies at pre-storm prices. Tens of millions of rand had been wiped off the shares of companies, including Food Consolidated. He had called to thank Minister Van der Vaal, who had not been available.

Walking briskly, cassock swishing softly in rhythm with his stride, Cardinal Enkomo saw lights burning in the prefecture of the pontifical household. The staff would be busy drafting formal letters of thanks to heads of state for their enquiries about His Holiness. Apart from hearing Cardinal Messner's statement on Vatican Radio, he had no real idea how the operation had gone.

He passed Swiss Guards who acknowledged him with a single stamp of their halberds on the floor. The *Vigili* strolling through the corridors nodded. He was just another prelate going about his business.

Reaching the corridor to the cardinal-secretary's apartment, he was greeted by a man in a well-cut lounge suit sat at a mahogany desk.

'Good evening, Eminence. Second door on the left,' murmured the *uscieri*.

'Thank you.'

The flunkey noted the cardinal's time of arrival in a log book.

The door was opened with a flourish by a cleric in a scarlet-buttoned and piped soutane. He looked as if he needed to shave only once a week.

'Welcome, Eminence,' he murmured. 'How very good to see you.'

The monsignor's blond wavy hair and haughty expression gave him the appearance of an over-fed, over-indulged and over-bearing cherub. He closed the door and led the way past a tapestry by Raphael showing Christ commissioning St Peter. The monsignor walked like a premature bishop.

Cardinal Messner was waiting in the main reception room, warming himself before the electric fire in the marble surround. Above the mantel hung a portrait of the mighty Charlemagne.

The ceiling mural, Renaissance wallpaper and Bavarian furniture made the room seem like a museum.

'Good evening.' Cardinal Messner came forward, glass in hand.

'Good evening, cardinal-secretary. Do you have any news of His Holiness?'

'He sleeps. We will know more when he awakes.'

'Do the doctors give any indication beyond what you said on the radio?'

Cardinal Messner gave a wintry smile.

'No. Doctors are worse than theologians when it comes to going out on a limb.'

'I will need to see His Holiness as soon as possible.'

'About this report of yours?'

'Yes.'

Cardinal Messner turned to the monsignor. 'Klaus, will you get His Eminence a drink.'

The cardinal-secretary turned back to his guest. 'How have you left matters in South Africa?'

While the monsignor went to a drinks table in a corner of the room, Cardinal Enkomo explained that food was now being distributed.

'A relief in every sense of the word. And this time your gamble paid off. But confronting a government is something I have never encouraged.'

'Sometimes there is no alternative.'

Cardinal Messner sipped his whisky.

'There's always an alternative if you look hard enough.'

The monsignor brought the wine to Cardinal Enkomo.

'Thank you Klaus, I won't need you again tonight,' murmured Cardinal Messner.

The priest inclined his head and walked from the room.

The cardinal-secretary motioned to armchairs on either side of the fireplace.

'Now this report of yours. Give it to me. I will make sure he receives it, Julius.'

'I really need to speak personally with His Holiness, cardinal-secretary.'

'Hubert, please. Away from the office, I prefer informality.'

Cardinal Messner gave another wintry little smile.

'Very well. Hubert.'

Cardinal Enkomo sipped his wine before continuing. 'We both know my report is out-of-channel. I was only asked to prepare it because of my specialist knowledge of Israel and the contacts I made there.'

'Of course.'

'Because this is a personal report ... Hubert, I really feel I have to give it to His Holiness myself.'

Cardinal Messner drank his whisky and looked at Julius Enkomo.

'It will be some time yet before he can read anything. In the meantime, as camerlengo, I have to keep things running. That includes reading all the reports intended for Nicholas.'

'Including those relating to Holy Cross, Hubert?'

The cardinal-secretary rose and walked to the drinks table and poured another generous measure. He splashed in soda and continued to speak.

'I will be frank with you, Julius. This plan of Nicholas's is doomed because even if Israel agrees to his visit, the new Patriarch of the Russian Orthodox Church is opposed to it.'

'Why?'

Cardinal Messner sat down and drank some whisky.

'You've forgotten your history, Julius. Our brethren in the Russian Orthodox not only connived but rejoiced in Stalin's suppression of our Church. Until Gorbachev, the Orthodox remained a pillar of the Socialist State. The present Patriarch is still having difficulty in coming to terms with the religious liberty sweeping many of the old Catholic republics. He's fearful that we will try and reclaim what was rightfully ours until 1946.'

'Will we?'

The cardinal-secretary drank more whisky.

'Let me answer your question another way. There's a dangerous movement which promotes the notion that we should be ready to sup with the old Communist devil now he's supposed to have lost his teeth. Everybody forgets how easy it is to get a new set.'

Cardinal Enkomo frowned.

'But there's nothing new in rapprochement. I remember when I was still a student we all felt Pope John's encyclical "Peace On Earth" paved the way to building links with the Russians. Even John Paul saw virtue in re-opening the old bridge between Rome and Moscow.'

The cardinal-secretary gave another wintry smile.

'That was his Slavonic emotionalism. It sounds exciting when you speak of re-opening an old bridge. But it's dangerous experimentation. And it goes against all the traditions. Rome has never spoken or decided in a hurry. No one denies we need to seek an accommodation with the old enemy. But this must be on our terms. Remember what Machiavelli said – that any change must leave a toothing stone upon which to secure the future. The time is not ready for us to perform such dentistry.'

'But how long can the raging toothache continue?'

'Now that's a big question, Julius. Why don't we explore it over dinner?'

Cardinal Messner led the way to the dining room.

In the Recovery Room, the specialist nurses worked as a quiet and efficient team. One regularly checked the pontiff's body temperature and his supply of oxygen, watching for any sign of a build-up of mucus in his bronchials. She regularly used a suction apparatus to vacuum inside the Pope's mouth.

A second nurse was making sure their patient's head remained in the exact position Dr Poggi had indicated. Great care had to be taken that the Pope did not turn on the side where the tumour had been. If he did, part of his brain could collapse into the cavity left by the excised meningioma – causing almost certain death. It would take about six hours for the brain to swell naturally and fill the cavity.

The third nurse continuously watched the monitoring equipment displaying Pope Nicholas's vital signs.

In the past few minutes, he had become restless. To keep his head in place, a bandage had been wound around his dressing and tied to the side of the bed-frame.

'His temperature's climbed a degree,' reported the first nurse.

'You think a clot could be forming?' asked the second nurse.

'Too early to tell.'

The risk of post-operative blood clotting was ever present despite the time and care Yoshi had taken to seal off bleeding points. It needed only one minute vessel not to have coagulated for a clot to form with fatal consequences.

The monitor nurse cast her eye over her screens. The Pope's pulse was weak, but not alarmingly so. But his temperature was still rising. The nurse at the bed head used her pencil torch to shine light into the Pope's eyes. He stirred and mumbled something unintelligible.

'I'm going to call Dr Poggi,' she said, walking quickly to the wall telephone.

While the dinner progressed through three courses, Cardinal Enkomo had glimpsed the nuns handing the valet dishes to be served. Fine food had been matched by choice wines; eaten and drunk from plates and goblets rimmed with gold.

Throughout the meal, Cardinal Messner had largely guided the direction of the conversation and he continued to as the valet removed the remains of the *dolci* and began to serve brandy.

'Today, more than ever, Julius, the Church is in an alien, hostile environment. Those of us who are entrusted with its destiny must walk a thin line between protecting her proper interests and not offending the civil regimes. It was never easy at the best of times. The Polish pontiff found that when he tried to impose his authority on Middle Europe.'

The cardinal-secretary sniffed his brandy.

'And look at the legacy he left us to deal with in Poland. An economic crisis that God Himself could not solve. All because he encouraged the local hierarchy to meddle where they had no hope of succeeding. They'd forgotten the basic rule of not getting involved unless you are sure you'll win.'

Cardinal Enkomo declined the offer of cognac and looked across the table at his host.

'If His Holiness taught me one thing, it was never be frightened of speaking out when you know it's right. He learned that from John Paul, his predecessor. All the great Popes have always spoken out – even if in the end they did not achieve everything.'

'Of course, Julius, of course. But I am speaking of something else. The danger to the Church if we become too involved with the secular authority. Every time we ask the State for something, we run the risk of compromising the Church.'

He took a mouthful of brandy and savoured it. 'You don't know what you're missing, Julius.'

Cardinal Enkomo made a polite movement with his hand. 'I was never one for spirits. I saw what the stuff did to my people in the shebeens.'

'Ah, yes . . . a world, I fear, a little beyond my experience.'

The cardinal-secretary cupped the glass between his hands.

'As I was saying, Julius, we cannot become embroiled with states like Israel and what remains of the Soviet Empire. And that is precisely what this Holy Cross operation will do.'

'His Holiness does not see it like that.'

'Of course not, Julius. But he's never taken the long view. He is simply concerned with the needs of the faith. He's more of a visionary than anything.'

'Not a bad thing, surely?'

'But not the only thing.'

Cardinal Messner drained his glass. The valet stepped forward from the credenza with the decanter. He refilled the glass then withdrew.

Cardinal Messner took a mouthful and continued.

'Not the only thing at all, Julius! And quite beside the point! The point is that Holy Cross will open a Pandora's Box!'

Julius Enkomo realised his host was a little drunk. But he had not come all this way to back down now.

'Hubert, I am convinced, totally convinced, that what His Holiness has in mind will not only benefit the Church by bringing it closer to the secular authorities, but will also have a huge impact upon the community of the faithful of all religions.

'He may not have as fine a grasp as you of the wider ideological subtleties of Vatican diplomacy. We both know he has never been one for detail. He has others for that. But he has a directness of purpose. And right now that purpose is to show how the Church can act as a great bridge builder between all the faiths! In that way he can teach the truth of religious freedom in the context of a real commitment to human rights. You are right. The Holy Father is a visionary. And I share his vision.'

In the silence Julius Enkomo saw no emotion in the cardinal-secretary's face.

Dr Poggi and Yoshi walked into the recovery room.

'Any change?' the Italian surgeon asked.

The monitor equipment nurse explained the Pope's restlessness had increased and his temperature continued to climb.

Yoshi ran his eye over the screens.

'Let's get a fan set-up, Claudio. We need to get his fever down. It's probably no more than post-op trauma or the effects of broken-down protein. But it could just mask a clot.'

The nurse stripped away the bedding and a damp sheet was placed over the Pope. A high-powered electric fan began to play on its surface.

Yoshi watched for a moment, then made another decision.

'I'll give him a cocktail.'

The mixture of drugs would help control the pontiff's temperature and keep him relaxed, so reducing his restlessness. The cocktail would also act as a subtle psychological booster in the twilight world Pope Nicholas was now in.

Monsignor Hanlon was about to leave his office. Every government with diplomatic relations with the Holy See had either telephoned or faxed expressions of pleasure at the successful outcome of the operation. Colonel Asmusson reported that the Swiss Guards had so far received over 20,000 floral gifts. These were now on their way to Rome's hospitals. One of the city's telephone exchanges had been hooked into the Vatican's phone system to help deal with the tens of thousands of calls from well-wishers all over the world.

In between handling high level calls, Monsignor Hanlon had arranged accommodation for Morton, Yoshi and Carina in guest suites identical to Cardinal Enkomo's. He had also asked one of the sisters who ran the papal household to find a change of clothes for Carina. A few moments ago the nun had phoned to say she had bought underwear and a dress in one of the boutiques just beyond the Vatican walls.

He had taken calls from several cardinals asking to be among the first allowed to see Pope Nicholas. The secretary had told them that any decision about visitors was entirely a matter for the Pope's doctors.

Dr Fortuti had called inviting him to supper. He had politely declined. The prospect of spending the rest of the evening listening to the papal physician give a blow-by-blow description of the operation was not appealing.

Now, as he was about to leave for a quiet meal in his own apartment behind the Apostolic Palace, the phone once more rang. When he picked up the receiver he was surprised.

'This is the Kremlin. Please wait for General Borakin,' instructed a man's voice.

A moment later the head of the troika was on the line.

'On behalf of my two colleagues and the people of our nation,

I convey our relief the Holy Father has been successfully operated on.'

He's reading the words, thought Monsignor Hanlon. But then he could not be certain. He'd never taken a call before from the Kremlin.

General Borakin continued to speak slowly and carefully.

'It is our great wish that when the Holy Father has fully recovered, he will travel here to bless all those who work with us. He will be most welcome as a symbol of peace between nations and the apostle of flexible and positive thinking.'

'Thank you, General Borakin. Thank you so very much. I will personally make sure this wonderful news is the first His Holiness will receive when he awakes.'

'Good,' intoned the voice from Moscow. 'Now goodbye and *mir* – peace!'

# 16

For the next three days Morton's life took on a pattern. Twice a day Yoshi continued to report that Pope Nicholas was making a routine recovery. The worry about a blood clot had passed.

After twenty-four hours of intensive care the pontiff had been moved to his own bedroom on the fourth floor of the Apostolic Palace. Yoshi had decided it would be psychologically beneficial for him to be in familiar surroundings. For the same reason he had ordered that the medical equipment at the bedside be reduced to an absolute minimum, and only one nurse need be present. Each worked an eight hour roster.

The cheap alarm clock was back in its accustomed place beside the Bible on the Pope's night table.

Early on the second day a nurse helped the Supreme Pontiff, closely watched by Yoshi, Dr Poggi and Dr Fortuti, get out of bed and gingerly stand up. Walking slowly, Pope Nicholas crossed the polished wooden floor to the window. The glass was covered with a net curtain to protect those inside against prying camera lenses.

At this hour the view was at its best, a hundred and more spires, towers, monuments and palaces and, glinting in the sunrise to his immediate right, the most magnificent of all the domes, Michelangelo's crowning glory on the basilica.

He glanced down at the crowded square, every inch as full now as it had been since news of his successful operation was announced. People stood in respectful silence, so that even up here he could hear the unique sound of Rome, the echoing hum produced by the city being built on hardened volcanic ash, the *tufo*.

Impulsively, Pope Nicholas pulled back a corner of the curtain and waved. A great collective gasp of recognition came from below then a thunderous cheering and clapping.

It had gone on long after Pope Nicholas returned to bed. Since then he had slept a great deal in between light meals. Apart from the medical teams he had no visitors.

The image of the pontiff at the window had appeared in newspapers and on television screens around the world.

Pope Nicholas was signalling business as usual, Morelli told Morton when he had next arrived in the security office to receive the first reports.

Marcus Baader and Jacques Lacouste both said their operatives had still turned up nothing incriminating about Wong Holdings. The other reports were more promising.

Norm Stratton's agents in Beijing had discovered Wong Lee had spent an entire day with the Chinese leadership before flying to Hawaii, where he remained in the penthouse suite of the finest of all the hotels he owned in the islands.

Swift Renovations in Los Angeles reported that the team assigned to run surveillance on the Church of True Belief complex had discovered the Reverend Kingdom was booked on the next flight to Hawaii.

In Tampa, Florida, an FBI unit, running unrelated surveillance on the mansion of Franco Umberto, overheard the head of the most powerful Mafia family in the United States order the pilot of his private Lear jet to file an immediate flight plan to Honolulu. The news had been routed to FBI headquarters in Washington DC and, because of Umberto's known links with international arms traffic, copied to Gates. He had come on screen to tell Morton.

Chantal had also appeared on the monitor. The operative she had sent to Hong Kong had learned that Wong Lee had told China's leaders it was time for the People's Liberation Army to reclaim disputed border lands with the Moslem republic of Kazakhstan. Her agents in Seoul, Karachi, Rangoon and Kathmandu reported that managers of local Wong Holdings companies had instructions from Lhasa to grant extended credit to clients in the republic – and to warn them that the Chinese army was poised to attack. The credit could be used to purchase arms from Wong Holdings.

Morton asked Stratton to intensify surveillance in Beijing, and Gates to have the FBI do the same with Umberto. Humpty Dumpty was told to add Umberto's name to his Hot Watch list and Lester Final's programmers asked to search for links between Umberto and Wong Lee, and any the Mafia boss had with Cardinals Messner and Muller.

A Swift Renovations operative in Los Angeles was ordered to travel on the same flight as the Reverend Kingdom, another to fly in and await the arrival of Umberto's jet.

Two more – posing as honeymooners – were detailed to stay in Wong Lee's hotel. Their luggage included a Samsonite suitcase identical to the one lost in the hotel fire in Istanbul.

Chantal was told to send a man to the borders with China and Kazakhstan.

Afterwards Morton read the revised psycho-profile the Professor had faxed. It contained an analysis of the great fulfilment Wong Lee derived from his personal killings. The number of his victims most certainly had increased as the predatory nature of his financial operations expanded. In both cases he was engaged upon the same process – destroying all those who stood in his way. It would be the only way he could still find pleasure.

Morton had finished reading when Percival West came on screen from London. In his crisp parade-ground voice, the MI5 chief detailed how, in a series of lightening, yet totally discreet moves, Wong Holdings had bought its way into Britain's armaments, electronics and shipping industries. The conglomerate's investment portfolio was also spread over the top one hundred British companies. Any time he chose to withdraw, Wong Lee could seriously damage the British economy. Morton was certain the same could be said of every stock market Wong Lee dominated.

After West's report, Morton went for a walk in the Vatican gardens. There he found Cardinal Enkomo walking across the grass and saying his breviary.

They had spent an hour together in the cardinal's apartment, talking about Steve and Dolly and their days together in Jerusalem. They had spoken as if it was only yesterday and not the three years which had elapsed since they last met. The cardinal showed him a copy of his report. Morton was impressed by its quiet authority.

Cardinal Enkomo said opposition to Holy Cross was growing

inside the Vatican. He had described his dinner with the cardinal-secretary and how, as he was leaving, Monsignor Hanlon telephoned Messner with news of the call from General Borakin. Messner's face had paled.

At that point the bleeper which Morelli had given to Morton had gone off. He had hurried back to the security office – only to find it was Bitburg on screen once more requesting the report on the incident at the dacha and asking when Morton was returning to Tel Aviv. He had been non-committal in both matters.

He had once more left the security office to walk through the grounds of the tiny city state. He needed time to think. Why did the troika want the Pope in Moscow? Given the troika's previous opposition to the Church, that was astonishing. Did the troika's change of mind have anything to do with Wong Lee's request to see Muller? The cardinal fiercely opposed the troika. And he would continue to oppose Holy Cross. But where did all this fit in with Umberto going to see Wong Lee?

By the time he reached the white painted pavilion dedicated to Pope Pius the Fourth, a new thought began to emerge. Was Muller the only contact Wong Lee had in the Vatican? Or was there someone else, someone who would be above suspicion?

He continued to walk past the buildings which had served as hospices, sacristies and residences down the centuries.

There were hundreds of prelates, scattered through the Sacred Congregation and Tribunes. Logically it would be someone in the Secretariat of State, the core of much of the policy-making of the Curia. That still left scores of priests. And what would be their motive for helping Wong Lee? Some secretly nurtured resentment against the rigid caste system they had chosen to live in?

He reached the summit of Vatican Hill and turned to walk back to the Apostolic Palace.

Was it someone who was tired of sitting in his Curia cubbyhole, watching the world pass by in an endless stream of memoranda, which he read and initialled, increasingly realising no one was interested in his opinion? Had Wong Lee flattered him? Given him the chance to talk, to explain his own views on where the papacy should be going? Or was it someone with an eye on the main chance? Tired of Church life, seeing a new one at Wong Holdings?

Was it a priest with a compulsion to run risks, who simply got a kick out of kicking over the traces? Julius had said the Vatican had its quota of such prelates.

Ahead, Morton could hear singing coming from the Sistine Chapel.

He entered the nave and stood for a moment staring at the awesome *Last Judgement*, Michelangelo's monumental act of atonement for the sack of Rome, which remained both an artistic masterpiece and a forceful warning of the terrible fate awaiting all heretics.

The choir was rehearsing in the stalls, their voices raised in plaintive song.

That call of Borakin's was strange. Why make the offer to Sean and not to Messner? Unless they wanted to test the water. Hoping the news would leak and stir up the opponents in the Vatican to the visit. That made sense. If things went wrong, the troika could withdraw the offer and lay the blame on those who opposed it. But that still did not explain why they wanted the Pope in Moscow.

The plainchant soared to the magnificence of the painted ceiling. Steve had been right: there could not be a more striking setting in which to celebrate God.

Sean had not mentioned Borakin's call. He had come across him twice in the past couple of days. Each time Sean had greeted him cheerfully as he had hurried on. Perfectly understandable of course. Sean was a busy man and had no obligation to keep him informed.

'Goethe said this was singing to nourish the soul,' Carina murmured behind him.

He turned. She was wearing the dress the nun had brought, with a pair of open-toe sandals on her feet. Her hair looked as if she had tried to comb some order into it with her fingers.

'You like it?' she asked, nodding towards the choir grouped before their maestro. 'It's how Allegri intended the *Miserere* to be performed.'

'You studied music?' he asked.

'My father wanted me to become a violinist. He said there were already too many doctors in Russia. If I became good enough as a violinist, I could travel abroad. That way I would have a chance to escape, seek political asylum, perhaps even get to Israel. Right to the very end he was obsessed with the idea that one of us had to go there. It never seemed particularly important to me.'

'It isn't,' Morton said. 'Being a Jew is a state of mind. Like being a Catholic. Or of any other faith or race.'

They stood for a moment listening to the singing. Then she turned and looked at him, very carefully.

'David, will you take me to dinner tonight?'

He smiled at how serious she sounded.

'For sure,' he said.

At that moment his bleeper went.

'I'll pick you up at eight,' he said, hurrying from the chapel.

When he reached the security office, Morelli said the Pathfinder had called.

The Pathfinder – Morton had never known anyone to call him anything else, a tribute to the man's skill at finding ways to eavesdrop – was the head of the small surveillance team Danny had sent to Rome. They were installed in an apartment opposite the Holy Office.

'What's up?' Morton asked when the Pathfinder answered the telephone.

'We are. Come on over.'

Morton walked out of the Arch of the Bells Gateway, where Swiss Guards were still receiving flowers, crossed the intersection and climbed the stairs to the third floor of the apartment block. It had been built in the last year of World War Two. An Italian Jew had bought the building in the fifties. Mossad had converted the corner apartment for its own purposes.

The Pathfinder opened the door. He had a shiny head and face, double chin and jovial eyes. He looked like an off-duty Santa Claus.

'Wong Lee's called Muller. The cardinal was praying and he was told to call back. He's due to do so in a few minutes,' the Pathfinder said, leading the way down a shabby hallway.

Morton glimpsed unmade beds through half-open doors. Surveillance crews were renowned for being poor housekeepers. Through the living room windows loomed the Apostolic Palace on the far side of St Peter's Square.

The Pathfinder grinned.

'We don't often get it this easy. Only problem was getting around the roof detectors.'

The CIA had installed them after the attempted assassination of Pope John Paul, to protect him from a kamikaze bomb attack or a snatch squad of terrorists while he walked in the palace's roof garden. The detectors would warn of approaching aircraft. Italian fighters were on constant standby to deal with such intruders.

In the living room the furniture had been pushed back against the walls to leave the centre of the floor clear. Spread over the carpet was foam rubber an inch thick. Standing on it was a pyramid-shaped steel structure bristling with antennae. Coaxial cables connected several small radomes positioned at various angles in front of the two windows. The radomes resembled outsize golf balls mounted on pedestals.

More cables ran to reel-to-reel recorders beside the pyramid. These were linked to a Merino computer. The CIA had provided the surveillance team with several. Each Merino could process up to 50,000 separate conversations.

The Pathfinder's two colleagues squatted on the foam, head-sets plugged into recorders. They waved at Morton.

'Park yourself down here.' The Pathfinder indicated a space on the foam. He handed Morton a headset, already attached to a recorder.

Morton placed the cans over his ears. A babble of voices filled his ears, mingled with singing.

'Sorry about this,' said the Pathfinder, squatting beside Morton and putting on his own headset. 'We're picking up every-thing going in and out of the Vatican. Including the Sistine choir. Right now the Merino's locked on to Muller's phone, and it isn't filtering. Once he gets his call we'll lose the background.'

They sat in silence for a few minutes. Then Morton saw one of the dials on the recorder begin to flicker.

'Here we go,' the Pathfinder said.

Suddenly the babble was replaced by a man's voice.

'*Pronto*? Who is calling?'

The reel on the recorder began to revolve.

'Muller's secretary,' the Pathfinder murmured. 'He's in his outer office.'

'One moment please, Mr Wong Lee,' said the priest-secretary. Morton heard a click.

'Hello, Mr Wong Lee. How can I help you?'

'How is your Pope?'

'He continues to improve.'

In the pause Morton heard Muller exhale. The man had the

232

beginnings of a smoker's wheeze. Wong Lee was once more speaking.

'I wish you to come to see me at once here in Hawaii.'

'I have already explained to you that I need to remain here.'

'I would not ask if it was not important, Your Eminence.'

Morton listened to the cardinal inhaling. His bronchial tubes must be well pitted.

'Very well. I will need a day or two to make arrangements.'

'Thank you, Your Eminence.'

Morton heard the click. He could not tell who had hung up.

Hal Lockman watched the afternoon sun spilling into the bedroom, creating wavering shadows as a gentle breeze from the Pacific slowly lifted the curtain over the window. The cloth bulged inward for a moment, reminding him of a half-full sail. One day soon he would have a boat, have anything he wanted. And he would not have to draw the drapes or lock the door as he had felt compelled to today in his bachelor apartment.

It was at the far end of Apostle Lane, one of a hundred identical box-like structures, furnished in the same spartan way. Each had a Rules of Residence framed on the back of the front door. No parties. No pets. No redecorating. No music between midnight and 7.00 a.m. No visitors between those hours. No visitors of the opposite sex at any hour. He had kept all the other rules except that one.

He watched the curtain hang limp and dull, the way he always felt after sex. Penny-Jane lay with her back to him, not stirring, her blonde hair damp from her exertions.

The curtain had started to move inward once more. The bed was narrow for two and he lay on his side, studying the curve of her spine, breathing in the smell of her skin. His fingers touched the nubs of her spine, pressing each one in turn, as if he was playing an instrument. She gave no response. But he knew she was awake.

Just as he had known they would come here – separately, of course – after he met her in the Hallway of Support, dusting all those ridiculous photographs and plaques.

He had seen her there before, but he had always been with Martha or Eddie, hurrying to or from some meeting. Now Martha had driven Eddie to the airport. He had been in his office when he saw them go. He had waved from the window then continued checking his transfers to his account at Credit Suisse.

After that last Investment Committee meeting he had decided the time had come to build up his deposits more quickly. He doubted if he could stand waiting a full year before quitting working for two such monsters.

He had removed 1,000 dollars from each of the 4,000 portfolios he managed. That gave him over 750,000 dollars on deposit. In another month he would have the million he reckoned he needed.

The transactions had fuelled his sexual drive, reminding him it had been a year now since the beast inside him had been satisfied. He had felt it awaken after its long winter, sniffing the air and telling him where to go. The beast came with him to the corridor and listened impatiently as he began one of those prefabricated conversations of which he was a past master.

'Do you like being with us ... everyone treating you nicely ... maybe one day you can come and work for me ... there's a tremendous buzz in being at the heart of things ...'

He had learned to spot the small signs. The way she had shifted from one foot to another. The intake of breath. The look in her eye. To anyone else the signs would be quite incomprehensible. But he knew. Soon, he had told the beast. Soon he would feed off all those hidden hollows and drink from that cave beyond the bushy thicket.

He had watched her tongue tip moisten a corner of her small mouth, balancing risk against discovery. Risk had won. He had given her his apartment number and told her to take the long route, behind the trees which sheltered the cemetery. He had taken the short way; past the site for the proposed new campus.

What he was doing was an acceptable risk, he had told himself. At this hour of the afternoon the apartments on Apostle Lane would be empty, their occupants busy with God's work.

By the time she arrived he had already drawn the drapes and produced two glasses and a bottle of Napa Valley champagne from the refrigerator. Then he changed into the loose fitting robe he liked to wear around the apartment.

They had drunk half the bottle, while their eyes consumed each other.

She had told him she had left the Mail Room because of Clara Stevens. He had been surprised. He had never thought Clara was lesbian. He had seen her a lot recently with Martha. Was something going on there?

The possibility opened up an exciting new avenue. If there was something going on, almost certainly Eddie did not suspect. He had an aversion to homosexuality, especially in women. So if Martha was gay, she would want to keep that very quiet. And that could be useful if she ever discovered about his bank transfers to Geneva. A little information was always useful in a matter like that.

Then everything else was forgotten as Penny-Jane slid her hand up inside his robe. He led her into the bedroom and stretched out on the bed, watching her undress.

From her personal history which he had retrieved from Records when he first became curious about her he knew she had led a full life. Even so he had not expected her to be so wild. Hers was a hunger which even outstripped his own.

Long after he finished, she continued to nibble and suck at him, grinding and gripping him with a ferocity which made him gasp. At last she had made a deep throaty sound, almost of disappointment, and turned her back on him.

Once more the curtain billowed. Soon the children on adjoining Testament Road would be coming home.

Hal shook Penny-Jane gently by the shoulders.

'It's time to go, hon.'

She sighed and shifted and her lips began small movements. She turned over and looked at him.

'I'm ready again.'

Her face was flushed, hair tangled in her eyes. She had started breathing fast again.

'I've got to get back to work,' he said.

She began to thrust against him, making soft mewing sounds.

'Again,' she groaned. 'Again . . .'

He felt his resolve weaken. Just one more time.


Flanked by Yoshi and Dr Fortuti, Cardinal Enkomo approached the corridor leading to Pope Nicholas's bedroom. The cardinal carried a buff-coloured file.

'Remember not to stay too long,' instructed the papal physician in a not quite approving voice.

The cardinal inclined his head.

Yoshi nodded at the file. 'Best you read to him. I don't want to put any pressure on his eyes.'

The cardinal nodded once more.

The *Vigili* seated outside the door rose to his feet.

Cardinal Enkomo knocked quickly on the door. It was opened by the duty nurse.

'His Eminence wishes to be alone with the Holy Father,' Dr Fortuti said, the hint of professional disapproval still there.

'If there's a problem, I'm sure His Eminence knows how to press a buzzer,' said Yoshi.

Cardinal Enkomo walked into the bedroom, closing the door firmly behind him.

It was a surprisingly small room, square with a high ceiling. Pope Nicholas's body, clad in a white nightshirt, barely disturbed the pastel bedcover.

'Julius, come forward, my son.'

Cardinal Enkomo did as bidden. Reaching the side of the bed, he knelt, his lips brushing the Ring of the Fisherman. He rose to his feet and smiled down at the Pope.

'I am relieved to see you so well, Holiness.'

'I feel well, Julius. Or at least better than I felt before.'

Pope Nicholas nodded at the heavy carved chair on the far side of the bed.

'Come, sit there. My nurses sit there. Seeing you is a blessed relief after hearing their tales of life in Rome. It seems to be more wicked now than in the days of Caligula.'

As the cardinal walked around the bed and sat in the chair, Pope Nicholas continued to speak.

'You're my very first visitor, Julius. I gather most of the Sacred College is ready to come and offer me their prayers. Not to mention the Diplomatic Corps.'

'I think half the world would like to come and convey their good wishes, Holiness.'

'God forbid,' Pope Nicholas said, sounding pleased.

'I've missed you, my son. Missed that honest face of yours and our arguments. Sometimes I have thought I should never have sent you to South Africa, but kept you here. But then if I had, I'm sure my doctors would have said you had to wait with all the others before being allowed to see me! But I told them you had come a long way and it was a matter of life and death.'

Cardinal Enkomo smiled.

'I'm sure they didn't believe you.'

'You have your report?' Pope Nicholas asked abruptly.

'I do. Dr Kramer said I should read it to you.'

The Pope sighed. 'He is a good man, but he's beginning to fuss like Fortuti. If I didn't stop them, they'd be in here all the time.'

Pope Nicholas paused for breath. The cardinal scanned his face.

'You are sure you are not tiring, Holiness? I could come back later.'

The pontiff's lips creased into a faint smile.

'After the struggle I had to get my doctors to agree to you coming here, I can't let you leave without hearing your report. Now read it to me.'

In a clear voice Cardinal Enkomo read his report on why the Holy See should formally recognise Israel.

When he had finished, Pope Nicholas stared at him.

'Thank you,' he said at last. 'That is exactly what I wanted. Have you discussed this with anyone else?'

'No one except Morton.'

'Ah, Colonel Morton,' the Pope said. 'And what did he say?'

'He approved,' Cardinal Enkomo replied, and sat quietly awaiting further inquiries.

'Have you seen Messner, Julius?'

The cardinal told Pope Nicholas about his dinner with the cardinal-secretary, and the call from General Borakin in Moscow.

Pope Nicholas frowned. 'Sean did not tell me about that in the note he persuaded one of the nurses to smuggle in here.'

'He probably didn't want to excite you, Holiness.'

'But the news does excite me, Julius! With the troika's support, I can make Holy Cross work!'

Pope Nicholas lifted his head from the pillows that supported him.

'I want you to stay in Rome and act as my ears and eyes, especially among the Sacred College. I'm not fool enough not to think my recovery will affect the plans of some of them.'

'I will, of course, remain, Holiness. But I think now that you are on the road to recovery, the opposition will wither.'

Pope Nicholas lifted a hand and sighed. 'I wish I could believe you, Julius. But in these past months my opponents have been scouring everywhere for support. They've even rounded up all those Jesuits who have given up being liberal, and are ready to use their manipulative skills to stop Holy Cross. Opus Dei is also totally against the idea. I fear the conservatives will go on mobilising, using their opposition to Holy Cross as the excuse to hold the line against a married priesthood and homosexuality . . . issues, which you know, I have at least tried to keep an open mind over.'

He sank back on his pillows.

'There are still the arrivistes like me, Holiness.'

It was their influence which had helped Pope Nicholas push through policies which the conservatives would otherwise have buried.

You selected us carefully, Julius Enkomo thought, judging our strengths, recognising our weaknesses. And we share your vision of a new Church, shaking off the centuries of deafness to the realities of the world.

'You are still too few, Julius.'

He was tiring. His right leg had started to throb once more. He had not mentioned it to anyone. He did not want any more fussing.

Cardinal Enkomo leaned forward. 'We've learned from you, Holiness, how to make the most of our number. We will use our own collective voice to convince others.'

'Thank you for that reassurance, Julius. Now I think you should go.' He suddenly felt very tired. Listening to that report had been exhilarating but exhausting.

Cardinal Enkomo immediately rose to his feet.

'Of course. Is there anything more I can do?'

'Just watch and listen.'

'I will, I promise.'

Cardinal Enkomo came to the side of the bed, knelt and once more made obeisance. When he rose he saw that Pope Nicholas's eyes were closed.

Treading softly, Cardinal Enkomo walked to the door. As he did so, the clock on the side table suddenly began to ring. He strode over and silenced the alarm.

During all this activity Pope Nicholas had not stirred.


Morton ordered the fish soup and pasta and a bottle of Frascati.

'I'm so hungry,' Carina said, leaning forward.

He had seen her do that before, letting her shoulders fall and her chest slump, as if she had thought of something she would share with you in a moment.

She wore a bandana and a man's jacket draped over her shoulders.

'I borrowed it from one of the choir,' she had said as they passed a Swiss Guard. He had brought down his halberd in a salute.

'We're becoming part of the furniture,' Morton murmured as they walked into St Damaso Courtyard.

The car Morelli had provided was waiting, a *Vigili* at the wheel, to bring them to Galeassi's. Morelli said Mussolini used the restaurant to entertain his mistresses.

Twenty minutes later they were in the old quarter of Trastevere. The last time he had come here he had missed cornering Abu Nidal by an hour. The *Digos* had turned the whole operation into a show and the world's most wanted terrorist had slipped away.

Out of habit he surveyed the restaurant. Two-thirds full. About half the patrons looked local. Morelli had made the arrangements and the *maître d'* bowed and led them to his best table at the back of the room.

Heads turned as they passed and Morton felt inordinately pleased at the admiration Carina attracted. She was doing so again as they watched the waiter make a show of displaying and then opening the bottle. His eyes never left her. Why did the Italians always have to put on a show?

After Morton played his part by sniffing and tasting the wine, the waiter poured them each a glass, then withdrew.

Carina looked across the table.

'Thank you for bringing me here, David.'

'I'm glad you could get away.'

'Then a toast,' Carina said raising her glass.

She leaned across the table, entwining her arm inside his, so that their faces were separated by little more than the diameter of their glasses.

'A toast to tonight,' she said softly.

'Tonight.'

Though their glasses merely clicked, their eyes remained locked as they sipped.

'The last man I did this with was my KGB superior. We were lovers for a while. Then he went back to his wife.'

She looked at him. 'Are you shocked?'

He did not know how he felt.

'Are you married, David?'

'No. I was. We've been divorced three years now.'

'You keep track?'

'Not really.'

She continued to press. 'Were you always faithful?'

'Yes.' Shola had said he was too busy to begin an affair. A month later she had left.

'So was I to my husband,' Carina said.

'Do you still love him?'

'Yes. But as a memory. And you? Do you love her?'

'No.'

She withdrew her arm, studying him.

'You're always under control, aren't you?'

He looked at her steadily. 'I wish you'd stop analysing me, Carina.'

She smiled. 'Does it make you feel uncomfortable?'

'A little, yes.'

She sipped more wine.

'You really don't know much about women, do you?' she asked gently.

'I don't think any man really does. But you sound like an expert on men.'

He saw Carina's eyes drop. Did she feel insulted? Hurt? He had never been able to tell with Shola or Nan. They knew how to conceal everything: anger, pleasure, any emotion. Maybe all women were equipped like that?

She looked up. 'At the university where he taught, my father ran the first class in love. Of course, he had to give it a proper name, like "Affection as a behaviour modifier" to make it sound more acceptable and scientific. But it was all about love. He was a wonderful teacher.'

He smiled. 'That's quite a leap from building roads in the Ukraine.'

She looked serious.

'The one good thing about the Stalin times was that everybody could get an education. My father graduated as a psychologist and was appointed to Lvov University. When my mother finished with the Bolshoi, she was dance director to the local theatre company.'

'What happened to them, Carina?'

She looked at him steadily.

'What happened to a lot of our people. They were shot in one of the purges. That was the other thing Stalin was good at. Purging the innocent.'

The words hung there, as raw and tender as a bruise.

'And your parents?' she finally asked.

Morton stared at her, his face set in cement.

They had come in the night, smashing down the door, smashing in his father's face, even though he had offered no resistance. When his mother tried to shield Ruth and himself, they had smashed their rifle butts into her body. His last sight of his parents was of their being hurled into the truck, still being hit by the rifles.

'The same.'

She reached across and held his hand and spoke in a small voice.

'I'm sorry.'

'I'm sorry for both of us. For all of us,' he said.

They looked at each other, saying nothing, knowing there was nothing more either of them wanted to say.

After a little while he made a deliberate effort to lighten the mood.

'Tell me more about your father's class on love.'

She shrugged. 'I don't remember too much. But I do remember he used to ask his students to write on the subject of if they were to die tomorrow, how would they live tonight.'

'How would you answer that?'

She sipped her wine, then carefully placed the glass between the candle and the bowl of flowers.

'That tonight I would like to make love to you, David.'

He felt a sudden visceral pounding inside him. Part of him was staring across the table at her – that part which had always been able to see with total clarity in the dark. To see what was going to happen. The part that always asked what it was asking now: where is this going to end?

Before he could answer she was speaking again.

'At this time of my life there's almost nothing I have not done with a man before. But this is the first time I have fallen in love at first sight.'

He reached across and took both her hands in his.

'This has never happened to me before either.'

'There's something else,' she continued. 'I don't want to go back. There's nothing there for me.'

He nodded, understanding completely.

'I'll call Savenko. And I'll speak to Yoshi. I'm sure there won't be a problem.'

If there was he would solve it.

She continued to look directly at him.

'Could I live with you?' She would never use him.

'For sure.'

The few friends he allowed in the apartment teased him he actually enjoyed living alone in spartan conditions. But she would love the view of the Samarian Hills through one window and an uninterrupted view down to the shore through the other.

'David, I love you.'

'I love you too, Carina.'

The waiter arrived with the soup. As he began to ladle chunks of fish and broth into their bowls, Morton's bleeper sounded.

In the next instant the pager in Carina's jacket began to signal urgently.

Morton was on his feet.

'Can I use your telephone?' he asked the waiter.

The surprised man pointed to the bar.

Switching off the bleeper, Morton strode to the counter and dialled the Vatican switchboard. He gave his name and asked for Morelli.

Morton was told to wait.

Carina had turned off her pager and was watching him intently. Then Claudio was speaking.

Morton saw Carina suddenly stand up and brush past the waiter. She was coming towards the bar, the eye of every man in the room following her.

The waiter was saying something. But all Morton could hear was Claudio's voice.

'We're on our way,' he finally said, putting down the phone.

He grabbed Carina by the arm and headed for the door. The waiter was shouting. Morton turned and thrust a fistful of lira notes into his hand.

Then they were back in the car and bumping over the cobblestones.

'He's dead, Carina. Yoshi says it was a massive blood clot. A pulmonary embolism. He wouldn't have felt a thing.'

Suddenly Carina was weeping softly. After a moment Morton placed an arm around her shoulders.

# 17

At the Arch of the Bells Gate, the crowd parted to allow the car into the Vatican. Many onlookers were tearfully reciting the rosary.

A Swiss Guard told the driver to go to St Damaso Courtyard, where Morelli was waiting at the entrance to the papal apartment.

'There's a problem,' he said, as he led Morton and Carina to the Pope's private elevator. 'Yoshi and Poggi are pressing for an autopsy. Messner's totally opposed.'

'Any reason?' Morton asked.

'He says there's no precedent. And this place runs on precedent, David. Besides, as camerlengo, Messner has the last word.'

They stepped into the elevator.

'Why do Yoshi and Dr Poggi want a postmortem?' Morton asked.

'It's standard in cases like this,' Carina replied.

Morelli pressed a button and the elevator began to ascend.

'There was also a theological problem,' Morelli continued. 'It boiled down to how long the Pope's soul remained in his body.'

'I don't understand,' Carina said, her brow puckering in puzzlement.

Morelli smiled briefly. 'It was Messner's first chance to show he's now really in charge. He's one of those who still believes the soul leaves the body at a certain time after brain death. In a healthy person who suddenly dies, that could be up to an hour. But in someone who has been seriously ill for some time, or has just had surgery, the time could be much shorter.'

Carina began to shake her head in bewilderment.

'He also used the business with the alarm clock. Cardinal Enkomo reported it rang unexpectedly just before he left the bedroom and Messner says it could have been a Divine Sign that the Pope was already dead.'

Carina's astonishment was complete.

'And that's important?' she asked.

'Yes. It means Pope Nicholas can't be given absolute absolution, the total granting of forgiveness of all his sins on earth. And that's important to any Catholic,' Morelli explained.

Carina had another question. 'Couldn't Cardinal Messner have relaxed the rule?'

'He lives by the rules. He made a huge thing of getting your colleagues to establish the precise time of death, and then pronouncing that in his opinion the soul had departed a good five minutes before he arrived.'

'Didn't anyone call him in time, Claudio?' Morton asked.

'Fortuti did. Linde said his master was in a meeting with Muller and they couldn't be disturbed.'

He glanced at Morton. 'They were discussing Muller's trip to Hawaii. That's off now, of course.'

The elevator door opened and they emerged in the papal apartment opposite its private chapel.

'When the Huns arrived in the bedroom they were more like a handler showing off his papabile than mourners,' growled Morelli.

He led them through a small salon. On a table was an open book, as if the Pope had left it to pick up later. The top of a credenza was covered with his family photographs. A wall was hung with photographs taken during his many pilgrimages. Everywhere was evidence of a man's long and full life.

'In a few hours there won't be a thing to show he ever lived here. This place will be as dead as an apartment waiting to be rented,' Morelli said.

He pushed open double doors and they entered the corridor leading to the pontiff's bedroom. Nuns covered from head to toe in old-fashioned habits and priests in black soutanes stood silently between the niches holding holy statues and icons. Several of the watchful figures looked in surprise at Carina. Apart from those who ran the papal household, no woman had ever entered the bedroom.

One of the nuns quickly stepped forward and placed a lace mantilla on Carina's head.

The bedroom was crowded, the curtains drawn, the silent figures ashen in the bedside light.

Yoshi, Dr Poggi and Dr Fortuti stood on one side of the bed. Across from them stood the camerlengo. With him were Cardinal Muller, Cardinal Enkomo and other members of the Sacred College.

Morton recognised Coffey of Philadelphia and Simmons of Los Angeles. They were still built like the pair of quarter-backs who had led Notre Dame to victory forty years ago.

The bespectacled Ospispo of Santo Domingo barely came up to the shoulder of Mongabe of Zaire. He was the only member of the College with tribal cast markings on his cheeks.

Beside O'Rourke, Primate of All Ireland, stood Berry of Scotland. They had been elevated at the same time as Julius and together they formed the front row of liberal thinkers among the College's 120 members.

To one side of them stood Koveks of Romania, Schwartz of Switzerland, Tovic of Czechoslovakia and Arnt of Belgium. Old men, whose eyes would cloud at the first unfamiliar sound of doctrine or the smallest deviation from orthodoxy.

Secretaries stood against the walls, a solid phalanx of black, relieved only by the white strips of their Roman collars.

Monsignor Linde turned and looked at Morton, but gave no acknowledgement. More than ever his unblinking eyes made him appear like a bird of prey.

At the foot of the bed stood Monsignor Hanlon. He glanced quickly at Carina as she passed. Morton glimpsed the secretary's face. It was calm and composed. But of course part of his profession had trained Sean to cope with death.

Cardinal Messner frowned and waited until Carina had taken her place between Yoshi and Dr Poggi. A nod from Cardinal Enkomo was her only recognition from the rest of the silent group around the bed.

Cardinal Messner reached into a small leather pouch he had placed on the bedcover and removed a vial of holy oil. He opened it and pressed it to his thumb.

In a sonorous voice he began to chant in Latin. As he did so he made the Sign of the Cross on Pope Nicholas's forehead, and rapidly moved his thumb up and down, back and forth, touching the body at each Station of the Cross.

'*In nomine Padre, et Fili, et Spiriti Sancti, Amen.*'

He recorked the vial and placed it back in the pouch. No one spoke. More cardinals were crowding into the room.

Morton recognised the towering figure of Leutens of Marseilles. Sean had said he was a future Pope – but only if he could survive the cut and thrust of the deal-making before conclave. With him was Saldarini, one of the Curia cardinals, and Posanos of Brazil.

Morton remembered what Steve had said. Every large organisation needed its wheeler-dealers. Saldarini was the Vatican's. But was it simply coincidence he had arrived with Leutens? Or was this the first move in the conclave stakes?

The stoop-shouldered Posanos had the suffering mouth and the shrewd, calculating eyes to know the virtues, and shortcomings, of any papabile.

Cardinal Messner waited until space was found for them at the bedside. Then he removed a small silver hammer from the bag.

He gripped it firmly for a moment, before lightly tapping Pope Nicholas on the forehead. In a loud voice he posed a question asked at this moment of all his predecessors.

'Are you dead, Virgilio Giovanni Enrico Antonio Marie?'

The camerlengo counted off the seconds in a quieter voice. After a minute he repeated his action and question. When a further minute had passed he completed the ritual a third time.

Morelli whispered in Morton's ear. 'A thousand years ago they almost buried a Pope who was still alive. Since then they've had this triple check.'

Cardinal Messner made a further pronouncement.

'As camerlengo, I pronounce Pope Nicholas is truly dead.'

Sighs came from those around Morton.

Cardinal Messner lifted the Pope's right hand and pulled off the Fisherman's Ring. From the bag he removed a jeweller's shears. Holding the ring between thumb and forefinger, he snapped the band in two, destroying Pope Nicholas's seal of office. The camerlengo placed the broken pieces and shears in the pouch.

The pontificate of Pope Nicholas the Sixth was officially over. Morton wondered if the bold initiative of Holy Cross had also died in this stuffy bedroom.

Then Yoshi was speaking.

'Camerlengo, Your Eminences,' he began. 'On behalf of my colleagues I ask that you reconsider the question of an autopsy.'

From across the bed, faces scored by age and the experience of being totally obeyed, frowned as Yoshi continued.

'While the cause of death is clear, a pulmonary embolism, we had no warning a clot was building up, so we need to establish its pathology –'

'Dr Kramer,' Cardinal Messner interrupted. 'Your medical curiosity cannot be allowed to intervene with something far more important. The sanctity of the papal body. A Pope has never been touched by a pathologist. I see no reason for it to happen now.'

Cardinal Koveks led the murmurs of agreement.

'There is nothing in the rule book explicitly forbidding an autopsy, camerlengo,' Cardinal Enkomo said quietly. 'And as I may have been the last to see the Holy Father alive, I would welcome confirmation that there is nothing suspicious about his death.'

'Suspicious? Who said anything about it being suspicious?' demanded the querulous voice of Cardinal Arnt of Belgium.

'That's how rumours start,' added Cardinal Tovic, fingering the gold cross on his ample chest.

'An autopsy would dispel any doubts,' Yoshi began again.

'Dr Kramer,' Cardinal Messner snapped. 'This is not a medical matter.'

The camerlengo turned and looked at Julius Enkomo.

'You are perfectly correct. There is no rule forbidding an autopsy. Just as there is no rule forbidding disinterment. But not since the days of Pope John the Fourteenth has anyone actually dug up a Pope!'

In the same icy voice he continued.

'And as no one has remotely accused you or anyone of any involvement in his death, I simply do not understand your remarks.'

He glanced surreptitiously across the bed.

'The doctors have assured us the Holy Father died of natural causes. Perhaps the only surprise is that they did not anticipate the outcome. But then, we on this side of the bed know that death is often like a thief in the night, coming at the most unexpected of times.'

Cardinal Enkomo shook his head. 'I am not disputing the

248

medical verdict – only asking for an autopsy to reinforce it.'

Cardinal Muller turned and spoke abruptly to Cardinal Enkomo.

'An autopsy would do quite the opposite. It would be a launch pad for rumours of all kinds: that we had an autopsy because there was a suspicion; that we covered up the suspicion to avoid scandal. An autopsy would cast an odium on all of us. We would be presented in the world's press as modern day Borgias hemlocking our leader!'

Cardinal Koveks led the nods.

'All the more reason to have an autopsy,' Cardinal O'Rourke said calmly. 'And it is a fact that the world has lost confidence in official versions of events. We saw that with Irangate and the assassination of President Kennedy. In this case an autopsy followed by a full police report would scotch any gossip.'

'What gossip can there be?' angrily demanded Cardinal Schwartz. He had a high-pitched voice as if he had spent his youth yodelling.

'Brothers in Christ,' interrupted Cardinal Leutens. 'This is neither the time nor place to conduct such a discussion. The matter should be placed before the full College.'

He looked around the bedroom, seeking support.

'Logistically, we cannot wait for the College to convene,' said Cardinal Berry. He had a pleasing burr and a fine-boned face. No one would have known that, as a boy, he had worked in his father's road-marking business.

Cardinal Saldarini was looking around, counting heads. He turned to the camerlengo.

'There are enough of us present to conduct a vote which will be binding on the College.'

'I would support that,' said Cardinal Posanos in a lawyer's careful voice.

Cardinal Muller and Cardinal Messner exchanged the briefest of glances. The camerlengo nodded.

'Does anyone wish to add anything before we vote?'

Cardinal Coffey thrust forward his lantern chin.

'I think I speak for all the North American members of the College when I say there should be no autopsy. An autopsy did not stop the speculation after Kennedy's death. All it does is establish foul play – not exclude it from the minds of those who see conspiracies everywhere!'

'Thank you,' Cardinal Messner said. 'All those opposing a post-mortem please raise their hands.'

By an overwhelming majority the vote was carried.

Wong Lee sat impassively in a tiny room none of the guests suspected existed in the 10,000 dollar a day penthouse suite in the Wong-Hawaii Shangri-La, the flagship of the dozen hotels he owned in the islands. The room had appeared on no floor plan of the suite that Pierre of Paris had furnished from a concept by Givens of Beverly Hills.

Inside the penthouse, over thirty pounds of 22-carat gold had been used to fashion door handles, taps and light fittings. The carpets were woven in China, the furniture culled from Europe. Other features included a constantly manned kitchen staffed by a chef and two assistants. A butler, footman and maid served and cleared away. There was a movie theatre, a 100-channel TV set and a library of 5,000 compact discs. The bathroom included a jacuzzi, sauna and a twenty-foot long pool with its own wave-making machine. The ceilings of the master bedroom opened at the touch of a button to observe the night sky through a telescope attached to a track over the bed.

It had cost over two million dollars to create this monument to high-tech vulgarity.

It had cost even more to equip the tiny room where Wong Lee sat. It was crammed with state-of-the-art communications and surveillance equipment which provided a constant view of what was happening elsewhere in the suite.

In the past this had proven highly useful in dealing with the politicians and industrialists who regularly used the penthouse. Many a tycoon had suddenly agreed to a deal after he received a copy of a video of his sexual indiscretions during his stay.

The room was kept constantly locked and could be reached only through a sliding door in the back of the kitchen pantry.

A few moments ago Chung-Shi had called on the surveillance telephone link from Lhasa to say the operative, Zong, had gone to his death still insisting it was only curiosity which had made him access the secret code. After his security chief had rung off, Wong Lee had continued watching the Reverend Kingdom and Franco Umberto.

The penthouse was designed so that two of its lounges remained entirely separate from one another, each with doors leading to elevators which gave access to the rest of the hotel. Access to either lounge could be gained from a larger, central lounge. Wong Lee had found the arrangement useful when negotiating deals with competing companies. He could keep their negotiators apart, yet close to hand.

At this moment – mid-afternoon Hawaiian time – several of the call girls the Wong-Hawaii Shangri-La retained for favoured guests, were entertaining the trio of bodyguards the Mafia godfather had brought with him.

The Chinese technician who ran the surveillance room continued to record the scenes of lovemaking in the central lounge.

'Good practice, singsung,' she grinned.

As he did with the shamaness, Wong Lee tolerated this bucktoothed woman because of her technical competence.

He watched a slim dark-haired young woman straddle one of the bodyguards.

'She new?' he asked. The woman technician was responsible for all the girls.

'Brought her in a week ago from Manila.'

Wong Lee felt a stirring.

'Send her to my room when I'm finished.'

The technician nodded. She always especially enjoyed filming those moments when the singsung gave vent to his drives.

Wong Lee continued to observe the scene in the other lounge. Umberto was pacing about. He had a dolphin's head and a whale's body. But for a *gweillo* he was no fool.

Not like Kingdom. Ever since arriving, he had behaved as if this was his own home, making phone calls to his sister, ordering the staff about. Always demanding. Now he was once more switching channels on the TV set, hunting for more news from Rome, laughing softly to himself each time there was a report.

The meddling fool was dead. That other *gweillo*, Messner, had come out on the balcony of the basilica and announced it. The bells had tolled. The pontifical body was in the hands of the embalmers so that it could be prepared for veneration by the faithful.

The shamaness's poison had worked its trick. That was all that mattered. Soon there would be another Pope.

Wong Lee rose to his feet.

'I'm going to number two room first.'

'Okey-dokey, singsung,' the technician said. 'You want a recording?'

'No. Just enjoy yourself filming the girls.'

Moments later Wong Lee walked into the lounge where the Reverend Kingdom was still switching channels. The pastor came forward, hand extended, beaming and looking like a host welcoming a guest.

'I'm really glad to see you, Mr Wong! Really, really glad,' the Reverend Kingdom said, pumping Wong Lee's hand. 'You're a hard man to reach!'

Wong Lee made a deprecating motion. 'Too many people to see and not enough hours in the day.'

The Reverend Kingdom nodded vigorously. 'I know the feeling. Martha – she sends her greetings – says I should delegate. But how can I? You can't delegate God's work.'

He paused and looked expectantly at Wong Lee, waiting for the response. When none came the Reverend Kingdom delivered it himself.

'And bless His name.'

'Please be seated, Mr Kingdom.'

Wong Lee indicated a sofa. He chose an armchair opposite.

'I'm sorry to bring you all this way for such a short visit. I had hoped we could have had dinner. But pressure of business dictates otherwise.'

For a brief moment an image of the dark-haired girl crossed his mind and he felt another stirring. He forced himself to concentrate on the *gweillo*. The man's disappointment was plain.

'I perfectly understand. I'm on a pretty tight schedule myself,' the Reverend Kingdom said.

He had planned to make his pitch over dinner for the money he needed to reinforce the new campus against an earthquake. There had been a tremor north of San Francisco during the night. Nothing big, just a reminder.

Out of a corner of his eye he glanced at the screen. CNN were reporting the Roman pontiff's lying-in-state would last three days. Then he would be sealed in three coffins – the inner one of cypress to symbolise the trees around Calvary, one of bronze to preserve his body, the outer one of elm so that he would appear to be like other men who go to their grave in a simple wooden box.

'You find all this interesting, Mr Kingdom?' Wong Lee asked politely.

The Reverend Kingdom turned and faced his host, his face beginning to suffuse.

'They can put him in as many coffins as they like, Mr Wong! They can wrap him in that fancy ermine blanket and cover his face with a purple veil. And place him in the deepest crypt of their Church. But that won't save him from the wrath of Edward Kingdom!'

'I understand your feelings, Mr Kingdom.'

'I hope you do, Mr Wong. I sincerely hope you do!'

The Reverend Kingdom leaned forward, placing his hands between his knees. When he spoke his voice had taken on its pulpit resonance.

'I want to waste no time in striking at the body of the Roman beast now that its head has been removed! There will be tens of millions out there who will be ready now to hear the Word! I intend to have the same effect as Joshua had on the walls of Jericho! And David had on Goliath. As –'

'Mr Kingdom!' interrupted Wong Lee, raising a hand to stem the flow. 'I know how powerful your sermons are. That was why I was happy to give you a satellite.'

The Reverend Kingdom nodded, somehow managing to convey both acceptance of the compliment and thanks for the gift.

On the screen another report was saying the last of the cardinals were expected in Rome shortly. And that the first questions were already being asked about what kind of Pope the Church now needed.

Wong Lee used the remote control to switch off the set. He looked at the Reverend Kingdom for a long silent moment. When he spoke his voice was without expression.

'I have brought you here to discuss a very important matter concerning the Church of Rome. The death of the Pope could not have come at a better time. He has been a troublesome meddler. In Africa and Asia. In all those countries where the Roman Church is struggling to maintain its authority.'

'And where the Church of True Belief is gaining converts.'

Wong Lee nodded impatiently.

'I am pleased to hear that, Mr Kingdom. But kindly do not interrupt any more!'

Could he really depend on such a fool of a *gweillo*? But there was no time now to invest in someone else.

Wong Lee resumed speaking.

'Soon they will elect a new Pope. I want you to devote your considerable talent to attacking one particular cardinal.'

The Reverend Kingdom felt a surge of excitement. Martha and he had both been wrong. This was what Operation Holy Cross was all about! And he was going to be at its very centre. Doing what he knew best. Attacking the Roman beast!

He forced himself to remain calm.

'Who is this person?'

For the moment Wong Lee ignored the question. Ever since he had heard the news from Rome, he had thought hard about how he could decisively influence the outcome of conclave. From what he now knew of past voting form, outside support for any one candidate would almost certainly doom his chances. That had happened in the past three elections, notably a newspaper campaign to promote the Cardinal Archbishop of Westminster. The English hope had gained only a handful of votes.

But to openly attack, even vilify a cardinal, would ensure the ranks of those who would gather in the Sistine Chapel would rally behind him. They would see him as a victim of unacceptable pressure. That could gain him a sufficient number of votes to ensure election.

'He is Cardinal Hans-Dietrich Muller,' Wong Lee finally said.

The Reverend Kingdom gave a little sound of delight.

'How deserving! He's little more than an old Nazi!'

'No doubt, Mr Kingdom, you will make use of that. Do not spare him. Scourge him like your Christ was scourged!'

Wong Lee rose to his feet.

'A car is waiting to take you to the airport. To save time, I have arranged for my own plane to fly you to Los Angeles. Please regard that as a measure of the urgency and importance I place on your task. I shall be watching most carefully to see how you handle it. Goodbye for the moment, Mr Kingdom.'

Wong Lee walked quickly from the lounge, already thinking of how he would handle Franco Umberto.

In the papal apartment, Cardinal Enkomo watched one of the nuns take down the stoup of holy water outside the dining room and place it in a box with the wooden cross. Both had been his gifts to His Holiness, carved from the tree which had stood beside his parents' kraal.

He had volunteered to supervise the removal of the Pope's personal effects while Monsignor Hanlon was clearing out the pontiff's official office a floor below. The process had begun immediately after the body was taken to the basement hospital for embalming prior to lying-in-state in the basilica. With the nuns weeping openly, and himself close to tears, Julius Enkomo had moved from room to room, helping to fill boxes and chests before they were wheeled away.

One held His Holiness's cassocks, another his modest collection of shoes. Two chests held his personal papers: the letters from his family and friends, old birthday and Christmas cards, notes from world leaders congratulating him on his election, letters from bishops and priests wishing him the long pontificate that was not to be, requests from children in his old diocese to come and visit him in the Vatican.

His books included a surprising number of contemporary novels – among them the incomparable Morris West. There were also files of clippings which His Holiness had used for those speeches which so captivated the world.

Into the same box went the cassette recorder and the tapes he had made to practise a phrase or learn a whole section of a particularly important address: he would play them back, listen and continue to record until he was completely satisfied he was word perfect.

The walls and niches had been stripped of his personal paintings and ornaments. In the kitchen a box had been filled with the tins and jars in which had been stored his coffee, sugar and biscuits.

After the stoup and cross were placed in a box, there was nothing left to pack. The nuns withdrew, to wait with the two Swiss Guards posted at the elevator. Cardinal Enkomo began a final check. Each room was as dead as a showroom.

The bedroom had been the very hub of activity following the formal pronouncement of death by the camerlengo: the vicar for Vatican City had blessed the mortal remains; the President of the Council of State had prayed over the corpse, as in turn had the prelates of the antechamber, the almoner of His Holiness and each cardinal as he had arrived in the Vatican.

Now the bedroom had a desolate air. The horsehair mattress

on its ancient frame was exposed. The alarm clock had been packed with His Holiness's toiletries from the bathroom.

But Julius Enkomo knew there was one item which had not been removed. He went to the wardrobe and, standing on tiptoe, felt around its top. His fingers found the envelope. He retrieved it and quickly shoved the envelope in a pocket of his cassock.

The night before he had left to take up his appointment in Cape Town, His Holiness had brought him to the bedroom and asked him to place the document in the most secure of all the hiding places in the Apostolic Palace. In the event of his death, His Holiness had said he was to make sure the envelope was given to the man elected to be the next Pope. The envelope contained the blueprint of Operation Holy Cross.

As Cardinal Enkomo stepped away from the wardrobe he became aware of someone standing in the doorway of the bedroom. He turned and faced Hubert Messner. In his hand the camerlengo held two lead strips.

'Is it all done?' he asked.

'Yes. Everything has been removed.'

The camerlengo turned and led the way back down the corridor. At the double doors near the elevator he affixed the strips across the door and its jamb.

The strips ensured no one would enter the apartment until a new Pope was chosen.


In the penthouse suite Franco Umberto broke off from what he was saying to fix himself another vodka from the lounge's cocktail bar.

What the hell was going on? First he'd been kept waiting for an hour. Then, when he was about to explain how hard business was, this fancy butler struts in to give the Chink a piece of paper on a silver tray and waltzes out again. Like something outa the movies.

The Chink had immediately excused himself and gone over to a window to read the paper. You couldn't tell from his face if it was good or bad news. Probably good. Nothing bad ever happened to the Chink.

Franco Umberto was wrong.

The hotel's computers had queried as security-suspect four registered guests. Their names had been faxed to Lhasa. Chung-Shi's even more sophisticated computers had identified the four as employees of Swift Renovations. His agents at the hotel had completed the checks.

The couple posing as honeymooners were in the Honolulu Suite immediately below the penthouse. The man who had travelled on Kingdom's flight had followed him back to the airport to watch the Lear jet take off, and was now in the room of the fourth man, who had been waiting to see Umberto's jet land.

Morton again. It was time to teach him a lesson, one this disgusting figure impatiently rattling the ice in his glass would appreciate.

He had allowed Umberto to kiss him on both cheeks, a familiarity no one else would have dared. And he had listened to his boring catalogue of losses. What did they amount to? A few hundred million at the most. The kind of money the man who had boasted to him he was the Cocaine King of America should easily be able to recover.

'Ya look like ya had important noos,' Umberto said.

Wong Lee smiled. Why did a *gweillo* always have to know? A Chinese person would never have been so rudely inquisitive.

'A small matter of no importance,' he said, folding the print-out and placing it in his pocket.

'I like it. "Small matta of no importance." I like it!' said Umberto. 'Wheredya learn such good English?'

Wong Lee frowned. There was a line over which no one crossed.

'Mr Umberto. Given the limited time I have, I would prefer it if we concentrated on more important matters.'

'Okay. Shoot.' The Mafia godfather sprawled in an armchair and slurped from the glass.

Wong Lee came and stood close to the chair.

'How would you like to recover not only all your losses, but also multiply them tenfold as profit? And that would only be a start.'

'Is dat a serious question?'

Wong Lee made a small gesture with his hand which Umberto found intimidating yet strangely reassuring. The Chink had done that before when he'd been about to outline a deal.

'The Soviet republics,' Wong Lee continued. 'I am speaking of the exclusive right to market drugs in all of them. From Kazakhstan to the Ukraine. From the Black Sea to the Arctic Ocean. I'm told the potential market is over two hundred million people, perhaps more. If they each only spent ten roubles a week to satisfy their craving, in six months you will have exceeded the profits I suggest.'

Umberto crushed a lump of ice in his mouth. Jesus H. Christ. You dream of this and then wake up. But he wasn't dreaming. He was sitting here, staring at the Chink, his mouth half-frozen with the ice, his mind at boiling pitch.

'Wad kinda deal you talkin' about?' he finally managed to ask.

Wong Lee saw that cunning had joined the respect. It was ever so. It would make no difference.

'I shall underwrite the setting up of your networks and the need to remove any local opposition. Those expenses will be recovered by me out of the first profits. All other expenses you will be responsible for and they are non-recoupable. I propose a straight fifty-fifty split on all gross profits. The usual monthly accounting.'

Umberto finished his drink and clinked the last of the thawing cubes in the glass. Two hundred million potential clients, say a hundred roubles a week. No, make that two. Jesus H. Christ. He would be a billionaire all over again in six months. It was the deal of a lifetime.

'Those are pretty tough terms,' he said, tipping the cubes into his mouth.

Wong Lee smiled. Make a *gweillo* an offer and he had to try and improve it.

'I understand, Mr Umberto. I'm sorry I brought you all this way only to disappoint you. But thank you for coming. You and your associates will, of course, be welcome to stay a few days as my guest –'

'Wayda minute! Jus' wayda minute, Mr Wong!' said Umberto, struggling to his feet. 'I only said the terms were tough. I didn' say I wasn' gonna accept them.'

'Then we have a deal?'

'Whadya think?' Umberto grinned. 'Les shake on it.'

'There is one other matter,' Wong Lee said quickly, moving back from the outstretched hand.

'Was dat?'

There was always something with the Chink.

'I need what I believe you call a . . . shooter?'

Umberto laughed in surprise.

'You wan' somebody taken out? Issat right?'

'Sit down, Mr Umberto,' Wong Lee said softly. 'I'll tell you exactly why I want your very best shooter.'

For the next ten minutes he spoke without interruption. When he finished Franco Umberto looked at him not only with awe, but also with fear.

'Jesus H. Christ!' he finally said.

Shortly before dawn, Cardinal Enkomo opened a side door and entered the nave of St Peter's basilica. His shoes echoing on the marble floor, he moved purposefully past some of the twenty-nine minor altars, the 148 colannades, the statue of St Peter whose right foot gleamed from constant kissing by the faithful, the black-and-gold monument teeming with Berberini's bees, the Pietà – past centuries of craftsmanship by artisans of every skill.

He eventually stopped before the purple draped bier on which lay the open coffin of Pope Nicholas. Four Swiss Guards stood motionless at each corner of the catafalque. At the head of the coffin a solitary candle burned with a steady flame in the still air.

Cardinal Enkomo stared at the body. His Holiness was dressed in full papal vestments, a mitre on his head, arms neatly folded. The embalmers had given him a colouring he had never achieved in life. Julius Enkomo thought the face had little resemblance to the man he had served and loved.

In an hour's time the basilica doors would open and, for the next three days, crowds would file past the catafalque.

At some point the members of the Sacred College would shuffle past to say their collective farewell. But for him this was the moment of farewell.

Julius Enkomo knelt beside the bier and prayed.

After a while he stood up and bowed deeply towards the triple coffin, the tears running down his face.

In the shadow of the tribune holding the ancient wooden chair on which the Apostle Peter was said to have sat, Monsignor Linde continued to watch as the cardinal retraced his steps. He had been following Julius Enkomo to see if he could learn more about the contents of the envelope the camerlengo had seen him retrieve from the top of the wardrobe.

# 18

In the Honolulu suite of the Wong-Hawaii Shangri-La, Sammy Blum crouched over the open Samsonite suitcase. After checking dials, he motioned for Rosie Adamski to move the directional mike on its tubular pole to another spot against the ceiling immediately below the penthouse.

A flat continuous tone continued to come through the headset fitted over Sammy's ears.

'The whole floor's lead-lined,' he said.

Sammy stood up and removed the headphones, frowning behind the horn-rimmed glasses which gave him an uncanny resemblance to Woody Allen.

'There has to be a way. That's what Danny always says.'

'How about drilling a hole in the window frame?' Rosie suggested.

She was a tallish woman with long auburn hair and a smile which had captivated Sammy from the day they were both transferred from Tel Aviv to the Los Angeles branch of Swift Renovations.

'You drill and send up a crab,' she continued.

A crab was a small listening device which could climb walls.

They were that rare couple who could work and live together in almost perfect harmony.

'Too risky. One of the hotel staff might spot it. And they've probably got bafflers on all the windows up there. They'd raise hell if a crab came close.'

He moved towards the bathroom.

'Let's try the plumbing. It's got to be connected to the rest of

260

the hotel. Maybe I can fish a broad spectrum mike up through a waste pipe.'

'Sounds fun,' sighed Rosie. 'You want I call Ken and Brian to say we're going to be late for dinner?'

Ken Rosen and Brian Lownes were the two other Swift operatives. They were in adjoining rooms three floors below.

'Why don't we cancel the restaurant and have them come up here?' Sammy suggested as he stooped to close the suitcase.

Rosie made a mouth. 'You see the room service prices? They'll give Bitburg a fit.'

'Who said we ever came cheap?' Sammy grinned.

As Rosie went to the phone, the door chimes sounded, playing a Hawaiian guitar version of the Wedding March.

They looked at each other quickly. Then, with practised speed, Rosie collapsed the pole and shoved the mike into the bedroom along with the suitcase, while Sammy went to the door. He peered through the security spyhole. A waiter with a room service trolley stood in the corridor. Chinese; the place seemed to be run by them.

On the tablecloth was an ice bucket with a bottle of champagne. Beside it was a box of chocolates and a tureen covering a silver platter. Two flutes stood between the napkins and a single red rose in a vase.

As the waiter's hand once more moved to the bell push, Sammy opened the door.

'Good evening, Mr Blum. A little gift from the management to congratulate you on your marriage.'

The waiter nodded at the display. 'Dom Perignon. Swiss chocolates. And canapes.'

'How nice,' Rosie murmured behind Sammy.

'Good evening, Mrs Blum,' the waiter said.

He was a lot more polite than some of the Chinese in West Hollywood where they lived.

'I'll just set it up then leave you folks to enjoy.'

The waiter pushed the trolley into the room, casually kicking the door closed behind him.

Sammy smiled. He had seen waiters do that before, in case one of their colleagues was passing and saw a tip change hands. This way the waiter could pocket it all for himself instead of putting it into the staff box.

The waiter opened the bottle and handed a flute each to Sammy and Rosie.

'A toast to a long and happy life together,' the waiter intoned. He unwrapped the box of chocolates. Sammy fished in a trouser pocket for his bill fold.

With a little flourish the waiter lifted the tureen, raised the small gas pistol from the platter and shot them both in the face with measured amounts of a paralysing agent.

Rosie and Sammy collapsed, unconscious, on the carpet.

At precisely the same moment, two other hotel security men, also both Chinese, and posing as room service waiters bearing gifts of welcome from the hotel, entered the rooms of Ken Rosen and Brian Lownes and rendered them unconscious.

Immediately more Chinese, dressed as maintenance men, entered the Honolulu Suite and the other two rooms. They pushed large baskets the hotel used for dirty linen.

Still unconscious, the Swift operatives were dumped into the containers, together with the suitcase and mike, and covered with bedding.

The Chinese then wheeled the baskets to service elevators and rode with them down to the basement. They took the baskets to the furnace room and placed them close to the huge oil-fired incinerators. The men remained on guard.

Once the sentry at the Kremlin's Saviour's Gate saw the permit signed by General Borakin, he gave Kramskay a crisp salute and directed the driver to Borakin's private office in the Sveadlov Hall. Another sentry was waiting to escort the prosecutor beyond the hall's imposing entrance of Corinthian columns decorated with bas-relief of tsars and princes long forgotten.

After they passed the entrance to the vast auditorium where the Soviet presidium had finally voted itself out of office, Kramskay found himself in a warren of passages, with anonymous doors firmly closed. They climbed a flight of flagstone steps and passed another door. When Kramskay saw the plaque screwed to the centreboard he knew where he was. The door led to the apartment where Lenin had lived after the 1917 Revolution. A few doors along was the door to the suite Stalin had once occupied. The guard knocked on that door, his ear close to the panelling and, when a muffled voice came from within, he straightened, flung open the door and motioned for Kramskay to enter.

The prosecutor saw Borakin was sitting behind the desk which, like the plate-glass window – as big as those in the Gum department store – was once a feature of this room. At night the window would be lit and the crowds had craned their necks and nudged each other and pointed out the familiar figure at the desk behind the plate glass. Untold millions of people had stood in Red Square and stared up in wonder.

Kramskay remembered his own mother crying the first evening she had brought him to the square urging him to look up there! Yossif Vissarionovich was hard at work! Planning a better world!

Only years later, when he came to actually work in the Kremlin, had Kramskay discovered the truth.

The Stalin in the window had been a dummy made from papier-mâché, so perfectly constructed, said those who saw it close-up, that there was no way of telling it was not real, from a distance. Even Stalin's pipe had a special device which enabled it to emit tobacco at exactly the same intervals as the one the real Generalissimo used. Day and night, often for a week at a time, the dummy sat at this desk, pipe firmly clasped between jaws, face wreathed in smoke, head bowed over some piece of paper, while the real Stalin had gone elsewhere on one of his secret missions which even now no one knew about. Immediately after his death, the window had been replaced so that it once more looked like any other.

Borakin looked up from what he was reading as Kramskay stood in front of the desk.

'Well?'

'Fung has telephoned me to enquire whether you or the other members of the troika are going to the Pope's funeral, comrade general.'

'Did he say anything else?'

Kramskay flushed inwardly. Borakin made the simplest question sound life threatening.

'Only that he will be representing Wong Lee.'

'The tone of his voice?'

'Tone? I'm not sure I understand –'

'Was he merely curious about who we might send to Rome? Or did you detect something else? Apprehension perhaps? Surely you know how to judge the tone of someone's voice?'

Kramskay nodded eagerly. 'Of course, comrade general. I would say his tone was . . . well, curious. Yes, definitely curious.'

Borakin continued to stare at the prosecutor.

Kramskay thought Borakin sat behind the desk the way Stalin must have sat: bolt upright, elbows on the desk top, eyes half closed.

Behind Borakin was the safe he knew was not really a safe. Stalin had installed it to hide the secret passage through which his cleaning woman had come three times a week, the same time every morning, to give herself to him. In all those years Stalin had not spoken a word to her before, during or after their coupling. But shortly before his death the old despot had written her a note, saying how much he appreciated her visits.

Kramskay knew the story was true because the woman was his aunt and she had shown him the note shortly before her own death. The note was now in a deposit box in Credit Suisse in Geneva. A few months ago he had asked the bank to investigate the possibility of selling the note to a Western collector.

Shortly after Fung's call he had received one from Geneva to say the bank had a client. He had asked who and, after some hesitation, the manager had said it was a Fräulein Clara Stevens in California. He had never heard of her. But he had instructed the manager to demand fifteen per cent above any offer Fräulein Stevens made. Fung had once said that was a standard practice in the Western business world.

When Borakin next spoke his voice was flat.

'Comrade Kramskay,' he began, 'do you know of a poison which can produce a brain haemorrhage yet leave no trace?'

Kramskay pursed his lips. There had been that doctor with a practice on Prospekt Marxa who had used an arsenic-based substance he had obtained in Afghanistan to murder several of his wealthier patients. Each died from a brain haemorrhage. But autopsies revealed the presence of the substance. And that waitress who had worked in the old Intourist showcase, the Rossiva on Razin Street. She had taken it into her head that all the foreigners who stayed there had come to Moscow to poison her. The woman had started to spike their food with a rat poison the hotel imported from China. She had been caught after three guests died. But again, post-mortems revealed the poison in their brain tissues.

A poison which left no trace? Kramskay shook his head.

'Maybe one of the old KGB chemists could answer your question, comrade general,' he suggested.

Borakin put another question.

'Do you know anything about Chinese traditional medicine?'

Kramskay gave a nervous little smile. What had any of this to do with Fung's call?

'Only what I picked up in my time in Mongolia, which was not very much,' he said hesitantly.

Borakin's voice remained soft, and yet it was filled with unnerving menace.

'Just tell me what you know, Comrade Kramskay.'

The general listened intently as the prosecutor explained about something called $Qi$ – vital energy – which Chinese doctors believe determines the ability of the human body to resist disease.

'A person's $Qi$ can be weakened by such things as overwork, anxiety, a need to make something happen, an incorrect diet or an excessive intake of stimulants such as alcohol or even tea or coffee.'

Borakin made a note. Then he put a further question.

'In your time in Mongolia did you ever hear of a Chinese drug which by itself would not be fatal, but taken with one of those stimulants would be lethal?'

Kramskay sat for a long moment, racking his brain. That Chinese doctor he met in Ulan Bator, who astonished him by performing a brain operation under acupuncture analgesia, had said something about how easy it would be to use the needles so that even a mild sedative could be lethal.

'Only with acupuncture. But probably only when done by an expert,' Kramskay said.

Borakin made another note. He looked up and continued to study the prosecutor.

'Do you know what a shamaness is?'

Kramskay hesitated. In Mongolia he had gone to that old woman who told him his sexual dysfunction was caused by his kidneys. She had prescribed a powder, which had not helped.

'Yes, I know what a shamaness is.'

'Did Fung ever mention Wong Lee had one?'

Kramskay shook his head.

Borakin abruptly stood up and asked the prosecutor to follow him from the office.

Minutes later they reached the forbidding structure of the Beklemischev Tower built into the southern corner of the Kremlin Wall. Outwardly there was nothing to show the importance of the tower, other than its historic significance. A small plaque over the door in Cyrillic script confirmed this was the place where the Mongol hordes had broken into the Kremlin in the seventeenth century.

The two armed sentries at the tower entrance remained at attention after one pressed a button for a heavy steel door to roll silently open.

Despite Borakin's intimidating silence, Kramskay felt a sudden surge of excitement. Whatever the purpose behind the baffling and unrelated questions, his answers had somehow been satisfactory enough for him to be brought to what was still one of the most secret places in Russia.

Beyond was a short, brightly lit corridor, featureless except for a surveillance camera. Borakin led the way to an elevator. Still in silence they rode down four levels and emerged in another identical corridor. At the far end was another steel door. Borakin pressed buttons on the coded keyboard and the door rolled back into the wall. They stepped into the Planning Centre.

Scores of men worked before computer terminals and video display units. One wall was covered with a map of the former Soviet Union, another with one of the world. Lights blinked brightly on both.

'You know what happens in this place?' Borakin asked.

'Only by reputation, comrade general,' whispered Kramskay.

'You can speak normally. The walls and ceilings are lined with lead. Not even the American antenna farms can penetrate here.'

Borakin waved a hand over the chamber.

'From Stalin onwards, your leaders have come here. And do you know what they all had in common, Comrade Kramskay?'

Borakin gripped the gantry rail tightly as he continued to speak.

'Failure! From Stalin's failure to outsmart Truman and Churchill at Potsdam all the way to Gorbachev's failure to hold the Federation together, the smell of failure has filled this place. That will not happen this time.'

He led the way down a steel staircase to the floor of the

chamber. Men looked up briefly and then returned to their screens.

Moving across the floor towards them was General Yuri Savenko. He wore the fatigues he had worn at the dacha. He gave Borakin a crisp salute and nodded quickly to Kramskay.

Savenko led them to an unattended work station. There was the usual computer and VDU screen.

'Give us the latest situation,' Borakin demanded.

Savenko reached forward and his fingers flew over the computer keyboard. On screen appeared a series of numbers which meant nothing to Kramskay, but which Savenko began to interpret in a calm voice.

'The Chinese are sending two armies to reinforce the one already in position along the Kazakhstan border. It will take between eight and ten days before they can be deployed.'

'And Beijing perfectly understands our position?' Borakin interrupted.

'Perfectly.'

Kramskay decided to ask a question. 'And what is that position, General Savenko?'

Savenko looked at Borakin.

'Beijing has been told that while we would normally regard any incursion as dangerous provocation, we perfectly understand China's wish, on this occasion, to protect her own borders.'

'So the Chinese deal with our troublesome Moslems?' Kramskay began.

'You are not here to discuss military strategy,' Borakin said. He turned back to the screen.

'What about those Wong Holdings companies in South Korea, Pakistan, Burma and Nepal?' Borakin asked.

Savenko typed rapidly. Fresh computerspeak appeared on the screen.

'With the exception of Nepal, we have persuaded the other governments to warn Wong Holdings that giving extended credit to our Moslem republics would be a breach of their local operating licences.'

'Why not Nepal?' Borakin demanded.

Savenko grinned. 'The Wong Holdings factory there only produces trinkets for the Asian market.'

Kramskay pointed to lights flashing on the wall map of the world.

'What is happening in Washington and London?' he asked.

'Comrade Kramskay, you really are very inquisitive!' Borakin sighed. 'But just this once, I will explain. The same as is happening in Paris, Frankfurt . . . in all the stock exchanges where this country has significant trading links. In each case we have discreetly warned the local central bank Wong Holdings might suddenly withdraw its investments.'

Kramskay continued to probe. 'Why should the capitalists believe us?'

'It's in their interest,' Borakin said shortly.

'I see. But I still don't understand why Wong Lee would wish to withdraw from markets which must be profitable for him,' Kramskay persisted.

'Comrade Kramskay, these matters do not concern you.'

Kramskay flushed as if he had been slapped in the face. Borakin was pleased. You crushed and humiliated a man first before you remade him in your image.

He turned to Savenko and began to give orders.

'You will go to Rome to represent the troika at the Pope's funeral. You will use your time to try and discover what support the next Pope will have for this Holy Cross operation. Take every opportunity to show we will encourage it to go ahead.'

Savenko nodded. Borakin turned to Kramskay.

'You will also travel to Rome and concentrate on Fung. Find out everything you can about Wong Lee's intentions. Use our embassy to communicate directly with me.'

He paused and looked at Savenko.

'There is one other matter. The Israeli, Morton. He is remaining in Rome. Almost certainly he will try and approach you.'

Savenko nodded. 'He has already. He called requesting permission for our doctor, Ogodnikova, to be allowed to go to Israel.'

'Did he give a reason?'

Savenko grinned. 'He didn't have to. I heard it in his voice.'

Borakin shrugged. 'Let her go. And encourage Morton to believe we wish this Operation Holy Cross to succeed.'

Kramskay was about to say something, but stopped when he saw the look on Borakin's face. And the prosecutor realised that, despite being admitted to this sanctuary, he remained very much an outsider when it came to understanding what was really going on.

*

Morton watched the light coming through the bedroom window change from grey to pale white and then a glorious gold which quickly became flecked with pink. Soon the sun would rise. But already he felt alive and awake, as though for the first time. Beside him Carina's body fluttered gently as she gave a little sigh in her sleep.

A few hours ago, they had left the papal apartment and found their way back to their hotel-like suites. They adjoined each other, with a connecting door. Morton had assumed the arrangement was for those cardinals who travelled with a secretary or servant.

From the size of the bed he guessed his was a cardinal's bedroom. The furniture was equally large, dark and oppressive. There was a prie-dieu in a corner; the only wall-hanging was a crucifix. The bedroom was like an overbearing penitential cell.

He had used the direct line phone on a bureau to call Savenko, who said there was no problem. Dr Ogodnikova would be one less mouth to feed, he had boomed over the crackling line from Moscow.

Afterwards Morton had turned off the light and stood at the window, listening to the night sounds of the city. A knock on the adjoining door disturbed his reverie. Carina had stood there. He was conscious she wore nothing underneath her dress. As she walked past him into the room she took his hand and led him towards the bed. For a moment she studied his face intently. Then in one graceful movement she removed her dress and he saw her naked body for the first time.

She slid between the sheets and, as he quickly shed his clothes to join her, a crushing excitement blotted out everything. When they made love all his feelings were focused on the silky strangeness of this woman who cried out in Russian at her moment of fulfilment.

They remained joined together, and he had tasted the salt of her tears and stroked her hair. After a while, they made love again, more gently.

They had fallen asleep, their bodies entwined, her soft lips open to his.

Sometime before the dawn turned to gold, she drew him into her again, whispering once more she loved him. And he had whispered back he loved her. After he lifted himself from her, their bodies separating with damp reluctance, she had curled up and fallen back to sleep.

He lay, eyes half-closed, the scent of her mingling with the sounds of the dawn. Low voices in the courtyard below; guards changing shift. A bell tolling. A priest murmuring his first prayers of a new day.

He thought of what Yoshi had said. *All the women I've known, David, want to own you. And that's not for me. You don't think she'll want to own you?*

He did not know and it did not matter. He felt he had known her for years. It was a strange feeling, something he had never experienced with any other woman.

Sex without affection he had always felt to be repugnant. He supposed it was the way he had been brought up. Steve and Dolly's love for each other had been such a vibrant thing.

The sound of the telephone seemed to fill the room. Morton slid out of the bed and padded to the bureau.

'David?'

'Yes.'

'Our Swift people in Hawaii have disappeared. We've run every check. The hotel says they all just suddenly left, to go to the airport. But there's no trace of them on any outgoing flight.'

There was silence for a moment and Morton thought they had been cut off.

'A surveillance team would never leave like that,' he said.

'Covert Action are flying in a team. But it's going to take the best part of the day before they're in place.'

They both knew it was a long shot. They both knew they had to do something.

Morton put down the phone. As he turned, he was in time to see Carina closing the connecting door behind her.

In a disused mine gallery in the hills of Montana, the shooter went about his preparations. In the eight hours since accepting the commission from Franco Umberto, in a phone call the godfather had made from one pay phone to another, the shooter had flown from Chicago to Omaha.

A private jet was waiting to take him to Denver. He had completed the rest of his journey by air in a helicopter. A jeep was waiting by the landing pad.

On the bench seat was a locked suitcase and the directions

to the mine, together with a sealed envelope containing bank confirmation that 1,000,000 dollars had been deposited in his name with Credit Suisse in Geneva. A further 1,000,000 dollars would be paid on completion of the assignment.

It was an hour's drive to the mine. He found everything had been prepared as he had instructed.

The rock wall at the far end of the long gallery was painted white. An old flatbed car which once carried miners to the workings, was waiting on the rails. Mounted on the car was a section of a window frame set in plywood. The overall effect was of a balcony. Inside the construction was a movie projector.

Placing the suitcase on the flatbed, the shooter stepped out the distance to the painted wall. Three hundred yards. He walked back to the flatbed and pulled it another twenty-five yards back along the newly greased rails. He opened the suitcase. The CQ sniper's rifle was in separate pieces: stock, barrel, telescopic sight, silencer. Fitted into the lid were clips of ammunition. The CQ was among the very best produced by Norinco, the State Armaments Corporation of China.

He quickly assembled stock and barrel and balanced it in his hand. Five and a half pounds. He clipped on a magazine. The twenty rounds of cartridges each weighed three ounces. Another four pounds. He screwed on the silencer and clipped on the sight. A couple more pounds. He always liked working with a heavy weapon. He had been doing so for ten years, the last five for Umberto.

In that time he had killed over twenty men and women in various parts of the world. Some had fled to its remotest corners. No matter; once they were located he had gone there and killed them. He never asked what they had done; that would be too personal an involvement.

His work had made him wealthy and, he knew, in his own world, totally respected. There was no one else like him. His present assignment had not impressed him. It was just another target.

The shooter climbed on to the flatbed and stood at the window frame peering at the white smudge almost a quarter of a mile away. He stepped back and lined up the rifle on the smudge. He made an adjustment to the telescopic sight. Then he turned on the projector. On the makeshift screen vague figures appeared.

The shooter once more peered through the gunsight.

Into view came a crowd in St Peter's Square. The film had

been shot from a high vantage point. Caligula's Obelisk was foreshortened, and the steps of the basilica ran off the smudge. But the faces around the popemobile were in sharp focus: priests, security men, all staring into the crowd who were waving ecstatically at the familiar figure of Pope Nicholas the Sixth.

Umberto had explained the news film was shot almost a year ago. It was really only intended as a guideline. You could never rehearse something like this. That's why you charged two million dollars.

The shooter watched through the gunsight until the film ran out. He rewound the projector, and once more ran the footage.

The shooter stepped back a couple of paces from the window frame and, feet comfortably apart, looked along the barrel. He waited until the image he wanted appeared. His finger tightened on the trigger. There was a little click and a flexing at his shoulder as the rifle recoiled.

At the moment of firing, the film freeze-framed; the projector was synchronised to stop at the sound of the click. The shooter lowered the rifle and walked down to the makeshift screen. Exactly where he expected, a piece was gouged out of the rock.

The shooter turned and walked back to the mouth of the cave, where he had parked the jeep. He used its mobile phone to call the number he had been given in Mexico City.

He had to raise his voice against the sharpening wind.

'*Puede hacerse!*' he said, hanging up.

It really could be done.

While he dismantled his rifle, he considered the one other matter he had to settle: the choice of a name. It was not until he was back in the helicopter that he settled on one. Father Juan Gomez.

His mother had always wanted him to be a priest.

# 19

On one of the monitors in Morelli's office Morton watched the door of the basilica close behind the last of an estimated one million persons who had filed past Nicholas the Sixth's bier.

It was almost noon on the third day after his death and Rome remained the focus of world attention.

The previous evening the Pope's will had been released specially in time for the evening television news. Morton thought the ten page document confirmed the essential goodness and simplicity of the man. The testament ended with Nicholas's plea for pardon from all those he had harmed.

Rome itself was now a citadel as the first statesmen arrived to pay their last respects. At times the Via della Conciliazione seemed as if it was playing host to all the bodyguards on earth.

Morton's time had been divided between Morelli's office and the Apostolic Palace. He had sat in on Colonel Asmusson's briefing for the Swiss Guards and listened to Morelli deploying his men. He was reassured by their thoroughness. In between he met a number of cardinals, introduced to him by Julius Enkomo, and was impressed by the way they balanced genuine sorrow with a sense of reality.

He had glimpsed Sean hurrying out of the Vatican by the tradesmen's entrance – the Santa Anna Gate. It was symbolic of the secretary's new status, Sean was now just another priest, living in one of the poky rooms the Vatican always had available around Rome.

Often late at night, Morton returned to the suite to find Carina waiting.

Sometimes there had been an unguarded frenzy to their love-making and afterwards he would lie with his face pressed against her stomach. Other times they were gentle, almost chaste and, when they finished, she would murmur snatches of Russian poetry to him. Each had a growing sense of wonder and joy they had found each other.

When she had finally shared her past with him, all he saw in her face was the complete honesty of someone who wanted to make the future work for them both.

They had lain on the bed and spoken of what it would be like. There would be no pressure, no rush to formalise the situation. Marriage, as such, did not interest either of them, but one day, perhaps, they would have a child. In the meantime she would continue to work. When he had warned her his job took him away for weeks, sometimes months, she had nodded, accepting completely.

Nothing he had previously experienced with any woman had prepared him for the extraordinary moments which had not only exorcised the past, but had promised him a future he had never dared think possible.

Before he had gone out this morning, he had given Carina money to buy clothes for the funeral, and those she would need for the journey to Tel Aviv. She would travel with Yoshi on the El Al flight which left Rome later that evening. Morton had already given her the keys to his apartment, and told her about its magnificent views of the sea and the hills of Judaea.

He turned to another screen. In St Peter's Square, on the balustrades of Bernini's colonnade, between the baroque statues, TV camera crews continued to rehearse the shots to bring the funeral to an expected audience of one billion.

On the square itself squads of Vatican workers were setting out over twenty thousand hardback chairs for the official mourners. The marble steps of St Peter's were already lined with velvet-covered kneelers for the cardinals.

The first police, carabinieri and *Digos* paramilitary squads were in position.

'They've sent ten thousand,' growled Morelli. 'They're calculating on one for every twenty mourners. That still leaves nineteen to worry about.'

A middle aged man with a boxer's physique turned to Morelli. 'I'll have a couple hundred of my best down there,' said Bill

Gates. 'They've done nothing else for the past three days but study every terrorist face we have on file.'

The CIA Director of Operations had arrived on Air Force One with the President of the United States and the First Lady, and representatives of the US church hierarchy.

The tall, patrician figure of Jacques Lacouste gave a grim smile. 'It's the ones we don't have on file that worry me.'

Murmurs of agreement came from the others. Marcus Baader glanced at them. His eyes were like yellow topaz, cold as the eyes of a cat.

'I have persuaded our Chancellor to arrive only an hour beforehand, and to leave immediately afterwards,' said the German Intelligence Chief.

A short, dark-haired man whose jaw line was beginning to blur with flesh turned away from the screens.

'There'd be no way the entire Cabinet could dissuade my Prime Minister from turning this into a photo opportunity,' groaned Percival West of MI5.

Britain's new Prime Minister was a notorious self-publicist.

A man with a gleaming white scar through one of his dark eyebrows turned to Morton.

'As far as the Middle East goes, everybody seems to be in his lair,' said Anwar Salim of Egyptian Intelligence.

'That still leaves a lot of people to do Wong Lee's dirty work,' murmured Norm Stratton. Canada's Secret Intelligence Service Chief had a mild-mannered expression which matched his voice.

One by one as they had arrived in Rome with their official delegations to the funeral, Morton had summoned them to report to him. Apart from the antenna farm over Lhasa confirming Wong Lee had returned there, frustratingly little was added to what he knew.

Gates had called the FBI Director to have his field agents in Honolulu join the search for the missing Swift operatives. The agents were working closely with the Covert Action team from Tel Aviv. Though the hotel had been searched from top to bottom, nothing had been found.

Stratton's operatives in Beijing had run into the proverbial bamboo curtain. Baader and Lacouste's agents still had turned up zilch in Germany or France about Wong Holdings.

The only development came from West. The Bank of England had received a priority message from Russia's Finance Minister warning Wong Holdings could be about to pull out of the London market.

'We can't let that happen,' West said crisply. 'So my government's taken steps to freeze all the key companies in which Wong Holdings has stock the moment he makes a move. The usual excuses. An investigation into suspected trading irregularities. God knows, we've had so much of that no one's going to be surprised. Our fraud people reckon they can keep enquiries going for months. In that time Wong Lee's money will just have to sit there.'

'Good thinking, Percy,' Morton said. 'If nothing else, that'll make him twitch. And might make him show us what he's planning next.'

Gates turned to Morton. 'The President's brought Greenberg, our Federal Reserve's top honcho with him. Greenberg's going to have a quiet word with Fung to explain our Exchange Securities people are going to run a check on all Wong Holdings operations in the US. They've started to do that with foreign-based companies after the Maxwell business. Wong Lee won't want to start rocking the boat while the Exchange investigators are on deck.'

Lacouste looked curiously at the others. 'Anyone any ideas why the Russians delivered that warning?'

Gates shrugged. 'Glasnost lingers on. And with the Russian economy in a downward spiral, the last thing it needs is to have its foreign investments rocked by Wong Lee.'

He glanced at Morton. 'Who're they sending?'

Morton told them Savenko and Kramskay were due in Rome shortly.

He glanced towards the monitor which had remained linked to Concorde even when the plane made the round trip to bring Karshov and the Israeli delegation to the funeral. The plane was now back on the ground at Rome airport.

The CCO was on screen.

'I have Danny. He says it's urgent,' the CCO said.

There was a sudden silence in the office.

A moment later Danny's face appeared from the communications room in Morton's Kingdom in Tel Aviv. There was a strained, haunted look on Danny's face.

'We know what's happened to our missing quartet. The Honolulu police got a call from people living downwind from the hotel complaining they'd been showered with ash. The police think it's bone fragments. They must have tossed the Swift people into the hotel incinerators, like it was Auschwitz all over again.'

Several of the men around Morton swore softly.

Leading the group through the Mail Room, Clara Stevens was increasingly aware the Reverend Kingdom's mind was elsewhere. Usually he used the weekly inspection to constantly remind everyone in Mail they were among his key staff – the first to know what the global congregation was saying and thinking. And, Martha would add, how much they were tithing.

Yet this morning he had asked none of his usual questions about returns on the latest video mail shot, or orders for copies of the Only Book.

They hurried through Prelim Sort, where thirty girls fed the envelopes through automatic openers. The machines slit the envelopes, snipped off the stamps, removed the contents and separated the letters from cash, cheques or money orders. The stamps were sold to dealers.

Clara consulted her clipboard. She was a woman in her late twenties, dressed in the pale blue tunic and pants of a head of department. The white silk scarf at her throat was held in place with a brooch bearing a small enamelled portrait of the Reverend Kingdom.

'We're up a mail sack a day, mostly from the Ukraine membership,' she volunteered.

'That's terrific, Clara,' the Reverend Kingdom murmured as they strode towards Second Count.

Neither Martha nor Hal Lockman spoke.

When Martha had arrived in the Mail Room, she had given Clara a perfunctory smile, then deliberately turned away. It helped turn Clara's hurt over Martha's rejection into a strong desire to hurt, first Martha and then her unctuous brother and, if that was not possible, someone close to them, someone they depended on, like the insufferable Hal Lockman.

'We're up a couple of thousand dollars on stamp sales,' Clara continued. 'That means Prelim Sort is now paying for itself.'

'Terrific, Clara,' the Reverend Kingdom murmured again as they entered Second Count.

A dozen women sat before electronic scanners, programmed to identify key words in the mail. Those letters with complaints went into one basket; those offering praise or suggestions into another. The baskets were sent on to Mail Analysis.

'What's the breakdown this week?' asked Martha abruptly.

'So far we're up five per cent on complaints,' Clara said sweetly. 'Mostly about the choir not sounding as good as they used to. We've also had an increase in the number saying they're finding it hard to meet the tithe.'

Hal glanced at the Reverend Kingdom.

'Maybe we ought to add a paragraph to the standard letter saying we're also feeling the pinch.'

He gave Martha a sly, sidelong glance.

'Perhaps you'd like to add a line about how we're always on the lookout for new Angels?'

She flushed. 'Thank you, Hal.'

As they moved down the row of scanners, Clara detected a tension in Martha and Hal she had not noticed before. But nothing like their fury would be after what she planned to do.

Clara had now decided how she could hurt them all. Eddie – because it would shake his judgement about never being wrong about a person. Martha – because it would drive her half-crazy that she had not spotted the scam first. Hal – because it would devastate his unshakeable belief in being able to carry off the almost perfect fraud.

Clara had discovered Hal's rip-off of Church funds purely by chance three months ago. One of the machines in Prelim Sort had rejected an envelope because its computer had identified the envelope as staff mail. That came in a separate sack. The girl operating the machine was new and had turned to Clara for help.

She had taken the envelope to her glass-walled office on a podium overlooking the work floor. For a while she had studied the envelope with its Geneva franking. Hal's name and address were printed inside the window flap. She had managed to make out the letter came from Credit Suisse. She had punched out the bank's name on her computer. Records did not list the bank as a contributor.

Clara had opened the envelope before she realised what she had done. It contained a bank statement, giving Hal's account number and access code, together with a list of deposits. Using the access code and then tapping more keys, Clara had unravelled the history of Hal's scam, uncovering every little theft from the portfolios under his control.

She had been neither shocked, nor surprised. She had always suspected Hal was that kind of creep.

Her discovery came right in the midst of her relationship with Martha. Sometimes, after they had satisfied their needs, she had been tempted to tell Martha what she had discovered. Instinct always stopped her. Now she knew why. God had given her this knowledge as an instrument to punish.

After Eddie returned from Hawaii – flushed with having flown in the unimagined luxury of Wong Lee's private jet and almost feverish with excitement over what he had been asked to do – Clara had run another check on Hal's secret account. It had almost doubled.

The same sixth sense which had made her open the envelope in the first place, told her that Hal could be about to disappear to enjoy his ill-gotten gains. His kind of large-scale larceny could not continue much longer before being discovered.

'Let's skip Mail Analysis and go straight to Banking,' the Reverend Kingdom said.

It had taken all of Martha's persuasion to get him to leave his office in the first place. For the past two days he had done almost nothing else but polish and hone his attack on Cardinal Muller.

He had combed the Only Book for evidence and found all he needed. The gospel texts would require a little editing and interpretation. But that was his forte, the reason God had chosen him.

The armed guard standing outside Banking opened the door.

'Still doing God's work, Billy?' asked the Reverend Kingdom.

'Right on the button, Reverend. And bless His name,' intoned the guard.

Entering the Banking Room, Hal had a sense of *déjà vu*. He had begun his career in a room like this, in those days when banks in the Midwest still had a formal counting room in which large deposits were weighed, banded and tabulated on strips of paper. A dozen women were doing exactly that on either side of the long polished table running the length of the room. Cash was going into one bin, cheques and money orders into another, credit card slips into a third.

'Despite the complaints we're still up on last year's weekly figure,' Clara said.

'How much?' Hal asked.

She glanced at her clipboard. 'Four point two per cent.'

Hal did the conversion in his head and turned to the Reverend Kingdom.

'That's six hundred and twenty seven thousand dollars, Eddie.'

'Terrific, Hal. Really terrific.'

Hal made another calculation. Once the money was banked, he would transfer ten per cent to Geneva. 62,700 dollars. He would reach his million target very shortly.

Martha was watching him between her slanting quick glances around the room. She still had not made up her mind what to do about the report from Fenton, who was in charge of security.

The former LA Police Department detective was both devout and dedicated and had a nose for trouble that enabled more than one potential scandal to be nipped in the bud. Earlier this morning he had come to her office with a story which, if not exactly unfamiliar, was still deeply disturbing.

Despite all her precautions, male staff had formed illicit relationships with female employees. Each time the culprits were swiftly dismissed. But she could not easily sack Hal. Next to Eddie and herself he was indispensable to the smooth running of the entire operation.

She could dismiss the girl, of course. Have her returned to the detention centre from which she had been plucked. Fenton had suggested that.

Again Martha had hesitated. That might not be the smartest move because it did not take into account Hal's reactions. Supposing the fool had fallen in love with the strumpet? Supposing Hal threatened to leave unless she was allowed to stay?

As the Reverend Kingdom turned to leave the room, Martha looked at Hal.

'You got time for a coffee?'

He studied her for a moment. As usual there was no way of telling what she was thinking.

'Sure,' Hal said.

After escorting them from her department, Clara went to her office and closed the door.

There was something else she had not shared with Martha: her passion for collecting memorabilia.

Since she was a small child, when her father had pinned up in her bedroom a fake vellum copy of the Declaration of Independence, Clara had collected such artifacts. She now had a drawerful of medals, coins, and other bric-a-brac, all of it reproduction and each item costing only a few dollars. With them were a stack of collectors magazines. She had ringed many of the ads offering items that often cost more than her annual salary. The most recent ad to catch her eye was one for an authentic letter in Stalin's own hand, written to his cleaning woman.

The thought that one of the most powerful men in the world had done that intrigued Clara enough to write to the box number. A few days later she had received a letter from Credit Suisse in Geneva explaining they held the document in trust for a client and would be happy to discuss a price for its sale. She had offered 1.000 dollars. The bank politely replied that they could not forward such an offer to their client. She had suggested 5,000 dollars, only to receive the same response. Her next offer of 10,000 dollars brought another refusal, with a closing paragraph saying no offer below 50,000 dollars would be entertained. The figure represented exactly double her annual salary. But that was no longer a problem.

Seated before her computer screen, Clara keyed the various stages of the operation until there was only one left. Then she locked off the sequence. When the time came, at the press of a key, she could begin to empty Hal's account into her own in the Bank of Southern California. Clara then began to compose a letter to Credit Suisse containing her final offer for the historic document: 100,000 dollars.

Wong Lee stood on the catwalk high above Central Operations. The chamber was a hive of activity. Tens of millions of dollars' worth of stocks were being traded back and forth across the stockmarkets of the world.

This was the time he enjoyed the most, watching his empire grow richer before his very eyes. It was more exciting than sex; more exciting than anything.

The girl in the penthouse had turned out to be surprisingly unimaginative when it came to the finer points of arousal. He had cut short her efforts and quickly strangled her. Her body had followed those of Morton's Zionists into the hotel incinerator. As a precaution, carcases from the hotel kitchen's butchery had also been fed to the furnaces.

Though the local police and the FBI had swarmed over the hotel, they found nothing except ash. There would be no way for them to forensically differentiate between the animal and human residue. Morton would only suspect – and that would add to his frustration, which would be one way to teach him a lesson.

Wong Lee's eyes were drawn to what was happening on that corner of the floor where the London stockmarket traders operated. He had ordered twenty million pounds' worth of shares in his UK portfolio to be sold. It was to be a test run.

Now the traders were talking animatedly among themselves and pointing to their screens. The floor supervisor was hurrying over to them. He listened for a moment, then turned and looked anxiously up at the catwalk. The man reached for his portable phone and a moment later Wong Lee's own portable purred. He put it to his ear.

'Singsung, something bad is happening in London. We cannot execute the sell orders,' said the supervisor.

'Why not?'

'The City Fraud Squad has begun another of its investigations. They say there may have been irregularities in the companies we have invested in. All movement is frozen.'

'For how long?'

'They won't say, singsung.'

On other parts of the floor traders were also beginning to stop work.

'What about the other markets?'

'What is happening in London is making them nervous, singsung. There is an overall volume drop in Tokyo, Hong Kong, Paris and Frankfurt. To buy or sell now would not be good, singsung.'

'Until I ask for your advice, do not offer it!' Wong Lee hung up.

A moment later the mobile purred again.

'Singsung?' Fung's voice was more high pitched than ever with nervousness.

'Did you deliver my message to Messner?'

'Yes, of course. But something else has happened. Mr Greenberg has spoken to me. The Exchange Securities Commission are to conduct a check on all our American holdings. Mr Greenberg says it is quite normal. Before he went to the Federal Bank, he had the same happen to him when he was running –'

'When is this review going to take place?'

'Soon, singsung.'

'How soon, you fool?'

'Mr Greenberg did not say, singsung.'

Wong Lee again broke the connection.

Morton was behind this; he had to be. The acceptance calmed Wong Lee. He began to give new orders over the mobile. It was time to teach Morton another lesson. By the time Wong Lee reached his office, Morton's personal file was on the onyx slab.

Seating himself on the log Wong Lee once more read the dossier. Afterwards he sat perfectly still, silently repeating the mantra which helped to further concentrate his mind. Then he spoke into the communications sphere to Fung. He asked only one question.

In an hour Fung was back with the answer. Wong Lee then sent for the shamaness and Chung-Shi. He told them what he wanted done.

Two hours later Chung-Shi, accompanied by a dozen of his best agents, lifted off from the helipad for the short journey to Lhasa's Freedom Airport. A 747 was waiting. As the plane climbed over the Himalayas, Chung-Shi began to rehearse the team by giving them the description Fung had provided of Carina.

Behind the Tabernacle was a small open patio with a dozen tables and chairs in front of a coffee dispenser. Hal brought their styrofoam cups back to the table where Martha sat.

'Some of the Angels been badgering me to have a doughnut machine installed,' he sighed.

'Is that why you suggested we needed new Angels?' she asked.

He shook his head and smiled.

'Heck, no! And I think you do a terrific job with the choir.'

Martha looked into his eyes and she saw, as always, only sincerity.

'It's not easy, you know, being responsible for so many young girls. They need constant watching.'

He nodded in sympathy. 'I can imagine.'

'Do you know a girl called Penny-Jane?'

The abruptness of her question did not startle him. He had subconsciously steeled himself for it. The question was not whether Martha knew – but how much.

'I know her, yes. But why do you ask?'

'She's been seen going and coming from your apartment,' Martha said, her eyes steady on him.

Hal continued to stir his coffee.

'I won't ask who told you this. Fenton, I guess. But it doesn't matter.'

He reached across the table and briefly touched Martha's hand as if to reassure her of the truth.

'Before I answer your question, let me ask you one. Have you ever, at any time, had any cause to doubt my total commitment to the doctrine of the Church of True Belief?'

She looked at him with lips pursed. She finally said, 'Until now, no.'

He held her gaze. 'Martha, what I am going to say is very personal and private. I want you to respect that.'

'I'll have to tell Eddie –'

'Of course. But hear me out first. Окау?'

After a momentary hesitation, she nodded.

'Ever since I came here, I've made no secret of wanting to be completely involved. To show the Good Lord I am ready to serve Him morning, noon and night. As much as Eddie and you, I believe in the Only Book and our Lord Jesus. And Jesus taught that the flesh is weak. And it's not just Penny-Jane we should be talking about, but Clara Stevens. Isn't that right, Martha?'

She felt the sky seem to darken for a moment and Hal's face grow several times its real size. How had he found out? His mouth continued to move, but she could not hear what he was saying. And then his words were clear.

'. . . Penny-Jane came to me because she was frightened of what had happened to her with Clara. She didn't want to come to you or Eddie because . . . well, she thought you wouldn't understand. Perhaps not even believe her. Clara's a deacon. And she's not supposed to behave like that, touching Penny-Jane and all that. The Good Lord only knows where it would have ended if Penny-Jane hadn't transferred out of Mail. But there she was. A street kid who'd found sanctuary with us – and suddenly it was all threatened if she said Clara was trying to turn her into a sexual deviant!'

He paused. He could see the sudden uncertainty on her face. And something else. Almost fear.

'What are you saying, Hal?'

He spread his hands. 'Against Clara? Nothing. I wasn't there. But I saw the look in Penny-Jane's face when she told me. She truly believed that Clara tried – well, to seduce her.'

Martha felt her cheeks flame. The bitch! How long had this being going on? While she and Clara had been lovers, had Clara been hopping from one bed to another?

'You feeling okay, Martha?'

She gathered herself.

'I'm fine. It's just that I'm stunned. There's never been any suspicion about Clara before.'

She was getting a grip on herself, remembering why she was here.

'Hal, it doesn't change the fact you've been accused of breaking the rules by taking this girl to your apartment.'

Smiling, he held up his hand, palm towards her.

'On that I plead guilty. But let me explain. When I happened upon Penny-Jane she was in a bad state. You can't calm down someone like that in a corridor with other people about.'

'You could have taken her to one of the counselling rooms.'

'You forget, Martha, that Eddie introduced a rule only deacons can now use them,' Hal said softly.

'But that still doesn't excuse what you did.'

He put down the cup and spoke unhurriedly. 'I broke your rule. And I apologise. But in breaking it, I saved Penny-Jane from making a whole lot of problems, for Clara – and for you.'

'What problems?' Martha whispered.

Hal smiled. Penny-Jane had been right. There had been something going on between Martha and Clara. He plunged on, confident now of how to handle the situation.

'Martha, I've spent all the spare time I have in counselling Penny-Jane. She trusts me because – well, I guess I'm like the father she's always wanted. Did you know her own father killed himself? And her mother died of a heroin overdose when Penny-Jane was just a kid? Those sort of things you don't talk easily about. I got her to speak only after I had built up trust between us, so I could achieve what I'm still trying to do – lead her to the Good Lord.'

'And bless His name,' Martha said automatically.

'Amen,' Hal added.

He leaned forward and looked intensely across the table.

'I just want to go on helping her, Martha. If that means you need to raise this with Eddie, that's okay. I'm sure he will understand what I'm trying to do. But I can only go on doing this in the peace and quiet of my apartment. And I can only really succeed if I keep this between Penny-Jane and myself. If you or Eddie were to speak to her now, why it could undo all I'm trying to achieve.'

Hal paused to sip more coffee, his eyes never leaving Martha's face. The fear on her face was more visible. His certainty grew. He put down the cup.

'Penny-Jane was badly scared by Clara, Martha. I guess you would have been, too. Eddie's right. 'Tain't natural for the same sex to . . . well, enjoy each other like that. I know some folks say consenting adults can do as they please in the privacy of their home. But Penny-Jane is just a kid!'

Martha felt her cheeks burning and she busied herself once more stirring her coffee. Her mind was racing. Hal knew. Hal was dangerous. Hal would have to be treated with extreme caution. She lifted her head and looked at him.

'I understand what you're saying, Hal. You know how much I value having you here. That's why I wouldn't want you to be the subject of filthy innuendo.'

He nodded fervently. 'Nor me, Martha! Nor me! But I just want to go on helping Penny-Jane. She really appreciates what I can do for her.'

Hal paused, sensing he was close to overkill. He gave a little shrug. 'But it's really up to you. And I guess Eddie, if you tell him.'

Martha realised how brilliantly Hal had manipulated her. The girl must have told him about Clara and her. And Penny-Jane could only have learned that from Clara. Clara would have to go. But how to explain that to Eddie? He thought Clara was doing a wonderful job in Mail.

Martha came to a decision. 'I don't think I'm going to mention any of this to Eddie. He's got so many other things to think about right now –'

'How's the campaign against Muller shaping up?'

'Coming along,' she said, thinking Hal is really expert at switching direction. He was more than dangerous. He was formidably dangerous.

'We need to stop the Romans dead in their tracks, Martha.'

She nodded. 'Okay. This is what I've decided to do. You will have special dispensation to go on counselling Penny-Jane in your apartment. But only during the day.'

'That's okay. I can work late to catch up with my other work.'

He leaned across the table.

'I'm really glad you raised this with me Martha, before it was allowed to grow in people's minds. It's so easy to get the wrong idea when all you're doing is trying to help someone.'

'I'm sorry if I sounded mad at you, Hal.'

He smiled at her.

'That's okay, Martha. In your position, I'd be just as angry if someone came to me and said you were stepping out of line with a member of staff.'

She felt her cheeks turn crimson.

Hal stood up. 'I'd better go and make sure God's money is properly invested.'

'And bless His name,' Martha automatically responded. For the moment she was still too shaken to stand up.


In a side room behind the great altar of St Peter, Hubert Messner and Hans-Dietrich Muller frowned at Fung. Monsignor Linde leaned against the door, arms folded, staring unblinkingly at Wong Lee's secretary. The cardinals had agreed to meet him here before robing for the funeral mass. Their vestments were hanging from pegs on the wall.

When Fung finished speaking he remained as stiffly formal as the morning suit he had rented, his top hat clutched in both hands.

'Please thank Mr Wong Lee for his condolences,' the camerlengo began. 'It is good to know the Church has such friends at this time of sorrow.'

Fung inclined his head.

'And thank him, too, for warning us about the attack we should expect.'

'May we know how your employer learned of it?' Cardinal Muller asked.

Fung shrugged. 'He knows many things before they happen.'

Cardinal Messner nodded. 'But it is no real surprise Reverend Kingdom should decide to attack the Church when we are filled with grief.'

Fung glanced at Cardinal Muller. 'But the attack will be against you personally, Your Eminence.'

Cardinal Muller sighed. 'It is not the first time a rabble-rouser has attacked me, Mr Fung. I expect it will not be the last. But I shall deal with any attack from the Reverend Kingdom the way I have always done. By ignoring it. And including him in my prayers.'

The camerlengo nodded. 'We have long learned to wear a crown of thorns in our calling. One more prick will not unduly trouble us.'

'And once again, please make sure Mr Wong Lee knows how grateful we are,' Cardinal Muller added.

The apartment rented in the name of Father Gomez of Mexico City was on the top floor of a block at the Rome end of the Via della Conciliazione. Like several of the other apartments on either side of the broad avenue Mussolini had ordered to be built, this one had a small enclosed balcony, identical to the one mounted on the flatbed car in Montana.

From the balcony, Father Gomez had the same high-angled view of St Peter's Square he had seen on the film in the mine gallery.

From one of the two locked suitcases waiting for him in the apartment he had removed a camera and several telephoto lenses. The other case contained the sniper's rifle. He had not concerned himself with how it had arrived in Rome.

Father Gomez mounted the camera and lens on a tripod which he pointed from the balcony towards the piazza. For the past hour he had been shooting test film, developing the strips in a makeshift dark room rigged up in the apartment bathroom. He hung the clips of film out on the balcony; just like he'd seen other photographers do.

In the apartment opposite the Holy Office, Morton crouched beside the Pathfinder, listening to the tape of the conversation between the two cardinals and Fung. Another of the surveillance team squatted in front of the Merino computer.

'We're close to overload,' the man called out.

'You'll just have to cut surveillance on the square and on the Via della however-you-say-it,' ordered the Pathfinder.

The third member of the team began to reposition the radomes. The needles on the Merino's dials began to swing back. Morton removed the headset.

'Any use?' asked the Pathfinder.

'Hard to say.'

Why had Wong Lee warned the cardinals about Kingdom's proposed attack? Reverend Kingdom almost certainly would not be making it without Wong Lee's approval. And why attack Muller? Morton stood for a moment longer watching the twitching needles on the Merino, before leaving the apartment.

There was no way for Morton to know that the repositioning of the radomes meant that Father Gomez, making his phone call from a pay phone on the avenue, was no longer inside the surveillance net the team had electronically draped over the Vatican and its environs.

The spiritual leaders of the former Soviet republics had timed their journeys to arrive at the same time in Alma-Ata, the capital of Kazakhstan. None of the dozen clerics wished to appear unusually eager for the meeting; all knew they could not risk the wrath of their host by arriving late.

Between them they exercised iron control over eighty million Moslems. But here, in the apartment's drab reception room, they were once more respectful pupils waiting for their master to appear. Waiting, they sat silent and watchful, each dressed in an identical robe and tarboosh, the pill-box hat which marked them as a mullah.

The tassels on their garments signified they were graduates from one of the most prestigious of Islamic universities, the campus of the holy city of Najaf in Iraq.

The Imam Nardash had been their teacher, in those years before he had become the most powerful figure since the Ayatollah Khomeini. Today the imam's influence ruled supreme over a Moslem world it took the sun six hours to travel across. He was acknowledged as a *murshid*, a master, to lead his people along the mystic *tariqa*, the path to Allah, the Holy of Holy Ones, the Most Merciful and Compassionate.

When he had last summoned them here it had been to tell them to unite with Iran and Afghanistan, to form the Islamic Confederation. It had sounded so promising, a pan-Islamic brotherhood stretching across the steppes of central Asia.

The reality had been otherwise. There was not a man in this room who would not agree that Tehran was now on a very different agenda. The mullahs there were obsessed only with seeking revenge on Iraq and Israel.

The Confederation was all but doomed. Was that why the

Imam Nardash had summoned them? Or was it because of the threat neighbouring China posed?

He came into the room the way he had once entered a class-room, crashing open the door, his coal-black eyes sweeping over them. As one, they stood, bowing in reverence, waiting until the Holy One had seated himself in an old armchair whose legs were as bowed as his own. His pot-belly, stretched taut the folds of his black robe. His beard was unkempt and streaked with white; his teeth and fingers stained from the Turkish cigarettes he chain-smoked. His protruding eyes continued to silently stare around the room.

Intimidation had always been his stock-in-trade. It was there in his Friday evening sermons broadcast throughout the entire Moslem world; in his books whose sales were only surpassed by those of the Koran. In everything he said or wrote his was the authentic voice of the street-corner demagogue. With it he had imbued millions with the unquenchable fire of religious rev-olution.

Surprise was his major weapon, supported by the reports of a network of spies that would be the envy of any intelligence service.

He greeted them formally in his coarse voice.

'*El hamda l'Allah*' – praise God.

'*Illah al hamda*' – God be praised, they murmured in respectful response.

He studied them for a moment longer, to remind himself of each man's record, his sermons, his standing in the community, his total fidelity to the daily observance of his faith. All of this, and much else, he had carefully studied before an invitation had been extended to come here.

These were the brightest and best of his students. They had shown that in the past. They had organised the radio stations to broadcast fear into the homes of the Russian infidels. They had made sure that after each explosion, their signature was left behind, a green Islamic crescent painted on a nearby wall or window. They had done everything he had asked.

'I believe the time has come for change,' he began in his usual abrupt manner.

'Your brothers in Iran are no longer to be trusted. The day has come when you must withdraw from the Confederation. It must be done quickly and without argument. At the same time you must retain the good will of the Iranian people. To that end you will begin to broadcast to them that their leaders have failed because they have too narrow a vision. In time, perhaps soon, that will provoke internal revolution that will remove the cabal in Tehran. But you must do nothing to lose the support of the people.'

He waited for the stir to come and go.

'I also believe the time has come to end your relationship with the Chinese, Wong Lee. His interest is not yours.'

A tall, narrow-faced mullah raised his hand.

'Holy One, the Chinese has made sure my own people are well equipped. From him we have weapons now that we never had before.'

Imam Nardash gave a cold smile.

'And what will you do with them, Kemal? You use so much as a single nuclear weapon and the American infidels will rain upon you death the like of which you last saw in Iraq.'

He stared around the room.

'When he sold you those weapons, Wong Lee was careful not to give you too many. All you have is just enough to threaten each other. Enough to allow the infidels in Moscow to claim you threaten the peace of the world.'

He paused to give his words the significance they deserved.

'I believe the time has come to reappraise your attitude to Moscow.'

A mullah at the far end of the room spoke. 'Holy One, in my own country we have sown fear in the hearts of the Russians. Only a week ago in Ashkhabad, our tribesmen killed a dozen more –'

'And how many are there left, Olmon? Two hundred thousand, maybe more? You will need years at that rate to remove the last Russian. By then your wives will no longer find you exciting. Perhaps they already don't for you to speak in such a manner.'

Chuckles came from the others. The Holy One's sarcasm was greatly admired.

Imam Nardash waved for silence.

'It is the same in all your republics. Your guerilla tactics have not achieved what I had hoped. Moscow has not sent its army to once more brutalise your people. That would have given you the impetus for a full revolution. For each one killed by their tanks and militia you would have a hundred, a thousand, rush to arms. But your people still hesitate – because as yet they have no stomach for revolution.'

He paused again, waiting for the truth to be absorbed.

'Holy One, are you saying we must give up our ambitions to spread the faith?' asked a heavily bearded mullah.

Imam Nardash sighed.

'No, Kum. I am not saying that. I share your dreams, but I only dream at night. In the day I don't allow the light to blind me.'

He once more looked around the room. How much should he tell them?

'The infidels in Moscow are planning to allow the next Christian infidel in Rome to stage some kind of religious ceremony in their city. I believe they will use the occasion to their own ends – perhaps even to stage some incident that could bring upon you all the wrath of the entire infidel world.'

This time he allowed the murmurs to continue. They needed time to discuss this among themselves, to reach the consensus he needed. When they were finally silent, he continued to speak.

'You are not yet strong enough to triumph over the infidel world. One day you will be, but not yet. But to prepare for that moment, you must do nothing that will provoke retribution now.'

Imam Nardash made a quick cutting motion with his hands.

'That you are here today is a good sign. But I know that when you leave here, you intend to go home and continue to attack each other in your sermons. That will now stop. You will put aside your differences and unite.'

He watched as they looked warily at one another.

'All of you! And you will pledge that to me now!'

One by one they murmured agreement.

'Good. The next thing is you must stop the attacks on the Russian infidels. You must lull Moscow into believing you mean no harm, that you are as they have always seen you – weak.'

They stared attentively at him. Theirs would be a difficult exercise in discipline and obedience to their master. But then, over the years of indoctrination and examination he had prepared them for no less.

The mullah Olmon had a question.

'Holy One, what do we do about this American infidel who

sullied the name of God with his preaching? There is great anger among my people –'

'Silence it! I have heard the American's words. Only a man of little faith would take them seriously.'

The mullah Kum spoke.

'What about the threat of the Chinese army –'

'Do not respond. That is what Moscow wishes!

'You must lull the infidels into believing you mean no harm. Then, when the time comes, you can strike in the knowledge the surprise is all the greater. It may not be tomorrow, or the day after tomorrow, or even the day after that. For some of you it may not even be in your lifetime. But remember it is written that verily when the time will come, the triumph will be all the sweeter for waiting. Remember that.'

In the silence heads began to nod.

By the time the Wong Holdings 747 landed at Rome's Leonardo da Vinci airport, Chung-Shi's agents were routine perfect. First they supervised the unloading of two containers, to which were fixed the diplomatic seal of the People's Republic of China.

The manifest Chung-Shi presented to Customs showed the containers held the household effects of a recently posted Chinese envoy to Italy. With the manifest was an authorisation from the Foreign Ministry in Beijing to bring back the effects of the outgoing diplomat.

Some of the agents accompanied the freight truck on which the containers were loaded. The others drove in several cars behind. A couple of miles beyond the airport, the truck headed north while the cars continued east towards Rome. In the lead car Chung-Shi spent the journey listening to the two women agents, chosen to spearhead the operation, going over what they were to do. They spoke to him in their native language, Japanese.

# 20

The truck with the containers left the Pisa autostrada to travel on a local road almost only used by peasant farmers whose rough-stone houses it passed. The men and their womenfolk working in the fields barely paused to give the truck a second glance. Every day trucks like this one passed on their way to and from the dreadful holiday homes being built for foreign millionaires in the barren hills beyond where the road became a track.

The truck continued along this road for another mile before the driver suddenly swung off the track and parked behind a screen of trees. The agents broke the diplomatic seals on one container and prized off the lid. They began to throw the cheap Chinese furnishings to the ground. When they had finished one of them fetched blankets and a portable oxygen cylinder which he placed in the bottom of the container. Then they sat on the ground, smoking and speaking quietly among themselves in Chinese.

An hour later and forty miles away Carina had all but completed her shopping in downtown Rome, around Largo Argentina. She had been captivated by the district's narrow streets; some she suspected were little changed from the days of Nero. Yet the traffic still roared through them as if they were as wide as Red Square. The noise was like a race track. She still could not quite believe she would never have to return to Moscow.

David had told her this morning after they had made love in the bath. They had scarcely moved in the water, joined together like sea urchins, looking at each other, not speaking, not needing to.

Later, much later, when he had wrapped and patted her dry with the soft towels, he whispered in her ear she was going to Tel Aviv tonight. Even now, she could feel his skin against hers, the taste of his lips when he had kissed her one more time before she had left to go shopping.

She had bought a long black dress for the funeral, and a pair of culottes and a blouse and jacket for the journey to Israel.

In the store a couple of Japanese women, weighed down with carrier bags, had smiled at her. Not at all like the Japanese tourists who marched through Moscow criticising everything they saw. But then, everybody in Rome was so friendly.

Passing a boutique behind the Pantheon, she saw a pair of shoes and matching handbag. These too, she bought.

Coming out of the shop Carina saw the women were watching their purchases being loaded by their chauffeur into the trunk of a limousine parked further up the street. The car was directly beside a No Parking sign. She saw its diplomatic plates and smiled. It was the same in Moscow. The wives of foreign diplomats were always getting their drivers to ignore regulations.

One of the Japanese gave a diffident little wave. Carina waved back. Then, clutching her parcels in both hands, she looked around for a taxi.

The few that roared past, forcing her back against the walls of the tall buildings, were full. The roar of the traffic had started to give her a headache. The last cab came so close that Carina dropped one of her parcels. Stooping to retrieve it, her eyes smarting from the car fumes, she failed to notice the keys Morton had given her to his Tel Aviv apartment had fallen from her handbag into the gutter. As she rose to her feet the limousine pulled up and the woman who waved was lowering her tinted window.

'Please, you like a lift?' she asked in broken English.

Inside the basilica, Julius Enkomo took his place in the procession of cardinals. They were paired off according to seniority. Koveks of Romania stood beside Tovic of Czechoslovakia; Schwartz of Switzerland with Arnt of Belgium. Beneath their mitres their faces looked even bleaker than usual. This was their fourth papal funeral since coming to office. Behind them came Walpole of Westminster and Terry of Sydney, followed by Coffey of Philadelphia and Simmons of Los Angeles, murmuring to each other.

The towering figure of Marcel Leutens of Marseilles was paired with Saldarini, one of the twenty-three Curia cardinals in the procession. Muller was paired with another. Julius Enkomo was beside Victor O'Rourke, Primate of All Ireland. Immediately behind them came Posanos of Brazil and Berry of Scotland; followed by Ospispo of Santa Domingo and Mongabe of Zaire. His mitre and bishop's crook gave him the look of a tribal chief.

Back they stretched: Martel of Manila, Anso of Tokyo, Reefer of Seoul, Camas of Madrid. Some spoke quietly together; others not at all.

At precisely the scheduled moment, Cardinal Messner led the procession towards the open door of the basilica. Ahead of them walked the frock-coated pallbearers with the coffin of Nicholas the Sixth.

Monsignor Hanlon was squeezed in the enclosure to one side of the steps of St Peter's with other members of the papal household. He, like the rest of them, knew nothing of what the future held.

Not like Heinrich Linde. He was standing in front of the basilica door, which was open again, imperiously surveying the Distinguished Mourners enclosure.

The new head of the Kennedy clan was seated behind the US President and First Lady. Nearby were the Archbishop of Canterbury and the Moderator of the Church of Scotland, amongst a hundred non-Catholic churchmen squeezed into the enclosure.

Monsignor Hanlon consulted the seating plan Colonel Asmusson had given him. The florid faced bemedalled general at the far end of the second row – that had to be Savenko. And the saturnine figure beside him? Kramskay, the Moscow public prosecutor. Monsignor Hanlon continued to identify the powerful and the merely rich whose donations to the Church had ensured them a ringside seat.

Would they be disappointed? Nicholas's will had stipulated there would be no catafalque, nothing to raise the coffin to public view. Instead it would be laid on the ground, bare and unadorned except for an open Bible on its lid. It was the Boss's reminder to them that he had always wished to reduce as far as possible the symbols of pomp and power which in the past had characterised papal funerals.

Monsignor Hanlon continued to identify the distinguished mourners and frowned. With the funeral Mass shortly to begin there was still a vacant seat among the Israeli delegation. He checked the seating plan. The chair had been reserved for Dr Carina Ogodnikova.

When the convoy reached the northern outskirts of Rome, the Mercedes and Fiat headed west, towards the airport. The limousine with the tinted windows continued north along the Pisa autostrada. Chung-Shi maintained his careful chauffeur's speed.

Father Gomez adjusted the telephoto lens and zoomed in on one purple-robed figure after another emerging from inside St Peter's basilica. None of them were of any interest to him. But he had told Franco Umberto from one of the pay phones on the Via della Conciliazione he would make no further calls. He wanted nothing to distract him from the job.

Yoshi sat between Karshov and Bitburg in the Israeli delegation. Several times the Prime Minister had looked at Carina's still vacant seat. Finally, he turned to the neurosurgeon.

'This is very embarrassing. I'm told there were a thousand applications for each place,' Karshov growled.

'She's usually very reliable, Prime Minister,' murmured Yoshi.

'The woman had no business being here,' Bitburg grumbled.

Behind them Dr Poggi leaned forward.

'I arranged it as one way of showing our appreciation for all Carina's help,' he explained.

Bitburg grunted.

The cardinals were forming themselves around the coffin resting on the basilica steps. Once more Dr Poggi leaned forward to provide a whispered commentary.

'One of the many new features of this Mass is that all the cardinals will concelebrate around the altar. The tall one is Leutens. He will be the main celebrant, that's why he is wearing a bright scarlet robe.'

For the next two hours Dr Poggi explained the various parts of the mass: the homily, the consecration, the singing of the offertory hymn, the litany of the saints, and the closing prayers, while the cardinals filed slowly past either side of the coffin. 'The remains of His Holiness will be laid to rest in the tomb specially prepared for him in the Vatican crypt. There he will remain to await his resurrection in glory,' Dr Poggi murmured as the pallbearers lifted the coffin.

While the burial party slowly climbed the basilica steps the choir sang the Magnificat and the bells of St Peter's tolled, as the pages of the Bible on the coffin lid began to rustle in the early evening breeze. Moments later the doors of the basilica were shut.

In all the enclosures and among the vast crowd beyond the steel barriers, as well as the worldwide television audience, the same question was asked. Who among the cardinals who had spent the past two and three-quarter hours burying Nicholas the Sixth would next emerge on the balcony above the doors of St Peter's as the new Supreme Pontiff?

Late in the afternoon the freight truck returned to Leonardo da Vinci airport. Both containers had new seals, indicating they had been affixed by the First Secretary of the People's Republic of China embassy in Rome. The official's name, translated from Chinese for the benefit of Italian Customs, was given on the weighbills as Chung-Shi. The contents were listed as the personal household effects of the outgoing diplomat. No one among the Customs men remembered that, when the envoy had left for Beijing a week before, he declared then he was taking all his possessions with him.

The containers were fork-lifted into the cargo space of the 747 freighter. Fifteen minutes later the plane took off. Once it was clear of Italian air space, Chung-Shi sent two of the agents to the container whose furniture they had scattered among the screen of trees. They broke the seals and removed the lid. Wrapped in blankets and breathing through a mask taped to her mouth, the oxygen cylinder propped beside her, was Carina.

The men removed the blankets and mask and carried her back to the passenger cabin and laid her on a stretcher bolted to the floor. The gurney's straps were secured across Carina's body. While the others watched, Chung-Shi busied himself at a trolley. In an enamel bowl were two ampoules and syringes. He carefully checked an ampoule to make sure he had the correct one, then inserted a needle and drew up the pale green liquid into a syringe.

The older of the Japanese women strapped a rubber tourniquet on Carina's arm and waited for the veins to show. There was a small collective sigh from the onlookers when Chung-Shi punctured the skin, concentrating on a slow, even delivery of the liquid. Afterwards the woman released the tourniquet and placed a small strip of plaster over the pinprick.

Everyone stood and waited. They had kidnapped before, many times. But never had they been asked to take such care of someone. Chung-Shi had said the foreigner was very special. After two minutes the body began to stir. Chung-Shi and both women timed it separately on their wrist watches. Forty-five seconds later, at the precise time the shamaness said it would happen if she had sustained no real injury during her abduction, Carina's eyes began to flicker. Thirty seconds later they opened into semi-consciousness, then tried to focus.

Carina began to struggle, but was held in place with the straps. When her lips began to move, one of the Japanese lent closer to hear better.

'She wants a drink,' she told Chung-Shi.

He shook his head. The shamaness had explained the original drug was combined with curare to produce this state of almost total relaxation of the central nervous system. It meant she could not yet swallow properly.

'Set up the drip,' Chung-Shi said.

The women prepared the saline drip.

Chung-Shi loaded the second syringe from the remaining ampoule and injected Carina with a liquid that was a darker shade of green. The shamaness had said it was most important to do so as soon as it had been established there was no physical injury.

As the plane continued eastwards Carina at first comforted herself with the shallow sound of her breathing. Then, suddenly, she could no longer hear it as the drug invaded her body. Her mind seemed to be opening and closing, forming and dissolving, as the drug continued to invade the fragile mechanisms of her brain, beginning to distort memory and destroy identity.

From a long way away, a face was peering down at her, endlessly repeating a word.

'Morton.'

She struggled to reply but her brain would not form the response. Carina had begun a journey in her mind she could never have dreamt was possible.

*

Pulling down the security shutters for the night, the owner of the boutique behind the Pantheon spotted the keys in the gutter. She recognised them as belonging to the foreigner who had bought the handbag and shoes. Because it was on her way home, the woman dropped them off at the police station close to Via Mercedes. The details were entered in the report book. Once a day all the entries were laboriously typed by a woman clerk onto a disc. This was then transmitted to the city's central police headquarters, to join the tens of thousands of other items reported lost or found every day in Rome.

A little after Nicholas the Sixth's tomb had been closed, and Carina was receiving her first injection some six miles above the Mediterranean, the clerk keyed on the disc containing the description of Morton's keys. Because she was still new at the job, the clerk had copied out in full the description – including the detail that the keys were attached to a ring in the shape of a six-pointed star and that engraved on three of the star points were names: Ruth, Steve, Dolly.

Cardinal Messner sniffed. Finalising the preparations for the conclave was exacerbating his allergy. Two days had passed since the funeral and in that time he had worked from before dawn to past midnight. There were now only a few hours left before he and the other cardinals would be locked into the specially prepared area around the Sistine Chapel to begin their deliberations. There was still much to do – including the discreet business of continuing to take soundings among the other members of the Sacred College to see who they wanted to become the next Pope. So far the camerlengo believed he could count on thirty votes for Hans-Dietrich Muller on the first ballot. His own formidable personality and authority would continue to play a decisive role in the strict isolation of conclave to persuade others to support his protégé. In the meantime a small mountain of paperwork on his desk needed attention. Nothing was too trivial to require the camerlengo's authorisation.

His spidery signature had authorised the purchase of toilet rolls, soap, hot water bottles and a hundred other items. Food for special diets; candles and matches in case of a power failure; portable heaters; barrack-room style beds and mattresses; a selection of wines and cheeses; all needed his approval. He was part quartermaster, part accountant and part hotelier, working to a budget that had barely kept pace with inflation since the last conclave.

On a wall of his office was the floor plan he had used then. It showed him at a glance the state of preparations. The floor of the Sistine had been covered with a thick underlay to reduce noise. Behind the chapel, an area was already prepared where the cardinals and support staff would eat and sleep. Each cardinal would have his own cell so he could meditate in peace on a stark unadorned prie-dieu beneath a simple wooden crucifix tacked to a partition wall.

Food had been purchased to feed conclave for a week from the glorified field kitchen set up in one of the Borgia apartments. Meals would be taken in the Hall of the Popes, once the armoury of the Borgias. Refectory tables had been set out below a fifteenth century fresco of Pinturicchio.

Cardinal Messner picked another memo from his desk and gave a louder sniff. Molins of Paris was asking for Vichy water, three bottles a day. The camerlengo checked a price list. Vichy cost more than Italian mineral water. But he approved the request. Molins was another of the cardinals who said he would vote for Muller.

The camerlengo picked up a handwritten request on Chicago archdiocese notepaper requesting a bedside ashtray. The note was penned by Michael Boylan, Archbishop of Chicago. He was now the only cardinal in the American hierarchy who refused to endorse Muller. The camerlengo consulted yet another list. At the last conclave, fifty ashtrays were permitted, together with a dozen spittoons for those prelates who liked to chew tobacco. Cardinal Messner dictated to a hovering priest-secretary a brief note telling Boylan to bring his own ashtray.

There were still more requests: for additional writing paper, for a club-bar to be installed and for *vasi da notte*, what the Americans called Uncle Joes and the English chamberpots. The camerlengo glanced at the wall plan. Against *vasi da notte* was a small tick. His staff had already combed Rome's monasteries and nunneries for all available pots.

In past conclaves, each cardinal had been allotted only five sheets of paper on which to scribble his thoughts. The camerlengo increased the figure to twelve. He compromised over the club-bar by authorising a well-stocked refrigerator of drinks be installed in the corridor outside the Hall of the Popes.

More lists: trash cans, vacuum cleaners, tablecloths, napkins, cutlery. He rummaged among the papers on his desk. One of Rome's leading stores had offered to loan tableware. He dictated grateful acceptance.

The phone rang. It was answered by the priest-secretary. He listened for a moment, then placed his hand over the mouthpiece.

'It's Kazuo Anso.'

The camerlengo hesitated. He had no time to listen to the Cardinal-Archbishop of Tokyo enunciating his textbook perfect English. But Anso was another of the uncommitted. Cardinal Messner took the phone.

'Good afternoon, Kazuo. What can I do for you?'

'Good afternoon, camerlengo. I would like to discuss with you the view from my room, or more precisely the lack of it.'

The camerlengo sniffed. 'There are only so many rooms with a window.'

'Exactly so. But I would like to be able to see the moon from my room. We are now in the first quarter period and at this latitude it should be clearly visible.'

'The moon?'

'Yes. I sleep very little, and I find being able to see the moon is helpful to focus my mind. The night sky can be very soothing to us insomniacs.'

The camerlengo stifled his irritation. 'One moment, Kazuo.'

He walked over to the floor plan. He would move Saldarini to a windowless cubicle to give Anso his view.

Cardinal Messner picked up the phone.

'No problem, Kazuo. I'll put you between O'Rourke and Enkomo.'

There was a momentary silence. 'Thank you. Can I ask whether the Reverend Fathers snore? That sort of thing can be very distracting.'

'I've no idea if they snore. That you'll have to find out.'

'I suppose I'll manage, camerlengo. But we all have a big responsibility, especially we who are newcomers.'

Anso had been among the last of Nicholas the Sixth's appointments to the Sacred College.

'We all have, Kazuo. And none of us wants to make the wrong choice.'

'Exactly so. I am praying hard, camerlengo.'

'I am sure we are all praying God will guide us to make a choice which will send a clear signal to the world.'

'There are many who could do that if chosen.'

Cardinal Messner gave a little laugh. 'Not that many, Kazuo. Very few, in fact. Many of our colleagues say Cardinal Muller could be the only one.'

'That is very interesting, camerlengo.'

'Think about it, Kazuo. And pray about it.'

'Of course. I am praying about it all the time.'

Putting down the phone, Cardinal Messner was once again struck by the thought that you could never exactly tell what an Oriental was thinking.

He turned to the secretary. 'Are we still within budget?'

The priest consulted a computer printout.

'Yes, Your Eminence. But we'll go over if we board up all the windows in the conclave area.'

The camerlengo came to another decision. 'Don't board them up. Nobody's going to be peering in.'

Across St Peter's Square the Pathfinder heard the decision with relief. He had already assigned two radomes to bug conclave.

For the watch officer in the bunker deep below the White House gardens in Washington, the camerlengo's decision made no difference. Even if the windows were boarded over, the antenna farm hovering several thousand miles above the Vatican would still have been able to silently gather up the deliberations about to begin in the Sistine Chapel and its environs.

# 21

In the Tabernacle's control gallery studio director Alan Milton turned to the new sound engineer.

'Level okay?'

'A-okay.'

'Right. Let's roll.'

Milton glanced around the gallery. 'Remember everybody. This is live. No retakes.'

He leaned forward and spoke directly into the microphone which linked him with the towering figure in the pulpit about a hundred feet below them.

'Fifteen seconds, Reverend Kingdom. God loves you.'

'And bless His name,' came the clear, confident response from the pulpit.

The Reverend Kingdom stood silent and still, jaw firmly clenched, silently counting down, staring into Camera One. A close-up shot.

Spread out on top of the lectern's open Bible, in deliberate view, was his script. It had been Martha's idea; it would help to convince his world-wide audience he had thought through every word of accusation. Some might even think the script was actually the evidence to back up the all-out assault he was about to launch.

Cameras Two, Three and Four were in a loose semi-circle; medium shot, a wider shot and a wide-angle to show the pulpit and the altar. A red light blinked steadily on Camera One. In the gallery the opening titles of the *Voice of Truth* hour were unfolding.

Out of the corner of his eye, the Reverend Kingdom saw the carefully edited news film of the cardinals in all their finery on the steps of St Peter's. Suddenly the shot zoomed in to freeze-frame on the face of Cardinal Muller. The editing made him look like a face on a Most Wanted poster. The effect was under-scored by the stark type-face.

HANS-DIETRICH MULLER

Up in the gallery Milton superimposed a dark-red question mark over the cardinal. The mark grew until it filled the transmission screen. Then the screen cleared to reveal the calm, confident face of the Reverend Kingdom. He waited a further three seconds before he began to speak.

Welcome to this special programme of the *Voice of Truth* coming to you as usual from our world headquarters here in Malibu, California. Today, I want to talk to you about an event which in the normal course of matters, would interest neither you nor me. It is the election of the next Roman pontiff.

He paused. The cue light on Camera Two was glowing. He pressed his palms down on the Bible.

We would say – let them have their secret meeting in that gaudy chapel of theirs. We would say – no matter who they choose, he will be no different to all the other Roman pontiffs elected in the past.

He counted off under his breath a full five seconds.

BUT NOT THIS TIME! THIS TIME THOSE DANGEROUS OLD MEN IN ROME COULD ELECT SOMEONE WHO WILL BE A THREAT TO US ALL. A MAN THE ONLY BOOK WARNS US ABOUT. SOMEONE WHO IS AS CLOSE TO THE ANTICHRIST YOU OR I WILL PROBABLY EVER MEET ON THIS EARTH!

YOU SAW HIS FACE AT THE BEGINNING OF THIS TELECAST.

WHAT YOU COULD NOT SEE WAS INTO THE HEART AND MIND OF THIS MAN!

I WOULD BE FAILING IN MY DUTY TO GOD — FOR WHOM ON BEHALF OF ALL OF YOU I SAY BLESS HIS NAME — IF I DID NOT NOW TELL YOU ABOUT THIS TRULY EVIL MAN!

The Reverend Kingdom let the silence lengthen, knowing that across the globe tens of millions would be watching and waiting, both enthralled and a little fearful.

When he next spoke the rage had gone from his voice.

Hans-Dietrich Muller. Cardinal-Archbishop of Berlin. A man of his church, most certainly. But a man of God? Most certainly not.

This man has served Rome well for over a quarter of a century. In that time the Roman church helped him as it has helped others. The Nazis it helped to flee in 1945. The Communists it gave sanctuary to in the sixties. Many people were given new identities. In return, they promised total fidelity to the Roman pontiff.

And so it was with Hans-Dietrich Muller. Once his past was buried, his future became assured. He rose steadily with the help of his patron. Hubert Messner.

He glanced down at his script as if to check a fact.

In the end Library and Research had found all too few. But that had never troubled him. Facts were like statistics: you used them as you wished. The important thing was righteous anger. With that, innuendo became an acceptable truth; the doubtful, all too certain. No one he knew used righteous anger with such skill and force.

Muller and Messner. Messner and Muller. No matter which way you put them, you have Svengali, and his disciple.

We will never know how Messner chose Muller. Was it that time when Muller told his mentor about those tens of thousands of acres of land he owns in Prussia and Saxony?

The Reverend Kingdom imperceptibly tightened his jaw and narrowed his eyes.

The history of that land interests me as much as it should you. It was a gift from Hitler to the Muller family!

A gift, my friends. A gift gladly given and gladly received because the Muller family – devout Catholics all – were among the first to pledge themselves to support their Führer when he came to power.

If that meant betraying their people, so be it. If that meant turning their backs on the atrocities, so be it. If that meant silently endorsing a thousand criminal acts – so be it.

Everything the researchers had been able to dig up on Hans-Dietrich Muller's family past filled no more than a page of script. A distant Muller had been in the office of the Gauleiter of Saxony in the first year of the war – before being sent to the Russian Front. A second cousin was the Bishop of Dresden who gave a qualified welcome to Hitler's plans to turn the city into one of the Third Reich's centres of culture. Some Mullers, even more distant cousins, had remained loyal to Hitler to the very end. In a series of deals their lands had passed into the hands of Hans-Dietrich Muller's family. It had been enough for the Reverend Kingdom.

The land gave them power. So much so that even when the Communists occupied Prussia and Saxony it was allowed to remain in the Mullers' possession.

The light was back on Camera One. Only his face filled the screen.

To my shame I must say our government, the governments of Great Britain, France and, of course, the former Soviet Union all knew about this.

He brandished the script so that Camera Three would have a clear view.

But because it suited them, just as it suited Rome, they chose to look the other way!

He put the script back on top of the Bible.

And so the future of Hans-Dietrich Muller was assured. In return for his family keeping the land, they gave him to Rome. Not as a sacrifice. But as someone who could use his power on their behalf.

Here the researchers were on firmer ground, able to uncover evidence that Muller, like any other politically astute churchman, had used his position in Rome to help improve conditions in his homeland. It was Muller who had confronted the Communists of old East Germany and won religious freedom; who had persuaded Moscow to rebuild Dresden. All this could be given a different spin.

He has worked hard, make no mistake. He has risen far and fast. And now he is poised to take the ultimate crown – to become the next Roman pontiff. To lead his Church and our world on a course that could be dangerous beyond belief.

The Reverend Kingdom spread his hands. Once more the thunderous denunciation rolled from the pulpit.

DANGEROUS BEYOND BELIEF! WHAT HE DOES TO HIS OWN FOLLOWERS IS OF NO CONCERN TO YOU OR ME. WE CAN ONLY PRAY FOR THEM TO FIND A WAY TO FREE THEMSELVES FROM THE HANDS OF THIS MAN.

BUT THE DANGER OF HANS-DIETRICH MULLER IS THIS. HE IS A RELIGIOUS CAESAR. A MAN WHO BELIEVES HE CAN DO WHAT CAESAR NEVER QUITE DID – CONQUER THE WHOLE WORLD!

Once again he waited for the words to have their impact. When he spoke next his voice was calmer.

What did Caesar say? *'Veni, vidi, vici'*, – I came, I saw, I conquered. But, my brothers and sisters, we will not know we have been conquered if Hans-Dietrich Muller becomes the next Roman pontiff. Because that is not his way.

Just as he hid that land from us – until the Good Lord led me to discover it – so he will work behind the scenes to make secret deals to benefit Rome. He will be like the beast in his lair that the good Book of Daniel warns us about. 'Then I would know the truth of the fourth beast, which was diverse from all the others, exceedingly dreadful, whose teeth were of iron, and his nails of brass; which devoured, broke in pieces and stamped the residue with his feet.'

Daniel was describing Hans-Dietrich Muller.

The Reverend Kingdom allowed his face to soften.

But do not be afraid! Trust in me because the Good Lord trusts me to protect you all from this man and his godless ambitions.

He paused and leaned forward, elbows on the Bible, face staring into the camera.

As news of the telecast spread through the Vatican, people paused in their preparations for conclave to watch. Cardinal Koveks had invited Boris Tovic, the Primate of Czechoslovakia, to his apartment behind the Apostolic Palace, to discuss their strategy in support of Hans-Dietrich Muller. Then Bernard Arnt of Belgium arrived.

'Quick! The television!' he cried, rushing over to switch on the set in a corner of the room.

They were in time to see the Reverend Kingdom raise his bowed head and continue his attack.

'Monstrous!' shouted Cardinal Koveks.

'But useful,' said Cardinal Tovic. 'It will draw support to Hans-Dietrich. You'd almost think he and our camerlengo had deliberately arranged this.'

'If so, it's a dangerous gamble,' Cardinal Arnt protested. 'All the newcomers could believe some of this and actually vote for someone else.'

They continued to listen to the diatribe pouring from the screen.

'Is any of this true?' queried Cardinal Koveks.

'What does it matter?' demanded Cardinal Tovic. 'It was all a long time ago.'

The Reverend Kingdom continued to make his connections between Cardinal Muller and the Nazis and Communists.

In the fourteenth century building which housed Vatican Television, Julius Enkomo was among a small group of cardinals watching a screen in a viewing room. They were waiting to record their tributes to Pope Nicholas the Sixth as part of a programme commemorating his pontificate. Cardinal Enkomo did not join in the growing murmurs of anger at what the Reverend Kingdom was saying. He was preoccupied over what more he could do to help Morton.

In the past two days he had seen a David he never suspected

existed. A man possessed. Someone unable to accept that for whatever reason, Carina had changed her mind about going to Israel and, rather than tell David, she had chosen to simply walk away from him. The lack of evidence any harm had come to her – no one of her description had been arrested or admitted to a Rome hospital or clinic – had only fuelled David's conviction something had happened to Carina.

The police had interviewed the boutique owner and every shop assistant around Largo Argentina. A few remembered Carina. One of them thought she had seen her getting into a chauffeur-driven car. But they couldn't remember sufficiently well to describe the car or its driver. A lot of chauffeur-driven cars came to the area every day. The one piece of evidence – David's keys – had deepened in him the conviction she had dropped them as a clue that she had been taken by force.

The *capo* in charge of the enquiries had politely pointed out that she could just as well have thrown them away as a symbolic ending to the relationship. Women did things like that. How long had he known her, the *capo* had asked? When Morton told him, the *capo* gave a man-of-the-world look. Such a short acquaintance.

Morton had insisted the search be expanded throughout Italy and then Europe itself. Every air- and seaport was checked. No one remotely fitting her description had been seen. David had called Moscow. She had not returned there. Interpol now had her on their computers. So did the FBI and a score of other police forces. Yoshi, Morelli, Gates and the others had put their considerable resources into trying to find her. No one spoke of wasting time. But everyone thought they were.

David had persisted; something had happened to her. Something so bad and unimaginable that it was not possible for him to begin to pinpoint where to look.

It was then that Cardinal Enkomo had visited Morton in his suite. At first they had sat together in almost total silence. Then, when it came, Cardinal Enkomo had made no attempt to deflect or dilute the awesome cold rage in Morton. He knew it was part of the healing process. Only time would make David finally accept the logic of what everyone was saying. It had been a desperately cruel thing to do. But a woman who suddenly felt she could not, after all, have a future with David, had probably not thought of the pain her action would cause him. David had finally admitted not knowing what had happened was worse than knowing she was dead.

After the anger had come his raw grief, Cardinal Enkomo once more had absorbed Morton's anguish. The process had gone on late into the night until, exhausted, David fell asleep. He had still been asleep when Julius Enkomo had left for the television studios.

On the screen the Reverend Kingdom continued to fulminate.

'The man's so patently a charlatan,' Julius Enkomo told the others.

'But there's usually no smoke without at least a little fire,' growled Cardinal O'Rourke. The Primate of All Ireland lit his pipe. 'When I was in Budapest last month, I heard some very strange stories about Muller more or less promising posts to some of the local hierarchy if he ever got the top job.'

'I gather he's got the other three Germans behind him, plus a couple of the Spaniards,' said Cardinal Berry of Scotland. 'At least that's what Messner's whispered in my ear. Of course he was careful to make it clear it was the Holy Spirit which moved them.'

'Our camerlengo thinks he is the Holy Spirit,' smiled Cardinal Leutens. 'But he won't get far unless he gets the Dutch behind Muller. And Horace Walpole of Westminster. He was the Pope-maker the last two times, breaking the deadlock by some very clever pleading.'

Julius Enkomo looked thoughtfully at the Cardinal of Marseilles.

'Cardinal Walpole cornered me after breakfast. He said it would be a good thing if we were to have an Acclamation. I told him I'd be ready to support that in your case.'

Acclamation was that rarity when one cardinal proposed another to become pontiff and all the others agreed at once.

Marcel Leutens quickly shook his head. 'No, no, no. Please do not even think of that in my case.'

'Many of us think that you are right for the job,' said Victor O'Rourke. 'You understand how the Curia works and your experience in the Third World would be invaluable in making sure the European and American Churches build proper and lasting bridges there –'

'Victor! Please stop,' implored Cardinal Leutens. 'Even if half what you say is true, I must still declare myself unable to go forward.'

'But Marcel,' interrupted Andrew Berry, 'only someone like you can stop the Muller bandwagon.'

Cardinal Leutens shook his head again.

'I appreciate the honour, Andrew, but I fear there are circumstances . . .'

'What are they, Marcel?' Julius Enkomo asked quietly.

Cardinal Leutens looked at them all. When he spoke his voice was as gentle as always.

'Last week my doctor told me I have a carcinoma. He thinks I have no more than a year, probably less.'

He cut off the shocked murmurs with a quick hand movement.

'The Church does not need another short-term Pope. It needs someone young enough to have the time to stamp his authority on us all and continue to lead the Church on from where Nicholas was going.'

He paused and looked at them carefully. 'You have heard of Holy Cross?'

Andrew Berry and Victor O'Rourke shook their heads. Julius Enkomo nodded.

'Very well, I will explain. If I leave anything out I'm sure Julius will remind me.'

Marcel Leutens told them everything Pope Nicholas had told him about his plan. When he finished he looked at Cardinal Enkomo.

'You left nothing out, Marcel.'

When Cardinal Leutens continued there was a new urgency in his voice. 'Now you will understand why you, all of us, must ask God to guide us to elect someone with the strength to enable Holy Cross to work. He will have to be a tough but a charismatic personality. Somebody who understands the new political map of the world. And someone who, above all, has the ability to bring together both our progressives and conservatives. And, of course, someone who can stand up to Messner and Muller.'

Cardinal Leutens glanced at the screen.

'And someone who can deal with that kind of bigot – and those behind him.'

He turned back to the others. 'If you can think of anyone who comes close to those basic requirements, then vote for him. Because that's what I'll be doing.'

*

Cigarette smoke poured furiously from Cardinal Muller's lips as he glared at the television in the library of his apartment in the Apostolic Palace.

'Lies!' he almost shouted, twisting in his armchair to look at Cardinal Messner.

The camerlengo was leaning against a wall of shelves.

He had interrupted his pre-conclave preparations to come here. He was glad now he had the foresight to have done so. Hans-Dietrich was badly shaken by the Reverend Kingdom's unremitting assault.

'Of course he's lying,' soothed Cardinal Messner.

The camerlengo walked forward and switched off the set. He turned to face Cardinal Muller.

'No point in upsetting yourself,' continued the camerlengo calmly. 'What damage there is has already been done. People will have heard enough to either believe it or not.'

'But he is lying,' protested Cardinal Muller hoarsely. He lit a fresh cigarette.

'But for who? And why now?'

Cardinal Muller sent another cloud of smoke spiralling towards the gilded ceiling.

'I think the answer to your last question is obvious. It's to stop my being elected.'

The camerlengo nodded. 'And why would Kingdom want to do that?'

'I can think of a dozen reasons! He sees me as a threat! He knows I'll fight his methods! He knows –'

'Operation Holy Cross,' interrupted the camerlengo. 'Somehow he has learned of it. And he fears if you are elected, you will stop it. Given what Kingdom's trying to stir up in the Soviet republics, that won't suit him at all. He needs us to go ahead with Holy Cross because it will provide the perfect excuse for him to accuse us of trying to foment trouble between the faiths in the republics – the very thing he is himself doing.'

Cardinal Muller looked quickly at the camerlengo. 'You think Wong Lee is behind this?'

The camerlengo began to pace the library, pausing from time to time to glance at the titles of the leather bound books.

'I fear he is, Hans-Dietrich. We know he gave Kingdom that satellite. We know he is encouraging the growing unrest in the

Moslem republics now that the Islamic Confederation is falling apart. It's his old policy of controlling by division.'

'But why did he want me to go to Hawaii?' asked Cardinal Muller.

'That's the one thing which doesn't fit,' the camerlengo murmured. 'Perhaps we should have another word with Fung.'

But when he telephoned the hotel where Wong Lee's secretary was staying, the camerlengo was told Fung was not expected back for some hours. By then conclave would have started.

In the Kremlin a television set had been positioned in front of the long oak table behind which sat Borakin, the former Chairman of the KGB and the ex-Party secretary. They continued to watch the Reverend Kingdom's telecast in silence. From time to time they made notes of something said, but otherwise gave no indication that the diatribe was of any interest to them.

Wong Lee had chosen to watch the broadcast in the solitude of his bedroom. He lay naked on the huge bed, believing that was the best way for the two mighty energy forces which governed his life – *Yang* and *Yin* – to penetrate his body and once more make him undisputed master of all he surveyed.

Only the shamaness knew how badly the business with the stockmarkets had shaken him. Hard on its heels had come the news that various governments had stopped his plans to provide extended credit for Kazakhstan to purchase more arms to resist the Chinese armies assembling on its borders. Then he had learned the troika had no intention of despatching what remained of the Red Army to defend the dissident republic. His plan to stir up a clash between Beijing and Moscow, which could leave them both weakened in the region, was doomed.

The People's Liberation Army could take Kazakhstan whenever it wished – giving China a power base which would seriously affect his own plan to rule through his chosen surrogates from the Pacific to the Arctic Ocean and the Black Sea.

On other fronts the news was also bad. The storms had abated in South Africa, and shares in the food manufacturing and distribution industries Wong Holdings virtually controlled in the Union had further plummeted. Acting on protests from neighbouring governments, the Zimbabwe regime had closed down the Zimba campus.

It had suddenly become even more important that the *gweillo*, Kingdom, should succeed.

Wong Lee forced himself to concentrate on the screen. The *gweillo* was a consummate actor. He knew how to manipulate an audience. But would it convince those old men in Rome to vote for Muller?

The uncertainty had begun to sexually excite Wong Lee. He clapped his hands towards the console beside the tank of carp. Instantly the voice of the shamaness responded.

'Singsung?'

'I need to be amused,' he said.

The shamaness chuckled.

On the screen the *gweillo* was once more staring into the camera. Then his thunderous voice rolled forward.

'Hans-Dietrich Muller, if you are watching this, I tell you now it is not too late to give up your naked ambition. It is not too late to turn your back on your evil mentor. It is not too late to walk out of the Vatican and come to me. We will pray together for your soul!'

The *gweillo* fell silent, head bowed, as if in prayer, as if he was asking his God to grant this should happen. He really was good, thought Wong Lee, as a knock came on the door.

'Enter,' he commanded.

The shamaness came in smiling and bowing in her mocking way. Then the old sorceress turned and beckoned to a woman. He could smell the yak's milk on the woman's body and see her naked body under the folds of the silk robe.

'She still cannot speak yet, singsung,' said the shamaness. 'The drugs have affected the part of the brain which controls speech. It is only a temporary thing. But they have also freed that which controls her sexual inhibitions. She is almost insatiable.'

Wong Lee nodded and smiled, smiled and nodded.

'Come here,' he said softly, 'come and amuse me.'

The shamaness stepped behind the screen to check the camera was ready for filming as Carina walked towards the bed.

Morelli watched four cardboard boxes being loaded into the trunk of a Vatican car. He had driven the Mercedes to the small nondescript looking shop behind the Pantheon where the House of Gammerelli had stood for over two hundred years and its tailors had dressed Popes for mourning and for rejoicing. Each box contained a complete set of papal vestments: extra large, large, medium and small; combinations of white silk cassock, red velvet stretch slippers with a small gold cross embossed on each, a white silk sash and a white skull cap and white cotton stockings.

The cassocks had not been completed; their backs and hems were held together by long looping stitches. The sleeves remained similarly deliberately unfinished. The sewing would be completed by Anton Gammerelli, the great-great-grandson of the firm's founder, before the cardinal chosen to be Pope stepped for the first time onto the central balcony of St Peter's.

As one of the tailors loaded the last box Gammerelli turned to Morelli.

'Think it'll be a long conclave? I've planned a holiday in a week's time.'

From the time conclave started, the tailor would remain close to a telephone waiting for the summons to rush to the Vatican to make the final adjustments.

'I think you'll make it,' Morelli assured him.

He nodded towards the pile of boxes. 'Which one are you betting on?'

'The medium-sized one. Though I'll probably have to switch caps. Muller's got such a small head for a man his size.'

Grinning, Morelli drove slowly away.


There was a polite, but insistent knocking on the door of Morton's suite.

He had kept the adjoining door to Carina's bedroom open, as if that would somehow retain her physical presence a little longer. He could still smell her muskiness, and taste the sweetness of her breath when they had kissed.

Lacouste had ridden shotgun on Interpol. Anwar Salim's people had combed the souks of the Middle East and North Africa for news of a white woman recently snatched into slavery. There had been several. None fitted Carina's description. Baader and Bill Gates had pulled in every favour they had left in Europe. Nothing. Danny had reprogrammed the weather satellite to include listening out for Carina's name on its orbits. Nothing. The antenna farms now had her name. Nothing.

This morning Claudio had come to tell him the hunt was being scaled down. The usual reason. It was simply too expensive in money and manpower to keep up this kind of pressure. He had told Morelli he understood. But he still refused to accept. A part of his mind would not let him.

When Morton opened the door to the corridor he found himself staring into the face of General Savenko.

'Comrade David, I am sorry to trouble you. But I need to talk to you before I return to Moscow.'

After a moment's hesitation Morton stood aside and closed the door after them. He motioned for Savenko to sit on a chair.

'How are you, Yuri?'

'Fine. But how are you, Comrade David? What can I say? She was a wonderful woman.'

'Thank you.'

Morton sat on the bed and looked at Savenko. He could feel the sudden tension between them.

'Where's Kramskay?' he finally asked.

Savenko shrugged.

'Did Borakin send you?' Morton asked.

After a moment's hesitation, Savenko gave a short bark of a laugh.

'He said you would come after me. Instead I am here.'

'Why, Yuri?'

The sigh rose from Savenko's belly.

'You saved my life once.'

'And you gave me Carina.'

Savenko rocked his head from side to side in that curious decision-weighing movement.

'But, how you say, I still owe one to you?'

'So tell me, Yuri.'

Savenko stood up and walked to the window. For a moment he stared down at St Damaso Courtyard, watching a detachment of Swiss Guards forming up, ready to mount guard over the conclave.

Lusia had said to him before he left for Rome not to forget to light two candles, one for Pope Nicholas, and the other for the new Pope. An hour ago he had gone into St Peter's and lit two tapers and placed them in their holders. Afterwards he had come here.

Savenko turned from the window.

'This Operation Holy Cross, David,' he said in little more than a whisper. 'I must speak to you about it.'

# 22

Monsignor Hanlon smiled blearily across the table at Fung and Kramskay. They were in the back room of Razellas, near the Spanish Steps and, as it was late afternoon, the restaurant was empty except for the owner polishing glasses at the bar out front.

The last of the cheese and a bottle of Razellas famed *digestif* were all that remained of a long and, in Monsignor Hanlon's case, an increasingly liquid lunch. He was now slightly tipsy.

It had been mid-morning when Fung had telephoned and suggested they meet. Monsignor Hanlon had been in his room overlooking one of Rome's minor squares, trying to read. But after the peace and comfort of the palace that came with the post of papal secretary, and which the camerlengo had ordered him to vacate until the new Pope decided who he wanted on his staff, the small and cheaply furnished room and the incessant traffic noise outside the window, made it difficult to concentrate.

Fung's call was a welcome interruption and, when he proposed lunch, Monsignor Hanlon immediately accepted. When Fung added he would have another distinguished guest, Kramskay, joining them, and would welcome a place where they could all eat well, Monsignor Hanlon knew why. He was being courted, something he was well used to. And, he had to admit, it was a good feeling after these days of being an outsider. Fung and Kramskay were the emissaries of powerful people. No doubt they wanted his opinion on who were the favourites for the conclave stakes.

So it had turned out. Over *negrinis* – Razellas potent cocktails – the others had listened respectfully while he set the scene for the deliberations in the forthcoming conclave. Over the first bottle of Chianti, Fung began to ask questions, while Kramskay kept his glass constantly filled. Like Fung, the prosecutor drank mostly water. A second bottle of wine arrived with the steaks and was rapidly consumed. He had told the others to call him Sean. A third bottle was called for.

'Now, Sean-san,' Fung said an hour later, 'who would your late master have liked to see follow him?'

Monsignor Hanlon once more smiled tipsily across the table.

'Someone who will be open to the world, a spiritual leader, an authentic pastor, a true fellow bishop, an ecumenical negotiator and a genuine Christian.'

Fung smiled at Kramskay, who smiled at them both.

The lunch was a fitting way to commemorate the outcome of his telephone call to Credit Suisse in Geneva. Herr Vogel, the Overseas Manager, had told him a staggering 100,000 dollars was being offered for the Stalin letter. He had told Herr Vogel to press for an additional fifteen per cent. Shortly before he had come here, Herr Vogel called to say he had settled with Fräulein Stevens.

Kramskay poured more wine for Monsignor Hanlon. In the space of an hour, he had earned almost as much as the master of this supercilious Chinese would pay him over two years. He could afford to sit back and let Fung do the work.

'And who, Sean-san, is the cardinal whom you think has all those attributes?' Fung asked.

Monsignor Hanlon drank his *digestif*. The Boss once said his successor would have to commission serious research into the workings of the Curia, not just in terms of its religious functions, but how it handled the vast sums of money at its disposal.

He assumed that was why Fung was asking his questions – he was worried that all those lucrative building contracts would no longer automatically go to Wong Holdings. And what had Morton said? Something about Wong Lee wanting to destabilise all those Russian republics? Maybe to get more contracts to rebuild?

He wished now he hadn't drunk so much. But no point in letting all that wine, the finest on Razellas' list of fine wines, go undrunk. Anyway, these two were perfectly harmless. All they wanted was to talk to someone they thought was still on the inside. So why not give them something to think about?

'Either of you read the report of Cardinal Saldarini's sermon at the English College last night? I don't know what the seminarians made of it, but the press have lapped it up. His Eminence served notice that while the Holy Spirit, and nothing else, is already hovering over every cardinal elector, he for one believes there has to be real power sharing between the next pontificate and the Curia. Most of the editorials see that as dancing on the Boss's tomb.'

Fung shook his head. 'I'm sorry, I don't understand such subtleties.'

Monsignor Hanlon offered the bottle of liqueur to the others. They smilingly shook their heads. He refilled his own glass and drank some of the dark, syrupy alcohol.

'Saldarini's saying the next Pope can have the glory but the power must go back to where it once was. In the Curia.'

He glanced at Kramskay. 'Right now, our Curia's a bit like your Presidium was – a rubber stamp for all those important issues the Boss believed in.'

Kramskay sipped water.

'Like his Operation Holy Cross?' he asked softly. Fung had agreed he would choose the moment to raise the matter.

Monsignor Hanlon stared at them both.

'Yes,' he said at last. 'Like Operation Holy Cross. But unless we get the right Pope, there will be no Holy Cross.'

Parked at either end of Via Razellas were two vans. One bore the markings of Rome's best known satellite TV rental company; the other had emblazoned on its sides the logo of one of the city's equally renowned electrical repair firms.

The TV van had followed Fung and Kramskay. Their destination established, the second van was called in. It arrived shortly after Monsignor Hanlon entered the restaurant. One of the TV repairmen had walked past Razellas and paused to retie his shoe lace. It was long enough for him to slap a coin-sized diode microphone at the bottom of the restaurant's large plate glass window. The mike's pick-up could be heard in both vans. At first, the reception had not been by any means ideal – the diode picked up passing traffic sounds as well as all those in the restaurant – but as the afternoon wore on, and the traffic eased and the restaurant emptied, the clarity of the surveillance improved.

The vans, their equipment and drivers had been provided by the Rome office of Swift Renovations. With one exception, the agents who made up the surveillance teams were CIA operatives, part of the task force Bill Gates had brought with him. The exception was Morton. He squatted on the floor of the TV rental company van, surrounded by the jumble of surveillance equipment, listening to the conversation in Razellas.

'Mind if we roll down the window?' asked the agent beside the driver. He had a bull neck and a Mississippi drawl.

The van was filled with the smell of sweat and confinement. In his headset Morton could hear Fung calling for the bill.

He shook his head.

The agent was looking in the rear view mirror.

'Is that a yes or a no?' he asked.

'A no.'

The agent shrugged and pulled a handkerchief from his pocket and mopped the moisture from his face.

'They're leaving soon,' Morton added.

The man grunted and turned in his seat.

'You want we follow?'

Morton looked over the agent's shoulder.

Kramskay was shaking hands with Sean. Fung was already climbing into the taxi the restaurant had ordered.

'Let the other team take the cab,' Morton said.

The driver spoke softly into a hand mike.

Monsignor Hanlon was walking a trifle unsteadily down the street. Morton tapped the agent on the shoulder.

'See where he goes. Probably home to sleep it off.'

The man climbed out of the van, as the taxi pulled away. The other van was edging out into the street.

Morton told the driver to take him back to the Vatican. He settled himself more comfortably among the equipment.

In his work you could not afford to believe too much in co-incidence, especially when it involved people like Fung and Kramskay. But instinct told him that it was no coincidence that, having raised Operation Holy Cross, Fung and Kramskay had not pursued the matter. The same instinct which made him refuse to give up on Carina.

Flanked by Morelli and Cardinal Messner, two *Vigili* walked through the conclave area. Each man held a slim black sensor in his hand, which he moved back and forth. The camerlengo carried a clipboard.

Suddenly the needles on the sensors began to twitch. The *Vigili* separated to get a cross bearing. Their instruments were programmed to lock on to each other so as to be able to better pinpoint a target.

Eyes intent on the needles, they walked up the corridor which led to the cells where the cardinals had already deposited their personal effects. They passed a dozen of the box-like structures before the needles steadied. As they reached a cell on their right, the sensors gave off a low, constant noise. The *Vigili* turned to the camerlengo. Frowning, he consulted his clipboard.

'It's Enkomo's,' he muttered.

He followed the *Vigili* into the cell. On the bed was an open washbag; visible among the other toilet articles was a battery-operated razor. One of the *Vigili* handed the razor to Morelli. He stepped out of the cell and walked back down the corridor. The buzzing of the sensors stopped. When he returned, the noise returned.

The shamaness had prepared a suite for her work with Wu. The sorceress had chosen the name for the foreigner because in the woman's state of mind it was easy for her to remember and pronounce. Wu had also been the name of the first recorded practitioner of Dark Taoism. The largest of the suite's rooms was the one where Wu ate and slept after her visit to the singsung's bedroom.

Wong Lee had behaved like a yak stag, and the shamaness had warned him that too much sex could endanger Wu. The singsung had reluctantly agreed he would make do with a succession of the bovine young girls he enjoyed killing.

Like everything else, the shamaness had carefully chosen the furnishings of Wu's room: There was a traditional reed mattress, quilted coverlet and a wooden block for a pillow. A screened-off corner hid the washbasin and toilet hole. The room was designed to deepen Wu's disorientation, an essential part of the process of removing the past from her memory.

Typically, the *gweillo* doctors of the West called this brain-washing, a word that suggested the process was a relatively simple one, instead of the immensely delicate and difficult manipulation of the brain's neuron-transmitting hormones and amino acids as they travelled through Wu's cerebral cortex, the seat of her senses.

The task of conditioning was carried out in the small treatment room. Every six hours the shamaness brought Wu into the room and strapped her into the heavy leather chair. Then she fixed leads to her temples and the nape of her neck, where the spinal column entered the brain stem. The leads were then connected to a large box-like structure, painted black and faced with dials and switches. It stood on the floor behind the chair and was the most sophisticated electro-shock instrument in the world.

In the West, the shamaness knew, the use of electricity as a means to eradicate memory had changed little since the crude experimentation of the CIA's doctors in the sixties. She had studied the reports of their work, briefly marvelling that they had been so freely published and, since a thorough understanding of electricity was part of her own work, she saw immediately why the experiments had failed.

It had taken her a year to design the prototype of the machine she now used. It had been built by the best medical technicians employed by Wong Holdings. Unlike the electro-shock machines of the West which only administered large shocks, to whole parts of the brain, her machine was highly selective. Like a laser it could pinpoint a tiny part of Wu's brain. And unlike those in the West which could only destroy, her machine could stimulate and subtly relax the autonomic nervous system which controlled Wu's bodily functions. But its greatest skill was being able to alter the activity in Wu's temporal lobes, the portion of her brain, located just above her ears, that gave Wu a sense of identity and personal integration. The electro-shocks were given in conjunction with drugs the shamaness knew were still undiscovered in the West.

In the treatment room she prepared another injection to increase Wu's conditioned response. The sorceress was pleasantly surprised how well Wu was responding; the girl was naturally suggestive. It had needed only two small shocks to Wu's hippocampus to produce a significant change in her emotions and motivation. The drug would further blunt Wu's ability to distinguish between right and wrong and deepen her sense of obedience to the shamaness's commands.

Syringe in one hand, she walked into Wu's room. As usual Wu lay naked on the mattress, the coverlet kicked to one side. The shamaness knelt at her feet and felt for a pulse in the sole. She massaged the skin with her thumb and when she could feel the pulse throbbing she injected it with the drug. Still on her knees, she moved to Wu's head and studied it carefully.

Her hair had been cut short and the eyebrows plucked. Already the face looked surprisingly Asian. Wu could be of Tartar or Mongol extraction. A few tucks around the eyes and the mouth would complete the impression.

'Wu,' the shamaness called softly.

The mouth stirred and repeated 'Wu'.

'Wu, listen carefully,' continued the shamaness. 'Who do you hate?'

After a moment's hesitation the mouth whispered again.

'Everyone you say,' Carina whispered.


With an old tape of 'Sounds of the Sixties' playing just within the range of audibility and the apartment's drapes firmly closed against the afternoon sun, Hal concentrated on Penny-Jane. She sat naked astride him, eyes closed and making small movements with her hips in time with his own. He sensed she was approaching climax, and with a few hard thrusts, he helped her achieve it, relishing her gasps and groans. Once more he had been able to delay his own release by focusing on something totally different. This time it was what was happening in the stockmarkets.

Before coming to the apartment he had called his contacts in New York and London. Hundreds of millions of dollars of shares and bonds he had invested were suddenly at risk: from Krupp and Aerospace shares in Europe to preference bonds in Singapore; from Eurotunnel units in London to Food Consolidated in Johannesburg; from Trusts and Futures, as geographically apart as Tokyo and Frankfurt, Hong Kong and Milan; in all these places, and a hundred other markets, Church investments were in danger. They were invested in the same companies in which Wong Holdings traded. The conglomerate had long been the barometer Hal used for the Church's investment strategy. Now Wong Holdings was at the centre of a serious investigation on both sides of the Atlantic. If Wong Holdings nose-dived, then the Church's financial empire would be wiped out. Far more important, to achieve his target of 1,000,000 dollars in Credit Suisse he must act at once.

'Hey, Hal!' cried Penny-Jane as he suddenly moved away from beneath her. 'You haven't finished yet.'

'I have for today, sweet one,' he said, rolling off the bed.

He saw the tears coming into her eyes.

'Don't cry, sweet one,' he urged, dressing quickly. 'It's just I've got work to do. There's always tomorrow.'

She shook her head. 'I'm not coming any more.'

Since his discussion with Martha, they had come here every afternoon, walking openly together, mentor and pupil, talking quietly to each other about what they were going to do, enjoying their mutual arousal, so that by the time he closed the apartment door behind them, the beast in them both was on the rampage.

He paused in dressing to look at Penny-Jane in surprise.

'What's the matter, sweet one? We've both been having such a good time.'

She shook her head. 'It's wrong, Hal, what we're doing. It's dirty and evil.'

He smiled at her as he continued to dress.

'You sound like the Reverend Kingdom! Or Sister Martha.'

She rolled off the bed, the tears spilling down her cheeks.

'And they're right! What we are doing *is* a sin. And you know it, Hal! Every time I leave here, I pray for forgiveness for what we've done. I tell the Good Lord, and bless His name, I'm just a weak creature and . . . and . . . I won't do it again.'

He went to Penny-Jane as she pulled on her skirt. He tilted up her head and tried to kiss her. She pulled back.

'No, Hal. That's wrong, too,' she cried. 'You don't love me. You just want sex, that's all. I'm younger than you, Hal. Last night, after I'd asked the Good Lord's forgiveness, I thought your sin is even worse than mine, because you're that much older!'

He winced inwardly. He gripped Penny-Jane firmly by the shoulders and stared into her face. He brushed away her tears with the back of his hand.

'Penny-Jane, listen to me. You know my work is very important to the Church? You know that, don't you?'

She nodded, uncertainly. He continued to hold her before him.

'Okay. Until I met you . . . I had a problem sleeping and eating properly. I guess I was worrying myself sick trying to do what was best. There were times I thought I wouldn't be able to carry on the Good Lord's work.'

'And bless His name,' Penny-Jane said quickly.

'Indeed so,' added Hal fervently. 'Then you came along . . .

and it was wonderful. And that's why I went to Martha about us.'

Penny-Jane gave a little gasp.

'You told her ... about us ... ?'

'I surely did!' he said even more fervently. 'I had to, don't you see, because I figured even then you would get to feel like you now do.'

He saw the look of new-found wonder in her eye.

'So what did she say?'

'Martha understands how important it is for me to relax, to have no worries, to be able to give my very best to the Church. You see what I'm getting at?'

Respect had joined the wonder, almost displacing the doubt.

'Maybe. But it still don't feel right ...'

He gripped her more tightly.

'It won't ... unless you see that what you are doing is good for the Church! By making me relaxed and able to work harder than ever before, you are helping to make the Church stronger and more powerful than it has ever been.'

He stepped back and looked at her intently.

'You know what the Only Book says about God moving in mysterious ways? Well this is one of them. God bringing us together like this is all part of that mystery. You believe me, Penny-Jane. You've got to believe me!'

She suddenly hugged him, clamping those long tapering fingers around his neck.

'Oh, Hal!' she cried. 'Oh Hal, I'm so glad you told me this!'

As he did almost every morning, General Borakin stood with his back to the window in his office, sipping the cup of scalding tea an aide had brought in with the overnight internal intelligence summary. The officer stood stiffly to attention on the exquisite Bukhara carpet and read in a funereal voice that Borakin had never known to change.

'Alma-Ata – nothing. Samarkand – nothing. Tashkent – nothing. Karaganda – nothing.'

Officials in city by city were reporting that for the first time in years there had been no violence. Total peace had fallen across the land – something that had not been known since those first days following the Red Army's humiliating retreat from Afghanistan.

But that had been followed by a period of savagery which had gnawed away at the underbelly of Mother Russia.

'Namangan – nothing. Ashkhabad – nothing,' intoned the officer.

General Borakin sipped his tea.

'Not even a report of a new daubing of their wretched crescent?'

The aide shook his head. 'Not one, comrade general. Their radios have stopped their attacks. Their mullahs have stopped their attacks, even against the American preacher.'

'Excellent.'

General Borakin turned and looked out of the window overlooking Red Square.

In his cell Cardinal Enkomo awoke to a sound he had not heard since boyhood. Then it had been the men of the tribe quietly going about their ablutions before leaving for work. Now it was his fellow cardinals preparing for conclave. From the cell on one side came the sound of Kazuo Anso pouring water into his washbowl, and from the other, Victor O'Rourke stropping an old-fashioned cut-throat. All around him other cardinals were struggling into wakefulness.

Many, he suspected had, like him, only slept fitfully, others perhaps not at all.

Over dinner the previous night in the Hall of the Popes, the lobbying had been low-key, but for all that intense. Hubert Messner had spent the entire meal moving from table to table, ostensibly enquiring if everyone was comfortable and explaining to newcomers the procedures of conclave.

This first night, he reminded them, was to be used as a time of spiritual cleansing, allowing the outside world to recede and the Holy Spirit to reach them all. As the evening wore on and the atmospheric fog thickened as cardinals lit cigarettes, cigars and pipes, and a few sent the serving nuns to bring spittoons, the lobbying continued.

He had smiled as Horace Walpole murmured that the camerlengo was trying to put flesh and blood on the Holy Spirit as he continued to promote the cause of Hans-Dietrich Muller. He had betrayed no emotion while this was going on, sipping his wine and wreathing his face with cigarette smoke.

As word spread that Marcel Leutens wanted no longer to be

considered, his supporters joined other groups. One of these mini-conclaves had begun to push the candidature of Horace Walpole, despite the quiet protests of the tall austere Englishman that he was too old for the job.

Lopez of Buenos Aires – who had smiled brightly at several of the nuns serving at table, a reminder, perhaps that his sexual transgression had in no way diminished his appreciation for a woman in a habit – had led a predominantly South American group in pushing the candidature of Enrique Camas. The Argentinian, they told anyone who would listen, was firmly opposed to vacillation over birth control, ordination of married men and especially ordination of women.

Another group had begun to promote Saldarini, pointing out that he understood that without a strong Curia, there could be no strong Pope.

Those who had approached Julius Enkomo received only a polite smile. Privately, he had wondered if anyone would receive the necessary seventy-five votes needed to win on the first ballot. He had been among the first to leave the dining hall. Over the next few hours lying on his bed, he had listened to the others slowly making their way to their cells, the night air filled with their whispers. Now as he dressed, the whispers again filled the air as the promoters and plotters went about their business.

The Mossad listening post in the apartment on the far side of St Peter's Square was crowded. In addition to the Pathfinder and his crew, Morton, Gates, Baader and Lacouste, Salim and Stratton were all standing among the surveillance equipment. Not wishing to embarrass Morelli, Morton had not invited him along. Not wanting to embarrass Morton, no one mentioned Carina.

Each man wore a headset plugged into the recorders, taping what the radomes picked up, which was converted by the Merino computer from a babble into separate intelligible conversations.

A few moments ago they had heard the cardinals begin to troop into the Sistine Chapel after a quick breakfast of coffee and rolls.

On one of the screens in the bunker beneath the White House, the watch keepers saw the cardinals kneeling and staring up at the majesty of Michelangelo's art, apparently riveted by the finger of God reaching out to Adam. This God was a virile, white-haired man, dressed in a surprisingly skimpy pink nightshirt.

Waiting for the proceedings to begin, Cardinal Enkomo found himself wondering about Michelangelo's *Last Judgement*. The way the artist's Adam is not circumcised – and perfectly right, too, for Adam preceded Abraham – but had been given a navel. Julius Enkomo decided this was more a demonstration of Michelangelo's grasp of anatomy than any doubt he may have had about the authenticity of the Book of Genesis.

When the 121 eligible electors were seated, Cardinal Messner remained in his seat, to the left of the *Last Judgement* fresco. Everyone knew what he was waiting for – to see whether anyone would propose the name of a cardinal to be elected by Acclamation. Then, if all the other electors felt similarly inspired they would together shout their assent with one word – *Eligio*.

Conclave would be over.

After ten silent minutes the camerlengo walked to a desk placed directly beneath the fresco. Another desk stood to one side.

'There has been no intervention by the Holy Spirit,' he intoned. 'Reverend Fathers, do you wish to proceed to delegation?'

The electors could appoint a committee of up to fifteen cardinals to select a new Pope. It had never happened. The silence remained unbroken.

'Very well, we shall now proceed to election by scrutiny.'

Cardinals O'Rourke, Ospispo and Martel were the first three names the camerlengo drew from a solid silver chalice before him which contained the names of every voter. They would be the 'scrutineers', who would examine and count the votes.

In the same manner further appointments were made: three 'reviewers' to check the work of the 'scrutineers'; three *infirmari* who, if the situation arose, would go to the cell of any elector taken ill and unable to come to the Sistine Chapel. The *infirmari* would collect his vote and bring it to the scrutineers.

Julius Enkomo and Hans-Dietrich Muller were to be two of the reviewers. The third was Cardinal Tovic.

Once the officers of the conclave were chosen, Cardinal Messner called forward the scrutineers to distribute the pile of voting cards before him. As Cardinals O'Rourke, Ospispo and Martel placed a card before each voter, the camerlengo outlined the voting procedure.

'You must make your choice in handwriting which cannot be identified. You will choose only one name. You will write in ink. Then you will fold your card down the centre.'

After placing a silver plate beside a second, empty chalice, the camerlengo returned to his seat.

Moments later came the first sound of scratching of pen on paper. As the others began to write, the camerlengo was the first to cast his vote. He walked to the desk, folded card held in his tightly clamped hands. Facing the fresco he loudly uttered the special oath of conclave.

'I call to witness Christ the Lord, who is my judge, that the vote I now cast is given to the one who, before God, I consider should be elected.'

The camerlengo placed the ballot paper on the silver plate, paused for a moment, lifted the plate and tilted it so that the card dropped into the empty chalice. He then sat at his desk.

Cardinals O'Rourke, Ospispo and Martel repeated the process and took their places at the scrutineers desk.

Julius Enkomo was the next to walk slowly forward, looking neither right nor left, his eyes fixed on Michelangelo's fresco towering over the altar. He had always thought the painting was weighty and overbearing, intimidating rather than inspiring confidence. He briefly wondered – and was surprised by the irrelevance of the thought – whether Islam was right when it forbade images or representations of the Divine.

As Julius Enkomo walked back to his seat, Cardinal Walpole rose to vote.

The Pathfinder glanced at his watch and grinned at Morton.

'Eighteen minutes so far. The Knesset could learn a thing or two about hurrying things along.'

Beneath the White House, the watch keepers in the bunker paused to watch the three scrutineers. The oldest one – Cardinal Martel – picked up the silver chalice and gave it a thorough shaking. Only those with the acutest hearing in the bunker fancied they heard the sound of the voting papers being swished around.

Cardinal O'Rourke sat to one side of the Archbishop of Manila, Cardinal Ospispo on the other. Cardinal Martel gave a slight nod and Cardinal O'Rourke removed a voting slip. As the Primate of All Ireland dropped the slip into his chalice, the voice of Cardinal Ospispo called out.

'One.'

If the total votes cast did not equal the number of electors, the cards would be destroyed and a second vote taken.

In the Sistine Chapel Cardinal Martel cleared his throat.

'Most Reverend Fathers, the number of votes cast equals those present.'

Cardinal Messner nodded. 'Proceed with the declaration.'

The reviewers moved to stand immediately behind the scrutineers.

Cardinal Martel switched the chalices so that the full one was once more before him. He dipped his hand into the receptacle and took out a card. He unfolded it and stared for a moment at the name handwritten on the two-inch square beneath the printed words: 'Eligio in Summum Pontificem' – 'I elect as Supreme Pontiff.'

The Archbishop of Manila wrote the name on a sheet of paper and passed the card to Cardinal O'Rourke. He, too, wrote down the name and passed the card to Cardinal Ospispo. Closely watched by all three reviewers, the Brazilian announced, 'The first vote is for Most Reverend Father Muller.'

Once more Cardinal Martel dipped into the chalice.

From his balcony on Via della Conciliazione, Father Gomez peered through a telescope lens at the growing crowd in St Peter's Square. Part of his skill included being able to estimate the size of a gathering. He reckoned there were about fifty thousand down there. When the time came there could be up to quarter of a million.

The balcony was now festooned with rolls of developed film; they obscured what he was doing from people in windows across the avenue. During the past two days he had tested the rifle's telescopic sight under various light conditions. It was mid-morning, and the sunlight hard and bright, when he made a

331

further test. He unlocked the suitcase containing the sniper's rifle and removed the sight. He clipped it to the mounting he had specially made and fitted on top of the camera.

Concentrating totally, he chose a number of faces to examine in the crosshairs in the area around Caligula's Obelisk. From time to time people looked up and pointed towards the temporary smoke stack fitted to the roof of the Sistine Chapel. He squinted through the sight at the stack. The sun's reflection on the metal dazzled him, and his eyes began to water. Wiping them, he reminded himself he would not be aiming at metal.

The Archbishop of Manila took out the last voting card from the chalice, unfolded it, wrote down the name, handed it to Victor O'Rourke who once more noted it before passing it to Cardinal Ospispo. His clear voice announced the name. It was another vote for Cardinal Camas of Madrid.

Everyone in the chapel knew what had happened. But no one dare acknowledge the fact by so much as a whisper. There was further protocol to follow. The three scrutineers began to pierce the voting cards with large needles which the most senior of the reviewers, Cardinal Tovic, had handed to them.

When the task was completed, Cardinal Tovic gathered up the cards, threaded them on a piece of string and placed them in one of the chalices. Escorted by the camerlengo, he carried the receptacle to the pot-bellied oven installed at the back of the Chapel. He lifted the lid and tipped in the cards.

Cardinal Messner selected one of the candles from a box beside the stove and lit it with the gas taper he had ordered for this sole purpose. He then popped the candle onto the paper and closed the stove lid. By the time he had returned to the desks, the voting record of each scrutineer had been checked by Cardinals Muller and Enkomo. The conclave officers returned to their places, leaving only the camerlengo standing beneath the *Last Judgement* fresco. Cardinal Messner gave the paper in his hand a final glance before announcing the result of the first ballot.

Through their headsets, Morton and the others heard the camerlengo speak.

'Reverend Father Anso. Twenty votes.'

The gasp sweeping the Chapel sounded to Morton like surf breaking against the shore.

'Anso? How'd he pull that many?' asked Stratton.

'A protest vote,' said Lacouste. 'The liberals trying to break the Muller bandwagon.'

The camerlengo's voice once more reached them.

'Reverend Father Saldarini. Twenty-six votes.'

'The Curia voting for its own,' murmured Baader.

'But where's Muller?' asked Gates.

Through the headsets came another response.

'Reverend Father Camas. Twenty-seven votes.'

This time no one spoke in the apartment.

'Reverend Father Muller. Thirty-two votes.'

Morton could sense the satisfaction in the camerlengo's voice. But Muller had only picked up one extra vote on those he had been pledged before conclave.

'Reverend Father Tovic. Ten votes.'

Another gasp came through the headphones.

'This has to make it anyone's race,' said Gates cheerfully. 'Tovic's splitting the conservatives. That's got to hurt Muller.'

The camerlengo's announcement of the final candidate who had received votes drew fresh murmurs of surprise within the Chapel.

'Reverend Father Walpole. Six votes.'

Anwar Salim, the Egyptian intelligence officer, turned to the others. 'The liberals are having a field day. The question is, can they keep it up? Anybody like to bet?'

There were no takers.


Father Gomez heard a great cry sweep the square. *Fumo! Fumo!*

He saw a wisp of grey smoke curl from the chimney on the chapel roof and swung the telescopic sight on the stack, feeling the familiar tension in his body which always came when action was close.

The smoke turned black and quickly disappeared. He did not need the collective cry of disappointment from the crowd to know the first ballot had failed. He forced his body to relax.


Hal stared at his computer screen, willing himself to remain calm. There had to be a mistake. He looked out of the window. Staff were making their way to the canteen for an early dinner. The thought of food increased the knotted feeling in his stomach.

Dammit! There had to be a mistake, had to be! You don't just lose 115,000 dollars.

An hour had passed since he had said goodbye to Penny-Jane outside the Records building, in a voice sufficiently loud for anyone passing to hear that their relationship was purely professional. Then he had hurried to his own office, locked the door and sat in the high-backed chair with thick rubber wheels which allowed him to scoot between the computers and the bank of modems, printers and racks of discs. He had selected one with the details of Church investments in South African Food Consolidated. On screen appeared the news that another half million rand had been wiped off the investment.

When he had sent a sell order to the broker in Johannesburg, back had come the immediate reply that trading in the stock had been suspended, pending what happened on the London market. Working with the speed and instinct which had once made him the most feared of traders on Wall Street, Hal had removed 70,000 dollars from Food Consolidated and placed it in Hold Corral. It was the name he had given that part of his computer's memory where he stored amounts of money before keying them on to his secret account in Geneva. In minutes a further 200,000 dollars had been placed in Hold Corral from other portfolios. He was now very close to the magical one million. With another practised shove of his foot, he had scooted to the cupboard for which he had cast a special key, removed the disc reserved for his Geneva account, scooted back to the computer and pressed keys.

The missing 115,000 dollars had leapt out at him. No matter how many times he reran the programme, the result was the same. He was down 115,000 dollars. It had to be a computer malfunction. He had pulled out the disc and fed in another. Everything on it was as it should be. He tried three more discs. The computer behaved perfectly. He re-inserted his Geneva account disc. The 115,000 dollars was still missing.

He removed the disc, unlocked the door and hurried to Mail. Clara had a computer. He'd use it to check the disc. He found her in Banking, watching the guard carrying the bagged cash, cheques and credit card slips out to an armoured truck from the Bank of Southern California.

She beamed at him. 'I guess God doesn't mind which computer you use for His work.'

'No, I guess not,' he said, forcing a smile. 'And bless His name.'

On Clara's computer the 115,000 dollars still remained missing.

She watched him burst out of her office and called after him. 'Hal, you look like someone just robbed your till!'

He looked at her, but did not break stride. If only she knew how close she was to the truth.

Watching him running out of Mail she thought how easy it had been. The nice man in Geneva had called her and said if she could agree to 115,000 dollars for the Stalin letter, he would have it couriered to her at once. She had said, no problem, no problem at all. A press of the key had transferred the money from Hal's Swiss account into her own. Another key shift had given the Bank of California central computer instructions to send the money back to the Overseas Manager of Credit Suisse. It really was so simple – and a lot of fun as well. Still smiling, Clara walked towards her office.


'Dammit,' Hal said aloud, when he was back in his office. 'The fault has to be their end.'

He picked up the telephone and dialled Credit Suisse in Geneva. An answering machine informed him the bank was closed. Hal looked at the wall clock. It was close to midnight in Switzerland. Making one last check on the disc, still unable to believe what had occurred, he was totally stupefied at what was now happening on the screen. Another 100,000 dollars had disappeared from his account.

In her office, Clara beamed happily as she prepared to remove a further 50,000 dollars from Hal's account.


Over dinner in the Hall of the Popes, Julius Enkomo heard several cardinals saying conclave might need several more days to produce a result. It had filled him with a sudden hope that what had happened in the Sistine Chapel on the second ballot was no more than an aberration. While Cardinal Muller had gathered the ten other votes previously cast for Cardinal Tovic, giving the Archbishop of Berlin forty-two votes, he was still a long way short of the necessary majority. Cardinal Walpole's votes had been divided between Cardinal Saldarini, giving him twenty-nine, and Cardinal Camas, who now had thirty. The first surprise of the second ballot was the elimination of Cardinal

Anso. Cardinal Molins of Paris had collected fourteen of those votes. He was a left-of-centre candidate. Then had come that totally stupefying moment when the camerlengo had announced that the other six votes had been given to the Reverend Father Enkomo.

All around him men had whispered and looked at each other, then at him. To avoid their gaze, he had bowed his head, filled with a sudden dread. All he could think of was that feeling he had experienced in the past of not yet having fulfilled the purpose God intended for him, the secret reason he had always feared death. But surely God did not intend this for him? The very idea of being His Vicar on Earth was too daunting, impossible to contemplate. Coming out of the Sistine Chapel he had been reassured, by Marcel Leutens.

'The liberals are maybe using you as a stalking horse, Julius. But you will need all our prayers, as well as your own.'

Half-way through dinner, Julius Enkomo had left his place and returned to his cell and knelt at the prie-dieu. He began to pray that God would indeed choose someone far more worthy and suitable.

In the early hours of the morning, alone in his suite in the Apostolic Palace, Morton continued to read the previous day's surveillance logs. The watchdog assigned to Monsignor Hanlon reported that after returning from Razellas, he had not left his room but had received one telephone call. It was from Monsignor Linde, asking if Sean wished to be present when the personal effects of Pope Nicholas were handed over to his family. The offer had been declined.

Fung had dropped off Kramskay at his hotel, and then gone on to his own. An hour later Kramskay had telephoned Moscow from his room and reported the substance of the conversation at the restaurant to General Borakin. Fung had made a similar call to Wong Lee in Lhasa. No mention had been made by anyone of Operation Holy Cross.

Morton had known this feeling before. The 'mocking god' had once more returned to taunt him, throwing up all the old questions which really came down to just a few. Was it boredom that was driving Sean? Was it shrewdness which had stopped Fung from pressing him about Holy Cross? Or was it something else – something that if he looked hard enough would hit him with the clarity of a muzzle flash in the dark? The way to find out was to deal with the mocking god the way he always had: accepting he had the right to be there, whispering his lies and disinformation, but allowing him to change nothing. And above all not letting the mocking god create a false sense of security. Or to give up on Carina.

He put aside the logs and turned to the reports of the second ballot. Morton shook his head. From all he had seen and heard the Church was not ready for someone like Julius. Those six votes were really no more than liberal scatter-shot.

General Borakin turned to the other two members of the troika. For several hours they had discussed the peace which had fallen on the Moslem republics. He turned to the former head of the KGB.

'Long ago I learned not to look for motive where there is none.' His tone was polite and deliberately unprovocative.

'I believe that what we see here is proof of what I have always said. That we were right not to respond to their provocations. You cannot keep a fire burning without fuel.'

The others nodded, accepting the wisdom of the axiom.

The old Party secretary toyed with a pen.

'But where does this leave a visit from the new Pope?'

'We have a little time yet,' Borakin said.

# 23

Julius Enkomo rose stiffly from the prie-dieu and turned to face the camerlengo, standing in the cell's doorway. A moment ago his knocking had interrupted a night spent in prayer on the kneeler.

'May I come in?' enquired Cardinal Messner.

'Of course.'

Julius Enkomo motioned to a chair.

'Thank you. I'd prefer to stand.'

The camerlengo walked over to a partitioned window; the other half provided a view for Cardinal Anso's cell. During the night Cardinal Enkomo had heard the Japanese praying quietly in his own language, while in the adjoining cell Andrew Berry twisted and turned in fitful sleep.

Cardinal Messner turned from the window.

'This is my fourth conclave and they don't become any more comfortable. Still, by tomorrow we could all be back in our own beds.'

Beyond the window the sky was still a pale gold, streaked with the first red at the edges, a precursor of another fine day.

'That depends how quickly I can see the new Pope and give him my report.'

Cardinal Messner gave a quick smile. 'Still worrying about this Holy Cross business, Julius?'

'I'm hoping the next Pope will see it through. My report could help him.'

In the momentary silence which followed, Julius Enkomo saw no reaction in the camerlengo's face.

'Your people need you back home, Julius. There's a lot of

338

work needing to be done after those food riots. Some of the government down there think the Church could be more supportive of its policies.'

Cardinal Enkomo sighed. 'I gather Minister Van Der Vaal must have phoned you?'

The camerlengo gave an ever briefer smile. 'He did, just before we all came in here. He wanted to reassure me a new Pope would mean, as far as his government went, that the recent past would be wiped off the slate. He sees the value of building proper bridges between Rome and Cape Town. Bridges that won't get washed away by the turbulent acts of agitators.'

'Is this what you've come to talk about?'

Cardinal Messner made a little hand motion. 'No, not really. I only mention it because people trust me to get things done. That's why if you'll give me your report, I'll see it gets the proper attention.'

'I would still prefer to explain the background myself to His Holiness's successor.'

The camerlengo pursed his lips. 'Let me be frank with you, Julius. We are a divided house as far as this business goes. And you know what the Gospel says. A house divided against itself is a house that will not survive.'

'That is why I want to explain everything to the new Pope,' Cardinal Enkomo said quietly.

'Very well,' sighed the camerlengo. 'But you must expect it will take a little while before he can see you. Perhaps it would still be more sensible to go home and return here when I can fix an appointment?'

Cardinal Enkomo gave a little shake of the head.

'I'd prefer to wait, at least a few days. Can I ask that you make every effort to convey to him the importance of what I have to say?'

'Of course.' But there was no warmth behind the camerlengo's words.

He glanced out of the window, then turned to Julius Enkomo.

'You have already made your mark, Julius, as the first African to collect votes in a conclave. Many Reverend Fathers go through their entire lives and never receive a vote in conclave.'

'I wish they had gone to someone else more worthy,' Julius Enkomo finally said.

'Really? That makes it easier to say what I've come to say.'

The camerlengo paused, trying to fathom what lay beneath the African's calm.

All around them conclave was stirring: the first signs of the day, water being poured, teeth brushed and faces scraped with a variety of razors.

The camerlengo's voice rose slightly to give added emphasis to his next words.

'Your votes were probably a tribute to Nicholas . . . that sometimes happens when a Reverend Father was particularly close to a Pope . . . but they're really no more. Just as I'm sure you'll agree we should all look deep into our consciences before we decide who is best suited to lead the Church.'

'I have prayed over nothing else all night.'

The camerlengo gave Julius Enkomo another careful look before continuing.

'Others have also sought guidance from the Holy Spirit to guide them to the right decision. Molins has declared he no longer wishes to be considered. And Saldarini has also asked to withdraw from nomination.'

'Why have they done that?' Julius Enkomo asked.

'For the sake of unity, Julius. Molins knows he can't go any further, even if all the arrivistes voted for him. I suspect some preferred Saldarini. But he realises they won't be there for the third ballot. By releasing his votes, he's become one of the Pope-makers of this conclave.'

'That still leaves Cardinal Camas. Why hasn't he withdrawn as well?'

The camerlengo shrugged. 'Spanish pride, perhaps. Or maybe he's not hearing what the Holy Spirit is telling him. That we need a strong pontiff who will implement his programmes with authority. A Pope who will be master in his own house – and one, as I have said, which will not be divided against itself.'

The camerlengo laid a hand on Julius Enkomo's arm. Did he not understand with Saldarini and Molins out of the contest, it was all but over? Camas, at best could only last another round? If Hans-Dietrich picked up only half the freed votes, he would be home and dry. Surely Enkomo could grasp that, would understand what he was driving at?

'Those first ballots were really only to test the waters. To see if the liberals would make a serious challenge. First they ran Anso. When they could see that was not going to work, they put up Molins and then . . . if I may say so, quite unexpectedly, you.'

The camerlengo withdrew his hand.

'In a way, those who voted for you are really reminding us all that anyone can become Pope.'

Cardinal Enkomo remained silent. The camerlengo continued, his voice cold like steel.

'But the reality, Julius, is that a priest must be carefully prepared for high office over a working lifetime. He must put aside friendship in favour of obedience. Those who will not cooperate, must be made to bend to his authority. Being Christ's Vicar on Earth was never meant to be easy. Today the job is harder than ever. We are a Church filled with inertia and over tolerance. The liberals are deeply embedded in the woodwork. I've always said the only person who can deal with them, with all our problems, is someone who has been properly trained at the very heart of matters, here in the Vatican.'

Cardinal Enkomo listened without interruption. The camerlengo continued in the same flinty voice.

'Whenever we have brought in an outsider, look what has happened. Pope Luciani barely lasted a month before the sheer responsibility killed him. And it took years to make the late Polish pontiff understand what we expected of him. Then, when your own mentor came along, we were back on the slippery spiral again. If Nicholas had lived, he would have presided over a Church increasingly divided.'

Again the camerlengo paused to rake Cardinal Enkomo with burning eyes.

'Now we have a golden chance to elect someone who understands he cannot be all things to all men, especially those who wish to further weaken the Church with their liberal policies. Mark my words, Julius, the world will see who we elect as a signal that the next pontificate will once more be like the great ones – uncompromising and not one that seeks popularity.'

Cardinal Enkomo began to rub his arm where the camerlengo had gripped it.

'Why are you telling me this?' he asked softly.

'Why?' asked Cardinal Messner. 'I would have thought it was obvious, Julius! I'm hoping you will see the sense of withdrawing your candidacy. All you need do is to tell me you now wish your votes distributed elsewhere –'

'To Cardinal Muller?'

'Yes, if you like. Hans-Dietrich would be the perfect choice to lead the Church in the coming years. He has all the attributes we need. And, if I may say so, those votes he has already received show all too clearly how the Holy Spirit is moving so many of us.'

'Can I ask you a question?'

'By all means.'

Cardinal Enkomo walked around the chair and placed both his hands upon the top bar.

'What will Cardinal Muller do about Holy Cross if he is elected?'

The camerlengo gave a little frown. So it was down to a trade-off. He had expected more of the African.

'I'm sure it will be something he will talk to you about when the time comes. And, of course, he will wish to study your report.'

Julius Enkomo gripped the chair more tightly.

'You frighten me, camerlengo. You and Cardinal Muller both. You really do.'

He stepped round the chair and stood close to the camerlengo, looking down into his eyes, seeing for the first time a sudden surprise and uncertainty.

'All my life I have believed in the absolute sanctity of what I was called by God to do. I came here to continue doing so by trying to choose the man I believe God wants to lead His Church. I am glad it cannot be me. But I hope it can never be Hans-Dietrich Muller.'

For a moment longer the camerlengo stared at Cardinal Enkomo, then he turned and walked from the cell.

It was 4 a.m. in Malibu when Hal was finally able to speak to Herr Vogel. The Overseas Manager of Credit Suisse in Geneva – where it was almost noon – had been tied up in bank meetings until then.

Hal had seen a further 385,000 dollars vanish from his account, making his total loss exactly half a million dollars. Almost all he had left was the 200,000 dollars still in the Hold Corral.

'So. Good morning, Herr Lockman. You are the early bird this morning! What can I do for you?'

Herr Vogel gave one of his Swiss laughs, which always sounded to Hal as if the banker had ice for blood.

'Something has happened in my account, Herr Vogel. Something very serious has happened.'

'Happened? One moment please.'

Hal could hear Herr Vogel calling up his account on screen. Then came a small intake of breath, followed by the suddenly overwound voice of Herr Vogel.

'So. Something has indeed happened, Herr Lockman. And you have made it happen. Why do you make all these withdrawals so quickly?'

Hal forced himself to remain calm. The neon-lit cross on top of the Tabernacle cast a cold blue light into his office. But it was Herr Vogel's words which made him shiver.

'I didn't make those withdrawals, Herr Vogel. Someone's got hold of my access code. And it has to be at your end!'

There was silence on the line.

'Impossible, Herr Lockman,' Herr Vogel said finally. 'That, you must understand, is not possible. We pride ourselves –'

'It's happened! Don't you hear what I'm saying! It's happened!'

'So. Please be calm, Herr Lockman. After all, we are only speaking here of money, and not a great deal –'

'Half a million bucks! That may not be a big deal to you. But it's my whole future! Do something!'

'I can close your account. But I will need your written authority, Herr Lockman. You can courier it here by tomorrow –'

'That's too long. Just take my money out now.'

Hal heard a reproving murmur on the line.

'Herr Lockman, our banking regulations do not permit such a thing. Interfering with a client's deposit is a very serious matter –'

'Don't tell me! Someone's done just that to me!'

There was another intake of breath from Herr Vogel.

'So. Herr Lockman, why do you play a game with me?'

'What! This is no game!'

'Herr Lockman, you have your account on screen?'

'No.'

There was a sigh on the line.

'Herr Lockman, even as we speak you have removed another 50,000 dollars from your account. Once more a cash transfer.'

'What ... what are you saying ...?'

There was a note of irritation in Herr Vogel's voice.

'All cash transfers, Herr Lockman. And of course with such

343

transactions, our computers keep no record. Now, if you wish to send me the proper authority I will close your account unless you wish to continue to remove your money in this way –'

'Wait. Please wait, Herr Vogel!'

Hal keyed his computer. He was in time to see a further 75,000 dollars disappear out of his account before his eyes.

Hal began to scream.

'Herr Lockman,' came the concerned voice of Herr Vogel out of the receiver. 'Herr Lockman, are you all right?'

Hal's screaming carried all the way to Mail, causing Clara to momentarily pause in her work. Her office was in darkness except for the glow from her computer screen. She smiled and, with a rapid movement of her fingers over the keyboard, completed the transfers from Hal's account into her own in the Bank of Southern California. This really was fun.

As she cleared the screen and stood up, a sudden flashlight beam caught her, making her squint and turn away from the light.

'Sorry, Miss Stevens,' called out the night security guard standing in the door.

He lowered the beam. 'Didn't know you'd be working this late.'

Recovering, she smiled at him. 'God's work knows no hours, Tim.'

'That's what the Only Book says, and bless His name.'

An unearthly scream rent the air, startling the guard.

'It's okay,' Clara said reassuringly. 'It's only Hal Lockman. When he's working late and alone he does that to let out stress. There's really nothing for you to worry about.'

'He sounds like he's in pain.'

Clara smiled sweetly. 'Pain is all part of trying to live a better life. Try and remember that, Tim.'

'Yes, ma'am.'

The guard touched his cap and walked out of Mail. He'd heard Hal Lockman was weird. But screaming like that? The guy had to be nuts.

Locking her office door, Clara left Mail, thinking that by this time tomorrow she would be almost a millionairess.

Another unearthly shriek pierced the night.

*

Dawn was reddening the sky when Morton strode into the Communications Centre on board Concorde. Swift Renovations had provided a car and driver to bring him to Rome airport where the plane was parked in a high security area. The decision to bring him here was Karshov's.

After Morton had briefed him, the Prime Minister said he wanted the Tribe, Israel's dozen most senior strategic planners, to hear. Only the Communications Centre possessed the technical facilities to link the planners in their widely scattered offices across Israel to the Situation Room in Tel Aviv.

Karshov and his own aides sat there. With them was Bitburg, in his usual position behind the Prime Minister. Several times the director had whispered in Karshov's ear during the briefing. That was Bitburg's way.

After reporting what Savenko had said, Morton gave a concise description of the reaction to the Reverend Kingdom's telecast. Finally he provided a report on events in conclave.

'God forbid I should ever again find myself grateful to Kingdom, but I am for his pointing out Muller's background,' said Bitburg.

The director sat, hands gripping his knees, the hard light of the Situation Room catching his thick glasses.

'It's all on file, Walter,' Morton said steadily. 'And Muller's no better or worse than others with his background.'

'They don't all have a chance of becoming Pope, David,' Bitburg snapped.

'How neatly you delineate things, Walter,' replied Morton.

He saw Bitburg's eyes begin to carom.

'Proof, David. That's what I use to delineate things. And that's once more what's sadly lacking here.'

Morton saw Karshov's brows knit.

'Walter,' growled the Prime Minister. 'Before we get to this issue of proof I'd like to hear what the Tribe has to say.'

The Prime Minister shifted his gaze. 'Izzy, would you like to start?'

A bearded face appeared on an insert on Morton's screen.

'General Savenko is perfectly correct in his assumption that the Soviet Islamic republics are on the verge of boiling over,' said Isadore Kuntz. He was the Tribe's expert on Mongol-Turkic relations, a man not yet forty with an old man's wavery voice.

'It's inevitable after Tehran's announcement this morning that the Islamic Confederation is being disbanded. That'll please Washington and London, but it doesn't mean we are out of the frame.

'But that said there is no evidence the republics will seriously carry their ambitions much beyond who will be top of their particular heap. I can't see that changing in the foreseeable future – especially now that the Ukraine and Byelorussia have really come together. So I tend to discount much of what else General Savenko postulates.'

Morton saw Karshov make a note and once more look up.

'Manny?' asked the Prime Minister.

Another face, beardless and bespectacled, appeared in a corner of Morton's screen. Manny Samuels was the Tribe's Kremlinologist.

'I agree with Izzy. Right now the troika's too busy trying to stay in power to start anything as ambitious as Savenko suggests, let alone confront the West. I think we should look at this from another angle. The troika could have deliberately used him to try and alarm not only us, but Washington and London. As we all know, no one there has so far really lifted a finger to help them while their economy goes on sinking by the day. Their war machine is rusting over. They're worse off than many Third World countries. Indeed, perhaps they are a genuine member of the Third World. Yet history shows there's no quicker way to get help than to yell your house is on fire and you've no water. This could just be the troika's way of forcing us to send the fire brigade.'

'Sally?'

A new face appeared on screen. Sally Deng was the Tribe's expert on China. She still dressed in a high-buttoning Mao jacket and wore her hair in a basin haircut.

'Prime Minister, I do not believe China will attack Kazakhstan,' she began.

For the next ten minutes the middle-aged sinologist provided a masterful insight into Chinese foreign policy.

One by one the other members of the Tribe gave their equally expert assessments. Each insisted that the scenario Savenko had given Morton was, in the end, most unlikely to happen.

Finally one strategic planner remained.

'Kevin?' Karshov prompted.

A moon-like face filled the insert. Kevin Sachs was the Tribe's authority on the deployment of nuclear weapons.

'The UN inspection teams are a long, long way from pin-pointing those nuclear weapons still remaining in the Islamic republics.'

'What sort of number are we talking about, Kevin?' Karshov asked.

'Oh . . . maybe five, six thousand. Mostly small battlefield tactical weapons. Maybe one or two bigger rockets. As time goes by, they'll become increasingly unstable due to a lack of proper maintenance. There's probably as much risk of one of them going accidentally out of control as there is of a deliberate launch. I've told the inspection teams where I see the real danger spots. But they're pushed to the limit. It could be months –'

'Excuse me, Kevin,' Bitburg interrupted. 'Have you any hard evidence the Tadjiks, the Uzbeks or any of the others plan to use these weapons as a direct threat against us?'

'No, director. But there's always the possibility one of the local war lords grabs some technician who knows enough to start up –'

'I'm talking about evidence, Kevin! Not conjecture!'

Eyes continuing to carom, Bitburg peered out of the screen at Morton.

'That's what's missing in what your general says, David. So why should we believe him?'

Morton looked directly into the small camera on the bulkhead above the screen.

'In someone like Savenko, patriotism counts for a lot, Walter. It must have cost him a great deal to blow the whistle on the troika. He probably doesn't know everything they're up to, but he's learned enough to know he doesn't wish to see them destroy what remains of his country.'

'Many of us wouldn't weep over that,' Bitburg replied. 'But then we don't have a sentimental attachment to Russia . . . though after what happened to you and your family, I can't imagine you feel much either. But that's beside the point. The only question is whether your general is telling the truth, David?'

Morton remembered what Savenko had said, each distinct, unforgettable statement.

'My instinct says he is. Either you accept that or you don't, Walter.'

'Instinct, David?' echoed Bitburg. 'Ah, yes . . . I'd momentarily forgotten about how important that is to you. It would be interesting to know if your . . . instinct supports the present voting pattern in conclave.'

Suddenly Morton wanted an end to this. It was more than sniping. It was something wider and deeper between them. Bitburg had ordered Carina's name to be removed from the weather satellite's watch-for list.

'It very much looks as if Muller's going to make it,' Morton said.

'Then in that case we have nothing to worry about!' Bitburg replied. 'This Holy Cross business will be dead and buried with Muller. And so will this . . . this delusion of your general's.'

Morton watched the director turn to Karshov.

'It really is too fantastic, Prime Minister. First Savenko says the troika wants this ridiculous Holy Cross operation to still go ahead. Then he says they want to use it as an excuse to reduce their Islamic republics to what they were in the Middle Ages! It's all just too fantastic! And he doesn't give David a rouble's worth of proof. Not that it seems to matter . . . not with David's . . . instinct working so well. But I fear I need a little more than that!'

Bitburg sat back, hands on knees.

Morton said nothing. There was nothing more he wanted to say. Bitburg had made another of his banker's decisions.

When Karshov finally broke the silence there was a rawness in his voice not there before. He stared sombrely out of the screen at Morton.

'Walter's right, David. What Savenko says is fantastic. In some ways it's little short of a blueprint for a new world war.'

The Prime Minister gave a sudden weary smile.

'But I have had to learn to live with the fantastic. If he did nothing else, Saddam Hussein forced me to do that.'

The Prime Minister cleared his throat. 'Yet if I go to the President in Washington or the Prime Minister in Britain, or anyone else who is still prepared to listen to me, they will also ask for proof – and who can blame them? And when I tell them we have nothing except General Savenko's word, I fear I will not get very far.'

The scar tissue over Karshov's eye had started to grow livid. When he continued there was a sudden weariness to his voice.

'Partly, of course, it's this whole business of the "new order"

George Bush started and which his successor has become fixated with. We all know it's created the kind of isolationism in America we haven't seen since the late thirties. As long as there's no real threat to the United States, Washington really doesn't want to become seriously involved.

'Once their hostages were finally out of Beirut, their interest in the region waned. We saw that over bringing Saddam to book. Over the Kurds. Over dealing with Gaddafi over Lockerbie. Over a dozen other issues.'

Karshov turned to Bitburg. 'So, yes, the President or anyone else, is going to want proof. And in the case of the President, he's going to weigh what I say against what those watch keepers in that fancy bunker under his rose beds are making of what's happening. So that's another problem.'

Morton saw Bitburg's eyes were steady as Karshov continued to speak.

'But there is also something else, Walter. And that is something I put a high value on. David's instinct.'

'Prime Minister, really –' Bitburg began.

'Hear me out, Walter,' Karshov said. 'David's instinct has proven to be right in the past. And because of what I have heard here today, I have given serious consideration to still going to the President and asking him to speak to the troika. Nothing formal, and certainly nothing on paper. Just enough to let them know we suspect.'

Morton saw Bitburg was once more starting to lose control of his eyes.

'Proof, Prime Minister! We have nothing –'

'Walter,' growled Karshov, 'stop interrupting!'

The Prime Minister addressed the screen.

'There is one other matter, David. Operation Holy Cross. Even if I was able to persuade the President to call Moscow, what would happen to Holy Cross then? Almost certainly the troika would refuse to receive the new Pope. Assuming, of course, he actually will go through with Holy Cross, and in Muller's case that is a very big assumption.'

Morton thought again how Karshov could sound like an Old Testament prophet as he developed an argument. He would neither be hurried nor side-tracked. But he had a politician's skill to say only what he needed to make a point.

Karshov continued. 'Without Holy Cross working we, and the

349

rest of the world, would be precisely where we are now: watching these Moslem republics tearing themselves apart.

'More than most, we have a vested interest in seeing that stop. We still have half a million of our own people there. And while Washington's geographically a long way from that cauldron, we are not. It would only need one flash point – like launching one of those undetected missiles which Kevin has spoken about against us. Then everyone would be sucked in.'

The Prime Minister stared into the screen, his eyes deeply troubled.

'I have listened most carefully to what you have said, David. And if General Savenko has got it wrong, then I'll be the first to say, thank God. And it may very well be that he has. But I can't take that chance, not for Israel or for our friends; not even for our enemies.

'We have to do everything possible to make sure the next Pope – even if he is Muller – goes through with Holy Cross. That means doing nothing, absolutely nothing, about Savenko's warning. To alert the troika we suspect them, and without more proof, we can't call it much more, would sink Holy Cross without trace.'

Karshov leaned into the screen, his face and voice suddenly softer.

'Everyone here joins me in saying how deeply sorry we are over your sadness with Dr Ogodnikova. From what I have been told it seems that whatever made her disappear like that, it is very unlikely she will now return. I must therefore ask you to put the matter out of your mind. I want nothing to deflect you from the task in hand, and that is to remain in Rome and make absolutely certain that once a new Pope is chosen, Cardinal Enkomo does everything possible to persuade him about the importance of Holy Cross.'

After Cardinal Messner had celebrated the Mass of the Holy Spirit, he addressed the electors in the Sistine Chapel.

'Reverend Fathers, many of you know only three names remain to go forward to the third ballot, those of Reverend Fathers Muller, Camas and Enkomo. I therefore now intend to delay the resumption of conclave until this afternoon so as to allow time for those of you who need to pray further or consult among yourselves.'

The camerlengo walked in silence out of the Chapel. The

others drifted after him. Soon only Julius Enkomo remained in his seat, head bowed. He had tried, God knows he had tried. But each time something made him hesitate about pledging his vote to Cardinal Camas.

Nicholas once said Camas was a Curia man in pastoral clothing. Someone like that could well abandon Holy Cross. And if Muller was elected then most certainly the operation would be doomed. That was all too clear from what Messner had said. Yet there had to be somebody who would carry on the torch Nicholas had lit. One of the Americans, maybe. He had heard good things about Michael Boylan. Or Philippe Martel of Manila. Both had administrative experience in the Curia, and would know how to handle any threat from that quarter. He would talk to them.

'Cardinal Enkomo, can we speak with you?'

Julius Enkomo stared into the faces of Walpole of Westminster, Leutens of Marseilles and O'Rourke of Armagh.

'How can I help you?' Cardinal Enkomo asked.

'By listening to what we have to say,' replied Cardinal Walpole cheerfully. 'And for a start, I propose we find somewhere a little more comfortable. It's a nice morning, why don't we go and sit in the Parrot Courtyard? They've put out some benches there, so we can enjoy the sun.'

Moments later they entered the small courtyard behind the Sistine Chapel. A number of cardinals were already strolling over the cobblestones, talking amongst themselves.

Cardinal Walpole led them to a couple of benches in a corner. He sat beside Julius Enkomo, the others opposite.

'May I call you Julius?' asked the Englishman in his diffident way.

'Of course.'

'And please call me Horace. I think we'd all welcome a little informality after the last two days of our camerlengo's formality.'

'Not to mention his style of politicking,' growled Marcel Leutens.

Horace Walpole turned and stared at Julius Enkomo.

'I fear we have a little politicking of our own to do. And it's very much in the spirit of the old adage – the Pope who goes into conclave comes out a cardinal. Have you heard that before, Julius?'

Cardinal Enkomo shook his head.

'For once it means exactly what it says. That the man who

goes into conclave most likely to be elected, isn't. We want to ensure that tradition continues.'

'In other words,' Victor O'Rourke said, lighting his pipe, 'we all want to make sure that Muller's bandwagon is stopped.'

'It's not just Muller, but Messner as well,' continued Marcel Leutens. 'It's clear from all the soundings I've taken that they will take the Church away from those perilous waters that ever since Christ we have been required to navigate.'

'But Cardinal Muller's got over forty votes,' Cardinal Enkomo said quietly.

Horace Walpole turned to look at him steadily.

'And he'll probably get more. But not enough to succeed if we can persuade you to remain as a candidate.'

Julius Enkomo recoiled as if hit.

'No!' he said emphatically. 'I can't do that.'

'Please, Julius,' Marcel Leutens said gently. 'More than any other conclave I have been part of, this one is divided between what we can call the "political" and "pastoral".

'The Huns are purely politically driven in all their thinking. You are the one pastoral candidate who still has sufficient experience to stand up to them. And you were closer than any of us to Nicholas. You knew his thinking, and what he wanted. Who better, then, than you to lead us forward?'

'Listen to me, all of you!' Cardinal Enkomo cried, his voice suddenly fierce. 'Ever since those six votes I have prayed that God would find someone else among us –'

'But he hasn't,' said Horace Walpole cheerfully. 'I saw it on your face this morning in chapel. The same anguish I saw on John Paul's face when we told him we wanted him to be Pope. And I'm going to tell you what I told him just before he was elected. Don't deal in factions but treat the Church as an entity. Look after the body of the Church and become the caring physician who will heal the wounds.'

'Julius,' Victor O'Rourke said quietly, 'in the end the decision is not yours to take. In the end it will be up to the Holy Spirit.'

Cardinal Enkomo stood up. 'Then I will only ask that you pray to him to make sure someone else is chosen.'

Head bowed, hands clasped across his chest, fingers stroking the pectoral cross suspended from the chain around his neck, Julius Enkomo walked out of the sunlight into the gloom of the corridors of conclave. He was glad for the shadows, glad no one could see the tears in his eyes.

Back in his cell he took from his pocket the envelope containing Nicholas's blueprint for Holy Cross. He began to read it one more time.

# 24

From the day he moved into his suite on the top floor of the manse, the Reverend Kingdom made it an absolute rule that no one, not even Martha, should disturb his first hour awake. It was his alone to follow a routine now so embedded he never gave it conscious thought. Climbing out of bed he lowered himself to the carpet and did thirty quick push-ups. He then performed his Chinese martial arts exercises, moving in slow motion around the bedroom. Next he spent a brisk ten minutes at the professional punchbag in a corner before working with the weights.

By the time he stepped into the shower he was breathing deeply. He lathered himself with pine scented soap and then set the shower to deliver alternate bursts of icy and steaming needles. Afterwards he put on a heavy towel robe and went to the den. Like all the other rooms in the suite it was painted yellow and white, colours he had read were the most soothing.

In the den he pressed a key on his personal computer to signal for Bridie to start preparing his breakfast. He shared the kitchen with Martha's adjoining apartment. It had been another of her cost-cutting ideas.

He switched on the den's TV to catch the sunrise headlines. There had been another small earth tremor in northern California, centred north of San Francisco, the second this month. In New York the markets had opened quietly. The top story in foreign news was that the Chinese People's Liberation Army had overnight pulled back from the border with Kazakhstan. There were unconfirmed reports that several Moslem republics were planning a new alliance. In Rome conclave continued. A clip showed the crowd in St Peter's Square pointing to black smoke emerging from the chimney on the roof of the Sistine Chapel.

The Reverend Kingdom switched off the set and placed a classical disc on the stereo turntable. The music soothed him and helped him think. These past two days had been particularly strenuous. The three further attacks he had broadcast on Muller required all his skill to rework the material, each time making it sound as if he was telling those hundreds of millions out there something fresh.

They had responded as he knew they would – faxing or phoning with messages of praise. The switchboard had logged over 20,000 calls, overwhelmingly urging him to continue exposing the man who wanted to be the next Roman pontiff.

The support came at a crucial time, the run up to the annual Church of True Belief Give For The Lord Telethon. Every year, for twenty-four hours, he stood in the pulpit of the Tabernacle urging his vast television audience to pledge, pledge, pledge. Martha had said that in one day he garnered more money than from a month of tithes.

The key to his success, he knew, was not just a thunderous denunciation of all that was evil, but to be able to produce before the cameras a living sinner of awe-inspiring wickedness who had repented. Down the years politicians, various sports stars and pillars of the business world had all, at the right moment in the Telethon, been brought to stand below the pulpit and publicly recant.

It was not only electrifying viewing for all those hundreds of millions glued to their sets listening to astounding confessions of sexual or financial wrongdoing. It enabled him to say: there but for the grace of God, and bless His name, go you, almost a billion of you. So give now to stay in His grace.

Though every year the telephone company put in more lines, from the moment the carefully chosen sinner ended his confession, the phones were jammed.

This year he had still not found a sinner who would once more make that happen.

When the music began to wash over him, the Reverend Kingdom bowed his head and once more asked the Good Lord to bring him such a person. Then, as the symphony built to its first crescendo, he walked over to the window to peer down at the complex. He wondered again whether Moses had enjoyed similar satisfaction when he had looked down at the Promised Land.

At this hour the complex was deserted. It would be another hour before the first worshippers went to the Tabernacle to give thanks for the night's rest God had given them.

The neon-lit cross still glowed above the Tabernacle. He had heard that on a clear night the cross was visible thirty miles out to sea, on those ships taking people from one Sodom to another Gomorrah. Soon he must preach another sermon about the evils of cruising.

The dawn already revealed the site for the new campus. While Hal and Martha had still not come up with the extra money to pay for the additional earthquake proofing, he had given the go-ahead to start work. In less than a week the first foundations would be dug; in a month they would be able to withstand a major tremor.

Last night the nightmare had returned again, as vivid as ever. He had tried to remain asleep to see what actually happened to him when he was buried under the rock. But once again he had been jerked at that point into sweat-soaked wakefulness. Soon he would be able to laugh off the nightmare.

'Eddie.'

The Reverend Kingdom turned, the startled look on his face making him suddenly appear older and more vulnerable than he ever did in public. Martha stood in the doorway, her hair unpinned and cascading around her face almost down to her waist. He had not seen her look like this since she was a teenager. Her cassock appeared as if she had slept in it.

'Martha, something wrong?' He came forward, smiling solicitously, trying not to show his surprise and irritation that she had interrupted him.

Her lips were trembling.

'What is it, Pumpkin?' He could not remember when he had last used her childhood pet name.

Behind Martha, Bridie had appeared with the breakfast tray.

'Like Bridie fix you something to eat?' he asked.

Martha shook her head, her mouth still working.

'Hal,' she finally said.

'Something wrong with Hal?' he asked.

Her whole body had started to tremble as she managed to whisper again: 'Hal ... he's ...'

He saw tears in her eyes and tried not to frown. Last night it had been Clara. He had been about to turn off the light when

356

Martha phoned to say she wanted Clara to go. She had given no reason, none at all, and he had pointed out, that with the Telethon coming up they needed someone experienced to handle the flood of pledges. Everyone in Mail did little else for a week after the telecast, and there was no one like Clara to keep things moving. He was still trying to explain when Martha started to weep and then hung up. Something was happening to her. But God knew – and bless His name – he could not afford for Martha to crack up now.

He took her by the elbow and gently led her into the dining room.

'An extra cup, Bridie,' he told the housekeeper.

After Bridie set a place at the table for Martha and left the room, he turned to his sister.

'Now what's Hal gone and done?'

Martha looked at him wordlessly, her mouth working but no words coming.

'What are you trying to say, Pumpkin?' he asked, trying to keep out the unease.

'Hal!' she said with a great effort. 'He's gone . . . gone and . . . ruined us.'

He looked at her incredulously. There was a sudden sharp pain in his chest.

'Ruined? What do you mean . . . ruined?' he finally asked.

'Our investments . . . millions lost . . . I don't know how many . . . and worse . . .'

The pain was like a band encircling his chest, tightening with every breath he drew.

'Worse?' he whispered.

Martha's lips were trembling almost out of control.

He closed his eyes and breathed in deeply, held his breath for as long as possible and then expelled it with as much force as he could. He felt the invisible band snap. He'd always handled panic attacks like this.

'Worse? What do you mean, worse, Martha?' he asked in his normal voice.

'Stolen,' she whispered. 'He's . . . stolen.'

As Martha started to sob, he reached across and gripped her hand.

'You better start at the beginning.' He closed his eyes, the better to concentrate.

'I found him on the office floor, curled up and whimpering like an animal,' Martha sobbed. 'It just all came pouring out. There was no stopping him . . .'

She told the Reverend Kingdom everything Hal had confessed to her. As Martha spoke, her brother occasionally interjected:

'Hal actually said he was going to quit when he'd taken a million?'

Or:

'When he tried to move the money out of this Hold Corral of his, that had also disappeared?'

And:

'There's just no way of finding out where it's all gone?'

And:

'He had sex with this child every afternoon until she saw the Light?'

But for the most part the Reverend Kingdom sat there, listening behind closed eyes. When Martha finished he waited a while before opening his eyes and staring into her stained and bloated face.

'Where is Hal now?' he asked softly.

It surprised her he could be so calm, and she started to sob once more.

'He's in his apartment. Fenton's with him in case he tries to cut and run. Fenton wants to call the police –'

'Fenton's not to do that, Martha,' he said firmly.

The Reverend Kingdom closed his eyes for a long thirty seconds and then opened them and looked once more directly at her.

'It's God's way, Martha. God answering my prayers – and bless His name.'

She looked in astonishment at him. What was Eddie thinking about? Hal Lockman had stolen a million dollars and almost wiped out the investment portfolios, and here was Eddie behaving as if this was part of some plan. As if there was something good in all this!

'Eddie, I don't follow . . .'

He smiled at her. 'None of us fully understands the mystery of the Lord. What you've just told me is terrible. Shocking and dreadful and downright criminal. And Hal of all people. Hal is our Judas. But remember Martha, what happened to Judas?'

'Judas? But I just don't see –'

'Judas repented, Martha! First he betrayed the Lord God. Then he repented. And *then* he killed himself. Haven't I always said on Easter Sunday that we should see Judas as the original sinner who repented?'

'Yes, but –'

'No buts, Martha!' He levelled a finger at her. 'Like I said, Hal is our Judas. Our sinner. And we need a sinner right now.'

She looked at him, realisation dawning.

'You mean . . . ?'

'Exactly, Martha! Hal can be our Telethon sinner! He's perfect in every way. The trusted right-hand man who stole. It's like a parable straight from the Only Book!'

He paused, gathering his thoughts. 'Of course, Hal will need a little coaching, a little reminder that it's either stand up and confess or spend the next ten years in some cell.'

He reached across and stroked her hand, the way he had done when she had been a child and frightened of the dark.

'When people hear him, Martha, they'll be deeply, deeply moved and they'll feel good in themselves, feel but for the grace of God they could be in Hal's place. Belief's a powerful emotion, Pumpkin. And it's human nature to give thanks when you realise you've had a lucky escape!'

She put her hand over his as he continued to speak in that quietly soothing voice, so different from the one he used in the pulpit, but every bit as potent.

'We'll not only get back the million he stole, but all that money he poorly invested. You wait. Once he admits his sins and repents, the good people will know what the Only Book said they must do. Give. I'm going to suggest they each give ten per cent more than they did last year. Just ten per cent. Nobody's going to crib at that.'

He smiled gently at her. 'Like I always say, Pumpkin, the Good Lord moves in mysterious ways, but he always takes care of his own.'

Martha started to sob again. Only this time she was laughing as well. He also had not seen her do this since she was a child.

The Pathfinder made another adjustment to the dials on the receiver and pushed the headset down over his ears.

'We keep losing him as he moves around among the others, David,' he apologised.

Then once more Morton heard in his own headset the coldly angry voice of Cardinal Messner.

'. . . it has been an interesting voyage of discovery, Cardinal Camas, but the time has come for your ship to drop anchor.'

'I feel reluctant to do so, camerlengo. At least until I have had further consultations . . .'

'I've spoken to the South Americans. Even Ospispo, who's done an excellent job to get you so far, says he doesn't think you'll go much further. What I am saying is if you pull out now there will be a place for you . . .'

'Lost him,' groaned the Pathfinder.

A babble of voices filled the headset.

'It's those damned walls in that courtyard. They're like baffle boards, bouncing sounds all over the place.'

The Pathfinder began again to tweak the dials.

Morton removed his headset and turned to the other technicians.

'Any sign of Cardinal Enkomo?'

Both men shook their heads. Julius Enkomo's voice had not been heard since he had walked out of the Parrot Courtyard.

'Got him again,' grunted the Pathfinder, 'but he's not very clear, David.'

Morton replaced his headset to hear what Cardinal Messner was saying.

'. . . it is not enough that our next Pope will strive to improve the perfection of Christian life. He must know how to come to terms with the great discipline of the Church.'

'You are saying we need someone who can put a stop to liturgical abuses?' asked a new voice.

Morton glanced at the Pathfinder.

'Posanos. He's the only one with a Brazilian accent,' murmured the Pathfinder.

'. . . Absolutely . . . someone who understands the separate roles of spiritual and ecclesiastical discipline,' the camerlengo replied.

'But what about Reverend Father Enkomo?' another voice demanded.

The Pathfinder nodded at Morton.

'Reefer of Seoul.'

'. . . a liberal. Look at that sermon on the liturgy Enkomo delivered when still a bishop. Hans Kung could have written it,'

Cardinal Messner was saying. 'And I happened to be at Enkomo's last retreat. Even some of our Dutch brothers were a little surprised at how relaxed he was over issues most of us hold dear . . .'

'You forget, camerlengo, I was at that same retreat and I recall that Cardinal Enkomo was very sound on the need for a strong Catholic identity and to issue a ringing proclamation of faith in a world which is increasingly losing its religious way.'

The Pathfinder identified for Morton the voice of Bertram Terry, Cardinal Archbishop of Sydney.

'You seem to have overlooked where our African Father stands on atheism, Bertram. He doesn't seem to favour outright condemnation. Instead he has what he calls this heuristic approach, trying to find common ground with unbelievers. Is that the man we dare entrust the future of . . .'

The Pathfinder swore softly. Once more he had lost the camerlengo's voice.

Wong Lee sighed and leaned forward on his log seat to speak into the communications sphere.

'General, when I tried to deal in all good faith with your predecessors, I found they did not understand the meaning of the phrase.'

There was another silence from Moscow. Fung had said this was how the troika negotiated. But they would find he could out-wait them.

'Mr Wong, we are different from Gorbachev and Yeltsin,' General Borakin finally said.

The grunt was the only acknowledgement from Lhasa over the speaker phone.

Borakin looked at the other two members of the troika seated with him around a desk in the lead-lined bunker beneath the Beklemishev Tower. Kramskay had warned them the Chinese would be a tough man to deal with. He had said so again when he called with news of the kidnapping of Ogodnikova.

That the Chinese could go to such lengths simply to punish Morton was an insight. He should be devoting all his energies to retrieving his position in the markets from London to Tokyo, Frankfurt to Hong Kong, where the stocks of Wong Holdings remained frozen.

'As you no doubt know, we have faced problems with our dissident Moslem republics,' continued Borakin.

'I am aware of that,' Wong Lee acknowledged. 'But you seem to have handled it successfully. And with the end of the Islamic Confederation, certainly, in my view, you do not need my help, nor the West's to help you subdue your Moslems. And, of course, this decision of Beijing must also have helped you.'

Borakin ignored the probe.

He had spent most of the night with the other two troika members in the bunker monitoring reports of the PLA withdrawal from the Kazakhstan border.

The reason for the withdrawal was as difficult to second-guess as what was going on in the mind of this Chinese.

'Your Moslems are like the Arabs who threaten Israel – they plot but in the end do little,' Wong Lee said contemptuously.

An hour ago he had received a phone call from the President of the fledgling Council of Islamic Republics to say they were holding a meeting to agree on a common policy towards Moscow. He knew what that meant. The weapons systems he had supplied them with had been a waste of time. As useless as the secret deal he had made with them on the very lines this *gweillo* in Moscow was proposing.

Borakin cleared his throat. 'We have also been assisted by what has been happening in the stockmarkets. It seems your . . . difficulties . . . have made it easier for the rouble to survive . . .'

'It would appear so, general.'

Wong Lee sat perfectly still staring at the sphere. Only because of what had happened on the markets had he allowed this *gweillo* to push matters so far.

His phone call had come as no surprise. That fool Kramskay had told Fung of the troika's dream to make Mother Russia once more a powerful figure – able to take on that other ridiculous figure admired by so many of the *gweillo* in the West. The one they called Uncle Sam. Just like children – and to be treated as such.

There was another phlegmy sound from Moscow.

'Once we have settled our problems, we are prepared to grant you long leases on mineral rights in the Moslem republics,' Borakin said.

Wong Lee reached forward and picked up a notebook off the onyx slab. On it was written the list Borakin had dictated earlier on in the discussion.

In the Planning Centre they heard another sigh from Lhasa.

'You are not only seeking strategic weapons, general, to replace those the UN inspection teams have destroyed. But support systems, early warning reconnaissance and communications. Both for defence and attack.'

'And you can provide all that?' Borakin asked quickly.

'Of course. That is part of our business, general. But let me come back to the question of mineral rights. You are proposing a straight fifty-fifty division.'

Borakin looked at the others. They both nodded for him to continue.

'That would make us equal partners, Mr Wong. Even the Americans when they offered us most favoured nation status did not get such a deal. The Japanese, Germans, British, none of them –'

'I have never been an equal partner with anyone, general. I do not intend to start now.'

Wong Lee put the notepad back on the slab. Fung was wrong. A Russian *gweillo* was like any other.

Borakin turned to the others. Kramskay had not prepared them for this.

The former head of the KGB and the ex-Party secretary began to write on pads before them. They glanced quickly at what each had written, then tore off the sheets and passed them to Borakin. He nodded and spoke into the speaker phone.

'We are prepared to offer you a sixty-forty division in your favour, Mr Wong.'

Another drawn-out sigh came from half-way across the world.

'The capital outlay my company would bear is considerable, general. As you say, the current stockmarket situation does not help me. And, I fear, none of us knows how long the situation will continue. Therefore, I must propose a division of profits to the ratio of seventy-thirty in favour of Wong Holdings.'

A sharp intake of breath emerged from the sphere. Borakin looked at the note he had made.

'But Mr Wong! Such an arrangement would leave us with very little – especially as you also wish to take your profits before we have recovered our portion of the capital outlay!'

'Then I fear we cannot do business, general,' came the cold whispering voice from Lhasa.

Borakin looked at his colleagues. They were writing furiously. They looked up and nodded.

'We would like to think our relationship with you is for the long term,' resumed Borakin. 'Therefore on this occasion we are prepared to accept the arrangement you propose. But I wish you to understand that any future deals will be renegotiated.'

'Of course.' It had always surprised him how *gweillo* put as much store on face-saving as did his own people.

Wong Lee leaned forward and glanced at the notepad. The military orders were worth twenty billion roubles. The potential profits from the mineral rights could be double that.

'In the matter of down payment,' he continued, 'the present ... difficulties ... preclude the usual bank to bank transfer. Therefore I propose you arrange to transmit the money to my surrogate in California, the Church of True Belief . . .'

He gave Borakin the details he would need.

'You are involved with this man – Kingdom?' Borakin asked, astonished.

'No more than I am with you, general. It is purely a business arrangement.'

'But this preacher is fomenting trouble for us, Mr Wong.'

'I am sure you can cope with it. Perhaps better than Cardinal Muller.'

Borakin looked at the others. Why had the Chinese raised this? They shrugged, as bewildered as he was.

The voice from Lhasa was asking another cold question.

'If this Cardinal Muller becomes Pope, will you invite him to Moscow, general?'

Wong Lee heard another intake of breath.

'It's much too early to consider the matter, Mr Wong,' Borakin replied.

For the first time in their discussion, Wong Lee smiled.

'If the new Pope does decide to visit Moscow, it would look very bad if one of your Moslem dissidents attacked him. I am sure you will take every precaution to make sure that does not happen.'

After the call ended, Borakin turned to the others and swore in Russian.

'Is he warning us off?' Borakin asked.

'Or maybe he is saying he will deal with the matter,' murmured the former chairman of the KGB.


Cardinal Messner tried to be reassuring. 'It still looks good, Hans-Dietrich.'

Cardinal Muller continued to stare out of the window of the small store room behind the Sistine Chapel that was one of the designated smoking areas in conclave. He had locked the door behind them so as not to be disturbed.

'Do you think it worth going back to Camas, Herbert?'

The camerlengo shook his head. 'No. We mustn't let him think we're anxious. That'll just keep him going. The important thing is that Ospispo knows the score.'

Cardinal Muller grunted as the camerlengo joined him at the window overlooking the Parrot Courtyard.

They watched Horace Walpole bring Cardinal Ospispo over to a mixed group of Europeans, South Americans and Asians.

'All Camas supporters,' the camerlengo murmured. 'My bet is that Ospispo is telling them it's all over.'

As Cardinal Muller lit a fresh cigarette, the camerlengo tried a joke. 'We'd get all the non-smokers if you promised to give up.'

Hans-Dietrich Muller gave another grunt and continued to watch the half dozen separate groups in deep conversation. Victor O'Rourke was over in one corner with the Americans and Canadians. Andrew Berry was talking earnestly to the Patriarch of Egypt and several of the Africans. Bertram Terry of Sydney and Michael Boylan of Chicago were strolling back and forth across the courtyard, sometimes breaking off their own discussion to listen to what others were saying.

'Look at Walpole,' Cardinal Muller said.

The tall Englishman had once more detached himself from the group to join another, in the centre of the courtyard.

'Our Dutchmen,' growled Cardinal Muller. 'That certainly doesn't reassure me. If they get behind Camas –'

'They won't!' interrupted the camerlengo. 'Just as they won't yet commit to you. The Dutch have always played a wait-and-see game. Wait to see how they can use their votes to get what they want.'

Cardinal Messner clasped Hans-Dietrich on the shoulder.

'I reckon Camas will get thirty-four votes at the most next time. I'm already very confident of you improving by another four.'

'And Enkomo?'

'He may squeeze another couple, no more.'

Cardinal Muller blew out a long spiral of smoke.

'That still leaves forty uncommitted.'

Sudden irritation on his face, the camerlengo turned to Cardinal Muller.

'We both knew this was going to be a slow business, Hans-Dietrich, but a couple more rounds and we'll have worn them down.'

Cardinal Muller tried to smile before turning back to the window.

'I don't see Camas or Enkomo out there.'

The camerlengo shrugged. 'They're both in their cells. Probably praying for the right words to make a graceful surrender.'

Behind them they heard the handle turn in the door, followed by a knock. Cardinal Messner walked over and unlocked the door.

Cardinal Camas stood in the doorway. There was a look of relief on his face. He spoke at once in a clear, unwavering voice.

'Camerlengo, I have decided not to allow my name to go forward. I believe the Church needs someone else.'

Cardinal Messner looked into Cardinal Camas's face to make sure there was no doubt. Behind him he could hear Hans-Dietrich's grunt of relief. He would really have to stop that grunting when he became Pope, learn never to show his emotions at critical moments.

'Thank you for coming to tell me, Enrique. If I may say so, yours is a decision that shows mature reflection. Would you prefer to tell your supporters they are free to vote for Hans-Dietrich, or would you rather I told them?'

'Camerlengo, I will tell them. I owe them that much for their support so far.'

Cardinal Messner inclined his head as Cardinal Camas continued.

'Whether they vote for Cardinal Muller is a matter for them. But I shall be making it very clear why I am not voting for him, but for Julius Enkomo.'

Cardinal Messner stared frozen-faced at Cardinal Camas. Behind him Hans-Dietrich made a noise very like a stuck pig.

Shortly after Morton arrived back in Morelli's office from the Mossad apartment, the CCO was on screen.

'Danny wants you, David.'

In a corner of the room Morelli looked up from his paperwork.

A moment later Danny's face appeared on the monitor.

'The weather satellite's just picked up a couple of items, David. The first's a call Wong Lee made to Franco Umberto in Florida. He phoned half-way across the world just to say "There are no exceptions!" And Umberto didn't even reply. Just hung up. Cipher says if it's code, it has to be on the letter permutation. That still leaves several million permutations to play with. Without a reference point, there's no real place to start.

'Chantal wonders if it could be drug related. She's picked up a hint that Umberto may have cut a deal with Wong Lee in Hawaii that gives him exclusive rights to supply all the old Soviet republics with high-grade crack and heroin. On that basis, "there are no exceptions" makes sense.'

'Got anything on what Wong Lee is getting in return from Umberto?'

'No.'

'Have her keep working on that. Get Humpty Dumpty to run a voice check for any previous reference to those words in anything on tape with Wong Lee. Have Lester's programmers do the same.'

He waited for Danny to finish writing. Morelli had stopped work and was listening.

'Now this second item?' Morton asked.

'In a way it's even weirder. The satellite picked up a conversation Wong Lee was having with the woman we've now identified as his shamaness. She was saying that considering how little time she'd had with someone called Wu, the progress was quite astonishing.'

Morton frowned. 'Wu's a pretty common Chinese name.'

'Then she went on to say "The Israeli wouldn't like Wu at all!"'

Morton reached for a sheet of paper. 'Give me that again, Danny.'

Danny repeated the words. Morelli was staring at the screen intently.

'Any ideas?' Morton asked Danny.

'It's a long shot. But I'll go with Chantal when she says you're probably the only Israeli Wong Lee worries about. And Wu was also the name of a kind of super-witch operating a couple of thousand years ago. But what she has to do with you is beyond us.'

When the screen cleared Morton turned to Morelli.

'You think anyone here could tell me more about who this Wu was, Claudio?'

Morelli considered. 'Your best bet would be our camerlengo. Dealing with witchcraft was one of his stepping stairs up the ladder.'

Morton shook his head. 'I think he's the last person who'll help.'

A moment later Bill Gates was on the phone from the office he had taken over in the US Embassy to the Holy See in Via della Conciliazione.

'The FBI monitoring team has picked up Umberto using a pay phone to call Rome. He told some guy he just called "Father" not to make an exception. Could be either a real priest or somebody pretending. He sure can't be Umberto's papa. He's been dead for thirty years.'

'This father say anything?'

'Nope. Just listens and puts down the phone.'

After Morton told Gates about Danny's call he asked: 'The FBI people any idea where Umberto's call landed?'

'Their best shot is somewhere between here and the Tiber. There's over a hundred thousand phones in the area. I've asked the *Digos* to see what they can come up with. But I wouldn't hold your breath.'

Out of a corner of his eye Morton could see Morelli waving a receiver at him. It was the direct line to the Pathfinder's apartment.

'Push then, Bill. Something tells me this is all connected,' said Morton.

He took the receiver from Morelli's hand.

'David, you better take a deep breath,' began the Pathfinder. 'Things have just blown up in Cardinal Messner's face.'

As the camerlengo completed reading out the result of the third ballot the stunned silence was followed by loud cries of excitement.

Hans-Dietrich Muller had received fifty-one votes.

Julius Enkomo had seventy.

The Primate of All Ireland was among those cardinals on their feet.

'Five more,' Victor O'Rourke was repeating to those around him. 'We only need five more to make history.'

Horace Walpole of Westminster was smiling warmly. Julius Enkomo sat, head bowed, eyes fixed on the floor. No one could see what he felt.

'Reverend Fathers! Please be seated!' commanded the camerlengo sternly. 'We shall go for a fourth ballot at once.'

Twenty-six minutes later he read out the result in a strangled voice. Cardinal Muller's votes had shrunk down to below those cast for him in the first ballot. Only twenty-six electors still supported him. Cardinal Enkomo had polled ninety-five votes.

Thunderous and sustained applause swept through the Chapel. Horace Walpole rose from his seat and crossed the aisle to stand over Julius Enkomo. The tall patrician Englishman reached out and touched the younger man's bowed head.

'Julius, this is right. For the Church. For Africa. For you. It means you can carry on where Nicholas left off.'

There was no response.

'You must publicly acknowledge you will accept,' said Marcel Leutens.

Julius Enkomo made the smallest of head movements, so slight, those around him could not be sure whether it was a nod or a shake.

'You've got to accept, Julius,' Victor O'Rourke said, more loudly. Others were gathering around the still bowed figure: Anso, Reefer, Martel, Berry, Saldarini and Camas.

The cheering continued. Only Cardinal Muller and those around him sat in stunned silence. The camerlengo was making his way towards the crowd around Julius Enkomo. The Archbishop of Madrid knelt in front of Cardinal Enkomo, holding both his hands.

'If you don't accept now, the camerlengo can declare you don't wish to be elected. Then we will have to have another ballot. I did not persuade my supporters to help elect you for that to happen!' Cardinal Camas said urgently.

Horace Walpole placed his lips close to Julius Enkomo's ear. 'I'll give you the name you should be called.'

After he whispered there was still no response.

'Reverend Fathers!' the camerlengo cried. 'Please return to your seats!'

Seated once more the cardinals stared at the isolated figure of Julius Enkomo, and the camerlengo standing before him.

There was growing tension. The unthinkable could be about to happen.

'Reverend Father Enkomo, do you refuse your election as Supreme Pontiff, which has been canonically carried out?'

Slowly, agonisingly slowly, Julius Enkomo raised his head, tears running down his face, which he made no effort to wipe. He turned and stared at Michelangelo's apocalyptic *Last Judgement*.

It was the only movement in the Chapel. He turned back and looked at the camerlengo. The two men continued to stare wordlessly at each other. Then in a firm and resonant voice that reached all corners of the Chapel, Julius Enkomo finally announced his decision.

'With obedience in full to Christ, my Lord, and with trust in the Mother of Christ and the Church, and with a humble heart, I accept.'

The camerlengo's eyes flickered, closed and opened again.

Renewed applause, more tumultuous than before, swept the Sistine. The camerlengo flapped his arms for silence and was ignored. Finally, eager to hear the answer to the last question the camerlengo would put, the cardinals once more became silent.

Cardinal Messner asked: 'By what name will you be known?'

In the same declamatory voice Julius Enkomo again gave his decision.

'Most Reverend Fathers, I shall be known as Innocent the Fourteenth.'

He looked around the Chapel. To where Cardinal Muller sat, eyes expressionless, with the Mid-Europeans who had remained loyal to him to the end. To Cardinals Coffey and Simmons, and the other Americans, smiling acceptance. To the South Americans, clapping in unison and the Asians, stamping their feet. Cardinal Saldarini and the other Curialists nodding to each other. To Horace Walpole, Victor O'Rourke and Andrew Berry, shaking each other by the hand. And Marcel Leutens and the Dutch, giving what seemed remarkably like power salutes. He looked at them all.

The camerlengo's mouth continued to work as if he had a rictus, but no words emerged.

Pope Innocent slowly stood up and spread his arms in a collective embrace.

'Reverend camerlengo, my brothers in Christ,' he began. 'I

ask you now to pray for me as we all go forward united into the uncertain future. I cannot succeed without you. I can still fail even with your help. But there is much we can do together.'

In the silence he walked across to stand beneath the fresco of the *Last Judgement*.

'I intend to begin my pontificate by sharing with you a secret only a few of you know. It was the dying wish of our beloved predecessor to see it fulfilled. He gave it the perfect name – Operation Holy Cross.'

From his pocket he produced the envelope, and in the same resonant voice Pope Innocent began to explain exactly what it was.

As the white smoke confirming the election drifted from the Sistine chimney into the air above the immense crowd in St Peter's Square, Father Gomez continued to pick out faces around Caligula's Obelisk through the telescopic sight. Now it was no longer attached to the camera but clipped on to the barrel of the sniper's rifle.

# 25

The last three hours had passed in a whirl for Pope Innocent. After addressing the gathering in the Sistine Chapel, Cardinal Messner formally presented him with a new Fisherman's Ring. It was the symbolic end of the camerlengo's role, and the start of a new pontificate.

After the tailor made minor adjustments to the white linen cassock, Pope Innocent stepped on to the balcony of St Peter's dressed in the full finery of the Supreme Pontiff, to bless the crowd and receive its ovation. His short speech, promising to carry on the work of his predecessor, was broadcast across the world.

He then dined with his cardinals, embracing many, having a friendly word for all. Hubert Messner had not been present. He assumed the camerlengo had retired early, exhausted from his duties.

After Colonel Asmusson removed the seals from the door of the Papal Apartment and presented the document which formally gave him the right of occupancy, Pope Innocent had signed the paper with his new name for the first time.

Together with the Reverend Mother in charge of the household, he inspected his home. She told him she had already telephoned Cape Town to have all his personal effects brought to Rome. A Father O'Sullivan was bringing them.

Pope Innocent had smiled. The young Irish priest was in for a surprise. He was going to offer him the position as his secretary. He had decided to offer Monsignor Hanlon the post of Nuncio-at-large, effectively the pontificate's roving troubleshooter. Nicholas had said Sean was perfectly suited to the job.

The Reverend Mother had brought him to the door of the room the Popes had always used as a study.

'Shall we continue our discussion inside?' he asked.

The elderly nun shook her head.

'For this first time, Holiness, you must be alone,' she murmured meaningfully.

He nodded, suddenly remembering. He wondered how many other Popes had felt the sudden tension he now did.

He closed the study door behind him. For a moment he stood staring around the room. In one corner was the desk where Nicholas had composed the blueprint for Operation Holy Cross. He had left the document in the Sistine Chapel for the others to study.

Only the desk's telephone console was a reminder of the times Nicholas had called him for advice. The bookshelves were empty, the side tables swept clear of their photos and mementoes. His eyes finally came back to a small old-fashioned metal trunk. It stood on the floor in the middle of the room and was painted yellow and secured with a lock through its clasp. Taped to the lid was a key. The trunk was the reason why the nun had gently reminded him he must enter the study alone.

He remembered what Nicholas had told him. How, within an hour of his own election, this same trunk had been brought up from the Secret Archives and left here. Nicholas had said no more; he could not.

Pope Innocent lowered himself on his knee before the trunk and bowed his head and prayed. Then, he peeled off the tape, inserted the key in the lock and removed it from the clasp. After a moment's hesitation he lifted the lid. The inside of the trunk was lined with heavy purple velvet. There were two objects wrapped in similar cloth.

Again he hesitated, not certain how to proceed. No one had told him. There were no instructions left in the trunk. Finally, he removed the smaller object and carefully unwrapped the velvet.

Inside was a manila-coloured envelope. In one corner was the Vatican insignia. He turned over the envelope. Across the flap were wax imprints, each identical to the one his own Fisherman's Ring could make. He counted them. Eight. One for each of his predecessors who had opened the envelope, read its contents and then resealed the envelope with their rings. Placing the envelope on the floor beside him, he unwrapped the second object.

The portrait of the Holy Family showed the faces of the Mother of God and her Boy Child without eyes. What appeared to be dried tears of blood ran down their cheeks from the empty sockets. Until this moment he had never quite believed the Godless Icon existed. Now, as he held it in his trembling hands, Pope Innocent recalled the story Nicholas had once told him.

The icon had hung above the main altar in St Basil's Cathedral, close to the Kremlin walls, and the eyes of the Mother of God and her Boy Child had been represented by the most precious jewels from the tsar's collection. As Lenin seized power in 1917, the icon had been smuggled out of the cathedral and brought in the utmost secrecy to the Vatican. It arrived on the very day the Mother of God had appeared to the children of Fatima to entrust them with her three secrets, telling them the reigning Pope was the one other person who could know what these were. When the icon was removed from its covering, the precious stones were missing, and the stains found on both faces.

The Russian priest who smuggled out the icon swore it had never left his presence. Before he could be questioned further, he had collapsed and died.

When he saw the damaged portrait, the reigning pontiff, Benedict the Fifteenth, had called it the Godless Icon.

Shortly afterwards, the details of the revelations at Fatima reached the Vatican with the instruction the children said had also come from the Mother of God: that the Godless Icon should be kept in the same safe place as the secrets. For a long time Pope Innocent held the Godless Icon in his hands, tears streaming down his own cheeks. Then he carefully wrapped it in velvet and placed it back in the trunk.

He picked up the envelope, his fingers tracing the seals. Benedict the Fifteenth had been the first to affix his mark. Pius the Eleventh the next to press the imprint in the wax on the envelope; that was in 1922 when the world must have seemed so trouble free. By the time Pius the Twelfth affixed his seal in 1939, the gathering storm was about to confirm the first secret, a second world war. In 1958, when John the Thirteenth had left his imprint on the envelope, the second secret of Fatima – the spread of Communism – was already a fact.

Communism had remained a force throughout the pontificate of Paul the Sixth and John Paul the Second. Only in the closing years of the Polish pontiff's reign had its death knell begun to

sound, and continued to do so through Nicholas's short pontificate.

Easing a finger under his immediate predecessor's seal, Pope
Innocent opened the envelope and removed the single sheet of
yellowing paper which contained the Third Secret of Fatima. He
scanned the contents, then read the words again more slowly.
His eyes began to cloud and he could feel his heart thumping.
The paper was fluttering in his shaking hand.

'Oh, Lord Jesus, grant that I can do what you wish,' he gasped.

Then, as he had done since a child in the mission school on
the veldt, he recited the most powerful prayer he knew, the Our
Father.

He was calm again when he placed the paper back in the
envelope. He looked inside the trunk for a means to affix his
seal. In a pocket in the velvet lining he found a pad and a tube
of wax. He squeezed some out and spread it on the pad, pressed
his ring against the wax, then fixed his seal on the back of the
envelope.

For a long moment he stared at the envelope, then wrapped
it and put it back in the trunk. He locked the trunk and placed
the key on his own ring of keys. Once more he started to think
about what he had read, understanding now why Operation Holy
Cross had taken on a new urgency and meaning.

In the gallery several floors below Wong Lee's office, the shamaness prepared to put Wu through another rehearsal. As with her
other conditioning, Wu had responded astonishingly well to the
instructions fed to her brain through the micro-transmitters
inserted in the folds of skin behind her ear lobes. Each transmitter was no larger than a pinhead, yet contained a synchro-
energiser sophisticated enough to sequentially affect Wu's
brainwaves.

She had revealed an unusually wide range and depth of
responses in beta, wide-awake consciousness, and alpha, alert
relaxation. Her theta responses – past memory – however were
shown to be almost non-existent.

The transmitters had been inserted during the minor surgery
to subtly tighten the skin around Wu's eyes and mouth to give
her an Oriental look.

In her white habit and with a wooden crucifix suspended on a
thong from her neck, Wu now looked like any nun on the streets

of Asia soliciting alms for the poor. She gripped the begging bowl firmly in one hand.

The walls of the gallery were covered with sykes, screens on which images are projected in television studios. The footage had been assembled from the crowd in Red Square watching old May Day parades and film of Pope Nicholas celebrating an outdoor Mass in St Peter's Square.

Editing had created the effect of the late pontiff standing at an altar in front of St Basil's Cathedral.

'Again, Wu,' the shamaness commanded.

She watched the woman walk towards a syke on which was projected the altar. The figure on the altar was extending his arms, as if to welcome Wu.

When she was still some yards away from the altar Wu reached into her begging bowl. As she did so the shamaness abruptly commanded her to stop. Wu was not yet fully conditioned for what she must do next.


Shortly before midnight Morelli and Morton entered Pope Innocent's study.

An hour ago he had watched Colonel Asmusson and a Swiss Guard remove the trunk and take it back to the Secret Archives.

Morelli came forward, knelt and kissed the Fisherman's Ring on Pope Innocent's extended hand.

'I wish Steve was here to congratulate you, Your Holiness,' Morton said.

Pope Innocent made a gentle little hand movement. 'He was never one for ceremonial.'

He looked at them both.

'You said it was important?' he prompted.

Morton produced a cassette tape from his pocket. The Pathfinder had made the copy.

'It's Messner, talking to Wong Lee,' Morton said.

He put the tape on the desk.

'Right after conclave Messner went to his office and called Wong Lee to say you had been elected. He said he was still ready to do everything to stop Operation Holy Cross, if that's what Wong Lee wanted.'

Pope Innocent picked up the cassette and looked at Morton.

'I won't ask how you obtained this, David.'

'Thank you, Your Holiness.'

'What did Wong Lee say?'

'He said he now wanted you to go to Moscow. It's all here on the tape.'

Pope Innocent handed back the cassette to Morton.

'I would rather not listen, David. But can either of you tell me why Cardinal Messner telephoned Wong Lee?'

Morelli sighed. 'It turns out he's been calling him for months.' The switchboard nun had confirmed it.

'In all probability, Your Holiness, Messner thinks what he was doing was for the good of the Church,' Morton said. 'He's more naive than wicked. And almost certainly he has no idea of the kind of friends Wong Lee keeps.'

'Such as, David?'

'For a start, the Reverend Kingdom, the Mafia boss Franco Umberto, and the troika in Moscow. Plus all the presidents of the Soviet Islamic republics. In one way or another, they've all got a vested interest in seeing Holy Cross fail.'

'Yet Wong Lee now wants me to go to Moscow,' said Pope Innocent. 'David, can you tell me everything you know or suspect?'

As Morton spoke, Pope Innocent sat with his chin cupped in the palms of his hands, elbows on the desk top, his eyes never once leaving Morton's face. Morton left out nothing and was always careful to distinguish fact from conjecture. When he had finally finished, Pope Innocent sat upright, his head perfectly still.

'Thank you, David,' he said.

He looked at them both with a steady gaze and began to speak in a quiet and measured voice.

'Cardinal Messner seems to have forgotten the first tenet of his calling is not politicking. Clearly he has spent too many years in this place. My predecessor used to say it can affect one's judgement as well as the spirit.

'My election will give His Eminence an opportunity to once more practise his pastoral duties. He will fill the vacancy I leave in Cape Town.'

'Who will replace him as Secretary of State, Holy Father?' Morelli asked.

'Horace Walpole,' Pope Innocent replied at once. 'He has all the qualifications as well as the humanity.'

He leaned forward across the desk and lowered his voice. 'It is now more important than ever that Holy Cross succeeds.'

'Prime Minister Karshov wants you to know he will do everything possible to make your visit to Israel successful,' Morton said.

Pope Innocent leaned his muscular upper body forward.

'David, I'm sorry. That visit will have to wait. There are other factors at play here. First of all, there is the obvious one. As you must both know, I have now read the Third Secret of Fatima. It is a blueprint for the Armageddon that Holy Cross is intended to stop. The one way I can ensure this is to go directly to Moscow and bring all the faiths together. There is no time for anything else. To go to Israel could be seen as an indulgence, perhaps even me favouring one of the other faiths. I must appeal to them all on neutral ground. That is the only way to make Holy Cross work.'

'What about the Imam Nardash, Your Holiness?' Morton asked.

Pope Innocent gave a quick smile. 'Whatever else he is, he is no fool. He will know that to stop any initiative will be very hard. Besides, I plan to appeal directly to the spiritual leaders of the Moslem republics to join me in this act of coming together. They will find it very difficult to refuse. I've had a lot of experience in persuading people to do what's good for them.'

'The troika?'

'They will not be a problem, David.'

Pope Innocent addressed them both. 'I must go to Moscow as soon as possible. But I want you both to come with me because I need everyone I trust to be there.'

He stood up.

'Now if you'll excuse me, it's been a long day. Tomorrow looks like being even longer.'

He came from behind the desk and walked them to the door. As Pope Innocent opened it, he turned to Morton.

'Any news of Carina?'

'None at all, Your Holiness.'

'I'm sorry, David. I really am.'

In his office the Reverend Kingdom paused over the next point of the telethon script. He planned a low-key introduction for Hal. What he had to confess was sensational enough.

Once Hal had realised the options, prison or publicly recant, he had co-operated fully. He was spending all his time in his apartment, writing his confession under the watchful eye of Fenton.

What he had read so far confirmed to the Reverend Kingdom that Hal was indeed a magnificent sinner. He reached for the reference book of Only Book quotations and turned to the section marked Sexual Transgressions. From the Book of Proverbs he began to copy out the timeless words about how the sin of lusting must eventually steal the soul of a person.

He underscored the word 'stole': it would be the one he would emphasise from the pulpit, the word which would lead him on to remind the television audience of that other great crime, of stealing from your employer. The Reverend Kingdom began to riffle the pages to find a quotation for that. He was so intent upon his work he had not realised Clara was standing in the doorway.

Watching him, Clara still could not quite believe what was happening to her. Not only had she, literally overnight, become wealthy beyond her wildest dreams, but this morning she had been awoken by a courier with a packet containing Stalin's letter. She could not understand a word of the handwriting, but she had counted the words, exactly one hundred. Over a thousand dollars a word. But worth every cent of Hal's money.

Then Eddie had called her in, told her what Hal admitted to and explained how the Good Lord had punished Hal by making his ill-gotten gains mysteriously disappear. Then Eddie had said he was entrusting her with the job of rebuilding the severely damaged financial empire of the Church of True Belief. He had given her Hal's job.

What about Martha, she had asked? Martha, Eddie had explained, was going to be resting until the telethon. The business with Hal had shaken her deeply. It is going to be just you and me to carry the burden for the Lord, Eddie had said. He had held her hands in his and smiled. She had smiled back, thinking if only Martha could see them.

Now, Eddie looked up and smiled at Clara. She really was a very pretty girl, really very pretty.

'You won't believe this,' Clara cried, walking into the office. 'But I've just seen a miracle actually happen.'

He sat back, still smiling. 'Let me guess. Like five billion dollars worth of roubles suddenly pop into your computer?'

She gave a gasp. 'How'd you know?'

Wong Lee had already telephoned him to expect the money transfer from Moscow.

'It's another way of God showing He's looking after us, Clara.'

'But five billion . . .'

'There'll be more, Clara.' Wong Lee had said so.

'Do I put it all on deposit with the Bank of California, or spread it around? In interest alone it could recoup most of what Hal lost or stole.'

Wong Lee's instructions had been clear.

'No, Clara. You just leave it right where it is. On your computer disc. Having it there is just like having it in the bank.'

'But Eddie –'

'That money's special, Clara. No one's supposed to know about it.'

'You mean . . . like the IRS?'

'Them most of all, Clara.'

'But all those hundreds of millions of dollars . . . just stored there . . . on that disc . . . if anything happens to it –'

'You just make good and sure nothing does, Clara,' the Reverend Kingdom said sharply. 'You just lock that disc in the safest place you know.'

'Sure, Eddie,' Clara said fervently. 'I sure will. I'll put it in our biggest safe, the one that's earthquake proof.'

He smiled at her.

'Good girl, Clara. And, if I may say so, you're also a very pretty girl.'

Clara managed to blush. It really was incredible what was happening to her.

By dawn there was an estimated 300,000 people in St Peter's Square. They gave a loud cheer when they saw a light come on in the Pope's bedroom. Pope Innocent had been awake for hours, padding from the bedroom in his old-fashioned nightshirt back to the study.

He had summoned and reassigned Cardinal Messner, and summoned and appointed first Horace Walpole and then Monsignor Hanlon. Both were now at their desks in the Secretariat of State.

Other appointments had swiftly followed. Victor O'Rourke had agreed to take over Vatican Bank. Andrew Berry would assume control of the Church's world-wide building operations.

His first job had been to send a fax to Wong Holdings cancelling all its contracts. Marcel Leutens, Michael Boylan and Kazuo Anso were all given Curial positions, replacing those held by Cardinals Arnt, Tovic and Koveks. Enrique Camas had accepted the post of head of the Doctrine of the Faith, after Hans-Dietrich Muller tendered his resignation from that office.

When this particular appointment became known, commentators pointed out that theologically, Enrique Camas possessed the outlook of Pope Innocent. Both were supporters of collegiacy and an open mind to the world.

Now, as dawn once more reddened the sky, Pope Innocent prepared for his first formal engagement of the day, a journey in his popemobile through the ever-growing crowd beneath his bedroom window.

Standing in his undershorts and vest he looked curiously at the garment which Morton had arranged to be delivered to the Papal Apartment. The bullet-proof vest was designed not only to protect his chest and back, but also the buttocks and pelvis, and arms down to the elbows.

The vest had been fashioned from measurements provided by Anton Gammerelli to the local specialist tailor employed by Swift Renovations in Rome. What the man lacked in intricate stitching he more than made up for by producing a protective vest which could absorb bullets from the most high-powered weapon. Sighing, Pope Innocent put on the vest and then his cassock.

A quarter of a mile away, Father Gomez rolled over, glanced at his watch, and went straight back to sleep.

In Morelli's office Morton finished briefing the others on what he had told the Pope. On one screen he could see Danny in Tel Aviv, on another the Director of the FBI in Washington. Both continued to listen attentively as Morton began to ask questions.

'Where's Fung?'

Bill Gates consulted his clipboard.

'Right now he's on his way to the airport. He's booked on the same flight to Moscow as Monsignor Hanlon.'

Sean was the Pope's advance man for Operation Holy Cross. Morton turned to Lacouste.

'How about Kramskay?'

'He left his hotel an hour ago after a call from Moscow. The surveillance team weren't able to hear what was said. But they've managed to stay close ever since. He's down in the square, rubber-necking like any other tourist come to see the Pope. Body contact confirms Kramskay isn't carrying a weapon.'

'Somebody can still slip him a gun,' grunted Morelli. 'The Turk who shot Pope John Paul was armed like that.'

'Good point, Claudio,' Morton said. He nodded at a screen. 'Danny, it's all yours.'

'Here's what we got,' Danny began without preamble. 'Our weather satellite picked up another couple of interesting conversations. She was right at the eastern edge of her Lhasa orbit, so we didn't get everything.'

Danny glanced down at a pad, then looked up.

'In the first pick-up the shamaness is having an argument with Wong Lee. She keeps saying that with this Wu person now so well prepared, there's no need to do anything else. The way she spoke, our voice analysts have a feeling this Wu is a younger person and someone the shamaness has been specially training for something. Chantal still thinks it's drug related. Her people have picked up a few more pointers that Umberto's gearing up to turn on the Russian republics in a big way to heroin which Wong Lee's supplying.'

On the screen Danny once more consulted his notepad.

'After the shamaness finished, Wong Lee used that fancy phone of his to call Umberto. He told Umberto to stop everything. Umberto sounded pretty upset and kept saying he was in for a million bucks and who was going to repay that? When he started to argue, Wong Lee reminded him who he was talking to and told him again to make sure everything was stopped. Then he hung up just as Umberto was about to really get going. That's it, David. By then the satellite was out of range.'

Morton looked around the room. 'Any questions?'

'Let's get the full picture first,' Gates said.

Morton glanced at the screen linked to Washington. 'Director?'

'Good morning gentlemen,' began the head of the FBI. 'Let me start where the gentleman in Tel Aviv left off. As soon as Umberto found he was talking to empty air, he freaked. Our surveillance people say they haven't heard him like that since he lost out to the Medellin cartel people in South America. In one way or another Umberto kept saying he was never going to do business with the Chink again. He let drop enough to give us some useful clues to the kind of business they have been doing.

'When Umberto called Rome again, our technicians couldn't pinpoint the actual number he was calling because there was no reply. They need a phone pick-up to begin to trace locally. All they can suggest is that the pulse tone indicates the call was being made to the same city area as before.'

The director paused and stared sternly out of the screen. 'If you have any questions I'd be glad to answer them.'

Morton supposed a man got like this after years of giving evidence before Congressional committees.

He turned to Gates. '*Digos* come up with anything on the previous call?'

The CIA Director of Operations shook his head and tapped his clipboard.

'I want to go back to this Wu character, David. She's been trained for something special. Umberto screams because he's going down for a million bucks he's paid to someone. Let's see if we can connect this Wu with this other someone.'

Morton glanced up at the Washington screen.

'Correct me if I'm wrong, director, but isn't Umberto supposed to have paid out that kind of money to take out some of the Medellin mob?'

'Nothing was ever proven, Mr Morton. But yes, that's the rumour. He got a couple of Colombians for his million then. We never found the hit man.'

Gates began to nod. 'So supposing Umberto's paid for another contract that Wong Lee's just heard about and doesn't want him to go ahead?'

'Because this Wu is going to do it?' asked Norm Stratton.

Baader frowned. 'The problem with all of this is that we don't know who Umberto was trying to call.'

There was the sound of the FBI director clearing his throat on screen.

'Maybe I can help you there. After he'd failed to connect, Umberto went into another crazed routine about how could the Chink expect him to stop everything at the last moment? He kept yelling at anyone in range that everything had a cut-out time, and after that nothing could be stopped.'

Baader smiled patiently at the screen.

'That still doesn't answer my point, director. Wu's still in

Tibet. So there's plenty of time to stop her, except that the shamaness wants her to do whatever she's supposed to do. And Wong Lee now accepts this. Just as he's changed his mind about trying to stop the Pope going to Moscow.'

There was a sudden silence in the office.

'The answer could be staring us in the face,' said Anwar Salim quietly. The Egyptian nodded towards the surveillance monitors relaying pictures of the scene around St Peter's Square.

'Anwar's right,' Morelli said. 'There just could be someone out there who still doesn't know the game plan has changed.'

On screen the FBI director was frowning. 'I can't buy that. Umberto's a Catholic, for Chrissake! He wouldn't raise a finger against the Pope –'

'You're probably right, Director. But I can't take that chance,' interrupted Morton.

He turned to Morelli.

'Reposition your cameras, Claudio. Forget the area around the colonnades and the basilica steps. Get extra cover along the route for the popemobile and include Via della Conciliazione as far as you can go without losing definition. Use the camera on the roof of the Apostolic Palace to sweep the adjoining roofs.'

Morelli reached for a phone and began to give instructions. Morton continued to brief the others on what he wanted them to do.

Gates would ride in the front of the popemobile. Salim and Baader would work the crowd on either side of the route. Stratton and Lacouste would each patrol the outer limits of the square. Morton himself would roam at will around the area.

When Morelli finished, Morton turned to him.

'We'll need our own radio network independent of *Digos* and the other police agencies down there.'

'No problem. You can use Godspeak.'

Godspeak was the network over which the *Vigili* communicated with Morelli's office. Morelli began to distribute earpieces and throat mikes. Each man already had his own weapon.

After his last visit to Concorde Morton had brought back with him the Luger. He knew of no better gun for precision shooting in a crowd.

Dressed in his caped cassock, a white skullcap firmly on his head, Pope Innocent strode from his bedroom.

Cardinal Walpole was waiting outside the apartment's private chapel. Together they walked to the altar to celebrate the first Mass of the day. Victor O'Rourke, Andrew Berry and Enrique Camas were seated with the Reverend Mother and the nuns of the papal household. After Mass, Pope Innocent led the cardinals into breakfast in the large, airy dining room.

While they each ate a full breakfast, he confined himself to coffee and a slice of toast. Cardinal Walpole forked a piece of sausage into his mouth before continuing.

'I've spoken to General Borakin and explained your visit is purely pastoral. I said that was the only way Holy Cross could work. He didn't have any questions, not even when I stressed you were coming as a religious leader, not as head of state. And that you wanted to co-celebrate with all the faiths. He's promised that the new Patriarch of the Russian Orthodox will co-operate fully.'

'What did General Borakin say when you told him how urgent it all is?'

'Nothing, Holiness. He just gave me a date. Two weeks from now. He said it was the shortest he needed to make all the arrangements.'

Andrew Berry buttered more toast.

'I fear once you get there, Borakin will still want to talk politics, Holiness. It was the same when I celebrated the re-naming Mass in St Petersburg. All the local priests could talk about was how did I see the political implications of having the city returned to its original name.'

Pope Innocent glanced across the table at the Scottish cardinal.

'Andrew, could you let me have a briefing paper on how you found the situation there?'

'Of course, Holiness.'

Pope Innocent turned to Cardinal Camas.

'I recall, Enrique, that Nicholas asked you to negotiate the agreements with virtually all the old Communist bloc countries before their regimes collapsed?'

The Archbishop of Madrid put down his coffee cup and looked pleased.

'Absolutely right. There was nothing on paper, of course. But when the collapse came, we were ready to fill the ideological vacuum in half a dozen countries.'

'Would you let me have a breakdown of how it is working?'

Cardinal Camas inclined his head. The Pope turned to Victor O'Rourke.

'Now, Victor. I want you to see how our bank can assist Russia with long-term, low-interest loans –'

Pushed and shoved by the crowd, Kramskay wished now he had not come to the square. Twice already he had felt someone quickly and expertly run their hands over his body. In Moscow he would have called for a plainclothes bodyguard to deal with the pickpockets. Here he had no one to protect him and soon, when he returned home, he feared he would also have lost his protection.

He had come to get a glimpse of this man Comrade Borakin had said on the phone would now be welcome in Moscow. The comrade general had said so just before ordering him home without a word of thanks for a job well done. Not a word of thanks for anything. Kramskay had been long enough in the troika's service to recognise the signs were ominous.

He continued to edge through the crowd until he reached the area in front of Caligula's Obelisk. He was pressed right up against the steel-mesh security barriers which kept back the crowd on either side of the route the popemobile would travel. He was unable to move either backwards or forwards.

Back in his study, Pope Innocent continued to explain to Marcel Leutens how he expected the Curia to work with him.

They sat in the pair of armchairs the Pope had ordered brought to the office.

'I feel more comfortable not sitting behind a desk,' he had smiled.

He had not smiled since he began to unfold his vision.

'I want more dialogue, more emphasis on serving God in a pluralist and secular world, Marcel.

'And I wish to make it clear to the Curia and everyone else, that my being a black African is of little importance. No one must be distanced from the universal character of my office and the message it proclaims. Everything I say and do is meant to reinforce the irreplaceable worth of life from within the womb to natural death.

'My function is to remind people of the importance of the timeless and awkward truths of our Church. That it has survived because of its core of strong convictions. Central to them is that a diluted faith cannot compete with the distractions of our modern world.

'To make all this work, it is essential that I avoid what happened to my predecessors. The Curia made them rely totally on its own channels. But I want to be exposed to what is going on outside the Vatican walls. And I don't want anyone screening out criticism. I want to know the good and the bad.

'Tell everyone to keep briefing papers down to no more than a page. I want all the Sacred Congregation to keep me updated on every current issue they are handling.'

Pope Innocent paused. When he continued his voice was gentler.

'I know it is asking a great deal, but I want you to make sure all this happens, Marcel, for as long as you are able. But please tell me when you feel the personal burden you bear is too painful. I want to make sure you have enough time to prepare to meet our Maker.'

'Thank you, Holiness.'

Pope Innocent reached across and grasped the cardinal's hands and studied his face.

'Do you fear death, Marcel?'

'I used not to. Now I do.'

'I used to, Marcel. Now I don't. I will pray you will once more come to feel the same.'

Impulsively, Cardinal Leutens knelt and kissed the Fisherman's Ring.

There was a knock on the door. Colonel Asmusson had arrived to escort Pope Innocent down to where the popemobile waited in St Damaso Courtyard.

'Come, Marcel. Walk with me, I fear we both need strength,' Pope Innocent murmured.

Morton continued to listen to the exchange over the Godspeak network in his earpiece. He was at the St Peter's Square end of the Via della Conciliazione, looking down the avenue. Its windows and balconies were filled with spectators.

People were still hurrying towards the square, streaming over the Tiber bridge and past the fortress-like Castel San Angelo. Even cynical Romans were excited at the idea of a black Pope.

'Anything?' Morton murmured again into his throat mike.

One by one the others acknowledged they had seen nothing untoward.

Then the voice of Bill Gates was in Morton's earpiece.

'He's here!'

Emerging into St Damaso Courtyard, Pope Innocent blinked and felt a sudden surge of emotion. The staff of the Apostolic Palace who could get away from work had formed two lines for him to walk to the popemobile. Priests and nuns stood shoulder to shoulder, clapping and cheering. Moving slowly down the lines, smiling, pausing to say a word, ask a question, Pope Innocent reached the gleaming white popemobile.

The box-like vehicle had a platform behind the open cab. Gates was already seated beside the blue-suited *Vigili* at the wheel.

'How fast does this thing go?' Gates asked.

'Five kilometres an hour. Usually slower,' grinned the driver.

Around the popemobile stood every cardinal of the Sacred College who had found an excuse to come to the square. Pope Innocent chatted with them for a moment, then climbed on to the platform. He gripped the steel white-painted handrail immediately behind the cab. The popemobile gave a little lurch as it moved off. Then the fat tyres were absorbing the unevenness of the cobblestones.

Gates whispered into his throat mike. 'We're on our way.'

Morelli continued to study the screens. One of the cameras was picking up the approach of the popemobile towards the Arch of the Bells Gate. When the Turk had shot John Paul, there had been another gunman positioned there. At the last moment he'd lost his nerve and fled.

As the camera panned over the area Morelli saw no sudden tension on a face, or unusual movement. He turned to the other screens. Nothing suspicious there either.

Morton was once more calling for reports.

Feet splayed and hands gripping the handrail, Pope Innocent stared ahead as the popemobile trundled towards the Arch of the Bells Gate.

The Swiss Guards were at attention. The blue-suited men were the only ones with their backs to him. Security. Same as those others beginning to trot alongside the crush barriers. He ignored them. Morton had said he should.

But which were Morton's Men? Then all other thoughts were banished as the first wave of cheers hit him like a living being. Even though the people on the other side of the square could still not see him, their voices rolled towards him in a great tidal wave of sound. Never had he imagined it could be like this. He began to wave and smile as the roar surged and surged again and grew louder each time. He reached down and tapped the driver's head and shoulder.

'Go slower! Drive as slow as you can!'

The driver nodded and grinned. Gates relayed the Pope's instruction to the Godspeak network.

Kramskay felt as if his ribs were being crushed as a solid wall of humanity pressed him against the crush barriers. The pope-mobile was still a hundred yards away. It had slowed almost to a crawl. The towering black figure, made still more black by the white of his robe, was reaching out to shake hands. Suddenly Kramskay had an irrational wish to also touch the hand of this man who could command such adoration.

Morton was half-way across Via della Conciliazione when Morelli began to speak urgently into his earpiece.

'Bill! Tell that driver to get back to his normal speed.'

Almost lost in the tumultuous sound, Morton heard Gates say the Pope was absolutely insisting the popemobile maintain its present speed.

Morton heard Morelli's groan and sympathised. Planning a security operation like this was a nightmare at the best of times. With someone so obviously having a good time as Pope Inno-cent, it was doubly so.

On the far side of the avenue, Morton paused to peer down towards Borgo Santa Angelo. Like everywhere else with a view on the square, the street's windows and balconies were crowded.

Morton turned and began to cross the avenue, heading towards Borgo Spirito, the street that houses the world headquarters of the Jesuits at one end and the Pathfinder and his eavesdroppers at the other. They, too, would be listening out.

Morelli was once more speaking urgently into his earpiece.

'David! There's someone on a balcony way down the avenue.

Left-hand side. Top floor. He seems to be crouching behind some kind of telescope! He wasn't there a minute ago!'

Morton was already running down the avenue, weaving past latecomers hurrying towards the square.

'Everybody go to yellow,' he instructed into his throat mike, his eyes peering up at the windows.

In the square the others would be increasing their vigilance while Morelli manoeuvred his cameras to focus better on that figure at the balcony window.

Until Morton tried to cover it in a hurry he hadn't realised how long the avenue was, or how many windows and balconies there were to look at and assess. He pounded on down the avenue.


'We've gone to yellow, so get this thing moving!' grunted Gates to the popemobile driver. 'Or I'll toss you into this crowd and drive myself!'

Pope Innocent felt the speed increase as he continued to wave and smile.

They were almost level with the obelisk. As far as he could see there was a solid cheering mass on either side. He turned and waved and smiled. His face was beginning to ache from just looking happy. No one had told him to expect that either.


Morelli was shouting in Morton's earpiece.

'It's a gun's telescopic sight and silencer! All on a tripod! Guy's dressed like a priest!'

Morton was sprinting and at the same time pulling the Luger from its holster. His eyes swivelled from balcony window to window.

People were pointing down at him and shouting in astonishment. On the street others were beginning to scatter in fear at the sight of a man running with a gun in his hand. The first cries could be heard for the police.

Morton ignored them and kept sprinting. The avenue seemed to stretch on and on.


As the popemobile drew level with the obelisk, Pope Innocent continued to reach into the rapturous crowd to shake more hands. His own hands ached and were beginning to swell from already being grasped hundreds of times.

Now there was this man pushing both his hands towards him. Like so many others he, too, had a shining look in his eyes. Pope Innocent felt increasingly humbled, and yet proud too, that he could reach out and touch all these people physically and, he hoped, spiritually.

Kramskay continued to extend both hands towards the smiling figure in the popemobile.

The Pope was moving and smiling, moving to get closer to shake one of his hands.

'David!' shouted Morelli. 'Where the hell are you?'

Morton could feel the sweat running down his face. Then he saw him – crouching, totally intent on what he was doing.

And Morelli was shouting again.

Then the Pathfinder's voice: 'Gunshot! We've got a gunshot!'

Pope Innocent felt the blow hit him in the chest. A hammer blow. So powerful it was making his knees buckle. He couldn't breathe. The pain was terrifying. Spreading ... Spreading ...

Kramskay watched the Pope swaying, saw the stunned look on his face, then the eyes close.

Gates half-turned, not able to believe, not wanting to believe, reacting instinctively. Drawing his gun. Out of his seat, reaching out to try and grab the falling Pope.

The first screams filled his ears. '*Il papa! Il papa!*'

They spread like a bush fire.

On the balcony, Father Gomez fired once more at the figure already dropping from view through the telescopic sight, down onto the floor of the platform.

He fired again.

The bullet caught Kramskay in the forehead. Blood, chips of bone and brain spumed over the people around him. He was dead but unable to fall, held upright by the press of bodies. The sight of his shattered head produced more screams.

Gates was hurling himself into the back of the popemobile when a bullet struck his shoulder. He sprawled on top of the Pope.

Father Gomez fired again, killing the *Vigili* driver, immobilising the popemobile. He'd gained a little more time.

He fired another round into the side of the popemobile. Through the telescopic sight he saw the shells ricochet off the steel plating. He would have to use armour-piercing rounds. He snapped off the mag, reached down and picked up another.

At the same moment he locked it in place, he became aware of the figure crouching below on the pavement.

Morton fired. And fired again. And again. He fired until he had emptied the entire chamber into the head and chest of the man on the balcony.

Behind him in the square the noise grew, a mixture of terror, grief and the special panic which comes after something totally unexpected has happened.

# 26

The Reverend Kingdom continued to make alterations to the telethon script spread out on the lectern of the Tabernacle pulpit. He had been forced to abandon what was to have been this year's theme for the fund raising: the launch of the Church of True Belief Moral Crusade to save godless Russia and the other Soviet republics.

Two weeks had now passed since that moment he reluctantly admitted, but only to himself, which could not be bettered for sheer drama. The moment when the new Roman pontiff had appeared on the balcony of St Peter's within hours of being shot, to reassure the world he had suffered no more than bruising, due to the protective vest he had worn. He then announced the details of his forthcoming historic visit to Moscow, so hijacking the Moral Crusade.

Since then the Reverend Kingdom had continued to consider and reject new themes for the telethon.

Now, with just over an hour to go he had still not decided on how to run the fund-raising broadcast. Yet he was not unduly concerned. That sixth sense which had always guided him said that when the time came, he would know what to say. In the meantime he continued to make changes in the script.

Some parts would, of course, remain – how could they not? Especially his attack on the preparations under way in Moscow for an unprecedented ecumenical service in Red Square to be led by the man the news media now called The Bullet Proof Pope.

His would-be assassin had been identified as Walt Kroker, a former US marine marksman. There was nothing to connect him with anyone. The media called him another Oswald. A nut with a sharpshooter's skill.

No details had emerged about the man scores of people had seen shoot Kroker dead. After running back along Via della Conciliazione the man had disappeared. Media suggestions he could have been a second killer, hired to shoot Kroker, had not been confirmed.

The wounded American in the popemobile was named as William Gates, and described as a protocol officer with the US Embassy to the Holy See. He was making a good recovery, but would not be giving press interviews.

The dead man in the crowd had been identified as Valentin Nikoloyevich Kramskay. No one had explained why the Moscow Chief Public Prosecutor chose to view the Pope's tragically interrupted tour of St Peter's Square down among the crowd rather than from the comfort and safety of one of the windows of the Apostolic Palace. Kramskay's body was due to be returned to Moscow on board the 747 bringing the Pope to the Russian capital. The plane was due to land at Rome shortly after the telethon ended, the following evening.

The attempted assassination had kept its place in the script – as an example of God warning the Roman Church to mend its ways. Other items had been dropped from the running order to make way for more up-to-date information.

A few hours ago came the news that the troika had asked NATO to defend Russia if it was attacked by the newly-formed Council of Soviet Islamic Republics.

The Reverend Kingdom had been wondering how he could make use of this news when one of the switchboard operators monitoring CNN called the pulpit phone to say the cable network was reporting that NATO had announced it had evidence the Islamic republics were actually disarming – destroying entire weapons systems no one in the West realised they possessed. It appeared the arms were a gift from Wong Holdings. He had tried to call Lhasa to find out what was happening, but as usual, he had not been able to speak to Wong Lee.

A short while ago had come the news that the Islamic republics, in response to the Pope's personal appeal, were sending mullahs and imams to take part in the Red Square celebration for Operation Holy Cross.

Thousands of men and women, representing all the faiths of

394

the old Soviet empire, would also be attending: Catholic nuns from the Ukraine would stand alongside Moslem clerics from Tadjikistan; priests of the Russian Orthodox Church would march with mullahs from Uzbekistan and Azerbaijan, Kirghizia and Turkmenistan were sending their holy men to mingle with rabbis from Byelorussia and Estonia. The religious leaders of Georgia and Moldavia had agreed to participate.

The Reverend Kingdom knew all he could do now was what he did best – attack the old enemy of Rome.

From the TV control gallery came the polite voice of Alan Milton, the telethon's studio director.

'Reverend Kingdom, can you show us that vest again, please.'

The Reverend Kingdom obediently picked up the bullet-proof vest off the floor of the pulpit. He had sent Fenton to buy one as soon as the Roman pontiff confirmed a similar one had saved his life.

'Okay, good. Now hold it up and turn to Camera Two ... and let me hear one more time what you're going to say.'

The Reverend Kingdom found the place in the script and held the vest high above his head in one hand. In the nave people stopped what they were doing to listen to the mesmeric voice thundering forth.

If the Roman pontiff had trusted in the Lord God to protect him, he would not have needed this! Just as the Only Book says, he would never have been able to face all the dragons and slingshots of the godless hordes he now tries to claim for himself! And look at his arrogance! He calls his devious operation Holy Cross. In doing so he takes unto himself the very symbol upon which our Church was founded.

The Cross of True Belief!

Remember how down the years we have all marched proudly behind that cross? Yet we could not have gone very far without that one essential which has destroyed so many who have mis-used it, but which the Only Book says is truly blessed when used in His name. To fight greed! To fight envy! And lust! And betrayal! My friends, I am speaking of the one essential I want you to give as generously as you always have in the past.

MONEY! MONEY FOR THE LORD GOD'S WORK! MONEY TO FIGHT ALL HIS ENEMIES! MONEY, MY FRIENDS, TO SHOW THE WORLD

The Reverend Kingdom hurled the vest from him and bowed
his head, as if in prayer.

From the gallery Alan Milton delivered judgement.

'Just perfect, Reverend Kingdom, just perfect. God loves you.'

'And bless His name,' said the Reverend Kingdom, opening
his eyes and continuing to work on the script.

In the nave, telephone company engineers continued to check
the last of two hundred phones they had installed on rows of
trestle tables which had replaced the usual seating for the congregation.

Clara was moving among the tables, checking the headsets of
her Mail Room girls were working and their desktop keyboards
plugged in, ready to transmit the pledges to the Honeywell positioned before the altar. Once the computer recorded a pledge
in its memory, the amount was automatically updated on the
giant electric screen suspended from the base of the crown of
thorns in the roof.

From time to time Clara glanced towards the pulpit, smiling
to herself. Eddie had asked her to dinner after the telethon. Just
the two of them, up in his suite. He had promised to cook for
her, and once more had held her hand and said it would be such
a pleasure to do so for such a pretty woman. She had felt her
cheeks warm and wondered what it would be like doing it with
Eddie. Doing it with any man. Part of the pleasure would be
making sure Martha knew she had done it with Eddie.

To one side of the altar, Martha continued to rehearse the
Kingdom Angels in the hymn she had written for the occasion:
'Give To The Lord And Rejoice'.

A compact disc, featuring it and other choir favourites, would
be sold during the telethon. Each copy carried the Reverend
Kingdom's signature which no one could tell was a machine-
made facsimile.

Martha had decided to deal with this business of Eddie and that
bitch straight after the telethon. She had seen them whispering
together on the way into the Tabernacle and Eddie behaving like
some kid on his first date, not the middle-aged pastor who owed
his success largely to her. And which she most certainly was not
going to share with that scheming little bitch. It was one thing

for Clara to have shafted Hal; quite another for her to dare to take on Martha Kingdom as she would find out just as soon as the final credits rolled.

Even now, while he was up there in the pulpit, going about God's work, the bitch was trying to catch Eddie's eye. Once more Martha put the choir through its paces, savouring what she would say to Clara.

Standing at the back of the nave, with Fenton as close to him as a man could decently stand, Hal continued to experience a wonderful peace.

He had delivered his script to Eddie who, after a couple of minor changes, had passed it to the autocue operator. The girl had transferred the words on to the roller caption machine of the camera. When the time came the caption would unfold at the same speed Hal delivered his confession. It was purely a precaution, Eddie had said, in case Hal forgot all he had to confess.

'What are you going to do when this is over?' Fenton asked.

Hal shrugged. 'Maybe head down to the Caribbean. Or South America. Someplace where I can start again.'

Fenton looked at him squarely. 'I guess you know I don't approve of the Reverend Eddie letting you go? It just don't sit right with me.'

Hal smiled enigmatically. 'What's right is what a man must do'.

'That's the trouble with fellas like you. Pretty good with words. Guess that's why you find it so easy to break the word of the Only Book.'

'Fenton, you should have been a preacher.'

Over the PA system Alan Milton reminded everybody it was exactly one hour to air time.


Close to midnight the Chinese Airlines Tri-Star landed at Moscow's Sheremetievo Airport. Its 300 passengers consisted of Chinese and Tibetan monks and Catholic nuns from various missionary orders who had recently been allowed to reopen monasteries and convents in several of the republics. Among the last to leave was the shamaness and Chung-Shi. They walked on either side of Wu.

Chung-Shi wore the robes of a Buddhist monk. The women wore the white habits of the Merciful Sisters of the Orient, a contemplative order which had recently established itself in Tashkent. The disguise was Wong Lee's idea, designed to cast the blame as far from him as possible. It was also the perfect cover for what Wu had been prepared for.

Like all the other thousands arriving in Moscow for the momentous event in Red Square, they were waved through airport formalities and directed to one of the buses waiting to take them to one of the many barracks in Moscow which had stood empty since the disintegration of the Soviet Empire.

As the bus entered the city suburbs, the shamaness turned to Wu.

'Do you recognise where you are?'

'No, Reverend Mother. I do not know this place.'

'You are certain of that?'

'Yes, Reverend Mother.'

The shamaness smiled. 'But as your Reverend Mother, you will obey me at all times?'

'Yes, Reverend Mother.'

The shamaness patted Wu's hand and sat back and closed her eyes.

Carina continued looking out of the window, wondering why a part of her brain allowed her to lie, to still think for itself.


On the catwalk above Central Operations, Wong Lee watched the traders continue to electronically transfer all his assets which had managed to escape the freeze on companies in which Wong Holdings held stocks. Once he knew the superpowers had joined forces to use their central banks to support the Russian rouble and, at the same time, try and crush him, he had moved swiftly.

From Central and South America, Australia and New Zealand and a score of countries around the Pacific Rim, from the continent of Africa and the Middle East, from them all, vast sums were being withdrawn and transferred to the safety of the Church of True Belief computer. In the past few hours over sixty per cent of the gross wealth of Wong Holdings had been safely stored on disc in Malibu.

Wong Lee found it amusing that the *gweillo*, Kingdom, was about to launch his annual appeal for funds when, for the moment, his Church was richer than many countries.

*

With less than five minutes left before air time, the Reverend Kingdom finally decided how he would conduct the telethon.

'Alan,' he called up over the pulpit mike to the production gallery. 'We'll open with the Sinner Spot. That way we get them at the start.'

'But we've always held that for the middle of the show. To get things going again when the pledges start to drop,' Alan Milton began to object.

'Do what I say, Alan. Or sure as hell will never freeze over, you'll be out of a job!'

'Okay. It's your show, Reverend Kingdom.'

'It's God's show! Don't ever forget that!'

'And bless His name,' Alan Milton said obediently.

He began to give orders to the floor crew. After cameras were repositioned, Hal was escorted by the floor manager to a mock-up of a courtroom witness box which had been wheeled into position immediately below the pulpit. The Reverend Kingdom leaned over the lectern, smiling reassurance.

'Don't be nervous, Hal. Just tell it like it was. Every detail. Spare them nothing. And remember the more shocking it is, the greater will be the response. Here's your chance to once more serve the Lord God, Hal. So serve Him well, my friend. From the moment the cameras come to you, hit the throttle!'

'I sure will, Eddie. Don't worry, I sure will.'

Satisfied, the Reverend Kingdom peered one more time around the nave. Clara stood in front of her girls, smiling up at him. She really was very pretty. Martha had her band poised to conduct the Angels. The lights on the electric screen were blinking.

'Ten seconds to air!' came the voice of Alan Milton over the PA system. 'Let's make it a good one for God.'

'And bless His name,' came the chorused response from everyone in the Tabernacle.

The Reverend Kingdom felt the first trickle of sweat on his ribs. On the pulpit monitor he saw the telethon's opening title sequence appear.

A panning shot of the girls waiting at the tables. Pause on Clara. Cut to the choir. Pan to the electronic screen. Hold on Martha. Then a succession of shots of the prettiest of the Angels singing.

Over their faces came the main title:

The transmission light on Camera One, the Reverend Kingdom's camera, was glowing.

He remained completely still, as if he was listening to the closing words of Martha's hymn.

When the singing stopped there was total silence. Then the rich and resonant voice began to roll out across the nave, filling the Tabernacle with perfectly amplified sound which, in the same moment, was being transmitted to over a hundred countries.

My friends, welcome! Here in Malibu it is evening. In Europe, the early hours. In Asia, still only this morning. But whatever the time on your clock, the real time is here and now.

He paused and gave his first smile.

Here and Now! The words of our opening hymn, specially composed for you by my sister, Martha.

A camera cut to her, smiling in her robe and hair pinned into a regal tiara. For one fleeting moment she reminded him of a statue in a Belfast public park of the young Queen Victoria. He continued to speak.

Here and now. That is our theme for this year. Think of the words. Here and now. We use them every day and probably never think twice about them. They're just little props which get us from one sentence to another. '*Here* we go', and '*Now* let's do this!' – *here* and *now*.

But for the next twenty-four hours I want you to think of them as the two great pillars holding up this telethon. Because for that time we will all be *here* and *now* with the Lord God. Ready to give and receive His bounty.

This year there are more compelling reasons than ever before that we give and receive that bounty.

Even now, as I speak to you, a third of our earth is about to fall under the spell of Rome. We know what that means! The Only Book tells us to beware of the Roman pontiff!

He paused again. He had set up one of his themes. He could return to it throughout the long night and day which lay ahead.

For a moment longer the Reverend Kingdom looked out from on high, until he saw in the pulpit monitor sadness had darkened his face.

But my friends, we also know that the Only Book also says never overlook the sinner in our midst. For that sinner is like a cancer, corrupting from within.

The choir had begun to croon a medley of old familiar hymns, each proclaiming the weakness of Man. As the Reverend Kingdom continued, the volume and resonance of his voice slowly increased to rise just above the harmonising of the Angels.

I had never thought it possible in all these years that I have stood here before you, that such a sinner could exist right here – here and now! – in our very Church!

After a pause he shouted.

A MAN I TRUSTED! TRUSTED TO DO THE LORD'S WORK! LIKE JESUS TRUSTED JUDAS!

He saw some of the Mail girls jump. All over the world they would be jumping. When that happened, you had them. Once you could make them jump, they'd stay right to the end. Give that extra ten per cent. Give more.

When he continued to speak his voice was once more only slightly louder than the harmonising of the choir.

Though almost none of you have met him, or even knew his name before tonight, he was someone you all trusted. He was in charge of your tithes, that portion of your hard-earned income you give to God, and gladly. The money we use to continue to spread the Word of the Only Book.

And what did this person do with that money? Give it to the Lord God?

The Reverend Kingdom stopped and leaned forward to look down at where Hal stood, staring into a camera.

NO! HE STOLE IT! I TRUSTED HIM. AND HE BROKE THAT TRUST. HE WAS OUR JUDAS! IN CHARGE OF THE LORD GOD'S MONEY WHICH HE TOOK FOR HIMSELF. BUT JUDAS WAS NEVER ABLE TO PUBLICLY REPENT. OUR JUDAS CAN! HE IS HERE NOW TO DO SO!

The Reverend Kingdom leaned further over the lectern.

Hal Lockman! Tell the world how you lied and cheated and fornicated. And tell them why, after all you have done, you wish now to repent.

TELL THEM, HAL!

In the silence, the Reverend Kingdom remained leaning forward, his hands clasped around the front edge of the lectern.

Hal began to speak, his voice no more than a hoarse whisper.

The Reverend Kingdom is right. I am guilty of all he says. I am a sinner . . .

The Reverend Kingdom gave a sigh and composed his face in the same look he imagined Jesus must have displayed over Judas's betrayal. He continued to listen to Hal.

. . . I have sinned in stealing your money. Almost a million dollars of it. It has all gone – and if I may say so, God only knows where . . .

The Reverend Kingdom frowned. Clara was smiling. He would have to tell her that was an inappropriate response.

. . . and I did have sex with a young girl . . . and I lied about that too . . .

Martha was beginning to glower, her eyes settling on Penny-Jane in the back row of the choir. As soon as this was over, she would be out.

Hal's voice had picked up strength.

But the Only Book also says, don't cast the first stone and beware of anyone who says she is without sin!

The Reverend Kingdom's frown deepened. That wasn't on autocue. And this reference to 'she' –

I am not the only sinner here in the Tabernacle! There are others here who have sinned!

Hal turned and pointed across the nave.

Martha Kingdom, for one! She has committed the very sin her brother preaches against – the sin of taking another woman. The woman who took my place, Clara Stevens. The woman who now hopes to end up in Eddie Kingdom's bed –

The Reverend Kingdom, Martha and Clara all screamed in unison. Lord God, strike this evil tongue dead!

At the same moment, they all felt their entire bodies begin to shake. Then the floor.

A split second earlier, eighty miles out in the Pacific, the sea bed had split open like a giant wound, making seismographs quiver as far away as Tokyo, London, Berlin and Moscow.

The earthquake rip travelled across the ocean floor at over 7,000 miles an hour, before coming ashore more or less beneath the complex of the Church of True Belief.

In that one millisecond since his body began to throb uncontrollably and the floor to heave, the Reverend Kingdom felt the pulpit break free from the floor and rise in the air at breakneck speed. In that same millisecond the towering cross above the Tabernacle crashed through its roof, bringing down the crown of thorns and the electronic screen on to the pulpit. One of the thorns severed the Reverend Kingdom's head from his body. Martha vanished forever from the face of the earth when the ground fissured open beneath her and then closed. The choir disappeared into the same hole.

The piledriving force of the energy travelling at supersonic force from the bowels of the earth hurled Clara and her Mail Room girls towards the Tabernacle stained glass windows at that same millisecond the earthquake hurtled Alan Milton and the production team out of the gallery. The bodies smashed against each other in mid-air before plunging back on to the crushed cameras in the nave and their already dead operators. By then Fenton was already buried beneath the first of the Tabernacle walls to collapse. The other walls followed at once.

Like some malevolent force, the earthquake carried Hal in his witness box out of the Tabernacle and tossed him to one side. No one would ever know if he was hurt, or how badly, or whether he had been in time to see the manse rise off its foundations and then disintegrate in the same moment it took for the Communications Centre and the rows of staff apartments to crumble. By then the stand of trees sheltering the cemetery had been split like kindling wood and the tombstones had begun to rise out of the broken ground.

No one would know how much – if any – of this Hal saw. Because at the same split second after it happened, the canyon itself began to heave and sway under the unstoppable force of the earth tremor.

With a roar that the Reverend Kingdom, if he had lived, might well have likened to the sound of Armageddon, millions of tons of rock and earth buried Hal and the ruins of the Church of True Belief.

The awful silence which eventually followed was only occasionally broken by the peculiar lapping sound of waves of soil, several feet high, undulating over the area.

Then they, too, stopped.

The earth looked as if it had been rearranged by an angry Creator, as if the Lord God had now returned it to its original form and expunged forever what had gone on here.

Shortly before dawn, Pope Innocent awoke to an unfamiliar sound – the changing of the guard in the courtyard of the Terem Palace, one of the smaller and certainly the most beautiful of the Kremlin buildings.

He had spent the night in the bedroom built for Tsar Mikhail Romanov, from whose collection had come the jewels for the Godless Icon. The icon now rested at the foot of the mahogany bed in its locked trunk which he had brought with him from the Vatican.

Throughout the journey he had received regular reports on the southern Californian earthquake. Miraculously, the loss of life turned out to be small, due to buildings in the greater Los Angeles area being properly earthquake-proofed. Most of the deaths had occurred in the Malibu area, with the greatest number being at the Church of True Belief. No survivors had been found there.

Rescue workers had made some bizarre discoveries. They had unearthed a safe containing a letter bearing Stalin's signature which had been established was a fake. In the same depository were a couple of computer discs containing details of deposits of billions of dollars. There was no indication where they came from, or to whom the money belonged.

The city of Los Angeles had filed claim to the fortune, to help pay for the massive rescue operation it had launched, and later, to help with the rebuilding. The mayor had issued a statement saying he believed that it was what the Reverend Kingdom would have wished.

Pope Innocent had sent a message of sympathy to the President of the United States. The President had responded by telephoning him at the Kremlin to wish his mission well. Similar messages had come from other world leaders. The troika had sent a formal welcome.

As the changeover of the guard ended, Pope Innocent climbed out of bed and went to the prie-dieu in a corner of the bedchamber. The kneeler had also travelled with him from the Vatican. After praying, the Pope sat at the desk the Tsar had used and continued to study the sermon he would deliver to launch Operation Holy Cross.

There was a knock on the door.

'Come in, David,' Pope Innocent called.

Morton remained in the open doorway.

'Good morning, Your Holiness. Did you sleep well?'

Pope Innocent nodded sympathetically. 'Probably better than you did.'

Morton had spent the night on a chair outside the door. Since the shooting he had remained close.

'Anything new, David?'

Morton shook his head. The Pope had asked the same question every day since the shooting.

There was nothing new. Nothing to tie in Umberto or Wong Lee. And nothing from Lhasa.

'I think the threat's over, David,' said Pope Innocent.

Everyone had said the same. That no one would try so soon after the last attempt when security was at maximum. In three months, the Professor and his behaviourists had said, that would be the time to start worrying.

'There's been such a world-wide response that I've even started to regard the attempt on my life as almost a blessing. It's concentrated the minds of so many people on what I'm trying to do.'

Pope Innocent gestured to a pile of letters on the desk.

'Mullahs, imams, your own Chief Rabbi, the Patriarch of the Russian Orthodox, leaders of all faiths have said in their messages that they will totally support Holy Cross. My feeling is that there's a great desire out there for it to succeed. And no one's going to be allowed to stop that. This time I think you're worrying needlessly, David.'

Morton nodded. Everyone had said the same.

'It'll soon be over, Your Holiness, and then I'll be out of your hair.'

Pope Innocent smiled. 'Right now, if you don't get out of here, I'll never get this sermon memorised.'

He turned back to the desk as Morton closed the door.

A mile away, on the other side of Red Square, the shamaness walked with Wu around the barrack courtyard. Both were well wrapped against the morning chill. Wu held her begging bowl in one hand.

'You understand exactly what to do?' asked the shamaness one more time.

'Of course, Reverend Mother,' Wu replied.

'Good, now let's join the others.'

Already figures garbed in the robes and habits of many faiths were leaving the courtyard.

Chung-Shi was waiting for the shamaness and Wu as they emerged into the street. He gave them the traditional sign of peace of a Buddhist monk. Then in silence they joined the throng heading for Red Square.

When he had finished reading, Pope Innocent went to the Cathedral of the Assumption, the Kremlin's main church, to celebrate Mass with his entourage. He had selected fifty cardinals to accompany him to Moscow and they waited in procession at the cathedral's western door, beneath an exact replica of Michelangelo's *Last Judgement*.

Pope Innocent led them past the wooden throne where Ivan the Terrible once sat, and into the private chapel of the tsars. Its walls were of white marble, cool to the touch, their hardness softened by diffused light coming through mosaics of religious scenes on the windows. Pope Innocent quickly genuflected towards the wooden cross on the wall, then bent and kissed the altar and began Mass with the timeless words: 'Oh Lord, I raise to you my prayer . . .'

In the salon where Napoleon once planned his retreat from Moscow, General Borakin continued to smile as he listened on the phone to Wong Lee.

'Of course I sympathise with you, Mr Wong. But I must say it was very ill-advised of you to have done that, given California's reputation for earthquakes.'

The former chairman of the KGB and the ex-Party secretary were also nodding and smiling as Borakin continued.

'There is, you will appreciate, no way we can pay you that money again. We did exactly as you requested in transferring it to Malibu . . .'

The troika continued to smile as Wong Lee went on speaking in a tone they had never heard him use before – defeated.

'But Mr Wong, really how could you have been so ill-advised?' remonstrated Borakin. 'Sixty per cent, you transferred. That is a huge sum to lose, even for you. Perhaps, especially for you.'

Borakin glanced at his colleagues seated on either side of him. They both nodded again.

Immediately prior to Wong Lee's call, there had been one from the President of the Council of Islamic Republics. He had confirmed the disarmament plans and had sought reassurances the troika would do the same. These had been given.

Borakin continued to speak to Wong Lee.

'Perhaps we can help you best by cancelling our order for those weapons systems. In that way you will not be under further pressure. Naturally, we would then be unable to go ahead with our agreement to develop mineral rights in our Islamic republics.'

Borakin's proposal to the Council that they should co-venture the exploitation of the rights on an equal profit-sharing basis had been accepted. Perhaps later they could discuss how to challenge the West. But perhaps, after all, that was not so important now.

'I warn you, general –'

'I really don't think you are in a position to do that, Mr Wong.

When you think it over, you will see why. In the meantime, our condolences again for your losses.'

Borakin hung up and smiled at the others.

In Red Square, police continued to marshal the crowds. The thousands of representatives of faiths were ushered to the front of St Basil's Cathedral. The shamaness and Wu were among those with passes allowing them to sit in the enclosure in front of the altar. To reach it they passed through one of the metal detectors. A guard inspected Wu's begging bowl before allowing it through.

Those in the enclosure would be presented to the Pope before he delivered his address. Drawn from all faiths, they represented the ecumenical nature of the occasion. Chung-Shi was seated just outside the enclosure.

The shamaness turned to Wu. 'You recognise this place?'

'No, Reverend Mother.'

The shamaness smiled. She really had succeeded quite brilliantly in blotting out Wu's past.

Carina continued to study the asymmetrical tent-shaped helmet and onion-domes of the cathedral, continued to remember. She was still too far away to have recognised the face of the man standing at a window high up in one of the cathedral's twin spires. Morelli continued to survey the crowd through binoculars. He glanced at his watch and spoke into his throat mike.

'Time to go.'

From his vantage point in another window in the cathedral's second tower-spire came a grunt of acknowledgement from Morton.

'Those people nearest the altar, Claudio. Their IDs been properly checked?'

'As far as we can. But the detectors would have picked up anything suspicious. Bill Gates had them specially flown in from Washington.'

Morelli continued to sound reassuring.

'Short of strip searching everyone down there, things couldn't be more buttoned-up. Everything we've learned after Dallas and the attempt on John Paul has been put into practice.'

'For sure.' But he just wished he could be as certain as everyone else.

For a moment longer Morton scanned the faces about the

altar, before focusing on the two nuns in their white habits. The younger one with her begging bowl reminded him of Carina. But he really couldn't tell from this angle, just as he couldn't tell how long he would go on seeing her face in all kinds of places.

Morton sighed and lowered his binoculars.

Pope Innocent returned to his bedroom after the Mass. With him was Cardinal Walpole.

The Secretary of State watched in silence as the Pope unlocked the trunk and took out the velvet wrapped Godless Icon.

'In returning this today, to its rightful place, I am fulfilling the first part of the Third Secret of Fatima,' said Pope Innocent.

He unwrapped the velvet. They both stared at the Godless Icon.

'Returning this is also the easy part, Horace. The second part, I fear, is not so simple. It requires that in one sermon I achieve what Christ Himself did not do: unite all the faiths.'

'You are His Vicar on Earth,' Cardinal Walpols said softly. 'If anyone can do it, you can in His name.'

Pope Innocent extended the Godless Icon to Cardinal Walpole. The Secretary of State kissed its frame. The pontiff did the same, and once more wrapped the Godless Icon in its velvet. Then he reached into the trunk and removed the other velvet wrapped item. He uncovered the envelope containing the last of the Secrets of Fatima.

Pope Innocent contemplated the envelope for a moment, fingering the seals.

'You are really going to do this?' asked Cardinal Walpole.

'I have to. It's the only way, Horace.'

Pope Innocent slipped the envelope into a pocket of his cassock. Then, clasping the Godless Icon to his chest, he left the bedchamber. Cardinal Walpole closed the door after them.

Waiting at the end of the corridor was the troika. General Borakin came forward. He bowed stiffly and introduced his co-rulers of Russia. With them was General Savenko.

'My colleagues and I welcome you to the Kremlin,' Borakin said in a formal voice.

'Thank you, general.'

'You will understand that we cannot accompany you on what is, after all, a religious mission. Though we were born into your faith, we long ago chose to relinquish it. But we will do nothing to stand in your way. I have asked General Savenko to act as your liaison.'

'Thank you, general.'

Borakin and the other troika members once more bowed stiffly and stood aside. Pope Innocent and Cardinal Walpole followed Savenko down the staircase which led to the connecting underground passage into St Basil's Cathedral.

From the gallery above the cathedral nave Morton and Morelli looked down on the cardinals standing before an empty space on the wall behind the main altar. They were talking quietly among themselves. Morton had come to know some of them well in these past weeks: O'Rourke and Berry, Boylan and Leutens, Martel and Reefer, Camas and Anzo, Simmons and Terry, Saldarini and Posanos. Dedicated men. He could not accept everything they believed in. But he would defend their right to do so.

'You had this place checked, Claudio?'

'Twice. Once by Savenko's people. Then Gates put a team in.'

Morelli squinted at Morton. 'Something still bothering you?'

'Force of habit, I guess.'

Morelli smiled. 'I know the feeling. But everything's taken care of. Savenko's got five thousand of his finest around the square. The troika gave Washington special clearance for an antenna farm to be positioned directly overhead. Gates and the rest have their best agents in the crowd. We've tried to cover every angle.'

'For sure.'

A door behind the altar opened and Pope Innocent emerged with Cardinal Walpole and Savenko. The general remained at the door while the others walked forward.

After Cardinal Walpole had taken his place among the other cardinals, Pope Innocent once more unwrapped the Godless Icon and held it up before them.

'Witness before God what I shall now do.'

Pope Innocent walked to the empty space on the wall and hung the Godless Icon back in its rightful place. Then he turned and, his eyes close to tears, led the cardinals down the nave towards the heavy wooden main door of the cathedral which had started to slowly open.

Beyond stretched a crowd larger than any seen before in Red Square. Pope Innocent reached the door and stood, arms extended in the timeless gesture of peace. When he began to speak there was a certainty in his voice.

'My dearly beloved friends, we of all faiths are gathered here today in the sight of one God. I ask you now to join with me in praying as you have always prayed to Him in your own mother tongue.'

Hesitatingly at first, then with growing conviction, voices began to pray in all languages.

To one side of the altar Morton watched bowed heads begin to lift and look towards the silent figure still standing with arms outstretched. In a moment the next part of this unprecedented religious occasion would commence when a selected few would come forward to the altar to be blessed by Pope Innocent. Then he would deliver his address.

Pope Innocent stared out over the crowd. In the distance, high up on the review stand set into the Kremlin walls, he could make out three tiny figures. The troika had come after all.

What had Stalin contemptuously asked from that same spot – how many divisions does the Pope have? That was when Marxism had flourished, when the dignity of man had already been debased. Other political systems had continued to erode that dignity. How many had died in the defamed name of national-ism? How many had been jailed and tortured because they had dared to protest mankind's inexcusable failure to solve the hostil-ity between differing ideologies?

In the end it came down to a hunger – a hunger for food for the body and soul. He could sense it here in the crowd, in all those expectant faces looking towards him. They wanted a miracle. All he could do was give them a sign.

From his cassock Pope Innocent produced the sealed envelope. He held it in both hands above his head, in a simple act of veneration. He had no doubt that all those years ago, in that then obscure Portuguese village, the Mother of God had anticipated this very moment. The wonder was that he had been chosen to execute it. He closed his eyes for a moment, humbled and proud at what he was being asked to do – lead the world back from the abyss.

A stir of expectation began to course through the crowd as they sensed something significant was about to happen.

Pope Innocent lowered the envelope. Then, using his thumb, he broke his own seal and extracted the single sheet of paper. He held it up between finger and thumb for a moment. Then he lowered the paper on to the altar. For a moment longer he studied the vast congregation. Then he leaned forward slightly, so that his lips were closer to the microphone, and began to speak in that same thrilling voice which had stopped the riot in Cape Town and with which he had accepted his nomination in the Sistine Chapel.

'Today, I will reveal to you the last Secret of Fatima. I do so in the certainty that God wishes me to share it with you. We have already seen the terrible results of the first two secrets. Global war and then the spread of godlessness.

'Yet, terrifying though they were, they pale into insignificance when measured against the Third Secret. It is literally a warning that we are on the eve of Armageddon.

'In the hope that mankind, each and every one of us, can avert that calamity, I have decided to make public the terrible consequences of ignoring the Third Secret.

'But before I do, I want to receive, on your behalf, the representatives of all faiths, to symbolise the coming together of all religions, both in the spiritual and secular sense, to work together to ensure man does survive and creates a better world.'

Pope Innocent beckoned to those in the enclosure below the altar. A black-robed Muslim cleric, a tarboosh on his head, slowly stood to his feet and came forward.

The shamaness saw an Armenian priest stand up, ready to go forward. In his hand he held a small incense burner.

'You are next,' murmured the shamaness to Wu. 'Remember everything I have shown you.'

Carina nodded. She remembered. Not all of it. But enough of the evil which had been done to her.

The shamaness slipped a plastic vial into Wu's begging bowl. A drop of the cyanide-based solution on the skin would be sufficient to kill. The plastic vial had escaped detection by the metal detectors.

The priest had reached the altar and was genuflecting before the Pope. Wu stood up. The priest was crossing in front of the altar and one of the stewards was beckoning her forward.

Morton was turning away to watch a Buddhist monk a few rows back who was leaning forward. He stopped, stunned.

'Carina!' he shouted.

'Carina!' he shouted even louder.

She paused, half-way up the steps, staring at him, unable to believe she could remember, that she was returning from the dead, that he was here.

'Carina!' he was moving towards her.

The Buddhist monk was on his feet and so was the old nun who had sat beside Carina.

'Now!' the nun was screaming. 'Throw it now!'

Morton saw Carina reach into her basket.

'No!' he shouted, plunging forward.

'Throw it!' the nun screamed.

Morelli was half-running, half-diving across the platform towards the Pope.

Carina turned and with unerring aim threw the vial. It broke against the face of the shamaness. Her hands began to work frantically to wipe off the liquid.

'Get down, Carina! Get down!' Morton shouted.

The monk had a gun in his hand.

Morelli sent Pope Innocent sprawling. Carina remained standing on the steps. Morton had almost reached her, could see the recognition in her eyes, could hear the word on her lips.

'David.'

Chung-Shi fired.

Carina spun, then fell into Morton's arms, as he fired the Luger. Chung-Shi crashed into the crowd, already dead.

Morton could hear Savenko ordering everybody to stand back, could see the Pope on his feet, and white coated figures with stretchers forcing their way towards him, could hear the familiar sounds of panic. And feel Carina's blood on his hands.

Pope Innocent, despite Morelli's protests, had come to the front of the altar to kneel beside him.

'She's dead, David,' he said gently.

Morton continued to hold Carina in his arms.

Later, people would marvel at what followed. As soon as the three bodies had been carried away – the shamaness had succumbed almost immediately to the cyanide poison – Pope Innocent addressed the crowd for a full hour. He revealed himself as both a prophet and a preacher, and above all, as truly charismatic. He spoke repeatedly of the transforming power of prayer and faith to create a better world. He shared with the millions listening in Red Square and the billions following his every word on radio and television around the world, the Third Secret of Fatima – that, unless a genuine effort was made to co-exist peacefully, the world as they all knew it would be destroyed. He had put a time limit before them for destruction: December 31st, 1999.

At times he paused, as if caught in the strong undercurrents of memory. At other times his whole body shook with the effort he was making.

He used images his audience could always understand. He spoke of the global chessboard and the worldwide game of pawn and dice played on it. Of the games of investment banking, foreign credits, stocks and shares, corporate financing, portfolios. Of the games of the power-brokers who tried to rule all their lives. But he had another game he wished them all to play. The game of salvation.

At times his voice was loud, clear and harsh, at times soft and gentle. But always he spoke with the force of total conviction. If the world did not change, the world was doomed. He ended where he had begun, saying he could do no more than warn. That others must act.

When he finished a roar of applause echoed around Red Square. Below the altar men and women of all faiths embraced and wept and pledged themselves. In the days following, that promise echoed throughout the capitals of the world.

How best to implement Pope Innocent's visionary concept of putting aside past hatred and working together for a better world took a little time to work out. Not for the first time it was the smaller countries who showed the way – allocating their surplus to feed the poor, opening their doors to the impoverished. The richer and more powerful nations followed, organising air lifts, offering extended credit at low interest, cancelling debts, providing technical help.

All this was activated without any help from Wong Holdings. Its shares had been dumped onto the market to try and raise the cash to meet its grave cash-flow problems. Its controlling interest in hundreds of corporations had been disposed of for the same reason. Wong Holdings, like its founder, was no longer a force to be reckoned with – at least for the foreseeable future. Diplomatically it was an exciting time. The Council of Islamic Republics announced from Alma-Ata that it was establishing full diplomatic relations with both the Holy See and Israel. The announcement came only hours after the Vatican announced the appointment of its own Ambassador to the Holy Land. Pope Innocent had urged, and Israel had agreed, their nation should be officially renamed the Holy Land – a land for all faiths to worship in harmony, with Jerusalem established as an open city. He had invited the Imam Nardash to join him on a visit there.

Early in the morning, Carina's favourite hour, Morton helped to carry her coffin to the cemetery with its view of the Samaran Hills.

Danny, the Professor and Lester Final were the other pall bearers. Chantal walked beside Monsignor Hanlon, representing the Holy See and General Savenko, representing the troika. They had been on the same plane which had brought the body from Moscow to Tel Aviv.

The service was short and simple, the chanting rising and falling, and then only the silence as the coffin was lowered into the grave.

Morton recited a final prayer. Then he produced from his pocket the keys to his apartment which Carina had dropped in Rome. Together with a handful of earth he cast them into the grave.

Those closest to him saw his lips move, but they could not be certain what he had said, except – 'for sure'.